THE BLACK TATTOO

THE BLACK TATTOO

SAM ENTHOVEN

razor
bill

The Black Tattoo

RAZORBILL

Published by the Penguin Group
Penguin Young Readers Group
345 Hudson Street, New York, New York 10014, U.S.A.
Penguin Group (USA) Inc., 375 Hudson Street, New York, New York 10014, U.S.A.
Penguin Group (Canada), 90 Eglinton Avenue East, Suite 700, Toronto,
Ontario, Canada M4P 2Y3 (a division of Pearson Penguin Canada Inc.)
Penguin Books Ltd, 80 Strand, London WC2R 0RL, England
Penguin Ireland, 25 St Stephen's Green, Dublin 2, Ireland
(a division of Penguin Books Ltd)
Penguin Group (Australia), 250 Camberwell Road, Camberwell,
Victoria 3124, Australia (a division of Pearson Australia Group Pty Ltd)
Penguin Books India Pvt Ltd, 11 Community Centre, Panchsheel Park,
New Delhi – 110 017, India
Penguin Group (NZ), 67 Apollo Drive, Rosedale, North Shore 0632, New Zealand
(a division of Pearson New Zealand Ltd.)
Penguin Books (South Africa) (Pty) Ltd, 24 Sturdee Avenue, Rosebank,
Johannesburg 2196, South Africa

Penguin Books Ltd, Registered Offices: 80 Strand, London WC2R 0RL, England

10 9 8 7 6 5 4 3 2 1

THE LIBRARY OF CONGRESS HAS CATALOGED THE HARDCOVER EDITION AS FOLLOWS:

Enthoven, Sam.
  The black tattoo / by Sam Enthoven.
    p. cm.
  Summary: When his best friend, Charlie, is possessed by an ancient demon, fourteen-year-old Jack,
accompanied by a girl with superhuman powers, battles all over London and into Hell to save him.
  ISBN-13: 978-1-59514-114-9
  [1. Demonology—Fiction. 2. Supernatural—Fiction. 3. Hell—Fiction. 4. London (England)—Fiction.
5. England—Fiction.] I. Title.
  PZ7.E72445Bl 2006
  [Fic]—dc22
                        2006021525

Razorbill paperback ISBN: 978-1-59514-133-0

Printed in the United States of America

To Laura
"My heart is in my hand.
. . . *Yuck.*"

DO I DARE
DISTURB THE UNIVERSE?
—T. S. ELIOT, "THE LOVE SONG OF J. ALFRED PRUFROCK"

FRESH BLOOD

LONDON. The West End. A little after four in the morning. At the base of the skyscraper known as Centre Point Tower, in the darkness at the end of a dank concrete walkway, something stirred. The shadows there began to ripple and coalesce. The dark became a manlike shape of pure liquid black. Then the demon emerged, taking its first leisurely step toward the woman who stood there watching it.

"Jessica," it said.

Hearing that voice again, and the way the sound of it seemed to take shape inside her head like black flowers blossoming behind her eyelids, it was all Jessica could do to stop her legs from trembling. She'd been so close! Another few minutes and she'd've made it! She gritted her teeth and told herself to concentrate. The demon took another step. It was clear of the shadows now, and the rainy orange streetlight glinted off its inky wet skin. Its face was a blank, but she could feel it looking at her.

"You should not have come back," it said.

Slowly Jessica put down the plastic bag full of fourteen years' worth of carefully hoarded tobacco shreds and cigarette ends that she'd been collecting and saving for this moment. She unbuttoned her filthy overcoat.

"Really," she replied. "And what makes you say that?"

"You must have realized that I can't let you warn them," the demon told her. "You must have known that if I found you you'd be killed, and what knowledge you possess would die with you—but you still came. Why?"

"Confident," said Jessica, "aren't you?"

Her amber eyes glittered. Her hard brown hands lifted fractionally from her sides.

The demon looked at her.

"Very well," it said. "Since you insist . . ."

It took one more step—

—blurred into motion—

—and attacked.

Jessica wasn't as young as she used to be. She'd been expecting the demon's charge, but her reactions had slowed over the years since they'd last fought. When she leaped, with superhuman speed, six feet straight up in the air, flinging herself in a twisting forward roll so tight it left her dizzy, she was, therefore, slightly too late. Her knackered old trainers clipped the demon's back as it flashed past beneath her. She was slightly off balance as her soles smacked back onto the concrete—and the first knife she threw as she landed went wide, spanging off the walkway's railing and spinning off into the night.

Smoothly her right hand whipped back and out again, but the demon had already recovered itself; it swatted her second knife out of the air with something very like contempt. Jessica held her breath as she reached for her third: the blade crossed the space in a flash of silver and struck the demon in the face, right between where its eyes would have been if it had been a person.

But it was not a person. Grimly she watched her knife vanish into the glossy darkness, leaving barely a ripple. The demon didn't even break stride. With the best speed she could muster, Jessica dived to one side. She just had time to notice that the demon had anticipated her . . .

. . . when she felt a blow that took her breath away.

The concrete wall at the end of the walkway was a clear twenty feet behind her; the blow flung her the distance in less than a second, and she smacked into the wall back-first. Helpless with pain, she slid to the floor, waiting for the follow-up that would finish her.

But it didn't come.

When she looked up, the demon was watching her.

"Feeling your age, Jessica?" it inquired.

Jessica didn't answer. Her bones were aching, and she could taste blood in her mouth, warm and coppery. She gritted her teeth and got to her feet, keeping one hand behind her back. *Magic,* she was thinking. All right: she was going to have to use magic.

"I sympathize," said the demon. "Truly, I do. As you see"—it gestured at itself with one ink-black hand—"I've taken what strength I can from my current host. But he, like you, is old now, and weak. He will not sustain me for much longer."

Jessica said nothing. She was concentrating. Behind her, slowly, agonizingly, the air above her palm wobbled, bulged—

then a light appeared. It was a tiny spark at first. The spark glistened and twinkled as she coaxed it into life, gradually becoming a little brighter, a little stronger with each passing moment. It was *herself* that Jessica was pouring into it—all of her determination, her power, and her hatred condensed into a single, glittering point. The spark grew to a sphere, a whirling globe of orange-flecked and sizzling silvery-blue, as the demon continued to speak.

"What I need," it said, "is a new vessel to work from—*fresh blood*," it added, "as it were. Someone vigorous yet . . . pliable. Someone spirited yet suggestible. In short, someone *young*. Why *did* you come back?" it asked again, suddenly. "Was it the girl?"

Still Jessica did not reply.

"Well," said the demon, "it doesn't matter." It waved wearily at the hand Jessica still held behind her back.

"All right," it said. "Go on, then. Surprise me."

Jessica bowed her head. She brought out her hand and what was inside it—

—and she smiled.

Already, a thin shell of softer blue was forming around the small globe of light that still danced and whirled over her hand. Another second and the shell seemed to harden, then *crush* inward, turning the light of the globe to an angry red, then white.

Then, suddenly, the demon was screaming.

Its head tipped back, the glistening liquid black of its jaws gaping so far they seemed to roll and fold back on themselves. Its body was flailing now, around where the light was hitting it, reaching and flailing as if being blown about in a wind tunnel, and all the time the scream went on and on.

The sound was one Jessica knew well. She had heard it in her dreams every night for fourteen years: a sound like paper tearing in your head; an intaken, wailing, braying sound that shot up in pitch like a rocket—a sound like nothing on Earth.

Her amber eyes flashed as she stared the demon down. Holding the light out in front of her, Jessica walked toward it. It was reaching for her: long, liquid-black fingers were grasping at the light, testing her will, checking her strength, but Jessica fought with all her heart, forcing the demon back, step by step. Without taking her eyes off it, she reached out and picked up her bag.

From her years on the streets, Jessica had learned to make the best use she could of whatever materials came to hand. Manifesting her power externally for any length of time was exhausting, but certain substances (Jessica had discovered) could be induced to hold magic, storing it up and releasing it slowly like a battery does an electric charge.

Tobacco, for example.

She began to pour the bag's contents out on the ground at her feet, a little at a time, as evenly as she could with just one hand. Slowly, steadily, she let the precious stuff fall, shaking it out, forming a line on the concrete between herself and her enemy. Holding the blazing light above her head, she forced herself to turn her back on the demon as she continued to pour. The bag went empty: her collection of shreds and dog ends flared briefly, then blackened as she completed the protective circle. She sat down and crossed her legs.

Suddenly, the demon seemed to realize what she was doing. It sprang toward her in a spreading flood of darkness—swallowing the walls, the rain, the world outside, and everything. Jessica took a deep breath. Forcing herself to blank out everything except the light of her will, forcing herself not to think of what would happen if that light went out . . .

. . . she closed her eyes.

The sound of the door buzzer, long and ugly, ripped Esme out of her sleep. The dream she'd been having was one she had often: a long, slow, freezing kind of dream, full of darkness and falling and cold that squeezed stony fingers round her heart. It was a frightening dream, but in a moment Esme had dismissed it as usual. She opened her eyes.

Her thick black curly hair had swung forward around her face, which meant she was on the ceiling again, where she always seemed to wake up. Parting her hair with her fingers, she floated soundlessly to the cushioned floor of her bedroom and walked the two steps to the intercom by the door. Just as she reached it, it crackled: her father had reached his first.

"Yeah?" he said, his deep voice managing to convey in that one syllable just how unhappy he would be if the person at the door turned out to have woken him up for no reason.

"Raymond?" said the voice from outside.

There was a pause.

"*Nick?*" said Raymond hoarsely—and suddenly, Esme's blood turned to ice.

She pressed the button. "I'll be down in a moment," she said.

Nick was small and thin and dressed in black from head to foot: he wore a black suit, black shoes, a black shirt open at the neck, and black silk gloves on his hands. His beard and mustache were as dark and neat as the rest of him, but there were deep lines of worry at the edges of his glittering blue eyes. He looked older than Esme had been expecting, old and very tired.

"Esme," he said. "Good to see you."

"You too," Esme lied. She and Raymond had been preparing for Nick's return almost the whole of her life. She was nervous.

"Can I get you anything, Nick?" boomed the grinning giant standing by the table. "Cuppa? Something stronger, maybe?"

Raymond, in contrast to Nick, was massive. His nose was squashed flat, his ears were out of shape, and he had no discernible neck of any kind, just an immense black beard with wispy white streaks in it, behind which his great bald clump of a head seemed to join straight onto his shoulders. In the army-issue undershirt he was wearing, his hairy arms looked huge. His meaty red hands, with their swollen knuckles, were resting easily on the back of a chair. But Esme knew from the way his fingers were clenching that Raymond was almost as nervous as she was.

"This isn't a social visit," said Nick.

Esme watched him. Nick took a deep breath and closed his eyes. Before he spoke, his face seemed to sag inwardly.

"I'm afraid," Nick said softly, "that the Scourge has escaped again." He looked up. "We're in trouble."

The grin fell off Raymond's face: a second later, he looked like he'd never smiled in his life. "How?" he said.

"I don't know," said Nick. "I can only assume one of the others must have released it. But one thing's for sure: the Brotherhood's in no shape to handle this as we are. We're . . . going to need some new recruits."

Surprised, Esme and Raymond exchanged a look.

"Have we time?" asked Raymond. He had never been very good at hiding his emotions, and the skepticism on his face was clear to see.

"No," Nick snapped, "I dare say we don't. But we'd be useless against the Scourge right now, and you know it."

Raymond blinked.

"We . . . do have young Esme here," he said carefully. He took a step closer to the other man and tried for a smile. "I'll tell you what: I've never trained anyone like her. You should see the way she—"

"Yes," said Nick, "but in case you haven't noticed, there's only one of her, and that's *not going to be enough!*"

His words echoed around the room. Raymond and Esme looked at each other uncertainly.

"I'm sorry," said Nick, "but we simply must have new recruits—*fresh blood,*" he added, "as it were." He looked at Esme. "Will you help me?"

"Sure," said Esme. "No problem."

CHARLIE AND JACK

The West End stank in the heat of summer: the smell came up at Jack in waves from the warm, gum-pocked pavement. A police sign on the corner warned in five different languages that thieves were operating near the cash machines—don't let anyone distract you, it said—but Jack had seen the sign plenty of times before, and besides, he was thinking. Any minute now they'd be at the restaurant. If he was going to get any answers about what was going on, then he'd better bite the bullet and ask now.

"Er . . . Charlie?"

No response. Charlie just kept striding ahead of him.

"Charlie?" Jack repeated. "Charlie, wait!"

Only now, when Jack had shouted, did Charlie stop.

Jack Farrell had known Charlie Farnsworth since they'd been put next to each other on the first day of school; Jack wasn't the kind of person who made friends easily, but he'd been impressed with Charlie straightaway, and they'd been best mates almost ever since. Both boys were now fourteen years old; Charlie was a month older than Jack and an inch and a half taller, and his cheekbones stuck out in a way that Jack's only did if he sucked his cheeks in. Charlie's hair was black as night and just tousled enough, whereas Jack's was blond and fluffy no matter what he did with it. Jack, like Charlie, was wearing black jeans and a blue cotton shirt, unbuttoned and untucked over his white T-shirt—but Jack didn't look . . . well . . . *cool*, like Charlie did. All these things were normal—*typical*, in Jack's opinion—and he'd pretty much learned to get used to them. But there was something else different about Charlie that day: it was obvious. Every step he took seemed to be filled with a kind of rage.

"Listen," said Jack, "you want to tell me what's going on?"

"What d'you mean?"

"Well," said Jack patiently, "what's the deal with having lunch with your dad? We haven't done that since we were kids."

There was a pause.

Suddenly, Charlie took a deep breath and said, "He's left."

Jack looked at Charlie carefully. "What?"

"He's *left*," Charlie repeated, making an exasperated face. "Look, you know how our answering machine's been on all day lately? That's 'cause the day before yesterday, Dad told me and Mum he was *leaving*—then he *left*. Okay?"

The words had come out in a rush. For a long moment after, there was silence between them.

"Oh, mate . . ." said Jack.

"Yeah," said Charlie.

"How did it—?"

"At breakfast," said Charlie. "Saturday morning. He comes

to wake me up just like normal—right? Only his voice is all funny and he's like, 'Come downstairs, there's something we've got to talk about.' So I go downstairs, and Mum's got this . . . expression on her face. . . ."

Jack could see Charlie was having trouble getting the words out—especially since, at that moment, a group of some forty tourists, all wearing identically ludicrous bright yellow fanny packs, were pushing past on either side of them.

"And Dad says . . . well, basically . . . he's going," said Charlie.

"Oh, mate," Jack repeated, uselessly.

"He says he's got this rented flat all sorted out, right? And him and this . . . woman he met through work are going to live over there for a bit while they work out what to do next. Then he packs a bag of stuff, and, well . . . " Charlie blinked. "He's gone."

"Mate, I am *so* sorry," said Jack. It sounded feeble, but what else was there to say?

"Mmm," replied Charlie and grimaced. "Listen," he said, "this is going to be the first time I've seen him since . . . you know."

"Oh, right," said Jack doubtfully.

"Well . . . I'd really appreciate you, you know, coming in with me. Backing me up a little bit." Charlie was looking at him. "What do you say?"

Suddenly, Jack began to feel awkward.

If Charlie had asked him to watch zombie films with him until four in the morning, he would've agreed like a shot, as always. Splattery team death matches on the Internet? Likewise, sure, no problem. This, however . . .

"Please," said Charlie.

Jack looked at him. Charlie was his friend. Of course, there was no choice, really.

"Well . . ." He shrugged. "Okay."

Charlie let out a sigh of relief and put his hand out. They shook.

"Thanks, man."

"Sure."

Charlie's smile faded quickly. "Well," he said, "here goes."

"Charlie," said Mr. Farnsworth, standing up as soon as he saw his son. He took a couple of steps across the room toward him, his arms opening for a hug—then he caught sight of Jack. His eyes widened for a moment: his smile stayed in place, but Jack knew, at that instant, that he shouldn't have come.

"And Jack!" said Mr. Farnsworth, letting his hands fall to his sides. "Good to see you. Come and sit down: the duck's on its way."

They sat. There was a very long silence.

"So . . ." said Mr. Farnsworth. "How are things at home?"

"Not great," said Charlie, "since you ask."

There was more silence for a moment as Mr. Farnsworth waited to hear whether Charlie had anything to add to this. Charlie didn't.

"And . . . how's your mum?"

"How do you think?"

Jack looked up from his plate to sneak a glance at Charlie's dad, but Mr. Farnsworth noticed, so he had to stare quickly down again. Jack heard him take a deep breath.

"Charlie," he began, "I—"

The waiter glided up with the Peking duck.

The small round straw box of pancakes arrived first, together with the dish of hoisin sauce and the plate of spring onions and cucumber. These were followed by the duck itself, which the waiter proceeded to mash into shreds with quick, well-practiced movements. This only took about thirty seconds, but to Jack, with Charlie and Mr. Farnsworth sitting there in silence, it felt like much longer.

"Right," said Mr. Farnsworth brightly, once the waiter had left. He rubbed his hands. "Who's going first?" When nobody answered, he lifted the lid on the pancake box and offered it across the table: "Jack?"

Well, Jack wasn't made of stone. . . .

"Thanks," he said. He took a pancake and spread a thin layer of the rich, sweet plum sauce across it with a teaspoon. Charlie took one too. Jack noticed a quick smile of relief on Mr. Farnsworth's face at this. Obviously he saw it as an encouraging sign.

"So, Jack," said Charlie's dad, turning heavily toward him, "how're things with you? Got any plans for the summer?"

"Er, nothing much," Jack said. He wanted to look at Charlie, to take his cue for how to speak to Mr. Farnsworth from him. Luckily, he had his pancake to work on.

"You still skateboarding much?"

"Dad, that was *years* ago," said Charlie.

"Oh," said Mr. Farnsworth.

By now, Jack's first pancake was ready to eat. He'd laid

out just the right proportions of cucumber, spring onion, and mashed-up duck on top of the sauce, and he'd successfully rolled the whole thing up into the proper cigar shape. He lifted it to his lips and took a bite: it was delicious.

"That's a very neat job you've done of that," said Mr. Farnsworth.

"Thanks," managed Jack through his mouthful. "Peking duck's one of my favorites."

Mr. Farnsworth smiled at him. Jack smiled back uncertainly.

Then Charlie threw his pancake down on the table.

"Dad, *why did you do it*?" he asked.

It was hot and bright in the restaurant, especially next to the window where they were sitting. Slowly, Mr. Farnsworth put down his pancake.

"Charlie," he said wearily.

"Yes?"

"Well . . ." prompted Mr. Farnsworth, "don't you think . . . ? You know, with Jack here?"

"Why not?" said Charlie, in a voice that made Jack squirm in his seat. "I want him to hear this too."

Mr. Farnsworth sighed. Then he dabbed at his lips with his napkin, spread it back across his lap, and looked up at Charlie again.

"All right," he said, and he took a deep breath.

"Your mother and I . . ." he began. "Well . . . we've never been really happy."

Now Jack *really* didn't know where to look. He certainly wasn't going to look at Charlie or Mr. Farnsworth, so he was reduced to fidgeting with his pancake. It was ridiculous and horrible at the same time—but suddenly he couldn't help wondering if he just had to sit there, or if it was okay for him to take another bite. Peking duck was his favorite, after all.

"I tried to make it work," said Mr. Farnsworth, staring earnestly at his son. "I tried to keep it going, for as long as I could. But, well . . ." He shrugged. "I'm not getting any younger. And when the chance came up for me to be really *happy*, I had to take it. Do you see?"

Charlie's mouth opened and closed a couple of times before he got his words out. His voice, when it came, sounded high and strangely muffled.

"But you left," he said, "so . . . suddenly."

Mr. Farnsworth sighed again. "Charlie, there's—"

"'Never a good time for something like this.' Yes, you said."

Mr. Farnsworth blinked, surprised.

"Good for who, though?" asked Charlie, his voice getting louder. "Good for who?"

"Charlie—"

"Mum was happy. She thought you were happy. We were happy! And all the time you were . . . making *arrangements*."

"Charlie—"

"Do you have any idea how stupid you've made us feel?"

"Now, Charlie," said Mr. Farnsworth, "you've got a right to be angry. . . ."

Charlie said nothing. Jack looked from his friend's expression to the last of the pancake—the perfect, mouth-size morsel of duck, rich sauce, and crisp, pale green vegetables. Slowly, he put it down.

"But you've got to let me make things right between us," Mr. Farnsworth was saying. "Charlie, you've got to understand that nothing's really changed between me and you, *nothing*. And if you'll just—"

"And I want *you* to understand," Charlie cut in, in a voice that made his father stop dead, "that I am never, *ever* going to forgive you for this. Do you understand that? *Never.*"

He paused.

"Come on, Jack, we're going."

He stood up. Hurriedly, Jack stood up too.

"Charlie, wait," said Mr. Farnsworth. "Please?"

But Charlie didn't wait. And Jack, of course, had to follow. When Jack looked back, Mr. Farnsworth was sitting absolutely still at the table, staring straight ahead. Then the door swung shut behind them, and they were gone.

"Er . . . Charlie?" said Jack.

Charlie didn't even turn, just kept stomping straight ahead, head down. Jack sighed.

For a good two minutes they strode on together without speaking, and before long they were coming out into Cambridge Circus. The big crossroads was packed as always, full of shuddering red buses, gaggles of tourists, brightness, noise, and heat. Looming over it all was the Palace Theatre.

The Palace Theatre is one of the most impressive buildings in the West End—a grand and ostentatious mass of stripy pink brick festooned with turrets, glittering windows, and fat stone cherubs. Jack was looking up at it, distracted, when—

WHUMP! A passerby barged into Charlie's shoulder, sending him staggering sideways.

"Hey!" Charlie shouted.

The man, who'd continued on his way as if nothing had happened, stopped and turned.

He was dressed in black from head to foot: black suit, black shoes, a black shirt, and black silk gloves on his hands.

"I'm sorry," he said. "Did I knock into you?"

"Why don't you watch where you're going?" said Charlie.

The man's eyes narrowed a little. "I've told you I'm sorry," he said.

"Yeah?" replied Charlie. "Well, sorry's not good enough!"

Jack held his breath.

The man raised an eyebrow. His face seemed to take on an odd, calculating sort of expression. There was a long, slow moment of silence, then—

"Suit yourself," said the black-clad man, and in another second he'd vanished into the crowd.

"Jesus," said Charlie. "Some people. Come on, I need to get some cash."

Jack followed without arguing.

The queue for the cash machine was seventeen people long. A very smelly, very dirty young man with sunken-in cheeks and a filthy blue sleeping bag slung over one shoulder was squatting in the alcove at the side of the machine.

"Spare any change, lads?" he asked when they eventually got to the front.

S
A
M

E
N
T
H
O
V
E
N

"Piss off," Charlie replied. He shoved his card into the machine and jabbed at the numbers.

Jack sighed again. It was going to be a long afternoon.

"'Scuse me," said a voice.

The boys looked round.

"'Scuse me," said the sleeping-bag man again. "It's just . . . I think you've dropped a fiver." He pointed at the ground next to him. The boys looked. It was true: lying on the pavement not two inches from the man's bare and astonishingly dirty feet was a crumpled green five-pound note.

"Er . . . cheers," muttered Charlie. He bent down to pick up the money, and then everything happened very fast.

The man shot out an arm, yanked Charlie's card out of the machine, leaped to his feet, and ran off down the street, shoving tourists aside as he went.

"What?" said Charlie. "He's got my card!" He ran off after him.

Jack watched Charlie haring up the road. The thief, it seemed to Jack, was impossibly far ahead. But then something amazing happened. The thief stopped running.

He'd stopped dead, in fact, in the middle of the pavement, right in front of another pedestrian.

It wasn't, was it? The black-clad man! And as, panting heavily, Jack arrived at the scene, he could hear the man speaking, slowly and carefully.

"**Give it to me,**" the black-clad man was saying, holding out a gloved hand. "**Give me what you've stolen. Now.**"

His voice was strange: it seemed to echo in Jack's head, making small flowering explosions go off behind his eyeballs.

For another moment, the thief just stared as if mesmerized. Then his hand was coming out.

No way!

"**Now go**," said the man, and the thief ran off, even faster than he'd been going before.

Jack gaped.

Charlie gaped too.

The black-clad man just smiled and handed the card back to Charlie.

"Whoa," said Charlie, looking at the card in his hand. "I mean . . . thanks," he added quickly.

The man shrugged, but he kept looking at Charlie with the same calculating, almost greedy expression that Jack had noticed before.

"Uh . . . listen," Charlie began, "I'm sorry about before."

"Think nothing of it," said the man. "You look like you're having a rough day. I'm Nick."

"Charlie."

"I'm Jack," said Jack—but suddenly, it seemed, no one was listening.

"I, uh, really appreciate you, y'know, getting my card back," said Charlie. "Is there anything I can do to, ah, thank you?"

"Well," said Nick, "there is one thing. I'd like you—both of you," he corrected himself, "to come with me and take a small test. It won't take more than a few moments of your time, and it's something you might find . . . interesting."

"What kind of test?" asked Charlie.

"Actually," said Nick, "words don't really help. It's something you have to see for yourself. But I rather think," he added, smiling at Charlie again, "that you're exactly the person I've been looking for. What do you say?"

Cynical, Jack crooked an eyebrow. But then—

"Sure," said Charlie, "why not?"

"Splendid. Well, follow me," said Nick, and with that, he set off across the road.

Charlie turned, but before he could follow this total stranger that he'd just randomly decided to go off with, Jack grabbed him.

"Charlie!"

"What?" asked Charlie, shaking Jack's hand off and scowling.

For a moment, Jack just stared at him.

Jack and Charlie were teenagers now. Maybe there was some point after which "talking to strangers" was okay, some point at which the rules changed and you were less likely to get kidnapped, murdered, or whatever.

Jack sighed. Of course there wasn't.

"Charlie, what are you doing?" he asked, gesturing and trying for a smile. "That guy could be anybody!"

"So?" Charlie asked.

Jack blinked.

"You coming?" Charlie asked. "Or what?"

Without waiting for a reply, he set off after Nick, leaving Jack staring at his back.

Well, thought Jack, there it was. With Charlie in this kind of a mood, there was no telling what he was going to do— or what kind of trouble he was going to get into. And just as before, when they'd been standing outside the restaurant, there was no choice for Jack, not really. Sighing uselessly, he set off after his friend.

They were heading back toward Cambridge Circus, back the way they'd come, but then Nick turned left, taking Charlie down a side street. When Jack caught up with them, they were standing outside an old and solid-looking black back door that looked strangely small in the mountain of red brick that surrounded it. Nick smiled thinly at the boys and pressed the buzzer. Jack looked up at the Palace Theatre again.

It was odd how different the back looked from the front. There were no fancy windows and statues here, just a vast Victorian clod of red brick with a cast-iron fire escape sticking out the top. The afternoon sun was very bright, so Jack looked down—and that was when he glimpsed something strange.

There was a weird kind of shadow on the back of Nick's neck: weirder still, it was *moving.* Curves and spikes of inky darkness were drifting across the man's skin. Jack blinked.

But when he opened his eyes again, whatever he'd seen was gone. Except for the glossy comma of Nick's long black ponytail, the back of his neck was bare.

Jack shook his head to clear it. *Should've brought my sunglasses*, he told himself.

"Yeah?" grunted a voice from the intercom.

"It's me," said Nick.

The door buzzed. The black-clad man pushed it open, and he gestured the boys inside.

THE TEST

Nick led them up a spiral staircase to a set of double doors. Jack had been feeling more uneasy with every step—but then the doors opened, and he suddenly found he was looking at the most beautiful girl he'd ever seen in his life.

She was dressed in a red hooded top and green combat trousers. Her thick black curly hair was tied back tightly in a bunch, leaving dark little wisps at her temples. Her face was angular and fiercely elegant, her skin was the warm color of milky tea, and her eyes were the most extraordinary shade of amber. They flicked from Jack to Charlie, and the fine black curves of her eyebrows arched at Nick in a quizzical expression: evidently, she wasn't too impressed by what she'd seen. As far as Jack was now concerned, however, following Nick didn't seem like quite such a bad idea.

"Esme," said Nick, "I'd like you to meet Charlie . . ."

"Hi," said Charlie.

". . . and, I'm sorry, what was your name again?"

"Jack," said Jack, annoyed.

"And this is Raymond," Nick said, joining the large and

frankly terrifying-looking hairy man who was standing by the long conference table in the center of the room. "There. Now the introductions are out of the way, perhaps we can get started."

"Hold on," said Raymond. "*These* are the new recruits you wanted? Two kids you just found on the street?"

"That," said Nick crisply, "is precisely what we're about to find out."

Esme frowned at the boys, shrugged, then closed the doors, leaving Jack and Charlie just standing there.

The room they were in was very big. The wide walls sloped inward toward a high, arched ceiling and were covered with a pattern of regularly spaced, strange-looking blotchlike things. The only light in the room came from a great round window at the far end, so Jack was having trouble making out the details.

"My colleagues and I," said Nick, leaning back against the table, "belong to a small yet ancient organization known as the Brotherhood of Sleep. We're . . . jailers," he said. "Of a kind anyway; our prisoner is a demon. We call it the Scourge."

At that, Jack gave up looking around and stared openly at Nick instead.

"I'm sorry," said Charlie, "but I don't think I heard you right. Did you just say 'demon'?"

"That's right," said Nick. "A demon. A being of pure liquid darkness, bent on a path of destruction."

Jack raised his eyebrows.

"Many thousands of years ago," said Nick, "the Scourge was defeated by a powerful curse. The curse kept the demon imprisoned where it could do no harm, and the Brotherhood's task was to make sure that it stayed that way. However, as the centuries passed, our order became complacent: our numbers thinned, and those who remained grew . . . weak. One day, over a decade ago now, one of our members betrayed us."

Nick walked slowly around the table until he stood at the far end, resting his black-gloved hands on the chair at its head.

"Hungry for power, the man—Felix, his name was— allowed the Scourge to possess him. The demon took him over and became very strong: we only just managed to recapture it. In the battle another member of our group—Esme's mother, Belinda—was killed."

Jack looked at Esme, but she showed no reaction. Her strange amber eyes were bright as she concentrated on what was being said. (She was, Jack decided, really very pretty indeed, actually.)

"In the years since that night, I've traveled the world," said Nick, "searching for new recruits to bring the Brotherhood back up to strength—without success," he added, with a wan smile at Charlie, "until today. But now, with the Brotherhood still in tatters, I find we have been betrayed again."

He sighed (a bit dramatically, Jack thought).

"The Scourge has been unleashed once more," said Nick. "For thousands of years it has been biding its time, waiting for the moment to come when it can put its terrible plans into action. Now, I fear, it will succeed. Unless we have your help."

Nick paused.

"I need the three of you," he said, looking at Esme, then Jack, then back at Charlie again, "to take a small test. This test will decide which of you is going to become the Brotherhood's next leader."

"But Nick!" Raymond spluttered. "You didn't mention this was about who's going to be leader!"

"Frankly, Raymond," said Nick, "I'd've thought it was obvious. You and I no longer have the strength to do what must be done: it is time to pass the burden to the next generation. The one who performs best in the test will take on as much of my own power as I am able to give, becoming the new leader of the group."

"But . . . that should be Esme, shouldn't it?" Raymond asked. "She's been training all her life."

"So you keep telling me," said Nick. Then, seeing Raymond's and Esme's shocked expressions, he sighed.

"Look," he told them, "I know this might seem strange to you. But the Brotherhood needs reinforcements and time is short. You've always trusted me before, Raymond: trust me now. *Trust me*," Nick repeated. "That's all I ask."

Raymond and Esme looked at each other but said nothing: already, Nick had gone back to concentrating on Charlie.

"Now, what you're being offered here," he went on, staring at Charlie intently, "is something in the way of a proper adventure. A chance to battle an ancient evil and—quite possibly—save the world. And all I need from you, at this stage, is a simple yes or no. So . . . what's your answer?"

There was a pause.

Jack had loved fantasy, science fiction, and horror all his life—the films, the games, and the books. He'd heard worse stories, and, frankly, he'd heard better ones, but no one had ever expected him to believe one was actually *true* before. He was so nonplussed, he wasn't sure how to react, so he turned and looked at Charlie.

To his amazement, Charlie wasn't even smiling: he was looking at Nick with fixed attention—giving every appearance of having listened seriously to every word Nick had said. Jack waited for him to say no. He waited for Charlie to burst out laughing—for him to do anything, in fact, except what he did, which was shrug and say—

"All right. Sure."

"Splendid," said Nick, already setting off back round the table toward them.

Jack stared at his friend.

"Wait!" he said, his voice coming out (infuriatingly) as a kind of squeak. "Er . . . what sort of 'test' are we talking about here?" he asked, in the gruffest voice he could manage.

"I'll show you," said Nick.

Slowly, grimacing with pain, he began to pull off his gloves, one finger at a time. Then, when the gloves were off, he turned his hands and held them out in front of him, palms out. There was a sharp intake of breath from everyone in the room.

The skin of Nick's hands was horribly burned all over. The palms were two masses of thick scar tissue—red, inflamed, and glistening.

"Could the three of you stand in a line, please?" asked Nick politely. "This won't take long."

Suddenly, Jack was standing with Charlie on his left and Esme on his right. Their faces were grim: to Jack's mounting dismay, everyone apart from him seemed to be taking this seriously. He looked at Nick, who had closed his eyes, concentrating—and Jack's stare widened even further.

Something was happening. Something weird.

The air in front of Nick's dreadful scarred hands began to wobble and shake. The effect was a bit like heat haze, but it only lasted for a moment, because just then a shadowy shape appeared, a shape that instantly began to thicken and stretch. In another moment something long and silvery had formed in Nick's hands, which were closing around it. Then, before Jack's brain really had time to register what it had seen, Nick was holding what appeared to be some sort of long metal bar, horizontally, so it stuck out to either side of him. The bar's length stretched along all three of them—Esme and Charlie too.

"Now," said Nick, "take hold of the staff."

Esme went first, taking her end of the object with both hands. Charlie took hold of his end too. *All right*, thought Jack, and followed their example. The object was smooth and cool in his hands—solid and real in every respect, save for the fact that it had just appeared out of thin air.

"Ready?" Nick whispered. His horrible burned hands were clamped on either side of Jack's. "Go," he croaked.

Jack felt a sudden pain, like red-hot scissors stabbing into his hands.

Before he could stop himself, he'd let go.

Nick's eyes snapped open.

"S-sorry," Jack stammered. "Wasn't ready."

"On three this time," said Nick, through his teeth. "Hold on for as long as you can." He closed his eyes once more.

"One . . . two . . . *three.*"

And it started again.

The pain was astonishing. It felt as though the skin of Jack's hands was being peeled off with red-hot pincers, like his palms were being devoured by ants. Jack resisted as long as he could—which was about two seconds—then he let go with a gasp.

This time, however, Nick did not stop the test.

Jack glanced down at his hands. They were completely unharmed. They weren't even tingling. Jack turned to Charlie, fully expecting his friend to have let go too.

But he had not.

Charlie's hands were clenched tight around the staff, the bones in his knuckles standing out white under the skin. His eyes were squeezed shut, and the muscles around his mouth were bunched into knots from the way he was clamping his jaws closed—but he wasn't letting go. And that, really, was when Jack began to get scared.

He looked from Charlie to the girl on his right, Esme. Her

eyes were closed too, but she appeared much more relaxed than Charlie. Her face was a mask of concentration and control, and Jack could see that she wouldn't be letting go of the staff anytime soon. What scared him was that he knew Charlie wouldn't either.

In the breathless hush of the big, dimly lit room, Jack suddenly became aware of a low, electrical humming sound. In front of him, under the hands of Nick and Charlie and Esme, Jack saw the blue-black surface of the staff give off a gunmetal glint—then begin, imperceptibly at first, to glow. Slowly, Charlie's lips parted and curled back, his face scrunching up even harder.

What is he thinking? Jack wondered.

In Charlie's mind, there was a soft, velvety rush of darkness.

When it lifted, he was at home, back in the kitchen, with his dad.

The scene was exactly the same as the morning when his dad had told him he was leaving, only the light was a bit strange and flickery. Charlie's dad's eyes too were different somehow. Darker. Almost black.

"Listen to me carefully, Charlie," said Charlie's dad. "It's time you heard the truth." The voice was a little deeper, a little louder than normal, and each word seemed to set off small flowering splashes behind Charlie's eyes.

"You know what it means," his dad began, "about me leaving?"

Charlie said nothing, just listened.

"It means that everything you know is a lie."

A shrill, cold sensation was filling up in Charlie's stomach. He stared, frozen.

"I don't expect you to understand this—you're young, after all," said his father. "But I think even *you* can get it, if I say that a lot of the time when you were growing up—for a lot of the time when we were together as a family—I was . . . wishing I was somewhere else."

He paused, giving Charlie a few moments to let this sink in.

"But—" said Charlie.

"Ah," said his dad, holding up a hand, "don't tell me. You're going to say that you had no idea. That you thought I seemed happy. Yes?"

Charlie said nothing.

"You know the answer to this one, Charlie," said his father.

"Oh no . . ." said Charlie. The cold feeling in his belly was getting stronger.

"I did it for *you*," said his dad slowly. "For fourteen years, fourteen years of living a lie, I kept the whole miserable thing going—for you. Now."

He smiled, the lips drawing back from his teeth.

"Parts of our time together as a family have been . . . nice. And I love you, Charlie. You're my son."

"Oh, Dad . . . please . . ."

"But the fact remains that every good memory you have, each and every good time you thought we had, has now changed."

He paused.

"From now on, whenever you think back to time you spent with me—whenever you look back to your childhood and anything good in it—you'll be wondering . . ."

He leaned forward, his eyes flashing darkly, the blackness in them widening.

"**Were we happy?**" asked his father.

"Oh no," Charlie whispered.

"**Were we really as happy as you remember?**"

"Please, Dad . . . no . . ."

"**Or was one of us just . . . pretending?**"

Charlie's hands were black shapes, clenched tight against the brightening orange-yellow of the staff. His head hung low, his shoulders were hunched—and Jack watched helplessly as, right in front of him, his friend started to moan to himself.

It was a quiet sound at first, a sound that Jack had never heard a person make before: a low, weird, keening kind of sound. Charlie's mouth was barely open. He was swaying slightly, as if the sound itself were making him move, as if the sound were a separate creature somehow, something that had been waiting and growing deep inside him, waiting for its chance to come out.

"Ohhhhhhh-ho," said Charlie. "Oh, Dad."

His face was red and sticky-looking, his tears glittering in the light from the magical staff. Jack stared, fascinated.

"Ohhhhhh, Dad," moaned Charlie, louder now. "Oh no."

He took one more rasping breath, threw back his shoulders, and tipped his head back—

—and *howled*.

It was a terrible sound, an indescribable sound—a dry, scratching, inhuman sound, like grinding glass and tearing paper. It went on and on, getting louder and louder. Jack wanted to shut his eyes but he couldn't, he couldn't look away, and now, suddenly, the staff was blazing white, and the humming was filling the room, almost loud enough to drown out the terrible, maiming sound that was coming from Charlie's mouth.

Esme's lips were pressed tight together now, turning pale with tension and effort.

"It's not right," said someone suddenly. It was Raymond. "Nick, this isn't right! It shouldn't be like this!"

"**Let it out,**" said a voice in Charlie's head. "**Let it all out, open your heart, and LET ME IN. *YES!*''**

And suddenly, everything happened at once.

Esme let go with a shout.

There was a thunderous, echoing CRACK.

And the staff, or whatever it was, vanished.

For a long moment, there was silence. Nick, still holding out his horribly scarred hands, stood swaying on his feet, blinking.

"What?" he said, looking at his surroundings and the people staring at him, as if taking them in for the first time.

"Where am—? Wait," said Nick. "This is . . ." Then he looked down at his hands. His face went suddenly white with horror, and his mouth fell open.

"Oh no," he said. "Oh, God. This is—wait! No! You can't! *The*—"

But before he could finish whatever he'd been going to say, his eyes rolled back, his knees buckled beneath him, and he sank, insensible, to the floor. Esme and Raymond rushed to his side.

Charlie, meanwhile, was looking at his hands.

The skin, from palms to fingertips, was completely, utterly black: an inky, glistening, polished-ebony black. As he watched, the darkness bunched and wriggled for a moment—then it shot straight up his arms, disappearing under the sleeves of his shirt. Slowly, Charlie let his hands fall to his sides.

"Charlie?" said a voice. It was Jack. "Charlie, what's happened?"

For a moment, Charlie didn't answer. His eyes, though red from crying, were shining strangely. He blinked, looked at Jack, and smiled.

"It's all right, mate," he said slowly. "It's all going to be all right."

Esme—who'd been holding Nick's wrist—looked at Raymond. There was a long silence. Then she said, "He's dead."

"Three o'clock tomorrow," barked Raymond to Charlie, as he bundled the boys through the door.

"But what about that guy?" spluttered Jack. "He's, you know . . . dead!"

"Not your problem, mate," said Raymond. "Three o'clock *sharp*," he emphasized, still looking at Charlie.

"What about me?" asked Jack, before the door closed.

Raymond paused.

"I don't know," he said, his eyes narrowing at Jack. "What about you?"

"He comes or I don't," said Charlie.

"Suit yourself." The big man turned and was gone.

Jack and Charlie stared at the door for a moment, even though it had slammed shut. They looked at each other, then they looked out at the street.

The sky was empty of clouds, and the afternoon sun was still hot and strong, making the pavement blaze uncomfortably. Traffic was heavy in both directions, and another long snake of sweaty-looking tourists was crawling its way west on the opposite side of the street.

Charlie turned to Jack. "It's too hot for the Tube," he said. "Let's get a bus."

"Oh," said Jack, surprised. "Er, okay." They set off, and soon they were safely wobbling their way north, back toward where they both lived.

They were sitting on the top deck of the bus, at the front, where they always sat, like everything was perfectly normal. It was almost as if—Jack thought—the whole episode had been some kind of dream. When he found that he couldn't stand it any longer, Jack spoke.

"Charlie, are you all right?"

"Huh?" said Charlie, drumming his hands on his knees.

"Are you *all right*?" Jack repeated.

"I'm fine, mate!" said Charlie. "Better than fine: I'm terrific. Fantastic. Amazing!"

Jack looked at him. Charlie's eyes were shining: his grin was huge. He certainly looked well enough.

"What about your hands?" Jack asked.

"What? Oh," said Charlie. He stopped drumming and showed them to Jack. "Look, they're fine too. Not a scratch!"

It was true. Charlie's hands looked perfectly normal; there were no outward signs of his ordeal. There was no sign in Charlie of anything that had happened, in fact, from the scene in the restaurant to . . . whatever the Hell had just taken place upstairs at the theater.

"So," said Jack. "Let me get this straight."

Charlie looked at him and grinned some more.

"Demons are real," Jack started.

"Apparently," said Charlie.

"And there's one on the loose. A bad one."

"'Liquid darkness, bent on destruction,' yadda yadda yadda," said Charlie.

"And *you*," said Jack, grinning back despite himself, "are now the new leader of an ancient brotherhood whose sole sworn purpose is to fight this . . .'scourge'—and bring it back under control."

"That's about the size of it, yeah," said Charlie. His grin widened. "Pretty cool, huh?"

Jack was doing his best: really, he was, and Charlie's enthusiasm, as always, was infectious. But a large part of his brain just couldn't help having doubts, and he knew that he had to say something.

"What about that guy, though?" Jack asked. "The one who just, like, *died* right in front of us?"

Charlie's grin vanished. "Jack, don't get boring on me, all right?"

Stung to the quick, Jack closed his mouth and fell silent.

Being called boring—especially by Charlie—was Jack's

Achilles' heel. The idea that he was boring scared Jack, because secretly, he was worried it might be true. Jack admired Charlie's ability to throw himself into things. It was part of the reason they got on.

Perhaps seeing the effect that his words had had, Charlie smiled again.

"Mate, this is what we've been waiting for," he breathed. "The chance to have a real adventure! Don't you see? Heh," he added, chuckling to himself, "and what about that Esme, eh?"

"What about her?" asked Jack, as casually as he could.

"Come on, man," said Charlie. "You were there."

Jack squirmed for a second as Charlie grinned in his face, and finally admitted, "She's all right."

"All right?" Charlie echoed with disbelief. "She's better than all right, mate. She's *gorgeous*. And did you see the way she looked at me?"

Jack hadn't, but his lack of reply didn't seem to stop Charlie.

"Oh yes," Charlie pronounced sagely. "Very promising, I'd say."

There was a pause.

"So," said Jack, giving up trying to sort it all out in his head. "This 'power' the guy gave you. You're, what, some kind of superhero now?"

"I guess we'll find out tomorrow," said Charlie gleefully.

"You going to start wearing your pants outside your trousers, then?" asked Jack. "Do you think we should get you a cape?"

"Tchah, *right*," said Charlie, looking out of the window again.

DARKNESS

People are used to seeing the homeless in the West End, and as the day passed and Jessica sat motionless in her circle, few people noticed her and none cared. That night, when the Scourge came to her for the second time, it just stood there at first, testing the protective ring of magic-charged tobacco and cigarette ends with long, wet, ink-black fingers.

"Do you believe in God, Jessica?" it asked.

Jessica had now been sitting cross-legged on the damp concrete walkway, without changing her position, for a full twenty-four hours. She did not dignify this with a reply.

"I've met him, you know," the demon told her conversationally. "Your 'God.' He's rather different from how you imagine him, I should think. Still, I'm looking forward to seeing him again. I want to tell him exactly what I think of him."

Jessica didn't answer.

"It was clever of you to suspect Nick all this time," said the Scourge, unperturbed. "No one else guessed he would never complete the ritual to reimprison me. Even he thought he was strong enough to resist—right up to the end."

Surprised despite herself, Jessica looked up.

"Yes," the Scourge told her, "Nick's dead. And I have found a worthy vessel at last."

Jessica said nothing.

"He's perfect," said the demon. "Young, hotheaded, and with a pain and fury inside him that is most"—it gave a liquid shudder—"invigorating. When the time comes for him to understand what I can offer him, there's no chance whatever he'll refuse me. You see, I'm not just going to make him into a god." It leaned closer. "I'm going to make him *stronger* than God."

The Scourge took a step toward her.

"I'm going to take your life, Jessica," it said. "I'm going to suck out your essence, to your last breath; I'm going to do the same to each of your little band until I've had my satisfaction from every one of you. And then, *then,* with this boy as my puppet, I'm going to open the Fracture, and—"

"And what?" Jessica interrupted, making a face. "What is your 'sinister master plan to conquer the world,' exactly? I wish you'd tell me straight, instead of all this posing."

"My dear woman," said the Scourge slowly, "I may still be stuck here in this ludicrous little science project, but I assure you, my horizons are somewhat wider. When I go back to Hell I'm going to wake the Dragon—and the Dragon is going to destroy *everything.* Well?" it asked. "What do you think of that?"

"Would you be quiet, please?" said Jessica. "I'm trying to concentrate here."

The demon froze.

"It's started, Jessica," it told her quietly. **"There's nothing anyone can do to prevent it."**

Jessica just closed her eyes again.

Esme was far too angry to sleep—and whenever she couldn't sleep, she trained. At this moment, she was using her makiwara boards.

The makiwara boards were the only pieces of actual training equipment that Raymond had ever allowed her to own or use. Five solid oak blocks screwed to the wall in the shape of a cross at the far end of her training room, their purpose was brutally simple. With her fists, her feet, her knees, her elbows—with every striking point of her body from the top of her forehead to the backs of her heels—she was hitting the blocks as fast, as hard, and as often as she could.

Students of martial arts have used makiwara boards—or their equivalents—for centuries. They are used to toughen the skin, to deaden and finally kill the nerve endings in the student's striking points—to make the student's body as resilient, as hard, as the wood. The purpose of makiwara training is also mental: thanks to her years with the blocks, Esme had learned to control her pain and not let it affect her.

She had been hitting the boards for about an hour. Standing behind her, Raymond noted wearily that each of the five dark oak surfaces now carried a telltale dark smudge of red.

"Esme?"

She ignored him, continuing to smash at the boards.

Raymond stood behind her, watching her, watching the way the muscles in her back bunched and moved as she worked: graceful, efficient—lethal. It was odd, he thought, how being so proud of someone could hurt you so much at the same time.

"I'm sorry, petal," he said quietly. "I . . ." He looked at his feet. "I didn't know the test would be like that."

"Don't make excuses," said Esme, without looking—without stopping. WHAM. CRACK. *CRUNCH.* A knee strike, an elbow smash, and a straight punch followed each other into the boards. Under the last, one of them splintered. "That's what you've always told me, right? No excuses."

There was nothing to say. Raymond looked at her helplessly. Should he tell her how astonished he still was by Nick's last actions? How bitterly disappointed he was too that after all these years, all the hard work he and Esme had put in, Nick should give the job of new leader to a novice? No. That was all just doubt. Nick had told them to trust him, and with the Scourge on the loose, doubt was a luxury. Still . . .

"Esme, I want to tell you something."

He looked back down at his feet and took a deep breath.

"I don't pretend to know a lot about magic," he said carefully. "That side of things is best left to those who have the gift, and that's fine with me, as you know. But in my time, I've met some very powerful people. I saw Nick in action in the early days. Your mum too. And I—" He stopped suddenly and took another deep breath.

"Well. Here's what I wanted to say."

He looked at her hard.

"There's something a bit special about you," he said. "I know it."

He paused.

"Now, if this 'Charlie' is the new leader, well, that's it, that's how it is. But I'm telling you, there's no chance we can recapture the Scourge without your help—no chance at all. This is still what we've been working and training for," he told her fervently. "This is still your moment to break out and spread your wings: your moment to shine. So . . . will you stop that now and get some rest? Please?"

He waited, trying not to let his smile waver.

After a long moment, Esme let her hands fall to her sides. Already the blood on her knuckles was drying up and vanishing: the physical damage she'd inflicted on herself was melting magically away, just as it always did—leaving only what was inside. Turning, she stood toe-to-toe with Raymond, her chin about level with his chest. Then suddenly, she stepped forward and wrapped her arms round his waist, as far as they would go.

Raymond gave a deep sigh and put his own arms around Esme's small, strong body, patting her gently with his big hands.

"G'night, Dad," said Esme, her voice muffled.

"G'night, petal," said Raymond. As soon as he felt her arms relinquish him, he released her and turned to go.

Felix Middleton, the man who'd first betrayed the Brotherhood, stood in his flat and waited. The Alembic House apartment was one of the finest and most expensive in the whole city, and Felix didn't like it. He didn't really care for its stunningly opulent furniture, its thick dark rugs and carpets. The panoramic view of the Thames and half of London, even lit up (as it was then) with all the glories of the city's nighttime lights, did little for him. From where he was standing, the wide picture window held two images: the city and a reflection of himself, standing in his room, alone. Felix wasn't relaxed. He wasn't happy or sad—but he was calm. After all, he had done all he could.

The logistics of arranging his not-inconsiderable personal fortune so that, on his death, one girl could have access to all of it, instantly, without fear of interference from governments, tax departments, or any other hindrances, had been no simple matter. But Felix was not a simple man. In the fourteen years since he had set himself on his path, Felix had cut a swath across the financial markets of the world, a trail of conquest no less devastating for its having been so quiet. But when the Scourge came for him now, as he fully expected it would, would that be the end of it? Would he have . . . atoned?

Felix allowed himself a bitter smile. Of course not.

He had done it, the unthinkable. By releasing the Scourge he'd unleashed a terror in the world, a terror that could be slowed but never put down. He had also destroyed a family. For him there could be no redemption, no forgiveness. He could only do what he could, use what he was good at as best he could, and never make another mistake, ever, ever again.

And he had made no more mistakes. His life was empty,

dry as sand, but he had made no more mistakes. He could take what comfort he could from that.

He gazed at the reflection in the window: the dim green of the glass-shaded lamps, the winged silhouettes of the dark leather chairs, and all the other expensive trappings. He gazed at them and past them, at the city beyond, until the ice cubes melted in his glass and, finally, in one corner of the room behind him, a patch of shadow began to move by itself. He fixed his eyes on the reflection of that piece of the dark as it bulged, swam, and took shape.

"At last," he said.

Felix gulped the remains of his drink: the fiery liquid slid down inside him as he put down his glass. Still smiling a bitter, grim smile, he now turned to face his nightmare.

"For nearly fifteen years, I've dreamed of you," he told it. "Every night the same dream. And every morning I've woken up knowing that I'm never, ever going to be free of you, and what I—*we*—did. So come on." Felix beckoned. "Come on and get it over with. Because frankly, I've got nothing left to lose."

"No," said the Scourge.

Felix frowned at the demon uncertainly. This wasn't how the moment was supposed to go. "No . . . what?" he asked.

"**No, I'm not going to kill you yet,**" the Scourge replied, "**and no, you still have something to lose.**"

Felix looked at the demon: its man-shaped body of liquid black and the shiny black blank of its face. "You're not talking about . . . Esme?" he asked.

The demon just waited.

"But I'm nothing to her," said Felix, smiling bitterly. "Less than nothing, I should think. Why, all she knows is that I released you, and through me you . . ." He trailed off suddenly and shuddered.

"Precisely," said the demon. It paused.

"Felix," it asked slowly, "have you ever wondered about Esme? About her power, her strength, her speed? Have you ever asked yourself where they came from?"

Felix turned pale. "No. Never. Why?"

"Felix, Felix," the demon admonished. "You never could lie to me."

There was silence between them for a moment.

"Oh, God," said Felix. "Oh please, no. No."

"This is one secret you don't get to carry to your grave, I'm afraid. She'll never take my word for it alone."

"But . . . please," said Felix. "Why can't you just—?"

"Quiet."

And there was quiet.

Presently, the demon stopped what it was doing and froze, crouched over Felix's body.

It was good enough. Felix wouldn't be telling any tales until the time was right. The demon stood up, took two steps, then vanished.

In his house, in his room, in his fitful sleep, Charlie twisted on the bed. Darkness spread through his veins like strong wine.

SKILLS

Charlie answered the door in his sunglasses. Once Jack was safely inside, however, he took them off—and Jack had his first shock.

"I know," said Charlie, looking away before Jack could even think of what to say. Charlie's eyes were red and puffy, with thick dark blue smudges underneath them. He looked awful.

"Mum was up most of the night again," he said. "She's asleep now, so we'll have to be quiet."

"Oh, mate," said Jack stupidly.

"Anyway," said Charlie, and a glint appeared in his eyes, "listen, before we go, I want to show you something. What do you know about tattoos?"

"Er . . ." said Jack—but Charlie had already got his T-shirt up round his neck.

"What do you think," he asked, "of this?"

He turned his back, and Jack had a second shock.

"Eh?" said Charlie, when Jack didn't answer at first, then again: "Eh?" He stretched out his arms.

"Blimey," said Jack finally.

From shoulder to shoulder and right down Charlie's back, almost as far as the waistband of his jeans, was a huge black tattoo.

Jack stared.

It was an odd sort of pattern. The tattoo's broad, curving shapes reminded Jack of certain tribal designs, Celtic or Native American ones, but it wasn't quite like anything he'd ever seen before. The shapes seemed to radiate out from Charlie's spine, scything across his back like a crest of broad feathers or a set of great curved sword blades. The shapes were black against Charlie's pale skin—completely, utterly black—and each and every one of them ended in a perfect, razor-sharp point. Charlie clenched his arms, and the black shapes seemed to bunch and shift of their own accord as his muscles moved underneath them.

Even apart from the fact that it had just appeared on Charlie's back, the tattoo made Jack uneasy. Still, he thought, with a twinge of envy, it was certainly impressive. In fact, no denying it, it was most definitely . . .

"*Cool,*" he breathed.

"Huh. Yeah," said Charlie, turning casually. "Got the surprise of my life when I caught sight of it in the mirror this morning."

"Does it hurt?"

"Naaah," said Charlie. "Not really."

"And that's the . . . thing? From yesterday?"

"Well, I don't think Mum drew it on me in the night."

"Wow," said Jack. He meant it.

"Come on," said Charlie, pulling his T-shirt down and getting into a short-sleeved shirt. He left it unbuttoned and untucked, hanging over the waistband of his black jeans, showing his black T-shirt underneath. He stuck his shades back on and turned to Jack.

"Let's go," he said.

"Yeah?" Esme's voice was cool and level through the speaker.

"It's me," barked Charlie.

"You're early." It was a statement, nothing accusatory, but Charlie said, "Well, I'm here. You letting me in or what?"

The girl didn't answer, but the lock on the door at the back of the theater buzzed loudly. Charlie pushed it open, then they were through.

"Raymond's not back yet," said Esme. "We'll have to wait." Then she just stood there, arms crossed, looking at the boys. An awkward silence began to develop.

Jack looked around the room. It was the same room they'd been taken to the day before, but this was the first chance he'd really had to get a proper look at it.

"That, er, pattern," he said, pointing at the regularly spaced blotch things he'd noticed previously. "It's . . . well, what is it?"

"Butterflies," said Esme, as if it were obvious.

"Oh, right," said Jack. "They're . . . nice."

Esme looked at him. "Thanks," she said. "I did them myself."

"Really?" asked Jack. "Mind if I . . . ?"

Esme shrugged. Jack walked over to the nearest wall.

Each butterfly was about thirty centimeters across and painted with incredible accuracy. The wings of the one that had first caught Jack's eye were quite beautiful: a powdery, electric-blue color on a background of deepest black. Its neighbor was different, orange and black this time, with wider, more elongated wings. In fact, although it was hard to see far along the wall with the light so low, it suddenly occurred to Jack that—

"Are they all different?"

"Yep," said Esme.

"I didn't know there were that many kinds," said Jack.

"Well, there are. Nobody really knows how many."

"How many have you got here?"

"Five thousand, four hundred and seventy-two," Esme replied flatly.

"Wow!" said Jack.

It came out much more loudly than he'd meant; both Esme and Charlie were now staring at him. Charlie rolled his eyes and gave Jack an exasperated look.

"Er . . . how long did that take you?" Jack mumbled.

"Seven years," said Esme (making Jack stare at her). "On a good day, I can do three." She gestured toward a shadowy point some distance away in the corner of the ceiling. "I haven't quite finished yet, though."

The boys looked up. The arched ceiling had to be a good sixty or seventy feet high, surely taller than the tallest stepladder, and yet it too was entirely covered in row upon row of painted butterflies—all except for a large empty patch at one end. *How on Earth . . . ?* Jack looked back down at Esme, but then the double doors opened and Raymond strode in.

"Right," said the big man. "Esme, Charlie—walk to the center of the room, turn, and face each other. It's time to see what Wonder Boy here can do."

Charlie blinked but did as he was told. Esme followed. Jack watched.

The butterfly room was cool and dark after the heat of the day outside. The sun through the great round window cast a long oval of creamy light across the hard matting of the floor. The conference table had been shifted out of the way, propped against the wall at the far end; there was nothing in the center of the room but the big padded floor, the pool of light, and Charlie and Esme, standing in the shadows to either side of it, some three yards apart. Charlie had taken off his button-down shirt so was now dressed in just his black T-shirt and jeans. He was smiling. Esme too was dressed lightly, in a fitted camouflage-green T-shirt and loose combat trousers, her hair tied back in a thick, tight bunch: her face was expressionless. Raymond stayed by the door, obviously keeping well back from whatever was about to happen, and Jack took his cue from him. The whole scene was beginning to remind Jack of pretty much every martial arts beat-'em-up game he'd ever played in his life. This was not a happy realization for him.

"Brotherhood members have different talents," said Raymond. "Our first job, Charlie, is to find out where yours lie, so let's start you off with a little sparring match. Esme?"

She turned. Raymond smiled, making his beard bristle alarmingly.

"Go easy on the lad to start with," he said. "We wouldn't want to hurt him"—his smile widened—"much."

Esme didn't smile back, just turned to face Charlie and dropped into a shallow crouch, one foot slightly ahead of the other. Her honey-brown arms were held loosely at her sides. Her hands were open, relaxed. Charlie, still grinning, if a little dubious, did his best to follow her example.

"Ready?" called Raymond. "Fight."

There was a blur, then—

"*GAHH!*"

It was Charlie who made this noise, as all the air exploded out of his body.

Jack gaped.

Charlie was now sitting on the floor, with his back against the wall, some ten yards behind where he'd been standing. His legs were sticking out in front of him, and he was gasping like a stranded fish as he tried to get his breath back. Esme's expression and demeanor had not changed in the slightest. She looked exactly the same as she had a moment ago, only now she was standing in the middle of the room, where Charlie had been.

Whatever had just happened had been so fast, Jack hadn't even seen it.

"Get up, you big jessie," said Raymond. "She barely touched you."

Blinking, then scowling as he realized he was being insulted, Charlie did as he was told—staring at Esme.

"Walk back to the center," said Raymond. "Esme, step back a little if you please. All right, face each other again."

He waited until Charlie and Esme were back in their original positions. Charlie's panting breaths sounded loud in the silence.

"Now," said Raymond. "Did you notice something there, Charlie?"

Charlie looked at Raymond. "How d'you mean?" he managed.

"That little side kick to the ribs," prompted Raymond. "Did it get your attention?"

Charlie scowled again.

"Good. Charlie, Nick must have picked you for a reason. As I believe I mentioned, we're here to see what you can do. If you don't concentrate, you're wasting our time. Plus, Esme'll clump you again. It's as simple as that."

There was a pause. Charlie stared at Raymond, then turned and raised his eyebrows at Jack, who shrugged back, helplessly.

"CONCENTRATE!" barked the big man, making them both jump.

Charlie shrugged and turned to face Esme, who was still regarding him calmly.

"Now, ready?" said Raymond.

Jack leaned forward, willing his eyes to catch something of what was going on this time. Esme and Charlie dropped into their crouches, just as before. Charlie frowned.

"Fight!" barked Raymond.

Jack stared, and time went slack.

Instantly, on the word of command from Raymond,

Esme had leaped forward, pirouetting in the air as she hurtled toward Charlie, the spin bringing her right heel out and round for a kick that should have taken Charlie's head off.

But it missed him. Without the slightest sign of effort apart from his continued look of hunched concentration, Charlie simply leaned back out of the way, just far enough for Esme's foot to flash harmlessly past, scant millimeters in front of his nose.

Esme dropped smoothly onto her left foot and sank, still spinning, converting the momentum of her first attack into a low, scything sweep at Charlie's feet, but this time Charlie hopped into the air like a kangaroo, and Esme failed to reach her target again.

Jack stared and kept staring as the fight continued. It was like nothing he'd ever seen. No, scratch that: he *had* seen what he was seeing, thousands of times—only that had been in films or in games, and not right in front of him when one of the people involved was his best mate.

Esme was moving so fast he could hardly see her—faster than he'd ever seen a person move before—and her skills were extraordinary. But the thing was, as quickly, smoothly, and gracefully as Esme attacked, daisy-chaining her moves into a constant, blurring barrage of fists and feet—Charlie was faster.

Every blow Esme launched at him, every hammering punch or slashing kick, somehow failed to land. Charlie had no finesse. He had no skill. Even Jack could see that the way Charlie fought was closer to the playground style of flapping your arms wildly in front of you than anything in the work of, say, Jet Li or Yuen Wo Ping. But the fact remained, it was working: he was holding her off. Charlie's face was a blank, a mask. His feet (when they were on the ground) moved slowly, almost mechanically, as he stepped back under the force of Esme's onslaught. But then suddenly—

Whoosh—SMACK!

It was over.

In a move that took a whole second after it had happened for Jack to work it out, Esme simply flipped through the air over Charlie, lashing out as she landed with a vicious high kick with her right leg. Charlie turned to follow her—just in time to receive the sole of her foot squarely in the middle of his face. His legs went out from under him and the back of his head struck the floor. He actually slid for a clear six yards before coming to a stop.

Esme jogged a couple of steps lightly on the spot, her hands dangling loosely at her sides again.

Suddenly, Jack remembered to breathe. His eyes were out on stalks.

Charlie reached a hand to his face and groaned.

"You okay there, son?" called Raymond, not sounding too bothered either way.

"My dose hurds," was the muffled reply from the floor.

"You poor dear," said Raymond. "Sit up, let's 'ave a look at you."

Charlie sat up, gingerly feeling his face, a stunned look in his eyes. His nose was a weird putty-gray color, almost as flat as Raymond's, and the blood was running from it freely. Jack was about to go and help him, but before he'd even completed the thought, he felt a massive and steely grip on his arm. Raymond had grabbed him without even looking.

"Take your hand away," said Raymond to Charlie.

Charlie looked at him.

"Take your hand off your nose," Raymond repeated, none too patiently, "and close your eyes."

Frowning uncertainly, Charlie did as he was told.

"Now . . . concentrate."

There was absolute silence in the room now. Wondering what was supposed to happen next, Jack looked at Raymond. The big man still had Jack's arm in a viselike grip, but all his attention was focused on Charlie.

"Stop the pain," said Raymond, almost whispering. "And *make it better.*"

Frowning, Jack looked over at Charlie, and his eyes went wide again.

No way!

Charlie's nose appeared to be *straightening itself.* The tip came out slowly at first, almost as if Charlie were pushing it out with his tongue, but the shape of it was re-forming and the color was going back to normal. In another moment Charlie opened his eyes, crossing them as he stared at his good-as-new nose. Then he wiped off the last of the blood in a long streak along his arm—and he smiled.

"No *way,*" said Jack, aloud this time.

"Haaaaaaaaaaaah," said Charlie.

"Get up," said Raymond.

Charlie did, still smiling.

Without looking at Jack, Raymond let go of his arm.

"Right," he said quietly. "Now, before Esme beat you again, what did I say?"

Charlie's smile faded. "You . . . said I should concentrate."

"After that," said Raymond.

"That I was wasting your time?"

"After that too."

Charlie frowned back at him, trying to figure out whether this was a trick question. "After?" he said.

"That's right," said Raymond. "*After* I told you to concentrate, *before* Esme beat you, what did I say?"

There was a long and heavy silence.

It was Jack who took a deep breath, then said, "'Fight'?"

Raymond turned on him with blazing eyes.

"Sorry," said Jack.

Raymond turned back to Charlie, who was trying for an 'isn't he ridiculous?' type of smile, in the hope of breaking the ice with him.

"Stop bloody grinning!" barked Raymond.

The grin vanished.

"Your friend here," said Raymond quietly again, "would appear to have been listening more carefully than you were." He turned to Jack and acknowledged him with a polite nod. Jack just stared at him.

"'Fight,'" Raymond went on, turning to face Charlie again.

"That's what I said. Now, which part of that didn't you understand?"

"What?" asked Charlie.

"God save us," said Raymond, looking up at the roof. "'Fight,'" he repeated, staring hard at Charlie. "'Come to blows,'" he added. "'Exchange a dose of fisticuffs.' '*Engage in single combat*,' for crying out loud."

"I don't understand," said Charlie.

"No," said Raymond. "You don't." He sighed. "Do it again," he said. "Face each other. Get ready."

Frowning, Charlie did as he was told. Esme stepped back to make way for him: she rolled her shoulders a little—Jack heard a soft *pop* from the muscles in her neck—then she dropped back into her crouch, waiting.

"Now," said Raymond. "We'll start again. Only for heaven's sake, I want you to lay one on her this time."

Charlie stared at him blankly.

"Hit her!" said Raymond exasperatedly. "If you can," he added, when Esme raised her eyebrows at him. "Ready?"

Jack blinked a couple of times to clear his eyes and leaned forward to watch. Charlie was scowling.

"Right. *Fight*."

Charlie pulled back his right arm and let fly.

No chance. Warding Charlie's fist off easily with her left hand, Esme stepped toward him, into the blow. Her whole body weight, therefore, plus whatever forward momentum Charlie had put into his punch, was concentrated in the heel of her right hand as it struck the point of Charlie's chin, palm open, hard.

The force of the blow lifted Charlie off his feet. He sailed a clear ten yards back through the air and hit the wall again, with a solid, sickening crack.

"Tch*uhh*," he said, or something like it, as he came to rest on the floor.

There was a pause.

"God's teeth," said Raymond. "What d'you call that?"

"But . . ." began Charlie, simultaneously holding his chin with one hand and rubbing the back of his skull with the other. "I . . . *can't*," he said, his voice coming out in a kind of whine.

"No," said Raymond, "if that's the best you can do, then maybe you're right. My gran could punch better than that— mind you," he broke off, turning to Jack with a wink, "she was a terror, that one."

Jack just stared at him.

"Come on, man: on your feet. I can see we're gonna have our work cut out with you. Have you no backbone at all?" he added, when Charlie didn't move straightaway.

Charlie picked himself up once more. His face was turning red. "Just how the *Hell*," he began, his voice going high and strangely quavery, "am I supposed to—?"

"I told you," said Raymond. "Concentrate."

Charlie stared at him, speechless.

"Now, again," said Raymond. "Face each other."

This time, however, Charlie didn't move.

Raymond grinned. "Face each other," he repeated.

Still Charlie didn't move. All the color seemed to have

drained out of his face. His mouth had hardened into a thin, bloodless line. He blinked once, but still kept staring at Raymond.

Uh-oh, thought Jack.

"Ready?" said Raymond, with elaborate sarcasm.

Esme looked at Raymond. Raymond's grin just widened. She shrugged and turned back to face her opponent, dropping into her crouch again.

Jack watched, holding his breath.

"Fight," said Raymond.

Esme leaped, sweeping her right leg up for a kick—

—but then something strange happened.

About two centimeters from the side of Charlie's head, her foot simply stopped in midair. For a moment Esme just hung there, off the ground, frozen except for the frown of incomprehension beginning to dawn across her face. Then, quietly—distantly at first, but quickly getting louder—a rumbling sound began to echo around the room.

Charlie had turned to face her. His arms were coming up either side of him, and as he raised his hands toward the hovering girl his face twisted slowly into a mask of sudden and absolute fury.

Esme sank to her feet. Her hands too were coming up as if to protect herself. Her eyes were wide. Her legs were bending as if she were pushing against some terrible weight. The air in front of her seemed to be shivering—rippling.

And now, slowly, Esme's feet were beginning to slide back across the floor.

Jack stared.

Charlie leaned forward, eyes bright with rage, his fingers clawed and stiffening. The weird shivering in the air around Esme's outstretched hands was spreading, turning a heavy bruise-black, stretching and folding back around her. The rumbling got louder: the beginnings of a grimace of pain appeared on Esme's lips, then—

"STOP!" roared Raymond.

Charlie turned, arms still outstretched—

Released, Esme dropped to the ground with a thump—

Something hot and electrical rushed past Jack, almost knocking him down. Then—

Silence.

Charlie's arms dropped to his sides. He was breathing hard.

"W—" said Raymond, then cleared his throat. The big man looked pale and shaken. "Well," he said. "That's certainly . . . more like it. You okay, Esme?"

She nodded. Lying where she'd fallen, propped up on her elbows, Esme stared up at Charlie for another moment before flipping smoothly to her feet.

"You're . . . obviously a lot stronger than I thought," Raymond told Charlie. "I can understand what Nick saw in you."

Esme's face fell.

"Your control could use a lot of work, though," Raymond announced. "And Esme'll need to put you through your paces till you learn some technique. Kicking and punching," he added. "Yeah, 'specially punching." He smirked. "You punch like a girl."

At this, Esme managed a thin smile.

Jack looked from her to Raymond and finally to his best mate, who apparently really *was* some kind of superhero. He noticed a hollow feeling in the pit of his stomach, and it took him a moment to work out what it was.

Jack was scared, he realized: scared of what was happening and scared of where it all might go.

Charlie just grinned to himself.

"So," he said. "Tell me about this demon."

KNOWLEDGE
AND POWER

"The Scourge isn't an easy thing to describe," said Raymond.

They'd set up the conference table again, and he, Esme, Charlie, and Jack were sitting around one end of it. The afternoon sunlight was streaming in through the butterfly room's big round window, making the dust motes sparkle in the air.

"Try," said Charlie.

"It's not . . . physical, like you or me," said Raymond, giving Charlie a look. "The Scourge doesn't have a fixed size or weight or shape. It's intangible: a thing of chaos and magic. That's one of the reasons it's so dangerous."

The boys looked at him blankly.

"The laws of physics—gravity and so on?" Raymond shook his head. "They don't apply to the Scourge. I've seen it be in two places at once, and it can travel big distances apparently instantly. It never gets old. It never gets tired, and we don't think it can be killed."

The boys' mouths started to open.

"However," Raymond went on, holding up a hand to forestall them, "it does have one important weakness. It's this."

He leaned forward, putting his beefy hands on the table.

"The Scourge seems to need a host body," he said. "Like a home base to come back to. A person," he emphasized. "Someone who'll let the demon live inside them and work its will through them."

He gave the boys a moment for what he was telling them to sink in.

"Do you mean it's . . . kind of like a parasite?" Jack asked.

"A little, I guess—yeah," said Raymond, nodding. "One thing, though: it seems like once it's got itself established in someone, the Scourge can also project itself out of them somehow. It can take a piece of itself and send it out into the world—like a ghost or a double or . . . a shadow. That part of it can go wherever the Scourge likes: it can speak and find out stuff; it has physical strength and it can fight. But for . . . certain things, the Scourge has to stay completely in its host. Or . . . that's what I think, at any rate."

"You think?" Charlie echoed, raising his eyebrows. "You mean you don't know for sure? Why not?"

"Because until fourteen years ago," Raymond replied bleakly, "the Scourge had never escaped before."

Jack frowned. "But . . . what about the Brotherhood?" he asked.

"Yeah! Didn't they know anything?" asked Charlie.

Raymond sighed.

"Look," he said, "there are two things you need to know about the Brotherhood. The first is that it's very old. The earliest written account we have is from Anglo-Saxon times, around fifteen hundred years ago, but the secret was passed down by word of mouth before then, and there's no way of knowing for how long. Nick always believed the Brotherhood began much earlier: centuries, even millennia earlier. And as to how it began—and who it was who first imprisoned the Scourge? Well . . ." He shook his head. "Nobody knows."

The boys gave him a skeptical look.

"The other thing about the Brotherhood," Raymond went on, regardless, "is that it's secret—perhaps the most closely guarded secret in the world. There are other groups that have powers. There are other groups that use magic or have dealings with what you might call 'the supernatural'—but there's nothing else out there like the Brotherhood. And no one outside this room—apart from two others who I'll come to in a moment—has the faintest idea we exist."

"Why?" asked Jack.

"Yeah," said Charlie. "If the Scourge is so dangerous, why don't more people know about it?"

"Think about it," Raymond replied. "The Brotherhood was founded with a single purpose: to keep the Scourge imprisoned. Everything we do or have done, for thousands of years, comes—or came, I guess I have to say now—down to that. The order's members, right down to Nick's father, Jeremy, believed that the more people who knew about the Scourge, the more likely it would be that someone would make a mistake—that the Scourge would be released and that the Brotherhood would fail in its purpose. And . . . well, when you think of all that's happened, who knows?" Raymond's face turned sad. "Maybe they were right."

"How did you get involved in all this?" Jack asked.

Raymond looked at him. "Nick chose me." He smiled wryly. "Against his dad's wishes, I might add. Nick chose us all: picked us out for our different skills. There was me, two sisters—Belinda and Jessica—and another feller called Felix. Four disciples, one master."

"Five's not really much of a brotherhood," Charlie commented.

"Believe me," Raymond replied, "even five was a lot more than there had been. By the time Nick's dad got round to telling him about the Scourge, there was no one else left who knew the secret but him. When Nick announced he was going to find some new recruits, they had a row so big that they even stopped speaking to each other—right up until Jeremy's death. But Nick did his best to make the Brotherhood strong again: if it wasn't for Nick, none of us would be here." He paused.

For a second—that was all, before Raymond's self-discipline took over—Jack had a glimpse of just how much the big man wished his old leader were there with them now. Frankly, this didn't make Jack feel any better about things.

"Now, our job, as I say," Raymond went on, "was to keep the Scourge from escaping."

"Escaping from what?" asked Charlie instantly.

"A tree."

"A tree?" said Charlie, looking from Raymond to Esme incredulously. "A *tree*?"

"The Scourge was imprisoned in the roots of a tree," said Esme.

"That's right," said Raymond. "A big oak, it was, in . . ." He hesitated, looking suddenly secretive. "Well, you don't need to know where now."

"But this tree," said Charlie, obviously having difficulty with the concept (and Jack couldn't blame him: he was too). "Was there something special about it? I mean, how did you actually know it had a demon inside it?"

Raymond ran a hand over his shiny bald scalp and frowned, remembering.

"Again," he said, "it's . . . hard to explain. You could sort of . . . feel it."

He stopped and thought some more.

"When you were out looking after the tree," he said, "pruning or what have you, you'd sometimes catch yourself . . . thinking things. Unless you were awake to it, you might not even've noticed you were doing it, but you'd find yourself getting . . . ideas."

"What ideas?"

"One time," said Raymond, "and I'm not proud of this—I caught myself thinking about the rest of the group. I started thinking about magic, about how rubbish I was at it compared to Belinda and Jessica and Nick—and I found myself wondering if the others thought . . ."—he frowned—"*less of me* for it."

He looked up at the boys.

"That's what it does, the Scourge," he said. "It manipulates you. It looks all through you for weaknesses—all your little hurts and resentments—and it exploits them. I think that's what happened to Felix," he added. "I think that's how the Scourge escaped."

"Nope," said Charlie, making an 'over my head' gesture. "You've lost me."

"How?" asked Jack. "How did it escape?"

Raymond sat back on his chair and looked into the past.

"Felix was jealous, that was his problem," he said. "He always took things personally. He saw coming second-best as a slur on his spirit—second in magic, in combat, in anything. And when Belinda and I fell in love," he added and paused. "Well, I think that's what pushed him over the edge."

"What happened?" asked Jack.

"Felix went to the tree and let the Scourge possess him," said Raymond. "There was a fight: the rest of us managed to force the demon out of him, and Nick recaptured it in his staff. But Belinda, my wife, was . . ." He trailed off. "Well, she died. Esme was only a baby at the time."

Quietly, without fuss, Esme touched Raymond's hand with one of hers. Jack was looking at them, but Esme noticed, so he stared down at his lap.

"Ever since then, we've trained," said Esme, taking up the story. "Every day since then I've worked and waited, perfecting my skills in case the Scourge ever escaped again. And now," she added, and her amber eyes glittered, "now, my chance has come."

Jack looked at Esme—at the way she held herself, the set

of her mouth and the cold hard glow of her strange amber eyes. At that moment, the gulf between him and her seemed so wide as to be uncrossable. What must it be like for her, living like this? Really, he knew, he could have no idea. To dedicate your whole life to one purpose, to spend every single day training and preparing . . . Sometimes, in the past, Jack had imagined himself doing something similar. Sometimes he'd even liked the idea. Just then, however, he knew that imagining was going to be as close as he was ever going to get. And to be honest, he wasn't very sorry about it.

"What about the other one?" asked Charlie suddenly.

Everyone looked at him blankly.

"The other Brotherhood person. You know . . . what's-er-name?" Charlie snapped his fingers. "Jessica?"

"Oh," said Raymond, surprised. "Well, Jessica and Nick had a row."

"What about?" asked Charlie.

"After . . . what happened," Raymond said, "Nick had . . . doubts. He must've felt guilty for what happened to Belinda: maybe he wished he'd done like his dad had said and never brought the rest of us into this thing in the first place. At any rate, he made a decision. He announced he was going to find a new place to keep the Scourge: another tree, but somewhere secret, where supposedly none of us would know about it. Now . . ."

He leaned forward in his seat, which creaked dangerously under his bulk.

"Jessica disagreed with him," he said. "She reckoned no one

should be trusted with the Scourge alone—none of us, not even Nick. And when Nick set out on his own anyway, Jessica stormed out too. She left the Brotherhood, left all of us. And no one's heard hide nor hair of her in what must be—"

"So," Charlie interrupted, "two suspects."

Everyone stared at him again.

He scowled. "Come on, people, *keep up*. Whoever let the Scourge out this time had to be one of the Brotherhood; otherwise how would they have known about the demon in the first place? Right?"

No one replied. Jack wasn't even sure he understood the question.

"Look," said Charlie with a sigh, "I assume we all agree it wasn't *Nick* who was possessed—right?"

Jack blinked—but Charlie was already pressing on.

"Well, if it wasn't *Nick*," he announced, as if to a room full of idiots, "and it wasn't you two," he added, looking at Raymond and Esme, "then who else is left? Jessica and Felix! Come on, it's not exactly complicated."

Jack winced inwardly. Charlie *was* making a kind of sense, he supposed, but he didn't have to be so smug about it.

"So," Charlie repeated, "which of those two d'you think's the baddie? Felix or Jessica?"

"Felix," said Raymond firmly. "He was the one who let it out last time, so—"

"I think Jessica," said Charlie, interrupting again. "Especially if you've no idea of where she is. That's right," he added, "isn't it?"

"What is?"

"That you've no idea where Jessica is," Charlie repeated sweetly. "Bit suspicious, that, don't you think?"

Raymond opened his mouth—and closed it again, annoyed.

"I'm afraid that's true," said Esme for him.

"*So,*" said Charlie again, grinning triumphantly, "how do we find her? How do we find this . . . Jessica?"

Raymond looked Charlie dead in the eye. "I'm open to suggestions," he said.

It wasn't the answer Charlie had been expecting. His grin became uncertain, then faded. An uncomfortable silence was just starting to develop, when Jack spoke.

"Er . . . can I ask something?"

In fact, Jack had a whole bunch of questions. How come Charlie was suddenly able to move at lightning speed and make magic powers come out of his hands? (He was still getting his head round that one, frankly.) And the enormous tattoo that had appeared on Charlie's back: was that some mark of the Brotherhood or what? But if Charlie wasn't going to ask about these things himself, Jack certainly wasn't going to do it for him. Not if it meant risking looking like any more of a spare part than he did already in front of Raymond and (especially) Esme.

Everyone was looking at him, and he could feel his face going red. Jack took a deep breath and said: "Um . . . what does the demon want?"

Charlie made a snorting sound in his nose.

"Actually," said Esme, "that's a good question."

"There's a place," said Raymond, "not far from here. We call it the Fracture."

"It's a weak spot in the fabric of reality," said Esme. "A magical gateway: a door. The Scourge wants to open the Fracture and escape back to where it came from."

"And where's that?" asked Charlie, with a skeptical expression—and to be fair, even Jack wasn't sure how much more of this stuff he could take.

Esme and Raymond looked at each other.

"The Brotherhood's earliest accounts speak of the Scourge as having come from a 'dark place,'" said Raymond. "An ancient place: a dimension of chaos and violence. This place, apparently, is where our universe began and it's where—the record says—it will end. The last time we fought, the Scourge spoke of the place by name."

"What place?" asked Charlie, becoming exasperated. "What are you talking about? What name?"

Raymond looked at him. "Hell," he replied.

For a long moment, there was silence.

"When you say 'Hell,'" said Charlie slowly, "you don't mean the real thing: fire and brimstone, eternal torment and damnation, that sort of Hell. *Hell* . . . do you?"

"That's the one," said Esme dryly.

"*Cool*," said Charlie.

Esme blinked.

"What happens if the Scourge goes back to Hell?" asked Jack.

"It could form an army of demons and invade the Earth," Esme put in. "That's what we've always thought—right?"

"We don't know for certain what the Scourge's intentions are," said Raymond, acknowledging her with a nod. "But if it's been imprisoned here all this time just to keep it *away* from Hell, well, you can bet whatever it wants to do can't be good."

Jack frowned again.

"But . . . Hell!" said Charlie. "Has anyone been there? I mean," he grinned, "what's the place look like?"

"I'm sorry?" asked Esme.

"This gateway," said Charlie impatiently. "Has anyone ever opened it and, you know, had a peek?"

"Listen, son," said Raymond, "maybe you don't understand—"

"We think only the Scourge has the power to open the Fracture," Esme explained.

"But even if anyone else could open it," said Raymond, his voice getting louder, "do you seriously think they *would?* This is Hell we're talking about! If the Fracture were to be opened . . . why, who *knows* what might happen?"

"Not *you*," snapped Charlie with sudden venom. "That's for sure." He looked at Raymond and shook his head in disbelief. "I can't believe you people!" he said. "Do you really mean to tell me that you've taken all this stuff, all this weirdness, on *trust*, without asking any of these questions before?"

"Yes," said Raymond flatly. "We trusted Nick completely."

"But now Nick's dead. And *you*, it seems, don't have the first clue about what's really going on!"

Jack was staring at Charlie now. Tact had never really been Charlie's strongest point, but the way he was acting was getting weirder and weirder. How did he manage to be so *certain* all the time? Where was all this confidence coming from?

"Where is it?" Charlie was asking. "This . . . 'Fracture,' I mean."

There was a pause. Esme and Raymond exchanged another look.

Raymond grimaced, then shrugged. "It's . . . a pub," he admitted.

Both Jack and Charlie gaped at him.

"But it's no kind of pub I'd be seen in, that's for sure," Raymond added quickly. "The Light of the Moon, they call it now. It's all chrome and steel and stripped pine floorboards, and about as much atmosphere as the *real* bloody moon." He shuddered. "Horrible."

"A pub," said Charlie.

"Yes."

"The gateway to Hell is in a London pub," said Charlie. "That's what you're saying."

"Yes," said Esme.

"And that's what this demon wants to do: to open the gateway to Hell."

"That's what we think. Yes," said Esme.

"O-*kay*," said Charlie. "Now we're getting somewhere."

Everyone fell silent. Charlie rubbed a hand across his brow, back and forth. His eyes were open, looking down. No one spoke.

"Well," said Charlie finally, looking up, "it's pretty obvious, isn't it?"

He began to grin wildly.

"What's obvious?" said Raymond.

"What we *do*," said Charlie. "It's simple! We wait at the Fracture for the Scourge to make its move, and then, when it comes, we *kick its arse*!"

There was another pause.

"You're going to kick its arse," echoed Raymond, looking hard at Charlie. "You," he emphasized, even more heavily.

"I said *we're* going to kick its arse, actually," Charlie replied, his smile vanishing as quickly as it had come, "but if it comes down to it, then yeah, that's *exactly* what I'm going to do. I'm going to wait for it to come, I'm going to square up to it, and then I'm going to kick its—"

And at that precise moment, a phone rang.

It was a mobile phone. For a dreadful second, Jack thought it might be his, but it was Charlie's. Everyone watched as Charlie fished his mobile out of his pocket, looked at the screen, and scowled. It was no use—the thing still kept ringing. He pressed the button and held it to his ear.

"Mum," he said, "this really isn't a good time."

Mrs. Farnsworth's voice was only audible as a sort of distant quacking. Everyone was pretending not to listen, but of course, they all were.

"Look, Mum, can I call you back in a minute?" tried Charlie. "Me and Jack are sort of in the middle of something here."

Listening, he frowned.

"Well, no, I'm not at Jack's *house*. And what do you think you're doing *checking* on me anyw—?"

Charlie sighed again and put a hand up to his brow.

"I'm with some friends of ours," he said. "Round their place. I'm in the West End, if you must know—"

Quack quack.

"Friends from school. Well, not school. I—"

Mrs. Farnsworth kept talking, and a horrible expression appeared on Charlie's face.

"No!" he said. "God! No! Look, I'm not with *Dad*. All right? Of course I'd tell you if I was with Dad!"

The silence in the room became even more awkward.

"What are you talking about, 'behind your back'? I *wouldn't*—"

Suddenly, Charlie just looked dreadfully, horribly tired.

"But Mum, I—"

Still the voice kept going.

"All right," said Charlie quietly. "All *right*. I'll be there as soon as I can. Yeah. You too. Yeah. See you later. Bye."

He pressed the button to end the call and looked up—just as everyone else looked away, pretending they hadn't been watching him.

"Listen," he said. "Me and Jack've got to go."

Jack was on the point of saying something about this, but the look on Charlie's face silenced him.

"All right," said Raymond. "On you go, then."

"We don't know whether anything would've happened tonight anyway," said Esme.

"But I want you here bright and early tomorrow!" called Raymond. But on 'tomorrow' the double doors of the butterfly room had already slammed shut. Charlie and Jack were gone.

"Well!" said Raymond after a moment. "A right little know-it-all, isn't he? Anyone'd think he was the one who'd trained all his life, instead of—"

"Yeah," said Esme glumly.

Raymond bit his lip.

"All right," she went on, once she'd had a moment to concentrate. "I'll take first shift at the Fracture, I guess. You go see if you can't track down Felix and Jessica."

Hearing the uncertainty in her voice, Raymond lifted his eyebrows at her.

"I know!" said Esme. "I just . . ." She paused, shaking her head to herself. "I guess I always thought that when the time came it would all be clearer somehow. This . . . " She shrugged helplessly. "This isn't happening at all how I expected."

"Me neither, petal," said Raymond grimly. "Me neither."

The train journey back to North London passed in silence. Charlie just sat there, staring ahead into space; he only looked up when other passengers jostled his legs, and the jostlers looked away quickly, perhaps sensing, like Jack, the fury that surrounded him like a storm cloud. The silence kept up as they left the station. The sky was starting to turn a darker, deeper blue as sunset approached, but Charlie just kept stumping on ahead, head down, and Jack found he was having to walk quite quickly to keep up with him. Only when they were almost as far as the front door of Jack's house did Charlie finally stop and turn.

"Well," he said, still not looking at Jack, not really, "I guess I'll see you tomorrow."

"I'll go across the park with you," said Jack.

Charlie looked at him.

"I need the exercise," added Jack as casually as he could. Lame as this was, it was the best excuse he could come up with. He had to get Charlie to talk to him, and keeping him company across the park might be the only way.

Charlie shrugged—then made a face. "I tell you," he said, "I don't. Esme gave me a real going-over." Slowly, creakily, he rolled his shoulders, trying to loosen them a bit.

"What about all that healing-yourself business?" Jack asked. "I thought you were supposed to be invincible now or something."

"Not invincible enough, apparently," Charlie replied, and smiled.

Jack smiled back.

"Come on, let's go."

They set off.

Their silence was more companionable now, but Jack was still finding it hard to ask what he wanted. In the end, he just blurted it out:

"Charlie, are you . . . okay?"

Charlie looked at Jack but didn't stop walking. "Yeah," he said. "Why wouldn't I be?"

"But isn't it . . . weird?"

"What, the superpowers thing?"

"Well, yeah!" said Jack. "Come *on*."

Charlie made a dismissive gesture with one hand. "It's not that weird, you know."

"No?"

"No," said Charlie, frowning now.

He thought for a moment.

"It's like . . . once you're into it—once you can do the stuff, you just . . . do it," he said. "You know? You just get on with it, and it all just feels right. Everything's straightforward. Clear. Simple. Until your mum rings up and tells you you've got to go home for *dinner*."

They crossed the road and went through the gate into the park. Jack said nothing.

"I swear," said Charlie, "you should've heard her. Nothing I could've said would've made any difference. Straightaway she's like, 'You're with your father, aren't you? You're seeing him behind my back!'"

"Oh, mate."

"Straight up," said Charlie. "I couldn't believe it."

Five or six older boys were playing football on the big stretch of grass to Charlie and Jack's right. At the end of the path, the church spire was already lit up for the night with its lights: it stuck out of the ground and into the evening sky like a giant, pale spike of bone.

"It's going to get worse, isn't it?" said Charlie. "This thing with my folks, I mean. Mum's going flaky on me. And Dad . . . well."

He stopped and turned to Jack. "You saw him in the restaurant. He just sat there looking all surprised, like he hadn't expected I'd be angry with him. Like I was just supposed to say, 'Yeah, sure, split up with Mum and go live with someone else, I don't mind!' Honestly, he doesn't have a *clue*."

Past Charlie's shoulders, Jack could see the footballers coming closer: one of them was lining up a shot at the goal—or the space between the two piles of jackets on the ground anyway.

"Saving the world's *easy*," Charlie was saying. "I'd rather fight a demon, you know? Better that than have to go through all this—"

Jack watched as the footballer took his shot: he knew, with a sudden and absolute certainty, where the ball was going to end up. And sure enough—

CLUMP!

It caught Charlie square on the back of the head, knocking him forward with the force of the blow.

Suddenly, all six footballers were laughing.

"Sorry, mate!" called the one who had kicked the ball, smiling broadly as his friends caught up with him. They all looked about sixteen or seventeen years old—certainly a lot bigger and stronger than Charlie and Jack. One of them was laughing so hard he was making little snorting noises through his nose.

Jack had seen these guys before. Year after year they spent the whole summer kicking their football around, and they never once seemed to get bored with it. Jack looked from them to his friend. Charlie was just standing there stiffly—head still forward from where the ball had knocked him.

"You all right?" called the lead footballer. The others were still sniggering.

Now, slowly, Charlie turned. "Who kicked it?" he asked. "You?"

"That's right," said the guy. His smile was cocky, not apologetic at all—and certainly not apologetic enough for Charlie.

"Come on," said Jack quietly, "let's leave it." But he knew he was wasting his breath.

"Why don't you watch what you're doing?" said Charlie. "You stupid sod!"

For a whole second the six lads stared at him. Then they burst out laughing again, all except for the one who'd kicked the ball, who just frowned.

"Listen, mate," he said, "I've told you I'm sorry."

"And I'm telling you, *mate*," said Charlie, "sorry's not good enough. Get on your knees. Right now."

Now everyone was staring at Charlie, even Jack.

"What?" said the lead footballer, grinning with disbelief.

"On. Your. *Knees*," said Charlie, and at the sound of his voice, the boy fell as if he'd been shot.

From where Jack was standing, he could see the back of Charlie's neck. He frowned. Weird black shapes were appearing under his friend's skin. Needle-sharp points of some inky-black substance were trickling up from under the collar of Charlie's T-shirt, widening into curved slivers of pure liquid darkness as they crawled up around his throat. Now the shapes were creeping down out of Charlie's sleeves, sliding past his elbows and down his forearms with an oil-dark, liquid eagerness.

Jack recognized the shapes: the curves, the hooks, the spikes. He'd seen them that morning on Charlie's back.

It was the black tattoo.

It was *moving*.

"**Now,**" said Charlie, barely speaking above the level of a whisper, but something in his voice made strange explosions go off behind Jack's eyeballs.

"**Wet yourself.**"

The eyes of the hapless footballer fell closed. A blissful expression crossed his face: there was a moment of silence, then a soft, trickling sound, and now everyone was staring at the dark stain that was spreading down one leg of his shorts.

"Euugh! Gross!" said someone.

The footballer woke up and looked down at his crotch, a look of total horror beginning to form on his face.

Charlie just grinned and turned his back. The moment was gone. The strange shapes of the black tattoo had vanished back to wherever they had come from. Jack blinked.

"Come on, man," said Charlie to Jack. "Let's go."

No one tried to stop them.

"Er . . . Charlie?" asked Jack, once they'd safely gone a few hundred yards farther down the path.

"Yeah?"

"Do you think it's safe? Using your . . . powers like that?"

Charlie smirked. "Who are they going to tell?"

In another moment, it seemed, they were standing outside the gate.

"Take care, mate," said Charlie, turning to go.

"Yeah," said Jack, to his friend's retreating back. "You too."

JESSICA

The demon didn't even bother to visit Jessica on the third night. By the fourth, she knew she was finished.

The Scourge just stood there at first, a scarecrow figure of rippling shadows. Its arms hung loosely at its sides; its long, liquid fingers twitched lazily.

"Humans," it told her, "with your little concerns: your tiresome and selfish preoccupations. I'd always thought demons were bad enough, but really—you people are something else."

"Don't you ever shut up?" Jessica asked, and closed her eyes.

She reached past the pain in her body. She reached past the terrible exhaustion in her head, the mental fatigue from keeping her circle going for so long—going further inside herself, further still. In her lap, her brown hands opened slowly. With a soft hiss, a thin blue spark appeared over her palms. She poured herself into it, and the spark began to grow.

"Think of it," said the Scourge, "what it'll be like when I succeed. Think of the peace: the pure emptiness. The silence. All Creation finally consigned to the Void. All the noise, waste, and pointlessness wiped clean in an instant, when this *witless boy* helps me wake the Dragon, and at last we finish what it began. . . ."

While the demon spoke, the spark had swelled to the size of a marble. The magical bolt was spinning, picking up speed, its surface becoming a rushing blur of scorching white and deepest midnight blue. Jessica sent more of herself into it, reaching down inside for everything that she had left. Now the bolt was the size of a squash ball and beginning to crackle and spit in the dark, stifling air of the tattered circle. Jessica was as ready as she'd ever be. Slowly, savagely . . . she smiled.

"It's a shame, in a way, that you won't be there to see what I mean," the Scourge was saying, "to see what your flyspeck of a 'brotherhood' has been supposedly preventing all these years, because—"

"Here's an idea," Jessica interrupted. "How about you stop talking and come and get me if you can, eh? Or are you planning on *boring* me to death?"

The Scourge looked at her. "I've kept you here long enough for my purposes," it said. "You were a useful false trail for the others while you lasted, but now I'm almost ready to make my move. In fact, there's just one more trick to play. Funny," it added, "isn't it, Jessica? All these years hunting me, preparing to face me, and that's all you were—a distraction. Still . . ." The demon shrugged, its shoulders and neck dripping together in long, tarlike strings. "If you're ready to die, I'll be happy to oblige you."

"Do your worst," she told it.

"As you wish."

Jack had been watching Charlie and Esme train all day. While Raymond kept watch at the Fracture, Esme had been putting Charlie through his paces on martial arts, acrobatics, weapons training, flying—the lot. Each new and amazing skill that Esme introduced to Charlie he seemed to master almost instantly, and without any particular effort. By the time evening was coming round, Jack was thoroughly, utterly *fed up*.

He'd asked questions, made comments, and tried to keep his end up—and Esme had been polite enough to respond, even when (as seemed painfully obvious to Jack) his remarks had come less from any wish to share wisdom or advice than the simple desire to remind her that he was still there. But the fact of the situation was, he knew, that both she and Charlie were far too engrossed in what they were doing to take any real interest in him. After all (as he asked himself), why should they?

They were superhuman: Jack wasn't. They were powerful and important: Jack wasn't. Charlie and Esme were getting ready to fight the forces of evil: Jack's job, apparently, was to sit there and watch. It was as simple—as *typical*—as that.

So the afternoon had passed. Jack was just letting out something like his three hundred and seventy-fifth sigh of the day . . .

. . . when everything started to go wrong.

"Oh!" said Charlie suddenly. He broke out of the complicated silat arm-trap-and-sweep combination he'd been working through with Esme up by the butterfly room's ceiling and dropped to the floor. His eyes were closed.

"What?" asked Jack, without much interest.

"It's . . . the demon," said Charlie. His eyelids were fluttering strangely.

"What about it?" asked Jack.

"I think I know where it is," said Charlie, frowning.

"How?" asked Esme, landing in front of him.

Charlie's eyes flicked open. "No time to argue: I can *feel it*, all right? It's at Centre Point Tower right now! You take Jack. Let's go!"

Esme stared at Charlie, but already she was looking at his back: in another second Charlie was out the door.

"Well, okay," she said, turning to Jack. "Come on."

Jack followed her out onto the landing—just in time to see Charlie throw open the door that led to the fire escape.

Jack saw him stand there for a moment. In front of him, beyond the black iron railing, was the West End—its roofs, the traffic, the lights, and the empty air. Charlie spread his arms, leaped, and plummeted from sight.

Jack hadn't had time to shout, or even move. He'd barely had time to register what was going on—namely that his best mate had just jumped off a tall building. Suddenly, Esme had taken his arm in a surprisingly viselike grip.

"Ready?" she asked.

Her face beside him in the half-light was hard, fierce looking.

"What?" Jack managed. "Now, wait. Hold on a second. Just—no! I can't fly! You can't carry me! And I am *not* just going to—*WhAAAAAAAAAAAAAAAAAAAAAAAGH!*"

His third step had been into nothing: his feet had left the ground.

He was flying.

The streetlights slid by in an orange blur below him. Jack saw what the roofs of red London double-decker buses look like from above, and the tops of trees seemed to skim his feet. He was still screaming, but his scream was lost in the roar of the exhaust-filled summer air whipping past him, turning hot on his face as they picked up speed. In front of him Jack could see Charlie's silhouette just ahead, blasting through the evening sky, his arms spread wide—and Jack suddenly found he had an enormous grin on his face.

It was only a moment. It would stay with Jack forever—

But then the huge, ribbed spine shape of an ugly skyscraper reared up in front of them. Charlie lurched out of sight. The earth was rushing up toward him—and they'd landed.

There was a woman sitting on the ground, holding her hand out. There was something in her hand, something blue and white and impossibly bright at first, but quickly darkening, weakening, as the strange and horrible creature she was being attacked by surrounded and began to swamp her.

Jack stared, trying to take it all in. *That*, he thought numbly, *must be the Scourge.*

At that moment, the demon was a shapeless splatter of darkness, gathering and battening and convulsing round the woman like something between a giant black cobweb and a bat's wing. Esme had let go of Jack's arm now and was rising in the air again, standing between him and the demon, ready to fight.

But Charlie got there first.

"HEY!" he called.

Abruptly the demon seemed to suck back into itself: now it was like a stick figure made of darkness. In a movement so dazzlingly fast that you could barely see it, it leaped straight up the side of the building, vanishing into its shadowy concrete alcoves, and Charlie—

"No! WAIT!" yelled Esme.

—leaped after it.

Jack watched with his mouth hanging open, seeing his friend haring up the wall of the big skyscraper, planting each foot as if he were running on the ground. It wasn't exactly "in a single bound," but Charlie was clearly well capable in the "leaping tall buildings" department. In another second, Jack's superhero mate had disappeared from view.

Jack looked down. The bolt of electric-blue something-or-other flickered out and disappeared, and the woman who'd been holding it sank back, unconscious. Esme only just caught her before her head hit the ground. Then, at last, there was a pause.

"Is she okay?" Jack asked, pointing.

It had been the first thing to come into his head, and he knew it was a stupid question as soon as he said it. Of course she wasn't okay. The expression on her face was calm, peaceful even, but as Esme took hold under her arms the woman's head lolled limply.

"Get her feet," said Esme. "One. Two. *Three*."

They swung her up off the ground. She was horribly light—in fact, she hardly seemed to weigh anything at all. Plus, Jack couldn't help noticing, she was . . . well, a bum. A homeless person. And to be honest, she didn't smell too good.

"Head toward the church," said Esme.

Across the street from the towering skyscraper a small old church was standing there looking stranded and abandoned. They shuffled hurriedly toward it, Jack struggling to keep up. Esme took them down a narrow alley at the side of the church and out into its tiny graveyard. They'd been lucky so far: no one else had been there to witness Charlie's lunatic charge after the demon, but it wouldn't hurt to keep away from any curious eyes on the street.

"Okay, put her down here," said Esme, stopping beside an ancient stone slab set into the grass. "You stay here with her," she told Jack.

"Wait!" said Jack. "Who is she?"

"It's my aunt," said Esme, softly. "It's Jessica."

Jack blinked.

"Listen," said Esme. She gestured at the unconscious woman lying on the grass between them. "Take care of her, okay?"

"Sure," said Jack, in the gruffest voice he could manage.

Esme gave him a wan smile. Then, with a graceful gesture, she let her hands fall to her sides, palms spread: she was already lifting into the air again. Jack blinked again—and she was gone.

"Be careful!" he shouted—and then felt very silly indeed.

He looked around himself, at the graveyard and the woman who was still lying on the ground.

"Right," he said. Then again: "Right."

Some time passed—Jack wasn't sure how much. It was only a few minutes, probably, but however long it was, it wasn't enough for him to get used to Jessica's smell. The combination of unwashed human being and (odd but true) *boiled cabbages* emerging from the unconscious body next to him was surprisingly powerful, even in the open air. It was getting dark too. The evening sun was setting fast, and what little light penetrated the graveyard from the streetlamps outside came through only as a thin kind of orange-blue haze. Plus, Jack had left his shirt behind at the theater and had only come out in a T-shirt. He was getting cold and hungry too. All in all, in his opinion, it was a pretty typical sort of situation.

He didn't get to be able to fly or do kung fu or chase demons up the sides of tall buildings—no, of course he didn't. *His* job, apparently, was to stand around waiting with smelly, trampy ladies in graveyards in the dark, while all the important stuff happened somewhere else. Typical.

"Ohhhh," said Jessica suddenly, making Jack jump. She sat up and, opening a pair of eyes that were every bit as astonishingly amber as Esme's, gave Jack a level look.

"Who are you?" she asked.

"I'm, er . . . Jack," said Jack.

Jessica just kept looking at him. Clearly, that answer alone wasn't going to be enough for her.

"I . . ." began Jack, then tried again. "We—I mean, the others—well, we, ah . . . rescued you, I suppose."

"You're from the Brotherhood?"

Jack nodded.

"Damn."

It wasn't quite the reply Jack had been expecting. He waited, watching Jessica look around at the graveyard, its empty spaces and its cold gray slabs.

"Listen," she said suddenly, "what was your name again?"

"Jack," said Jack.

The amber eyes narrowed at him. "I don't like our position here, Jack." Jessica gestured at the old black stone of the back of the church. "If the Scourge comes back, we'll be better off over there, with the wall behind us." She looked at him again. "Can you help me?"

Jack's brain was still coping with the possibility she'd mentioned of the demon's return. "Er . . ." he said.

"I've been sitting cross-legged on a cold concrete walkway for seventy-two hours straight," said Jessica. "My legs went numb after the first four."

Jack blinked.

"You're going to have to carry me," Jessica added, seeing that she wasn't getting her point across.

"Right," said Jack, standing up. "Of course. Right."

Jack was fourteen years old and of an average height for his age. His mother was always telling him that he was about to grow in huge spurts, but it hadn't happened yet: Jessica was taller than him, if only by an inch or two. He looked down at her, at the thin brown skin of her hands and face, and her narrow bony wrists jutting out of her filthy old overcoat.

"What?" she asked him.

"Nothing," said Jack.

"Come on, then." She beckoned.

Jack did as he was told. Jessica's hands in his felt dry, waxy, and horribly delicate, like he could crush them by mistake if he wasn't careful.

"Now, up we go."

He did his best.

"Wah!"

But her legs wouldn't support her: Jessica slid out of his grip and sat back down on the edge of a gravestone, hard.

"Oooh," she said, grimacing with pain.

"Sorry!" said Jack. "Sorry! Sorry!"

"Don't you get taught anything anymore?" she asked. "Telekinesis? Levitation?"

"No," said Jack. "I mean—well, not *me*." He broke off. Jessica was staring at him again now. "I'm just . . . kind of tagging along," he said miserably. "I don't have any . . . you know . . . powers."

"Wonderful," said Jessica. "Oh, that's just wonderful."

Seeing Jack's expression, she softened a little.

"Look," she said. "Here's what you do. You just crouch down in front of me here, with your back to me. . . . Yup, that's right. Now, let me get a grip on you."

Quickly, she slid her arms around Jack's neck. Jack did his best not to flinch.

"Right. Now stand up."

He did, taking Jessica with him. She was now hanging off his back. Her head was perched next to his, on his right shoulder. Her breath was warm and nasty, and her hair was itchy on his cheek.

"Reach up and grab my elbows," said Jessica. "Right. Now put me down over there."

Jessica weighed next to nothing, and her body was so swaddled in clothes that Jack couldn't really feel her at all. It was okay, he supposed. Weird but okay. Apart from the smell, obviously.

"Listen," she said, once he'd set her down, "I don't think we have much time."

"Why?" asked Jack. "What do you mean?"

"I know what the Scourge is going to do," Jessica told him. She paused and shook her head. "This thing—it's bigger than the Brotherhood. It's bigger than you or me—it's bigger than anything! Now, I've sent for help, and for what it's worth, help's on its way. But someone's going to have to follow the Scourge to Hell and stop this before it's too late. I just wish I could figure out *who*."

She sat back against the black stone walls of the church and sighed.

"The Brotherhood's finished," she said. "Raymond, the rest of us—and that *idiot*, Nick—we're useless. Worse than useless. Maybe we always were."

She looked up—and froze.

"Oh no," she whispered, making Jack stare at her again. Then, "Look, quick. Help me up."

Jack looked in the direction Jessica was looking and blinked.

A patch of shadow in the darkness at the far end of the graveyard was behaving . . . oddly. As he watched, the darkness seemed to wobble and shake. It *bulged*, taking on a strange kind of shape—and then a figure was standing there at the end of the graveyard. A weird stick figure made out of liquid darkness—completely, utterly black.

"Help me up, Jack," Jessica repeated.

It was the Scourge. It had obviously doubled back somehow and had come back to finish Jessica off. There was no sign of Charlie or Esme. And now—as Jack continued to stare at it—the demon began to walk toward them.

"Jack, *help me up*, dammit!"

"Right," said Jack. "Right."

"Get behind me," Jessica told him.

She was only standing with an immense effort of will. Taking a deep breath, refusing to let her legs buckle beneath her, Jessica looked away from the demon that had come to kill her and down at the boy instead.

"Okay," she said. "It looks like this is it."

She smiled sadly.

"I'm sorry, Jack," she said. "You shouldn't have got into this. None of us should."

She turned, took another deep breath, then, with more

venom than Jack had ever heard in a person's voice before, she said:

"I hope you choke, you piece of—"

And suddenly, the Scourge was on her.

It leaped, crashing into Jessica, instantly knocking her flat. For a second or two Jessica and the demon wrestled with each other before the Scourge pinned down her arms and brought the blank black shape of its liquid face right up to hers. Jessica fought as hard as she could: she wriggled and snarled, but as Jack stared, utterly helpless, a strange haze of light began to emerge from Jessica's face, a smoky gray light that crossed the space between her and the demon—crossed it and was instantly *absorbed*. Suddenly, Jessica gave a long, gasping sigh—impossibly long, as though all the breath were being sucked out of her body.

The demon was sucking out her life, Jack realized. The Scourge was sucking out Jessica's life, right in front of him! Before he could even think about what to do to stop it, Jessica shuddered and went rigid. The dreadful noise stopped; there was a long, frozen moment—then Jessica went limp and fell back.

The demon lifted its eyeless, blank black face from what it had been doing.

And it looked at Jack.

Now it was getting up.

And now it was *coming for him*!

What? said Jack's brain. *No way!* This was totally unfair! *His* job wasn't dealing with demons! *His* job was sitting and watching! Numb with fear, Jack backed away, tripped over a gravestone, and fell over. In a kind of ecstasy of panic, unable to take his eyes away from the demon, he kicked out frantically with his feet, trying to push himself away back across the ground. But it still kept coming. The ink-black figure kept walking toward him, a step at a time. Closer it came, closer still, until suddenly—

"HEY!" said a voice. "HEY, YOU!"

Jack looked up. Standing behind the demon . . . was Charlie.

With a soft thump, twin balls of flaming orange light appeared in his hands.

"EAT *THIS*!" Charlie yelled, and flung them, catching the demon square in the middle. Suddenly, to Jack's utter amazement, the demon's body was a mass of flames.

And then the Scourge began to scream.

It was like the screech of brakes, like paper tearing slowly in your head. The black shape of the demon turned fluid, shooting out in all directions and snapping back in an effort to escape the magical fire, and the flames made great *whoomph*-ing sounds in the air as the Scourge flung itself about. The screaming kept going, on the same dreadful single note. The demon flapped wildly, pounding on the ground. The flames seemed to tear upward, straight through the demon's body, then—

WHUMP!

They vanished, leaving nothing but a few twinkling blue sparks floating in the empty air.

Silence.

"HAH!" yelled Charlie. "HAAAAAAH!"

Esme elbowed past him and leaned down over Jack.

"Are you okay?" she asked.

Jack looked up at her, at her lovely face staring down at him in concern.

"Yeah," he said. "I'm fine."

She smiled at him!

"But I think it got Jessica," he said, watching her smile vanish with an ache in his heart as she caught sight of Jessica's lifeless body.

Esme felt for a pulse.

"Is she—?" said Jack.

"Yeah," said Esme miserably. "She's gone."

"I got it, though!" said Charlie, dancing on the spot. "I *got* it! *The Scourge is dead!*"

SWORDS AND PIGEONS

They were back at the theater. At last, the doors opened. It was Esme.

"You can come in now," she said.

Jack looked at Charlie. They'd been waiting outside in the passage for almost twenty minutes while Esme gave her report to Raymond about what had happened with Jessica. Still, for a moment Charlie stayed where he was, leaning against the wall. Eventually, making it perfectly clear that it was in his own time and not because anyone had asked him to, Charlie detached himself and made for the door. Esme stood aside to let him through. Jack sighed, followed him, caught sight of the room beyond—and blinked.

The room they were standing in now wasn't quite as big as the butterfly room, but it was still impressive. A large, coal-fired forge, presently unlit, with a wide, blackened metal flue poking out of the top of it and leading up through the ceiling, dominated the center of the space. The forge was surrounded by workbenches, racks of tools, and several large pieces of machinery, one of which Raymond was standing over and adjusting. He had his back to them, and as the boys came in he didn't turn round.

"This is the armory," said Esme. This didn't really need explaining, Jack felt, because the walls of the room were entirely covered in weapons.

There were axes: single- and double-headed, from small throwable hatchets and tomahawks to a five-foot-tall thing with giant gleaming steel half-moons that could probably chop Jack in half just by him looking at it. There were throwing stars, glaives, and knives of every description—some sheathed, some hanging in their cases with their blades exposed. Most of all, there were swords.

There were foils, with long blades stretching to points so sharp you could hardly see them. There were cutlasses and scimitars—curved and wicked looking. Every edged or stabbing weapon Jack had ever seen or heard about seemed to be represented somewhere—and a fairly high proportion that he hadn't.

"Nice collection," said Charlie, pretending not to be impressed. "Where'd you get 'em all?"

"One or two of the older pieces belonged to the Brotherhood," said Esme. "But most of them Raymond made himself."

"Come 'ere," growled Raymond without turning around. "I've got something to show you."

Winding their way between the long workbenches, the boys went over to take a look. On the table beside Raymond lay a long bundle of thick black canvas, which the big man proceeded to unwrap.

"This," he said to Charlie, as the contents were revealed, "is what I've been working on for you."

It was a sword. A big one. It had no grip, no handle yet: the long, gently curved, dull-blue-colored blade stopped abruptly, revealing the short, rough oblong of the naked tang beyond that. But it was already an impressive-looking weapon. It was shaped like a katana, a Japanese sword, the ones samurai warriors used. Even unfinished, the sword looked beautifully proportioned and elegantly, utterly deadly.

"*Cool*," breathed Charlie, and reached out to touch it—but he suddenly found he'd grasped a pair of goggles instead.

"Put 'em on," grunted Raymond.

"Jack?" called Esme.

Jack turned as Esme tossed another pair of goggles to him: he caught them—just—and smiled at her. She didn't smile back, just pulled her own pair down over her eyes and walked over to join the boys in watching what Raymond was about to do.

The big man flicked a switch. A low electrical hum sprang up from the machine, rising to a whine as it gathered speed. The machine had a small wheel, not much bigger than Jack's fist, and it was this that was being spun by the motor.

"Watch this, now," said Raymond, lowering his goggles. He took Charlie's unfinished sword and pressed it, gently but firmly, against the wheel's surface.

The wheel screamed, and an instant shower of sparks sent

bright blue splashes across Jack's retinas, even behind the dark goggles. The sparks sprayed a clear two feet ahead of the wheel as Raymond ground the long blade twice, once for each side of the sword's traditional single edge. His strokes were smooth and easy looking, following the curve with a steadiness born of years of practice. Then he turned the sword over and started again, grinding twice more.

Jack frowned, looking at the sword as best he could through the gusting sparks: was he imagining it, or was the sword actually getting smaller?

Raymond turned the sword over and ground it yet again. And again.

Now Jack was sure of it: the sword *was* getting smaller. And then the realization hit him: Raymond wasn't sharpening the blade. He was destroying it. He was destroying Charlie's sword!

The wheel ground and shrieked as it bit into the steel. Fat sparks flew as Raymond pressed at the remains of the sword mercilessly. Jack watched where the sparks fell, watched their glow fade from white to orange and finally to black on the pitted surface of Raymond's workbench. The long, curved blade became a stumpy blunt nub. Then Raymond tossed the last bit of it aside, laid his goggles down carefully, and switched off his machine.

As the whine of the machine dropped back down to silence, Raymond unhooked a dustpan and brush from under the workbench. He swept at where the sparks had landed, collecting the filings into a neat pile before transferring them to a nearby bucket. Then he picked up the bucket and set off for the door at the far end of the room, before the boys had time to do anything other than stare.

"What the Hell did you do that for?" spluttered Charlie finally.

"Just watch," said Esme quietly.

They followed Raymond into a storeroom of some kind. Long metal shelves lined the walls to either side. Raymond reached up to the top right-hand shelf and brought down a small sack of something, which he proceeded to pour into the bucket, mixing it in well with what remained of Charlie's sword.

"Mind how you go," he said to Jack, surprising him. "There's no railing or nothing, so don't be getting too close to the edge now." Then he opened another door, which took them out onto a roof.

The night air was cool, and the sky was stained a weird kind of violet by the orange color of the London streetlights. The roof at the back of the theater was wide and flat, and at its center stood a big square crate made out of roughly nailed wooden slats. The crate was almost as tall as Jack was, and there were fluttering and cooing noises coming from inside it. Jack could hear the noises even under the sound of the West End traffic, which was surprisingly loud now that they were outside, even up where they were.

Raymond had turned his back again and was sprinkling great handfuls from the bucket over the top of the crate, provoking a frenzy of flapping and cooing from inside it.

There was a pause.

"Erm . . . what are you doing?" asked Jack.

"Feeding these pigeons," said Raymond.

"We can see that," snapped Charlie. "What we want to know is, why're you feeding them bits of sword?"

"They haven't eaten since I caught them," said Raymond. "They're hungry." Then he went back to the feeding—smiling and making absurd little kissing noises at the pigeons, while the boys kept staring at him

The boys looked at each other. Then they looked at Raymond again. Presently, he turned around and looked at Charlie.

"I've been making swords," he said, "for thirty years now, near enough. I'm going to tell you how it's done."

Charlie stared at him, then shrugged. "All right," he said.

"Find yourself a nice bit of metal," Raymond began. "I'm simplifying, obviously. Then you heat it up in a forge. Around fourteen hundred degrees is best, I find, but 'bloody hot' will do for a rough description. With me so far?"

"'Bloody hot,'" said Charlie. "Right."

"Then you take a big hammer and you beat it. Hard. And when it's the shape you want, you quench it."

"You *what* it?"

"You stick it in something to cool it down," muttered Jack.

"That's right," said Raymond, nodding to Jack.

"Next," he went on, "I *grind* it. I keep grinding, till there's nothing left but filings. Then I sweep the filings up, I mix 'em with seed, and I feed 'em to some pigeons."

"Why?" said Charlie.

Raymond's beard bristled as he grinned. "Because the next day, when nature's, ah, 'taken its course,' as it were, I can collect what's under the pigeon coop, melt it down, and then start the whole thing again."

"*What?*"

"The Saxons were where I heard it first," said Raymond blithely. "They used chickens. But the Arabs, Toledo—most everyone was at it at some time or another. Some Eastern swordsmiths even used ostriches, if you believe the stories."

"What are you talking about?" Charlie asked.

Raymond frowned. "The droppings," he said, as if it were obvious. "The feces. The birds' mess—the poo."

The boys just stared at him.

Raymond sighed.

"Let me ask you something," he said. "What does bird poo smell of?"

"Ammonia," said Jack, surprising himself.

"Right!" said Raymond. "That's because it's full of nitrogen. Well, feed the filings to your birds—with a nice bit of seed, of course—and when they, ah, come out, the nitrogen will've reacted with the metal, hardening it. Melt down the result, beat it into the shape you want, and you end up with a sword that's smaller, sure, but it'll be unbreakable, near enough. Do the whole thing three or four times and it'll be stronger still. Now . . ."

He paused.

"I make good swords, some of the strongest, hardest, toughest swords in the world. I'm not one to boast. Other people's swords may be nicer to look at. But my swords, you can trust your life to 'em. Which, after all, is what a sword is for."

"Good swords," said Charlie. "Right. What's your *point*?"

"By the time I'm done with a sword," said Raymond, looking hard at Charlie, "it's been heated red hot, smashed flat with hammers, ground down to nothing, crapped out by pigeons, heated red hot, smashed flat with hammers—et cetera, et cetera, *et cetera*. Seven times is my record."

"Seven?" echoed Esme with sudden interest.

"Never mind that now," said Raymond. "My point is," he went on, turning back to Charlie, "*you*'ve had your powers since . . . when? *The day before yesterday*."

Charlie frowned at him, not understanding.

"Why did you chase the demon, Charlie?" asked Raymond patiently.

"What?"

"Why did you chase the Scourge by yourself instead of waiting for backup?"

For another long moment Charlie just looked at him.

Then he scowled.

"All right," he said. "Well, I don't know if Esme mentioned this to you, but it was going *quite quickly*. If I'd waited, we'd've lost it."

"No," said Raymond quietly. "If you'd waited, you could've helped get Jessica back here. Instead of which, you took off, forcing Esme to follow you, and Jessica—and Jack—were left unprotected."

"I didn't *force* Esme to—" Charlie began.

"The day before yesterday, Charlie," Raymond repeated. "Understand? Esme's been training her whole life. You're not qualified to make those decisions. She is."

"But—"

"Plus, of course," Raymond went on, ignoring him, "you lost it anyway."

Charlie's scowl deepened.

"You lost it," said Raymond. "Yes or no?"

"All right!" said Charlie. "All right! Yes, I lost it!"

He paused.

"I followed it across the rooftops," he said. He turned to Jack. "You should've seen me, mate, it was amazing!"

Jack looked at him.

"But then it . . . vanished suddenly," Charlie went on. "It happened when we were back near the theater. And that's where . . ." He trailed off.

"That's where Esme caught up with you," said Raymond.

"That's right," said Charlie.

Raymond looked into the pigeon coop at its cooing, fluttering occupants for a whole minute. Then, obviously satisfied by what he saw, he put down the bucket.

"Let me ask you another question," he said wearily.

Charlie just looked at him.

"If Esme hadn't decided—"

"Raymond," said Esme softly from the doorway. "Don't you think—?"

"No, petal, this is important," said Raymond. "He may

be new to all this, but he's got to realize what's at stake." The big man turned his gaze back onto Charlie. "If Esme hadn't decided that the first priority was to get back to Jessica, what do you think would've happened?"

Charlie scowled but didn't answer.

"Shall I tell you?" Raymond asked. "Your friend here"—he gestured at Jack without looking at him—"would be dead. And it would be your fault, just like it's your fault that Jessica's dead."

Raymond kept looking at Charlie.

"What do you say to that? Eh?"

Jack too looked at Charlie. Charlie's mouth had turned into a hard white line. When he spoke, it was quietly.

"Look," he said slowly. "In case it slipped your mind, that demon of yours, the one that you've been making all this fuss over—is *gone*. I killed it." He paused. "Now, I'm sorry about . . . what's-er-name, Jessica. But we know now for sure that what happened to her isn't going to happen to anyone else, ever, because it's *over*. And I won."

Raymond said nothing.

"I'm the boss," said Charlie, looking slowly around the room. "I *rule*," he added, as if extra emphasis were needed. "So . . ." He shrugged. "What's next?"

There was another long silence—broken only by the sudden sound of Charlie's phone, ringing again.

Charlie sucked his teeth, pulled out the phone, looked at the screen, and scowled.

"You'd best run along home to your mum, son," said Raymond quietly. "It's late."

For a moment, Charlie just stared at him. Then he stamped his foot.

"I don't *believe* this!" he shouted. "What's wrong with you people?"

No one answered.

"Come on, Jack, we're going," said Charlie. In another moment he was heading back for the door. He waved a hand and it swung open for him: it flew round on its hinges and smacked into the wall, hard.

Jack set off after him quickly, but before leaving the roof he cast one quick look back. Both Esme and Raymond were standing perfectly still, apparently lost in thought, with the great wooden coop standing between them. Then the door swung shut.

There was a pause.

"So," said Raymond. "What do you think?"

"I'm going to get my paints," said Esme, and set off, not looking at Raymond.

Raymond followed her through the storeroom and then through the armory. Then, when Esme turned left, heading for her room, he crossed the landing and opened the doors to the butterfly room. He walked over to the long conference table and sat down. Presently, Esme returned: in one hand she was carrying a paint-spattered tray that held a small jug of water and a large palette spotted with a variety of colors—blues, mostly. In the other, she held a clutch of fine, red-handled paintbrushes. Raymond sat scratching his beard as, still not looking at him, Esme walked past the long table and off toward the shadowy far corner of the room, the place where the pattern ran out. She stopped walking, closed her eyes—

—and lifted off the ground, floating smoothly up toward the high ceiling.

Her thick black curly hair was tied back in its customary tight bunch, and she was wearing a thin scarf of some dark material to catch any splashes. Quickly, easily, she let the rest of her body swing upward until she was lying flat in the air, facing the ceiling, with the tray resting on her belly. She chose a brush, dipped it in the water, and dabbed at the thick black poster paint she was using for the outline of tonight's butterfly. When it was the consistency she wanted, she set to work.

All this while, Raymond said nothing. Esme was concentrating on her butterfly. Raymond waited.

Finally, Esme said, "I don't know."

Still, Raymond just waited.

"All my life . . ." said Esme, working the fine brush around the butterfly's outline with a rock-steady hand. Only when it was roughed in to her satisfaction did she turn to look at the man at the table below her. "You know?"

"Mm," said Raymond.

"I don't—" began Esme, then frowned.

"I *didn't*," she corrected herself, "think I'd feel like *that* when it was dead."

Raymond looked up at her. "Like what?" he asked.

"Like nothing," said Esme.

Raymond waited.

Esme dropped the first brush into the water jug and chose another. Frowning, she began filling in the butterfly's outline, laying the paint on thick.

"Maybe we've been wrong all this time to think the Scourge couldn't be killed," she said. "Maybe Charlie really *is* that strong. I mean, the Scourge *died*—or it certainly looked that way: I watched it die; it was screaming. But I . . ."

She sighed and shook her head.

"I should have *felt something*. Not . . . happy or anything. You know I wasn't expecting that. But there should have been something—shouldn't there?"

She looked down at Raymond.

"Mm," he said again.

She turned back to the butterfly—and blinked. There was nothing there now but a great butterfly-shaped splat of darkness: not a glimmer of the ceiling's original cream showed through. The thing she was going to say was growing inside her, pushing to get out, so she gave up what she was doing and looked down at Raymond again.

"I just can't believe it's dead," she said.

She waited, holding her gaze on him until he looked up at her again.

"Not like that," she added.

"No," said Raymond finally. "Me neither."

"I think you'd better find Felix," Esme said.

"Yeah," said Raymond. "I think you're right."

THE CHANCE

Charlie and Jack were walking back across the park toward Charlie's house. There were no lights in the park, and when Charlie left the path, his steps becoming suddenly inaudible on the grass, the silence settled around the boys like a cloak. Charlie stopped by the lake that ran along the park's south side. Jack caught up and stood beside him, and they looked out at the water: it was as black as ink, and Jack could hear it whispering to itself.

"So," said Charlie suddenly, his voice sounding bright and crass in the quiet. "That was a pretty classy bit of rescuing, eh?"

"Yep," said Jack. "Just in the nick of time too. I think this superhero business is starting to suit you."

"*So,*" repeated Charlie, with sudden savagery, "why the Hell didn't you stick up for me back there?"

Jack stared at him, astonished. "What?"

"For Christ's sake, Jack, I saved your life tonight! You might at least've said something to back me up with Raymond—but instead you're all, 'Stick it in something to cool it down.'" Charlie's voice had gone high and singsong as he threw Jack's words back at him. He sounded nothing like Jack whatsoever.

"Well?" he asked.

"Well what?" asked Jack, unable to fathom where all this was coming from.

"Why didn't you say anything?"

Jack looked at Charlie. Charlie's face was in darkness. Jack thought for a moment, then said quietly, "Do you think it would've helped?"

"I mean," he went on, when Charlie didn't reply, "it's not like you or the others have ever really listened to me before. Right?"

There was a long pause.

Charlie sighed.

"I'm sorry, man," he said. "I didn't mean to have a go at you. I just . . ."

He turned to face Jack suddenly.

"You know," he announced, "you're my *best mate*."

"What?" said Jack again.

"You're the only one: the *only one* who I know'll stick by me, no matter what. Like at the restaurant," Charlie went on, speaking so fast he was almost babbling. "You know, when you came in with me. I don't think I could've said what I did to Dad if you hadn't been there. In fact, maybe I'd never've been able to tell him how angry I was if it wasn't for . . . well, if it wasn't for you."

Jack squirmed a bit. Charlie had never spoken to him like this: it was weird.

"Er . . . sure," he managed. "No problem."

"I can't tell you how happy I am that you're with me on this, man."

"No worries, mate," said Jack, frowning. "You know, whatever." He shrugged.

Apparently satisfied, Charlie turned to look out at the lake again.

"What do you think's wrong with them?" he asked after a moment. "Esme and Raymond, I mean.

"I mean . . . you *saw* me. Right?" he added, before Jack had time even to think, let alone reply. "I killed the demon! I made fireballs come out of my hands and I burned it to death! Right?"

"Mm," said Jack. "About that. How did you *do* that?"

"Oh," said Charlie with a dismissive *fff*ing sound, "that sort of stuff, I don't even have to think. It's just . . . you know, simple."

"Yeah," said Jack uneasily. "But it sounds like sometimes you sort of *have* to think too. Don't you?"

"What d'you mean?" Charlie shot back, instantly defensive.

"Well," prompted Jack carefully, "they didn't sound too happy with you just now."

"But that's just what I'm saying!" said Charlie. "I mean, I know it must've been a shock for them, all this. Me passing the test and not Esme. Me coming along out of the blue and just whacking this demon when everyone else has been running scared of it for years. I can see that'd be hard to take, 'specially for Esme, with her mum and everything."

"Hm," said Jack.

"But, you know, they've just got to deal with it! Right? Like tonight, f'rinstance. I mean, I didn't want them to make a big thing out of it, right? Of course not. Not my style. But still, you know, job well done, credit where credit's due—and what do I get? A bollocking!"

Charlie looked out at the lake again.

"Jack, can I ask you something?" he asked suddenly.

"Sure," said Jack. "'Course."

"Do you ever wish that the world just . . . didn't exist?"

Jack stared at him again. "How d'you mean?"

"Well . . . all this *stuff*," said Charlie. "The Scourge. The Brotherhood. My *folks* . . ."

The list was an odd one and Jack might have smiled if it weren't for what Charlie said next.

"Don't you think it'd be simpler if . . . none of it was here anymore?"

"Sorry?" said Jack.

"Wouldn't it be better if there was *nothing?*" Charlie asked, turning to face him. "Don't you ever feel like it'd be better if one day everything, the whole universe, just came to an end—pop!—like that?"

Jack looked at him. He didn't really know what to say.

"Sometimes," said Charlie, frowning, "I just feel like . . . I don't know. . . ."

He bunched his fists.

"Like I want to reach out and smash everything," he said. "Like I want to rip everything up. Tear it to shreds, burn it all down and dance in the ashes. Do you ever feel like that?"

Jack looked at Charlie carefully.

"Not really, mate, to be honest," he said. "No."

Charlie sighed. "Ah, forget it." He grimaced. "Listen, it's late. Mum'll be having kittens. I reckon I'd better just head home by myself."

"Sure?"

"Sure."

Jack looked at his superhero friend and attempted a smile.

"'Faster than a speeding penguin,'" he told him.

"Yeah, right," said Charlie, attempting a smile back. "See you."

"See you."

They parted.

Later, Jack would look back at this moment and wonder if he could have done things differently. By this point Charlie was already helpless under the Scourge's influence, but even so, if Jack had said something, if he'd obeyed his instincts telling him that something was badly wrong with his friend and stayed with him until they'd talked things out somehow, then maybe the rest of what was to come might not have happened the way it did.

Now it was too late.

BUTTERFLIES

Esme was most of the way through her third butterfly of the night. Her eyes were tired, and her eyelids were beginning to droop—but as soon as she heard the noise, she was wide awake.

She slid to the ground soundlessly, placing the tray of paints and brushes on the floor. At that moment, the only light in the butterfly room came from the single lamp she'd left glowing in the center of the long table. Crouching well back in the shadows at the far end of the hall, she watched as the double doors swung open, and a dark figure strode in.

"Esme?" said Charlie. "It's me."

"Oh, hi, Charlie," said Esme, stepping slowly out into the light.

Charlie gestured behind himself vaguely: "The, ah, door to the roof was open. Mind if I . . . ?"

"Sure," said Esme. "Come in."

They stood at opposite ends of the table. Charlie put his hands on the back of the chair in front of him.

"Been painting, I see," he began.

"Yeah," said Esme. "There hasn't been much time the last

couple of days, so I had a bit of catching up to do." She smiled at him politely. The grin he gave back was very eager.

"Butterflies, eh?" he said.

"Yes."

There was a pause.

"What made you choose them?" asked Charlie. "Butterflies, I mean."

Esme, surprised, looked at him for a moment, then shrugged.

"It's partly because there are so many kinds," she said. "Also, they're hard to paint: getting the colors right used to be pretty tough, especially when I was starting out."

"But the main reason," Charlie interrupted, "is that they're like *you*." He grinned. "Aren't they?"

Esme frowned at him. "What do you mean?"

"You've been waiting your whole life to fight the Scourge," said Charlie, his eyes never leaving hers for an instant. "Every day you've been training, preparing, perfecting your skills: you said so yourself."

"Yeah," said Esme. "So?"

"Well, you're like them, aren't you?" said Charlie delightedly, gesturing at the walls. "You're there in your cocoon, waiting to come out. Waiting and waiting—waiting all your life for the moment when you can spread your wings and fly."

For a second, Esme just stared at him.

"What on Earth are you talking about?" she said. "I . . . just like butterflies, that's all." To her horror, however, she could feel her cheeks beginning to go red.

The thing was, though she'd've died before admitting it . . . Charlie wasn't entirely wrong. The life cycle of caterpillar to cocoon to butterfly had fascinated Esme ever since Raymond had first explained it to her. It was the reason she had started painting butterflies in the first place, seven long years before. And Charlie knew. He was grinning at her now smugly, pleased with himself for making her lie like that. He *knew*.

"They're beautiful," he said—looking at her.

"Thanks," said Esme, infuriated.

"How many was it again?"

"Five thousand, four hundred and seventy-five," said Esme, "now."

"Wow," said Charlie softly.

Esme took a breath. "Charlie, don't take this the wrong way, but . . . do you mind if I ask what you're doing here?"

Charlie's grin grew wider.

"Do you like surprises?" he asked.

Esme frowned at him again.

"I don't know," she replied. "It depends."

"Because I had this idea," said Charlie. "A surprise for you. As soon as I thought of it I came straight over."

"That's . . . nice," said Esme.

"Just you wait," said Charlie, still smiling. His fingers clasped and unclasped on the back of the chair.

"You know," he said, "I was thinking. It's all happened very fast, this whole thing."

"Uh-huh."

"And the way things've been going, you and me haven't

really had much of a chance to . . . get to know each other."

"No," said Esme. "I suppose that's true."

"Well, I don't know about Raymond," said Charlie quickly, "but I think you and me could . . . get on. You know?"

Esme looked at him.

"I want us to be friends," said Charlie. He shrugged—a study in elaborate casualness. "What do you say?"

His stare was very intense. Esme found herself looking away.

"Sure," she said, shrugging carefully back.

"Great!" said Charlie, delighted. "Great! Well! About that surprise I mentioned . . ."

"Oh yes."

"It's the classic. You know—you've got to close your eyes. No peeking!"

Esme just looked at him. "What?"

"Come on," said Charlie. "Just close your eyes for a moment."

"Charlie—"

"You'll love it! I promise!"

"Well . . ."

It was odd, but Esme really didn't want to. Still, what could she do? Pursing her lips, she did as she was asked and closed her eyes.

"Now," she heard Charlie say, "just give me a second here."

She heard him take a breath and hold it. Then the air in the room seemed to be heating up.

She could feel it from where she was standing. It was as if the atmosphere were thickening or swelling somehow. There was a weird smell, like ozone or hot metal, and the air was crackling with something like electricity: it made her scalp tingle. Esme tried opening her eyes but found, with a shock, that she couldn't. Then—

"*Ffffffff*," said Charlie suddenly, as he let out a great breath—and as quickly as it had come, the weird feeling in the air vanished.

"You can open them now," he said.

Esme did and looked around, but the only difference she could see was that Charlie's big, satisfied grin was even bigger and more self-satisfied than before.

"What?" she asked uncertainly. "What am I looking for?"

"Just a second," said Charlie. His eyes were darting little looks around the walls, as if he were searching for something. Then—

"There!" he said, pointing, almost jumping up and down, he was so excited.

Esme looked, and her breath caught in her chest.

On the ceiling above her, one of her butterflies, the one she'd just been painting—was moving.

It was nothing more than a tremble at first. Very faint. But in another moment the unfinished butterfly, one set of markings on the lower part of its right wing still not properly inked in, was twitching convulsively. Its small black body was straining and pulling. One thick powdery wing came free, then another, and then the butterfly was flapping its wings experimentally, each flapping movement revealing the wing-shaped gaps in the surface of the paint underneath. Now, suddenly, the movements were spreading, being followed and imitated all across the ceiling and down the walls. All over the room, all Esme's butterflies, all seven years' worth of them, were rippling and twitching, jerking and straining—and coming free. She looked back at the first one, the unfinished one, just in time to see it tense itself, then leap away from the ceiling. It plummeted like a stone, and Esme thought for a second that it would hit the ground—but then, as if with a heart-stopping effort, the oversized butterfly flapped its wings once, twice—and bobbed back up into the air.

And *then*—

—suddenly—

—they *all* took off.

"WHEEEEEEEEEEEEEE-HEEEEE!" screamed Charlie, disappearing from view in a blizzard of fluttering wings. The air was thick with them now, thick with the butterflies and the soft clattering sounds they made as they flew—a sound like the slow, soft crumpling of a million sheets of paper. They followed each other, swinging round the room in a great arc, a seething, shivering, whirling mass of blurring bright painted colors.

Charlie danced on the spot, still screaming and waving his arms in the air as the butterflies dived and swooped all around him.

Esme, however, stood still.

For a second, as the air cleared between them, Charlie saw her. Still grinning, he called out to her.

"What do you think? Huh? How about this?"

He made a casual gesture in the air with one hand, and

suddenly tens, hundreds of the painted creatures were landing on her shoulders, on the skin of her bare arms.

Esme watched one on her hand. She recognized it: it was an early one. Her brushstrokes had none of the finesse she'd developed later. Without legs or antennae, it bumped against her blindly, each contact shaking tiny flakes of paint dust from its dark wings.

"They're alive," she said slowly. "They're really alive."

"Yep," said Charlie.

"You can do this?" asked Esme. "You can bring things to life?"

"Looks that way to me," said Charlie, smirking. He too was covered in the oversize butterflies now, all over his arms and his hair. Behind him, the rest of the great flock suddenly changed direction at once, sweeping the other way around the sides of the room.

"And you've done this," said Esme, "just to impress me?"

Charlie looked at her.

"It's a present!" he reminded her. "Why? Don't you like it?"

"Do you have any idea what you're doing?" asked Esme. The butterflies leaped off her as she rounded on him, her hands shaking with sudden rage. "Stop it!"

Charlie stared, his face slack with surprise. "What?"

"Stop it!" shouted Esme. "Turn them back!"

"Why?"

"Do it NOW!"

"All right!" said Charlie. "All right!"

He blinked.

For a second, the butterflies froze in the air.

Then they fell.

Each one shattered into powder as it touched the ground. In a moment, the floor was a mass of tiny flakes of paint. The walls were covered in butterfly-shaped silhouettes. These things were all that remained of Esme's seven years of work.

From opposite ends of the table, Esme and Charlie stared at each other.

"Don't ever," said Esme, "*ever* do anything like that again."

He stared at her for a moment. Then he scowled.

"I'll do what I like!" he said.

"No, Charlie," said Esme quietly. "You won't."

Something in her voice made Charlie stop dead.

He looked at her and grinned uncertainly.

"Come on," he said. "I don't want to fight you, Esme."

Esme just looked at him.

"I mean, it was a present—right?" Charlie's grin was wide again now, as if he were sure she'd still come round. "I didn't mean anything by it. I just wanted us to be friends."

"Well, that wasn't the way to go about it."

The silence between them then lasted for a long time. At last, Charlie's smile went hollow—and faded.

"Fine," he said suddenly. He looked up and shrugged. "*Fine*. Well . . . *bye*, then."

He turned. Already the double doors were opening to receive him.

"Charlie?"

He didn't answer.

"Charlie! Wait!" she called.

But the doors clicked shut. He hadn't looked back.

Esme was still staring when a loud, ugly buzz from the intercom broke the silence. She went over to the door and pressed the button. "Yeah?"

"It's me," said Raymond. "Can you come down here and give me a hand a second?"

"What is it?"

"I've found Felix."

Raymond had only really wanted Esme to talk to: even with Felix's unconscious body over his shoulder in a fireman's lift, he still climbed the stairs to the headquarters two at a time.

"He was in a private clinic out in the suburbs," he explained. "He was checked in there by his housekeepers two days ago; that's why we couldn't find him till now."

"Is he . . . ?"

"Dead?" asked Raymond. "No. It's the Scourge's doing, that's for sure, but it's some sort of coma, like—*blimey*," he added, as Esme opened the doors to the butterfly room and he caught sight of the scene beyond.

"Yeah," said Esme grimly. While Raymond laid Felix down on the table, she quickly told him what had just taken place.

"But how?" Raymond asked. "I mean, I don't think even Nick had that much power."

Esme was pacing the floor. "What worries me is the way Charlie was afterwards," she said. "The way he left seemed awfully, I don't know . . . final." But then, noticing Raymond's look of dawning horror, she stopped. "What?" she asked.

For another moment Raymond just stood there by Felix's unconscious body, frozen by what had just occurred to him.

"Esme," he said—and gulped. "I've never seen anything like this." He gestured woodenly at the remains of the butterflies. "I mean, bringing things to life! Nobody in the Brotherhood's ever done anything remotely like this. Ever!"

"So?"

"Well, what if . . . ?" Raymond began—and fell silent.

Esme stared at him. "Wait a second," she said, "let me get this straight. Jessica wasn't the host, and neither was Felix—not if he's been in a coma for two days."

"Right."

"But the only other person who the host could have been is—"

"Nick!" Raymond finished for her.

"What about the test, though?" Esme asked. "Choosing a new leader?"

Raymond shook his head. "Nick wasn't looking for a new leader. He wasn't even looking for new recruits: the Scourge was controlling him! What it wanted was a new *host*!" He paused. "And it found one."

They looked at each other.

"Oh no . . ." Esme whispered.

SORRY'S NOT GOOD ENOUGH

It was the same night: it was stiflingly hot, and Jack was having bad dreams when the knocking sound got loud enough to wake him. He sat up in bed suddenly. Still wrapped up in his dream, it took him a while to realize that the knocking wasn't in his head, it was coming from the window.

Jack's curtains were thin. Normally, the orange of the streetlight outside came through them quite strongly. At that moment, however, a large black shadow was blotting out most of the light.

Jack got up and pulled the curtains open. Jack's room was three floors up off the ground, but there, waiting outside as if he were standing on solid ground, was Charlie.

He was smiling. His arms were out at his sides; ink-black tattoo shapes were dripping down them, coiling restlessly under his skin.

Jack opened the window. "Charlie, what the hell are you doing here?"

Charlie just smiled. "Nice to see you too," he said.

"What time is it?" asked Jack. When Charlie didn't answer, he looked back at the glowing red digits of the clock on his bed-side table.

"Jesus, Charlie! It's four in the morning!"

"Yeah?" said Charlie. "I didn't check. You were certainly out for the count."

"Yeah, well, that's because it's *four in the morning*," Jack repeated, since the information clearly hadn't got through the first time.

"Jack," said Charlie, "we've got to go somewhere."

Jack looked at him. "What?"

"You and me," said Charlie. "You see, I've just had the most amazing idea. But I want you to come with me."

"Come with you where?"

"To the demon world," said Charlie. "I want you to come with me to Hell."

There was a pause.

Jack looked at Charlie carefully for a moment. Then he put both hands on the windowsill and leaned forward, look-ing out and down. Charlie slid back in the air a few inches to make room. Jack looked past his friend's feet, at the ground below, then he looked up at him again.

"You're steady as a rock," he said. "Getting pretty good at this flying thing now, eh?"

"Jack," said Charlie, "help me on this. I don't want to do it alone."

"Do what?"

"Open the Fracture."

"Ah," said Jack.

"Raymond'll never let me do anything," Charlie spat. "And Esme . . ." His expression turned hurt and puzzled looking. "Well, I don't think me and her are ever going to get on, man. That's all."

"What are you talking about, Charlie?"

"A real adventure," said Charlie. "Don't you see?"

His eyes took on a weird gleaming quality that Jack didn't like one bit.

"You and me," said Charlie, "we don't need the Brother-hood. We're better at fighting demons than they ever were. And now we've got the chance to go somewhere *no one's ever been*. So how about it? What do you say?" Charlie had got so excited that he'd actually started bobbing slightly in the air. Now, however, as he leaned forward for Jack's answer, the bobbing subsided until he hung still once more.

Jack looked at him.

"Give me a minute," he said. "I'll get some trousers on."

Jack changed out of his pajamas quickly. He was thinking quickly too, and his thoughts went something like this:

There was no point in saying no. That was obvious. What-ever Charlie was intending to do, he was almost certainly still going to do it whether Jack came with him or not. But if Jack did go with him, then there might be a chance to warn the others or stop him somehow before it was too late.

In moments, he was ready. He was dressed lightly: black jeans, black T-shirt, and his favorite trainers. In his back pocket, he also had his phone, with Esme and Raymond's number already programmed into it.

"Okay," he told Charlie. "I'll meet you outside."

Charlie shook his head. "No good, mate," he said. "Your folks are downstairs, asleep in front of the telly. You might wake 'em when you go past." He held his arms out. "Give me your hands," he said.

"Okay," said Jack. "But listen, erm . . ."

"What?" said Charlie with a flash of impatience.

Jack was thinking about his parents—two lumpish shapes sprawled across the sofa in the light of the TV screen, their heads lolling. He almost smiled. They'd be snoring. They'd be stiff in the morning too: his dad was always particularly bad when they'd spent the night on the sofa.

Should he tell them he was going? *Yeah, right,* he thought: what would he say? Besides, if he managed to warn Esme and Raymond in time, then maybe he'd be back in his bed before his folks even woke up. But Jack sighed: somewhere in his heart, he knew already that that probably wasn't how the night was going to end up. Not with his luck.

Typical.

Grimly, he swung his legs up onto the windowsill, took hold of Charlie's hands, and stepped out into thin air.

"Let's go," said Charlie.

"All right," said Jack. And they were off.

Jack's home, his street, shrank below his feet and vanished into the night. There was a rush of hot air, a sensation like huge black wings closing around them both—then they were stepping out of the shadows onto Charing Cross Road, in London's West End.

From the front, the Light of the Moon looked a bit like a cinema. The entrance was a sort of wide stone porch, supported by three fairly ridiculous-looking cream-colored pillars. The doors themselves consisted of six panels of thick sheet glass, with large and ugly vertical brass handles stuck onto them. The darkness beyond the glass was total: everyone who worked or drank there was long gone—but the street itself still had a few stragglers passing by. The boys waited until no one was looking. Charlie put his hand on one of the heavy locks, Jack heard a soft *click*, then Charlie was pushing through into the dark, empty space of the pub that was a gateway to Hell.

Jack sighed and—a little unsteadily—followed Charlie in. The light from the street quickly shrank into the enveloping darkness of the empty pub. The sensation that they weren't supposed to be there was, Jack found, very strong.

"Charlie?" he asked, in that ridiculous hoarse whisper you use when you want to be heard but don't at the same time.

"Over here," came the reply, in Charlie's normal speaking voice. "Come in. Mind the steps."

By the light of the street behind him, Jack could just make out a wide flight of steps, and he followed them down until his trainers made squeaking contact with the bare floorboards.

"Charlie, how about a bit of light?" he asked, in his best casual voice.

"Sure."

Whump! A ball of light appeared over the open palm of Charlie's hand. Charlie grinned.

Jack looked at the glowing fireball, still trying not to bog-gle too much. Then he looked around himself.

The light of Charlie's fireball thing showed a space that was surprisingly big, maybe even as big as the butterfly room. To Jack's left, a long chrome bar top spanned about two-thirds of the length of the room, and there was a partitioned-off section of tables and sofas along to his right. Charlie stood in the middle of the wide, largely bare open area that took up most of the room. The whole place stank of stale cigarettes and booze. But what Jack really noticed was the high ceiling, which, in the flickering yellow-orange light of Charlie's fire-ball, seemed very far away.

Jack looked back down at Charlie, who was doing some-thing weird—well, even more weird anyway. He was hunched over, his head sticking out forward as if he were sniffing for something. His hands were groping about in the air. The fireball thing hung over him, following him smoothly as he moved.

"Charlie, what are you—?"

"Here," said Charlie suddenly, turning to Jack with a huge grin. "Here. Feel."

Jack shrugged and walked over, his trainers squeaking loudly as he crossed the bare wood of the floor.

"Put your hand where mine is," said Charlie.

Jack gave him a sideways look but did as he said, putting his arm out.

"Can you feel it?" asked Charlie, still grinning wildly.

Jack felt about a bit. "I can feel . . . a draft," he said.

"It's not a draft," said Charlie. "See? If I stand in front of it. Here. Or here. Where could it be coming from?" His smile got even wider. "It's not a draft."

Jack frowned. It certainly was very odd. There was a cold space in the air, just above waist level, like putting your hand in a fridge. It was a very small and very defined sort of space: if he moved his arm so much as a few centimeters anywhere around it, the sensation vanished. He'd read stories about supposedly haunted houses that had "cold spots." He wondered whether that was anything to do with this.

"This is it, man," said Charlie, so excited he was practically vibrating. "The Fracture. The gateway to Hell."

"Mm," said Jack, straightening up and looking at his friend. He took a deep breath. "Listen," he said, "are you sure about this? I mean, really?"

"I've never been more sure of anything," said Charlie, "in my entire life."

"But—"

"I can feel it," said Charlie. His face glowed weirdly in the light of the fireball that was still hanging in the air above him. "In my heart," he said, "in my head—and in my blood." He closed his eyes, sniffed in a great lungful of air, and his eyelids fluttered.

Jack frowned at him. "Er, right," he said. "But don't you think, you know, that we should maybe call the others?"

"No," snapped Charlie, his eyes flicking open. "No others."

The two boys looked at each other.

"Don't you get it?" asked Charlie, with a smile that was

blatantly false. "The others don't want us. They don't want us to do this."

"But Charlie—"

"Come on, Jack!" Charlie's voice turned desperate. "There's nothing for us here. Nothing! And what we've got—right?— what we've got is a chance to leave it all behind." He stared at Jack, eyes wide.

"Come *on*, man," he repeated. "People never get the chance to do something like this. Not for real. The others had it, but they blew it. We're not going to make the same mistake."

Jack said nothing.

"All right?" said Charlie.

"I guess," said Jack.

"Cool. Now take a step back. I've got to do something here."

Jack did as he was told.

Charlie turned his back on him. He spread his arms, and the ink-black shapes of the tattoo slid down under his skin like they were being poured there.

Jack watched the tattoo. In seconds, Charlie's skin was a mass of black shapes—twisting, curling, and caressing.

Then the whole room started to hum.

It was a sound that seemed to come from everywhere. The air in the room seemed to be tightening around Jack like polyethylene. Charlie's outstretched arms began to make strange, jerky coaxing gestures—and an eggshell-thin line of light began to form in the space in the air in front of him.

It was just a crack at first. But as Charlie jerked and

weaved—as if he were a puppet being pulled by invisible strings—the line was widening and filling the room with an unearthly red glow.

Slowly, carefully, Jack eased his phone out of his jeans pocket.

Not taking his eyes off Charlie, he pressed the buttons that would bring up and dial the number he wanted.

After three long rings, Raymond answered. "Yeah?"

His voice sounded tiny and far away.

"It's Jack," whispered Jack.

"Hello?" said the big man. "Who's there?"

"It's *Jack*."

"Jack? I can't—"

"I'm at the Fracture," said Jack. "Charlie's—*hkh*—"

And a blow struck all the air out of his body, immediately followed by a stunning impact from behind that almost made him black out.

When his vision cleared, he was staring into Charlie's face, down Charlie's arm. Charlie's hand was locked round his throat.

Charlie's eyes were full of blood. His face was like a mask: the black shapes of the tattoo seethed and boiled under his skin, wriggling like eels. The corners of his mouth lifted in a strange grin, before the mouth opened, and a horrible voice said:

"No, no, *no*. That's quite out of the question, I'm afraid."

Jack forced himself to look down, away from the eyes, and saw (past his own dangling feet) that he was now some distance off the ground, pinned to the wall over the bar, on the other side of the room from where he had been standing before. He guessed Charlie must have grabbed him and just flown through the air with him until they'd hit the nearest wall. He looked back up at Charlie as, slowly, Charlie's head tipped to one side. The burning blood-filled eyes glanced at the phone in Jack's hand—

—and it tore from his grasp, shattering somewhere out of sight.

Silhouetted against the low, red glow of the Fracture, Charlie's face turned sad.

"You called them, Jack," he said, in his own voice—slowly, as if he couldn't believe what he was saying. "Why would you do that? Why would you . . . *betray* me like that?"

Jack said nothing. It was hard to speak when someone had you by the throat. He grabbed Charlie's arm with both his hands, but he might as well have been squeezing an iron bar. The grip tightened, cutting off Jack's breath, and in another second Jack's vision was closing in: great swaths of velvety black were swishing in from all around, surrounding Charlie's face until it was all that he could see.

He was losing consciousness, he realized.

Charlie was strangling him.

Jack felt a pressure on the inside of his skull, a squeezing in his heart, a tearing, thickening, swelling in his blood as it pounded in his ears—and he suddenly felt very stupid indeed. Now, at last, it was obvious: everything, from meeting Nick for the first time, all the way up until this moment, had been nothing more than a trick. Nick hadn't passed on any powers to Charlie: he'd passed on *the Scourge*. It was *Charlie* who was the Scourge's host body. It was *Charlie* who'd been harboring the demon inside him all this time. And though Jack had *known* there was something wrong with Charlie all along, he'd done and said nothing. He'd been so stupid! Stupid, stupid, stupid, *stupid*—

WHAM!

He glimpsed something slam into the side of Charlie's head.

The grip on his throat was suddenly released.

And Jack fell to the ground, hard.

He sat there in a crumpled heap, gasping for air.

"Esme," he heard Charlie say, surprised.

"Yeah," said Esme, and her amber eyes flashed fiercely. "Me."

Jack looked up. Esme was standing off to his right, on the steps that led down from the pub's entrance: Jack had never been so glad to see anyone in his life. Opposite her, to Jack's left, on another flight of wide steps that were the mirror image of the first, stood Charlie. Across some twenty yards of bare, polished floorboards, Charlie and Esme faced each other.

"I should have known about you," said Esme quietly. Her hands hung loosely at her sides. She shifted her weight from one trainered foot to the other slowly. "I should've spotted you from the start."

"Oh yeah?" said Charlie. "And why's that?"

"It's all come pretty easy for you, hasn't it?" said Esme. "Didn't it ever occur to you to wonder why?"

"What are you talking about?"

Esme shook her head, smiling.

"You're nothing more than an *accident*, Charlie," she said. "The wrong person, in the wrong place, at the wrong time." She leaned forward a little, staring at him hard to push home every word. "The Scourge needed a puppet. Someone who was easy to push around. You—with your little tantrums—fit the bill perfectly. That's why you were chosen, Charlie. Not for any other reason. And certainly not—God forbid—because you had any *talent*."

"Is that right?" asked Charlie.

"It's like you said, Charlie," Esme told him. "I've been waiting for this moment my whole life. Ever since the thing that you let inside you took my mother from me. You?" she added, and shrugged. "You're here by *mistake*."

And she lunged.

She leaped straight off the steps, hurling herself through the air toward Charlie.

Charlie too leaped toward her, a fraction of a second later.

Jack saw a blur of limbs.

There was a resounding and sickening *crack*.

Then the two of them landed again, on the opposite sides to where they'd been standing before.

Charlie looked shocked: his eyes were wide and staring, and his left arm cradled his right, which was sticking out at an alarming angle.

Esme's mouth was twisted in a sneer of rage: her killing hands twitched at her sides. She leaped again.

Charlie flung up his arms to ward her off.

And then the fight really began.

It was almost too fast for Jack to watch. He could see Charlie doing his best to block her, but Esme was too quick: for every blurring blow of foot or fist that landed relatively harmlessly on Charlie's shins or forearms, there seemed to be twice as many that cracked into a rib, hammered at his face, or smashed the air out of his belly, leaving him gasping. Esme spun on the spot and drove her trainered foot squarely into Charlie's mid-riff, doubling him over, taking him off his feet and hurling him through the air, straight back into the stairs he'd started off on. As the rest of his body hit the steps, his head snapped back, cracking against an edge. Charlie's hands fell to his sides, his eyes rolled up in his head, and he lay there unconscious.

Snarling, Esme leaped again, straight up this time, ready to stamp Charlie, when she landed, right through the floor.

Charlie was out for the count, defenseless.

Jack held his breath. But suddenly—

—at the moment of impact—

—Esme stopped.

Jack stared.

Esme began to struggle, but she was stuck fast. Hands like steel pincers gripped her waist: Charlie's hands.

Instead of dodging or rolling Charlie had simply caught her.

His face just inches from hers, Charlie's eyes flicked open, filling with blood. The black tattoo shivered, then rippled through his whole body.

And the thing inside him smiled.

Still grasping Esme, Charlie swung upright. Now he was hovering off the ground. Esme stared back in horror as Charlie continued to grin at her. Then Charlie began, slowly at first, to spin.

He spun once. Esme's hands began to pluck uselessly at his.

He spun twice. Esme's legs were already beginning to trail out behind her as the terrible momentum took hold.

He spun a third time, still grinning at her.

And then he let go.

Like a stone from a sling, Esme was flung across the room. She crashed to the floor in a pile of tables and chairs.

Charlie's awful smile remained frozen in place. Slowly, easily, he looked around the room—

—and the furniture, the bottles, the glasses, everything in the pub that wasn't screwed to the ground rattled in its place for a moment, then lifted into the air. The cloud of objects began to move, picking up speed, converging on Esme.

She sat up, blinked—and sprang to her feet as the blizzard of objects came whistling toward her. Instantly Esme became a blur of flailing limbs—ducking, twisting, and blocking as she used every ounce, every minute of her years of training and preparation to defend herself. When the first bar stool hit her she was ready, warding it off with a combination of a backward roll and a scything kick that sent it winging away into a corner: it smashed into the wall leaving a large hole in the plaster. The second and third met similar fates. Then the first table caught her in the small of the back.

Jack heard her gasp.

She missed a step.

And now, suddenly, she was down. The stools and tables and bottles and chairs kept coming, smashing into her, sending her sliding across the polished wooden floor under a burgeoning mound of twisting, twitching furniture. At the wall, not five yards along from where Jack was lying, she stopped.

The furniture stopped moving. She was trapped.

Charlie's smile widened further, in a ghastly grin that showed all his teeth. Then—

"LEAVE HER ALONE!"

In a blinding white burst, all the lights of the pub went on at once.

There, at the top of the steps above Esme, stood Raymond.

"KHENTIMENTU THE SCOURGE!" he roared. "TO ROOTS THAT BIND AND TO THORNS THAT CATCH I CONSIGN YOU!"

Charlie froze.

"By the light of the world," said Raymond, quieter now. "By the strength of my will and the curse that first stilled you, I command that you return to your prison. *Get you hence, and trouble us no more!*"

Charlie—or the thing that was wearing him—smiled again.

"**Do you know,**" said Charlie's mouth, though the voice that came out of it was nothing like Charlie's now, "**what it's *like* to be imprisoned for nine thousand years?**"

Charlie's eyes, as the Scourge glanced around the room, were completely black, like marbles: Jack looked at them and shuddered.

"Just try and imagine it," said the demon. "Nine thousand years, a day at a time. You can't do it," it said. "Can you?"

"Kh-Khentimentu the Scourge," began Raymond again, less confidently this time.

"Quiet," said the Scourge, and there was quiet. "I've been planning my revenge for longer than you could possibly comprehend. *You*—" it paused, and the eyes in Charlie's face seemed to bore into Raymond's, "are my finishing touch. When you're gone, your little 'Brotherhood' will have ceased to exist."

"Yeah?" blustered Raymond. "What about Esme?"

The demon smirked.

"It's already too late for her." Charlie looked down at Esme, who was still trapped under the pile of furniture.

"It's *always* been too late for her," said his mouth. "Just ask Felix."

"What are you talking about?" began Raymond, then stopped. He turned pale.

"That's right," said the Scourge, grinning delightedly. "Haven't you ever had your doubts about where her powers come from? Her strength? Her speed? Her *spirit*? Well, now, at last, you can begin to understand. Now, when it's too late."

"No," said Raymond quietly. "Ah, no. Surely not." He looked at Esme.

"You're going to die now, Raymond," said the demon. "You are harmless and weak, and you pose me no threat, but vengeance is vengeance and I will not be denied. If you have anything left to say, say it now."

Raymond looked at Esme.

"Listen to me carefully, petal," he said quickly. "Remember what I told you about your mother, all right? *Remember your mother.*"

"Dad," said Esme, "I—"

Raymond shook his head. "Look in my room," he said. "There's something for you. I was going to give it to you for your birthday, but that doesn't matter now: when you're ready, when you know what to do, you *use* it. All right?"

"Dad, I don't—"

"There's *more to life than this*, petal," said Raymond urgently. "Don't ever forget that. And don't ever forget . . . well, that I love you."

"Oh no," said Esme. "Oh, God. *Dad!*"

"All right," said the big man, straightening up and pushing his chest out. "All right, you bastard: do your worst."

The demon spread Charlie's arms. Its smile faded. The air in the room heated up suddenly, crackling and popping in Jack's ears with an awful electricity. A blast of pressure blew out all the lights of the pub, leaving it in darkness once more except for the dull red glow of the Fracture.

Then there was silence.

Raymond was gone. There wasn't even a body. It was as if he'd never existed.

Charlie's hands fell to his sides. The light from the Fracture was brightening now: it was widening, opening, the red

glow changing quickly to orange, then yellow, then a freezing, icy white. Charlie looked down at his hands. His face was
blank.

"You're dead," said Esme, sitting up. "I'm coming after
you, and when I find you . . . you're *dead!*" Her voice cracked
as she said it.

Charlie turned. The tattoo had subsided. The demon
inside him had let go for the moment, and it was Charlie the
boy who was looking at Esme now. A pang crossed his face,
and his jaw began to tremble.

"I . . . didn't . . ." he said.

Esme just looked at him.

"I . . . what . . . ?" said Charlie. He looked back down at his
hands.

"Oh no," he said. "Oh, God."

He turned to look at the blinding white gap in the air that
had appeared, silently, behind him. It was now wide enough
to step through.

And suddenly, watching him, Jack knew what he had to do.

There's nothing for us here. That was what Charlie had said.
It wasn't true—of course it wasn't. But Charlie had let himself
forget: the thing that had used him had made him forget. Jack
got to his feet.

Charlie looked at him: a begging, pleading look that
twisted in Jack's heart like a knife.

And instantly, the black shapes were swarming up Charlie's neck again. Charlie's face went slack as the demon took
control once more, ensuring that its victory wouldn't slip

away at this, its most triumphant moment. Charlie turned away woodenly, facing the Fracture. He stepped forward—

—and vanished.

Not pausing to think too much, Jack ran. The Fracture was already closing. He could hear a screaming sound as the freezing white space loomed up in front of him, a screaming he suddenly (with an odd sort of clarity) was able to identify as coming from Esme, begging him not to do what he was about to do.

But it was too late. He had done it already.

The light had him now. The shouts behind him were getting fainter, and soon there was nothing but light.

Right, thought Jack, waiting for the next bit. *Here we go, then.*

He was on his way.

On his way to Hell.

END OF

BOOK ONE

"IF SOMEONE COMES AT YOU WITH A SWORD, RUN IF YOU CAN. KUNG FU DOESN'T ALWAYS WORK."

BRUCE LEE

BOOK
TWO

THE PIGEON SWORD

WELCOME TO HELL

Some time later, Charlie opened his eyes. The first thing he saw was the demon.

It was the same black figure he'd chased over the rooftops. The same one that had pretended to die when he'd struck it with magical fireballs—a slim, narrow, but man-shaped thing made out of absolute darkness, its face a shiny black blank. It was looking at him.

"**Good,**" said the Scourge. "**You're awake.**"

"Er . . . yeah," said Charlie.

"**Did you sleep well?**" The voice came directly into Charlie's head, with a sensation like icy fingertips behind his eyes. Before answering, Charlie sat up. The tattoo was still there in the skin of his arms, but it wasn't moving now; it was still. The room he was in didn't appear to have any walls or ceiling or even a floor that he could see. There was himself, the bed, and the demon: everything else was just featureless white.

"I don't know," he said. "How long was I out for?"

"**There's . . . something I want to show you,**" said the Scourge gently, ignoring the question. "**It's a sight that I promise you'll never** forget as long as you live." With a smooth, liquid movement, it stood up and offered an ink-black hand. "**What do you say?**"

Charlie looked at the Scourge's hand.

"All right," he said, and took it.

The demon's touch was cool but firm. Charlie felt a rush of hot air, a sensation like huge black wings closing around him, then—

"**There**," said the Scourge. "**Open your eyes.**" Because as soon as Charlie had glimpsed what was there, he'd closed them tight before he could stop himself. The demon lifted one of its arms in a wide, sweeping gesture.

"**Welcome to Hell**," it said.

Charlie looked down at his feet. He was standing, unsupported, on a lip of black stone barely as wide as his trainers. Above him and around him there was nothing but starless sky, warm and thick and strangely still. And in front of him . . .

In front of him, and below him, stretching as far as he could see in any direction, was Hell.

"Buh—buh—" Charlie gibbered.

"**Take your time,**" the Scourge advised. "**Take it in slowly.**"

Charlie did his best, but it was difficult.

It's one of the strangest things about the human mind that, when it sees something really impressive—the Grand Canyon, for instance—the first reaction, often, is simply to dismiss it. "Naaah," says your brain, "it's a *backdrop*. Painted scenery. Special effects. It's not really there." You have to stand and look for quite a long time sometimes, just to let the realization sink in that what you are looking at *is* actually there.

That what you are looking at really is many millions of times bigger than you. And *it* doesn't care whether you believe in it or not.

"This place is known as the Needle," said the Scourge conversationally. "It's the highest point of the palace and, therefore, the whole of the realm."

Charlie didn't reply. He was too busy staring.

It was like standing on the summit of a mountain, he decided. Only instead of being made out of rock, the crags and peaks below him were actually buildings. Keeps, turrets, and towers of all shapes and sizes, from slender spires to things like giant cathedrals, all seemed to be jutting nonchalantly from the palace's gargantuan tapering sides. From the foot of it, miles below him, five vast and arrow-straight white-lit lines struck out into the landscape as far as his eyes could see. These lines were linked by smaller curved paths that split the land into a series of roughly concentric rings, broken up into sections by the five great roads. Charlie's attention was immediately caught by a country-size chunk that was the only bit of Hell so far that was anything like what he'd been expecting: the whole section appeared to be made out of flames. The flames were a beautiful rushing red and orange and yellow, and they slid up the walls of the pit that contained them and slipped back down again, heaving and subsiding like coastal sea on a stormy day. At every seventh great convulsion the waves of fire leaped even higher, sending a great gout of flame bursting up into the night sky before it crashed back into itself, leaving blossoming purple flashes on Charlie's retinas as he stood watching, spellbound.

"It could all be yours," said the Scourge quietly.

"What could?"

"All this," said the Scourge, gesturing again. "All Hell."

Charlie stopped looking at the sea of fire and turned to look at the demon.

"What are you talking about?" he asked.

"Here," said the Scourge. "I'll show you." Without further warning, it grabbed Charlie's hand—and they stepped off the edge.

Charlie's heart rose in his chest and his breath caught in his lungs as, for a full ten seconds, they plummeted straight down. Past his feet, the sheer black stone blocks of the tower they'd been standing on blurred past with sickening speed. His eyes were streaming, but when he looked ahead he could see the spiked roof of the next-tallest turret rushing up to meet him and—apparently—impale him. A scream pushed its way out of his throat. But it wasn't fear.

It was joy.

"HAAAAAAAAAAAAAAAAAAAAAH!" screamed Charlie, or something like it, as, with a pressure that made his insides feel like they were being squeezed flat, he and the demon suddenly leveled out and swooped round the turret. For a wonderful fraction of a second, Charlie actually felt his foot brush the edge of the roof—then they were diving, swimming through the air. The Scourge swung him out to their left, taking him in a wide circle, as the spectacularly fanged and spiked and crenellated and twisted towers of the palace rose to meet them, and pass beneath their feet.

"These are the High Reaches," said the demon, and Charlie heard its voice perfectly clearly even over the din of the rushing air. "From here all Hell's affairs are managed and directed."

They were now level with the highest windows of the palace. What Charlie saw didn't make a lot of sense to him. Up where he was, the turrets all seemed very small—individual structures separated from each other by the yawning spaces below—and they were all different from each other. He glimpsed windows of all shapes and sizes, and all were brightly lit, but he and the Scourge were flying too fast for him to be able to make out any more than a blur.

"This actually isn't the best way to see the palace," said the demon. "To appreciate it fully, one really needs to get away from it a little."

And with that, the roofs dropped away beneath them, and he and the Scourge swung out over the clear skies of Hell.

The night sky was a deep and tender purple-blue, warm and clear apart from occasional tiny wisps of strange cotton wool–like clouds that tickled past them as they continued their strange descent. Charlie gave himself up, letting the demon take him where it would, until the rushing air on his face slowed to a breeze—then, suddenly, they stopped.

Perfectly still, floating in the air, they turned round to face back the way they'd come.

"There," said the Scourge. "Impressive, don't you think?"

And Charlie had to admit, the Scourge was right.

The palace was unquestionably the biggest thing in the whole landscape. It was so big that if he hadn't been told what it was, Charlie wouldn't have been sure it really qualified as a single building. From where he was, hanging suspended high in the air, still holding the demon's hand, Charlie saw his earlier impression confirmed: the palace *was* more like a mountain than a building, with hundreds, maybe thousands of individual structures seemingly growing out of it in an astonishing profusion, a bewildering and chaotic array. The harder Charlie looked, the more detail there was to find.

So he stopped himself.

A small, thin stream of cloud drifted past: Charlie felt the moisture of it on his face and stuck out his tongue to taste it on his lips. It was salty, like tears.

"So this is Hell," he said, as casually as he could.

The Scourge didn't answer.

"Listen," said Charlie, his voice sounding high and strange in his ears. "Before we go any further, you're going to have to clear a few things up for me."

He took a deep breath.

"First of all, and I'm sorry if this comes out sounding a bit stupid, but—are we dead?"

"No," said the Scourge. "Not dead. On the contrary: for the first time, I think, you are truly *alive*."

"Sure, whatever," said Charlie, "but . . . well, you know, isn't Hell supposed to be where you go *after* you're dead? I mean, normally?"

The demon thought about this for a moment.

"Mm," it said finally. "You are referring, perhaps, to some sort of belief system in the place where you come from."

"Sorry?"

"**What do your people believe?**" asked the Scourge patiently. "**What do your people think happens after death?**"

"Oh," said Charlie, surprised. He had to think for a moment.

"Well, some of them," he began. "Not *me*, obviously, but some of them believe that, you know, when you die, there's a couple of possible things that could happen. If you've been good, if you've led a good life, then you go to, er . . . Heaven."

He broke off and looked at the demon, to see if he was getting this across properly. It was impossible to tell.

"It's supposed to be a nice place," said Charlie, doing his best. "You know, eternal happiness. That sort of thing."

"**I see,**" said the Scourge.

"And if you've been *bad*," said Charlie, "then you go to this other place. A *bad* place, where bad things happen to you. Fire. Brimstone. Eternal torment or whatever. And that's Hell."

"**That is what you believe?**" asked the Scourge, with a smile in its voice.

"Not me," said Charlie quickly. "Just, you know—some people."

Slowly at first, but with gathering speed, something strange was happening to the demon: it was trembling. In another moment, it was quaking all over, big shudders running all over its liquid black body.

"What?" asked Charlie. "What is it?"

But then he realized what it was. The Scourge was laughing.

"I'm sorry, Charlie," it said, once it had managed to get itself back under control a little. "But that's very funny."

"Why?" asked Charlie, annoyed.

"I knew your people were primitive, but really," it said, "that's—"

"*What?*" said Charlie.

The Scourge stopped laughing and looked at him.

There was a pause.

"In backward, *unenlightened* societies," it said slowly, "it is possible to control people by means of what they believe. This belief system of yours: it's a perfect example."

"Oh yeah? And why's that?"

"Think about how it works," said the Scourge. "If you're *good*, if you do what you're told, then when you die you'll go to . . . where was it?"

"Heaven," said Charlie.

"Yes," said the demon. "But if you're *bad*, if you don't do exactly what everyone says is the right thing to do, or behave as you're told to behave, then—"

"You'll go to Hell," finished Charlie.

"Exactly. Charlie," said the Scourge, "you must understand that beliefs like those you've described are for the *weak*. They make you easy to control, and they can be comforting too: it's so much simpler to make decisions about how to live your life when all the guidelines are set out in front of you. Look at me."

Obediently, Charlie turned to look at the Scourge's face. In the blank shiny blackness that he found there, his own reflection stared back at him.

"The only way to make a decision is of your own free will. You yourself must weigh up the consequences for and against and make your choice accordingly, without anyone else telling you what is right and what is wrong. That is what free will is all about."

Charlie didn't answer; he just stared at himself, reflected in the demon's face.

"There is something," the Scourge began, "that I need you to help me to do. It will not be easy, but the rewards will be great."

"What is it?" asked Charlie.

"I will tell you," said the demon, "but not just yet. I have something else to ask of you first."

"And what's that?"

"Charlie," said the Scourge, "I want you to trust me."

Charlie stared.

"Trust you?" he echoed. "*Trust* you? Well, let me think about that for a second. *No.*"

"No?" said the Scourge, surprised.

"Come on!" said Charlie. "What do you think I am—stupid? It's all very well, you coming on like 'the Snowman' and giving me the guided tour *now*. A little late, though, don't you think?"

"Charlie—"

"You tricked me! You made me think I had superpowers, when all the time you were possessing me! Taking me over! *Using* me so you could get what you want! And *then* you . . ." He remembered the moment he'd realized what the demon had done through him. He remembered Esme's face as she'd vowed her revenge. He shuddered.

"Give me one good reason," he said.

"Because I'm offering you the choice," the Scourge replied.

Charlie stared again. "What?"

"You know what I can do, Charlie," said the demon simply. "You know the power I can wield over you. And yet you see that I do not use it."

"So?"

"I think that by the time you have seen what I plan to do," the Scourge explained, "you will want to do it every bit as much as I do. And we can work so much better, I think," it added, "as a team."

It paused.

"Let me be your guide," it said. "Let me show you what I'm planning. Trust me that much at least."

"And if I decide I don't want to help you with whatever you're doing, then what?" asked Charlie. "You'll let me go home?"

"Back to your world?" asked the Scourge, surprised again. "Back to your family, or what's left of it?"

"Hey!" said Charlie.

"I'm sorry," said the demon, "but it seems hard to believe that you'd want to return, with things as they are right now."

"That's not the point!" said Charlie—loudly, because the Scourge had reminded him of something he didn't want to think about.

"Of course," said the Scourge soothingly, "you are free to choose. You have my word." It looked at him, waiting.

Charlie thought about it.

He looked down at Hell, far below him, laid out under his feet as if just for him. He looked at the palace and the surrounding fantastical landscape that spread to the horizon in every direction. No one on Earth had been where he was. No one on Earth had seen what he was seeing. Looking around, Charlie suddenly had a very powerful impression that the whole world—the whole universe, maybe—revolved around where he was standing (or floating, to be strictly accurate).

Then he thought about a Chinese restaurant in London's West End and the last time that he'd seen his father. He thought about the abandoned meal and the things that they'd said to each other—things, in his opinion, that could never be taken back. He thought about his mother, who was probably still waiting for him at home and wondering already where he was. He thought about the hateful mess his father had made of their lives by leaving them the way he had—and he briefly considered whether, frankly, he could really be bothered with any of it.

Stay or go back. Those were his choices.

No contest.

"Okay," said Charlie. "Show me."

FRESH MEAT

Jack woke with a jolt, looked up—and stared.

He was in a throne room of some kind—that was the first thing he noticed: an immense, cavernous, dome-shaped space with a raised circular dais at its center. Jack was kneeling on a narrow strip of bloodred carpet, and to either side, forming the rest of the floor of the room, was a huge and glittering gray-blue expanse of . . . what? Jack frowned as he realized that the floor was *moving*—bulging and rippling like an oily sea. But then he looked up and found himself staring even harder.

Just next to the throne, dipping slightly in the air as it made a small movement of its tail, was what appeared to be . . . a shark.

The shark was very big—thirty feet long at least. Its torpedo-like body was crisscrossed with a network of horrible puckered scars; its blank gray eyes glinted at Jack like gun barrels—and it was floating in the air, just hovering there, as if this were the most natural thing in the world.

The shark—and the throne room—were already, frankly, just a little bit more than Jack felt able to cope with at this point. But as if these things weren't enough on their own, there was the throne itself and the strange figure that sat on it.

He looked like a man—or most of him did. His gleaming white three-piece suit was immaculate and well cut; his jet-black hair was elegantly tousled, and his goatee beard and narrow sideburns were so neat they looked like they had actually been sharpened. But there were also, Jack noticed, several weird things about him, too. The skin of the man (if *man* was the right word) was unmistakably red. His hands, which were folded in his lap, were actually more like hooves, with stubby black spur things instead of thumbs. And the worst thing—the thing that made Jack actually shiver as he looked at him—was his eyes.

They were golden, with black vertical slits in them instead of pupils. They were not human eyes, and the look they were giving him was not a friendly look: the expression on the man's face was the kind you might give to a really large spider that you've just found in your bath. "Who are you?" he said.

"J—" said Jack, then found his voice. "Jack Farrell," he said. "Sir."

The man arched his perfect black eyebrows. "That's not much of a name."

Jack found he didn't really have anything to say to that, so there was a pause.

"Are you . . . the Devil?" Jack asked finally.

The man frowned. "I've never heard that word before. Say it again."

"The Devil."

"No. The name means nothing to me. I may add it to my collection, though." The man sat up straight on his throne, and his chest swelled as he prepared to speak.

"I am Ebisu Eller-Kong Hacha'Fravashi," he said. "God of Rulers, God of the Dead, God of Darkness, God of Gods. I am the Voice of the Void, whose breath is the wind and whose rage makes all worlds tremble. I am Lord of Crossing-Places, King of All Tears, and the Suzerain Absolute of the Dominions of Hell."

"Er . . . pleased to meet you," said Jack.

"You will address me as 'Emperor,'" said the man on the throne. Beside him, the shark's mouth hinged open in a wide and meaningful grin—and Jack decided that now wasn't a good time to argue.

"Pleased to meet you," Jack repeated, "Emperor."

"This," said the Emperor, gesturing at the giant flying shark with one cloven red hand, "is Lord Slint. You find his presence . . . off-putting?"

"A little bit," Jack admitted, "yes."

The Emperor smiled. "You may leave us, Slint," he said. And as soon as the words were spoken, the shark lunged.

Jack ducked—he couldn't help himself—but the shark, all thirty feet of it, had already passed over him and away, making for the giant doors that stood behind where Jack was kneeling. They were a hundred meters off, maybe more. In the second or two it took to cross the distance, Jack watched the shark's easy, undulating movement and the sinuous way it slipped through the doors and out of sight.

"Now," said the Emperor, leaning forward on his throne. "We have a rather pressing matter to discuss, do we not?"

"We do?" queried Jack. "Er, Emperor?" he added.

"Indeed we do."

There was another pause.

"Come now," said the Emperor, when Jack continued to stare at him. "You have just made use of the same crossing-place that the Scourge employed to return from your world. It may interest you to know that the Scourge's reappearance has come as something of a surprise to me. Khentimentu's banishment was long ago considered purely a matter of myth among my people: the Scourge's very existence was cause for conjecture, right up until its return. And the discovery that its incarceration took place in a world of which all records appear to have been lost is of no small interest to me also."

Jack just kept looking at the Emperor, waiting for whatever he was going to say next.

The Emperor sighed. "It appears I must be blunt." The golden stare narrowed and sharpened. "*Why are you here?*"

"Oh," said Jack. "I'm, ah, here for my friend. Emperor," he added, as the man on the throne continued to stare at him.

"You don't mean the Scourge's *vessel*," said the Emperor, with an expression of distaste. "Do you?"

"His name's Charlie," said Jack. "Emperor," he added again (getting a bit tired of doing it, to be honest).

"And what, may I ask, do you propose to do when you find this 'Charlie'?"

"Well, I want to rescue him," said Jack, feeling his ability to deal with this whole situation finally begin to leak out of his ears. "You know, take him back home."

"Let me get this quite clear," said the Emperor, sitting back. "You've come, alone, unaided, into my kingdom, to find your . . . 'friend,' release him from the Scourge's influence, and bring him back with you to wherever you came from?"

"That's about the size of it," said Jack. "Yeah."

For another long moment, Jack and the Emperor just looked at each other.

"Your story is ridiculous," said the Emperor finally. "And this encounter has already taken up more of my time than I am prepared to waste."

He drew himself up, staring down at Jack.

"You will be taken to Slint's gladiator pits," he announced. "There you will be pitted against the finest fighters of all my dominions, and we shall see how well you fare. If your performance proves diverting, I may perhaps grant you a boon, such as a privileged position from which to watch the invasion and conquest of your world. But it is my suspicion," the Emperor added, "that you will fail and die. Goodbye."

Like most of the rest of the conversation, this last bit had pretty much gone over Jack's head. At any rate, the Emperor sat back on his throne, and Jack suddenly found that he did not have time to think about it any further.

The surrounding stuff from the floor of the throne room—the stuff that he'd noticed moving earlier—was now flooding out over the sides of the carpet and *running up Jack's legs.* In another second, Jack's whole body was covered in a weird, clammy, grayish-blue jellylike substance that clung to him all over, locking him in position: any effort to struggle produced no result whatsoever. He was helpless as the jelly stuff ran up his neck, quickly spreading all over his head and then—revoltingly—his face. There was a squeezing sensation. A moment of unbelievable tension, then—

Darkness.

Presently, Jack opened his eyes again and sat up.

The room he was in now looked very small after the throne room: more like a cell, really. The floor was bare earth, reddish and dusty. The walls were smooth yellow stone, forming the room into a perfect square of maybe fifteen feet by fifteen, with no door, no apparent way in or out, except through the ceiling, which, Jack suddenly realized, wasn't there. The walls simply stopped, some thirty feet above him. Obviously his cell was only a part of some much larger room—and that, for the time being, was all Jack really cared about in that direction.

Not wanting to stand up just yet, Jack crawled over to one of the walls and sat there, with his back to it, his arms huddled round his legs.

He was frightened. Terrified, in fact. Large parts of his brain were wibbling and gibbering to themselves, quietly yet with gusto. Single words like *Hell* and *shark* played leapfrog in his head, amongst the more prosaic ones like *Help!*, *No!* or *AAAAAAAAAAARRGH!*

There were, he decided after a moment, two main approaches to this thing.

The first, the obvious one, was to give up: to burst into tears, scream himself hoarse, or start banging his head against the wall. All these options were certainly tempting. There was a strong swelling sensation in his chest and stomach and a hot wetness behind his eyes that wouldn't need a lot of encouragement. He was alone, in Hell. Approach one was very attractive indeed.

But then there was approach two, which went something like this.

Whatever was going to happen was obviously going to happen whether he liked it or not. (*Easy,* he told himself, as he started to panic again. *Easy. Come on, think it through.*) Well, if that were true, there was a *possibility,* however remote it might turn out to be, that he might—at some future moment—find some way of making things *less* unremittingly awful for himself. Opportunities might come (he told himself): chances might present themselves—and it would be a lot easier to spot these and take advantage of them if he *didn't* let himself go completely off his chump and start gurning like a man whose nostril hairs were on fire. He was in Hell, he told himself. All right, that much was obvious. But what that meant, what that would actually involve, was yet to become clear. Besides, there was something else about this situation, he saw: something familiar and, oddly, rather comforting.

Here he was, on his own in, apparently, an ultimately horrible position. And why was that?

Because, simply, that was the way things always seemed to turn out for him.

It was an extreme example, the scenery was different and so forth, but the fact was that, really, when it came to the sort of luck Jack had come to expect in his life, this was nothing more or less than *business as usual.*

What this *was*, in fact, he thought, as he flexed his legs and (using the wall for support) pushed himself upright, was absolutely, devastatingly . . .

"Typical," he finished aloud.

"Hello?" said a voice, making Jack nearly jump out of his skin. "You awake in there? You hear me?" The voice was high and scratchy, like sharp stones grating against each other.

"Y-yes," croaked Jack. Then he tried again. "Yes!"

"Shhh! Not so loud!" hissed the voice. "What's your name?"

"Jack," said Jack.

For a moment, there was silence. Then, "Hur," said the voice.

"What?" asked Jack.

"Hur, hur, hur."

Jack frowned.

"Hur, hur, hur, hur," he heard. "Hee hee hee HEE!"

"What's so funny?" asked Jack, an irritating whining note coming out with the question before he could stop it. The scratchy laughter ceased abruptly.

"Thass not your name," said the voice.

Jack stood in silence, staring at the wall in the direction the voice was coming from.

"*Fresh meat,*" said the voice. "Thass your name."

HOME

Esme lay on the floor of the Light of the Moon, in darkness, remembering.

"You lost," said Raymond.

Esme lay flat on her back. What had just happened had happened so fast that she hadn't even broken her fall properly: her head still rang from the impact as she'd hit the floor, and her vision was full of darkness. In the middle of it, she could see the big man standing over her. His face was flushed and sweaty but he was grinning from ear to ear, delighted.

"You lost," he repeated. "How?"

Grimly, biting back frustration, Esme closed her eyes. The last move, the kick—that was where she'd overextended herself and left herself vulnerable, obviously. But how? How had it been possible? Concentrating, she played the fight back in her head.

This latest bout had begun much like all their others. Throughout the opening exchange, she'd pulled back before committing herself to every attack she'd started. This was for the simple reason that each time she'd started a move, Raymond had already been moving to anticipate her, just as he always did. But this time, Esme had tried something new.

Gradually, as the bout continued, she'd allowed a little desperation to come through into the way she was responding. To a spectator, the two of them would have been moving almost too fast to watch—but as the fight went on, Raymond would have noticed (she hoped) a little raggedness, a little roughness in her usual glassy-smooth technique. In due course, her strategy had been rewarded: the big man had apparently become more confident, letting himself come a little further into her striking range than he usually did. So Esme had launched her main attack.

She'd begun the move in textbook style, leaping off her left foot into a spinning midkick with her right. If it had all gone according to plan, Raymond should have lowered his hands to protect himself, at which point Esme could have completed the feint by folding her right leg into a further 180-degree spin, letting her left foot scythe up over Raymond's guard to take the big man up under the chin.

Pretending to attack with one foot only to surprise one's opponent with the other was a classic move. It had taken Esme many months of hard training to master it, but she had pulled this one off, she knew, flawlessly. There was no way, therefore, that Raymond could have anticipated what she was going to do.

And yet, he had read the feint for what it was.

He had not reacted to the approach of her right foot in the least—just stayed absolutely still.

And when Esme was fully committed to the follow-up—when she was in the air, well and truly past the point when she could pull back on the kick or prevent what was about to happen from happening—Raymond had stepped *toward* her. His hands were in exactly the right place to catch her left foot effortlessly as it passed its target. Keeping an easy grip around her ankle, transferring his weight smoothly, he too had spun, once—

—and released her, letting her own momentum hurl her halfway across the room, to land in an undignified heap on the butterfly room's hard, matted floor.

"You *knew*," Esme spluttered up at him, furious.

"About the kick?" Raymond pretended to think for a moment, then grinned again. "Yup."

"How?"

Raymond's bushy beard bristled as his smile widened further.

"I'll tell you what it wasn't, if that's any help," he said. "It wasn't magic. I didn't read your mind or anything like that." He leaned over her. "And I hope you're not going to tell me about *strength*. Are you?"

"No," said Esme sulkily.

"Well?" Raymond held out a beefy hand to help her up. "How do you think I knew?"

Esme looked at his hand, made a contemptuous sucking noise with her tongue against her teeth, and got to her feet by herself.

"I failed," she said. "I wasn't good enough, that's all. Something in the execution must've told you what I was planning. I need more practice. Obviously."

"No, petal," said Raymond, shaking his head. "You're wrong there. For what it's worth, it was beautifully done."

"Oh yeah?" Esme stared at him, exasperated. "If it was *that* beautifully done, how come I didn't *get* you with it, then?"

Raymond's smile faded. He sighed.

"Petal," he began, "just answer me this one question. Who do you think taught you about feints and combinations? Who do you think taught you all about putting your opponent off guard? About anticipation? About control?"

"You!" snapped Esme, not seeing what he was getting at. "It was you, of course."

"So," said Raymond, putting his beefy hands out to his sides in a small shrug. "How did you think you were going to take me by surprise?"

Esme froze.

"Eh?" added the big man.

There was a long pause.

"I . . ." began Esme, then fell silent.

"You've been a pleasure to teach, petal," said Raymond quietly. "I've never met anyone to touch you for dedication, concentration, or focus.

"But right now," he added, "everything you've got comes from *me*."

"So how am I supposed to *beat* you?" asked Esme.

Six years later, lying on the floor again, she realized she'd spoken aloud.

For a long time, she just lay there. The light from the

Fracture had vanished when it had closed. Every lightbulb in the Light of the Moon had exploded in the battle that had just taken place. Esme lay on the ground, in the darkness, alone. After a while, though, as if from far away, she began to be aware of the pain of her injuries as they started to heal themselves. It was the pain, really, that brought the facts of the situation home to her.

The Scourge had escaped.

Raymond was dead.

She, strangely, was alive.

Slowly, carefully, Esme freed herself from the pile of objects that had held her trapped and stood up. Then, because no better ideas seemed to occur to her, she started walking, a step at a time.

She went up the stairs. She went out of the door, out of the pub, out into the warm, sickly air of the London summer night—and she set off back toward the theater.

Her insides felt like they were filled with broken things. Shattered clockwork, jagged glass: the wreckage moved and ground and ripped at her with every small step that she took, and something cold and dark was in the place where her heart had been. But she kept walking. And soon, almost before she'd expected it, she was home. She climbed the stairs up to the Brotherhood's headquarters, and to her it was as if she were walking into a dream.

It was no different, she realized. Her home still looked and smelled and felt exactly the same as it always had, in all the years of her life that she had shared it with Raymond. It seemed inconceivable to her that it could still be the same, when the man at its heart, the man who had made it what it had been to her, was gone. It was incredible. Enormous. She felt like she was balancing on the edge of the world and could fall off it into nothingness at any second. The nothingness feeling was too much. It was going to swallow her. So she got enough of a grip on herself to make a decision.

It was now nearly five in the morning. On a normal day, in a couple of hours, she would be waking up.

She would act as if it were a normal day.

First, she set off toward the bathroom. She stripped, got under the shower, and turned the hot tap on full blast. Hard jets of scalding water drove at her skin like needles, but Esme hardly felt them. She stood under the shower numbly till she'd had enough, then she switched it off and got out.

Next she combed her hair—then pulled it back, hard, and tied it in place with six ordinary rubber bands, just like normal. She hung up her dressing gown on the back of her bedroom door and changed into the gear she always wore for her morning workout—a clean pair of loose white cotton trousers with a thick elasticized waistband and her second-favorite red hooded top. Then she headed down to the butterfly room.

Esme opened the doors and flicked on the lights. Then she paused.

The room was empty.

Felix—the man who was supposed to be lying on the table in a coma—wasn't there.

He'd gone.

Strange.

Esme frowned for a moment but decided she couldn't deal with that right now. Setting all thoughts of Felix aside for the time being, she concentrated on preparing herself for her morning workout. She fetched a broom and, mechanically, trying to ignore the gaping butterfly-shaped holes in the paint on the walls, she swept her dojo clean. Then she got started.

Ever since that day six years ago, the day of her failure with the feinting kick, Raymond had let her set her own training regime, contenting himself only with a few judicious suggestions once in a while. For six years now, therefore, Esme had always started the day in the same way, with her own combination of yoga, Pilates, and tai chi. After about thirty minutes, when her circulation was up to speed, she moved onto some gymnastics: slow handstands to begin with, followed by rolls, cartwheels, and finally some combination handsprings from one end of the room to the other. Next she turned to the makiwara boards. After perhaps an hour, when she had built up the speed and power behind her attacks until she was outpacing her body's magical ability to repair itself—when all five of the dark oak surfaces carried their telltale smudges of red and the muscles of her body ached with strain—she stopped and picked up her sword.

It was a bokken, a heavy, Japanese-style training sword, a rounded, gently curved black pole exactly two feet eight inches long, also made out of solid oak. Raymond had given it to Esme for her sixth birthday, when the sword was not much smaller than her: back then, she'd been unable to lift it for more than a few minutes at a time. Now, for the next part of her morning regime, Esme assumed a horse stance (feet parallel and apart, with her legs well bent) and held the sword out in front of her. Though she had built up her strength until she could stand like that for much longer, nowadays she was content to keep the horse stance for just another hour. This, she had found, was long enough for the energy of her workout to spread around her body and for her mind to settle. Standing alone in the butterfly room, Esme waited for the spreading warmth, the sensation of being alive and awake, the relaxed-yet-focused singing of her blood in her veins that time in this stance usually gave her.

It wouldn't come.

It was a mess, she decided, after a time. Her whole life was a mess. Her whole life she had trained, her whole life she had waited for the chance to defeat the Scourge—and she had failed. The Scourge had escaped to Hell. She had failed, and Raymond had died.

Esme felt sick inside: sick and empty and confused and hopeless. She didn't know what to do. And the longer she stood there, hoping for some peace and calm to return to her through the act of going through her daily routine, the more hopeless she felt.

Still, she stood there.

Still, she waited.

And suddenly, the doors to the butterfly room burst open.

Kicked in by heavy boots, the doors swung round on their hinges and smacked into the walls. Ten—no, fifteen—men, all dressed identically in black, with gas masks covering their faces, poured in and fanned out, the noise of their combat boots on the floor resounding round the room. Seeing Esme, they froze, and there was a lot of ostentatious ratcheting, racking, and clicking from the several varieties of guns that the men appeared to be carrying, as they pointed them all at her.

"Freeze!" barked the leader, dropping into a firing crouch and leveling a fat-barreled black pistol at Esme. "Stay where you are!" he added, in case she hadn't known what he'd meant.

There was a pause.

Esme looked at the group with a strange kind of detachment. Everything was unreal to her after Raymond's death: for a moment, she had the urge to laugh. Slowly, not breaking her stance, she took one hand off the sword and pulled her hood back.

"Hello," she said evenly. "Who are you?"

"Oh," said the man, lowering his gun. "You're a girl."

Esme's eyebrows flew upward. *Now* she was surprised. "And?" she inquired.

"It's all right!" called the man. "Weapons down, gentlemen: she's a girl." Instantly, the rest of the group flicked the safeties on their MP5s back on and snapped to attention.

"All units, this is Number Two," said the man, holding one hand to his ear. "We have a civilian in the main room of the top floor. Lone female, young, apparently harmless. Testing for possible contamination now."

Esme glanced around at the rest of the men, noting their positions. Holding her stance, keeping both her hands on her practice sword, she looked back at the man who had spoken.

"What do you mean," she asked, "'possible contamination'?"

"We are sorry, mademoiselle," said a second man, stepping forward. (He spoke slowly and calmly, with a pronounced French accent.) "We believe you may 'ave been in contact with something rather dangerous."

"Really," said Esme, still not moving in the slightest. "And who are you people, if you don't mind me asking?"

"We are the Sons of the Scorpion Flail," the French-accented man replied, "a secret international rapid-reaction force, sworn to protect the world from supernatural—"

"What have I told you, Number Three?" the first man interrupted, rounding on his comrade. "For the last time, what is our first rule of engagement?"

There was another pause.

"But she is 'ere, sir," said Number 3, gesturing awkwardly at Esme. "She must be part of zis 'Brotherhood' the informant mentioned, so I see no reason for—"

"Our first rule, Number Three," the man repeated.

Number 3's shoulders slumped. "'Operational information may be divulged to civilians on a need-to-know basis only,'" he quoted miserably. "Sir."

"Thank you, Number Three," said Number 2. "So, enough talk. Number Nine? Number Twelve? Give her the test." Obediently, two men began to advance on Esme from either side.

"What test?" Esme asked.

"A blood test," Number 3 told her quickly. "It will

determine in moments whether we 'ave anything to fear from you. And we would feel better," he added, "if you would lower your weapon."

"I'm afraid," said Esme quietly, "that that's just not going to be possible."

Halfway across the floor toward her, Number 9 and Number 12 stopped and turned to look at their leaders.

"Drop the stick, honey," said Number 2. "We're not fooling around here."

Looking at the men, in their black gear and gas masks, something inside Esme came awake with a *whoosh*: a soaring, sizzling, sparkling sensation that flushed through all her senses and left her tingling.

"No," she said.

"Sweetheart," said Number 2, "you have no idea who you're dealing with. We're the Sons of the Scorpion Flail. We travel the world, looking for evil, and wherever we find it, we kick its butt. Now, I'm telling you, girl, drop that thing and take the test; otherwise I'm going to have to get nasty."

"No," Esme repeated, with a predatory smile. She was going to enjoy this now.

"I'm going to count to three," Number 2 announced brilliantly. "ONE!"

If shouting was supposed to make Esme flinch, it didn't work.

"TWO! Look," said Number 2, when Esme still didn't move, "you want to do this the hard way? Fine! You asked for it. *THR—*"

That was as far as he got before Esme's bokken smacked into his face.

It had happened so fast that no one had seen it, but the faceplate of the man's gas mask now had a jagged spiderweb crack. Esme deliberately hadn't thrown the practice weapon hard enough to do more than give Number 2 a surprise, but he staggered backward, holding his hands up to his face. In the sudden silence as the rest of the men stared at him, the clatter the bokken made falling to the floor seemed very loud indeed.

"Whuh. What?" said Number 2. "T-uh. Take her down!"

Number 9 and Number 12 looked at each other. Then they lunged.

Number 9 got his hand on the girl first. His black-gloved fist closed around her left elbow, and for a fraction of a second he felt pleased with himself.

The feeling didn't last.

Esme's first move was minimal, a single small step, turning on the balls of her feet—but Number 9 suddenly found himself off balance, stumbling toward her. To his further surprise (it was supposed to be *him* grabbing *her*, after all), Esme took hold of his wrist with both her hands—and now she had control of his arm.

Esme could have broken Number 9's arm in a number of different places. She could have hurt him so badly that he never did anything with the arm again—but instead, she contented herself with a simple but well-executed aikido move. Number 9 was a good foot and a half taller than Esme, but her utter command of her weight and balance made this no problem: she flipped him, straight into Number 12, his partner, and the two Sons of the Scorpion Flail crashed to the ground, astonished, in a tangle of black-clad limbs and military equipment.

The third man to reach her didn't fare any better: a bare heel on the end of a whiplash kick exploded under his armored ribs, and, still reaching for the girl, he found himself lifted off his feet, climbing into the air, flying back over the heads of his fellows.

A scything low sweep cut a fourth man's legs from under him.

A snapping back-smash with the point of her right elbow dropped a fifth without Esme even needing to look.

Then, while the rest of her attackers piled at the place where she'd just been standing, Esme sprang into the air, flipped over once in a tight forward roll, and came down in a crouch beside where her practice sword had landed.

Perhaps a whole second had passed. The man she'd kicked, Number 24, was just hitting the wall: surprisingly high up, he slid to the floor with a crash. At any rate, by the time the rest of the group turned round, Esme had retrieved her bokken.

The remainder of the fight happened very quickly indeed.

She struck at knees, and elbows, and necks and ribs and ankles. She struck the breath from lungs and the strength from bodies. She kicked, she flipped, she swept, sliced, and smashed—and all with a fierce and easy joy, because it was what she was good at, what she did best. The heavy black weapon blurred in her hands and—silent and unconscious or howling and clasping themselves—the men toppled helplessly around her.

Suddenly, it was over. In her right hand she still held her bokken. In her left, she held the group's leader by the collar.

She had him off balance: she was supporting his entire weight easily with one hand—if she let go of him, he would fall flat on his back. Tucking the bokken's tip under the black rubber edge of his shattered mask, she ripped it neatly off his face and looked at him.

The man looked to be about forty years old. He hadn't exactly been handsome to begin with, and his face was now disfigured by terror: his piglike eyes glittered at her from under their beetling black brows, and his mouth was opening and closing like a ventriloquist's dummy's. Number 2 was plainly frightened out of his wits—by her. He was frightened of Esme. The sensation was strange to her, and a little uncomfortable.

"You're . . . not . . . *human*," the man gibbered.

Esme just looked at him. Hurting the man suddenly didn't hold quite the same attraction for her as it had a few moments ago—and now, to be honest, she didn't really know what to do instead.

"You're not human!" Number 2 repeated. He cast a wild-eyed glance at what remained of his troops and heard the moans and whimpers of those who were conscious. "We need backup," he added to himself. "We need more men. My—yes!" He put a hand up to his headset. "All units, this is Number Two! We are under attack! Repeat! We are under attack! All units converge on the first-floor main room! Get me backup—now!"

Esme's eyes narrowed. She dropped the man (he hit the ground with a thump) and took an uncertain step backward. "How many of you are there?" she asked.

"Hundreds!" said Number 2, crawling back from her. "Thousands! Keep away from me!"

"We 'ave another twenty men," said a voice from behind her. "Mademoiselle? Please listen to me."

She turned round and saw Number 3, the French-accented man. Like the rest of the group, he'd been wearing body armor: nonetheless, Esme was reasonably certain that she had cracked at least two of his ribs, and he could only be sitting up with great difficulty. Strangely, this didn't seem to have affected how polite he was being.

"We were told of this," he said. "An ancient evil, and a secret Brotherhood pledged to stop that evil from being released. It seems the informant spoke the truth."

He paused, and all Esme could hear was the sound of heavy boots pounding up the stairs and outside the doors, onto the landing.

"When the others come, do not fight them," said Number 3. "If you fight, they will shoot you: it is useless. We are 'ere to 'elp you!" he added desperately. "And all I ask in return is that you trust me."

"Why?" asked Esme.

Number 3 pulled off his mask. His jet-black hair was

cropped short, and running just above his right eyebrow half-way down his cheek was a long, angry scar. The eye crossed by the scar was a pale grayish-blue color, but the other, Number 3's left, was a deep, warm brown with flecks of gold in it. He was looking at her and—strangely—smiling.

"Jessica sent for us," he said.

Esme stared at him. But then the doors burst open, and more men filled the room.

"Fire at will!" shrieked Number 2.

"Non!" yelled Number 3. But the guns were already coming up: black-gloved fingers were tightening on the triggers.

And now, Esme saw, these people were shooting at her.

Time went slack.

Esme watched the flowering muzzle-flash of the guns with a weird kind of breathless concentration. The clattering bubble-wrap pops of the MP5s seemed to have slowed to rhythmic gluey thumping in her ears. She could see the spreading black stream of bullets stitching the air; their trails sticking out of the barrels like stair-rods, like banners that would unroll and say BANG. She caught a long glimpse of them all, the men firing their guns, and—*There's something a bit special about you. It's always been too late for her*—strange words seemed to be echoing in her ears.

She dropped the sword. Faster than time—faster than the world—but with an easy grace that felt as natural to her as breathing, she leaped.

And by the time the first bullets reached the place where she'd been standing—

—Esme wasn't there.

Rising now, her arms out to either side of her, Esme swung her legs up, flipping backward this time. As she reached the height of the butterfly room's great round window, she was in position: with perfect precision, the bare soles of her feet struck the exact center of the circle.

Then the world sped up around her once more.

Metal struts buckled and split: glass exploded, and cool air hit her like a shock wave. Ignoring the bullets buzzing around her, Esme completed her back flip, coming upright, outside now, high above Cambridge Circus. Her thoughts were now utterly focused on the one place in London she had left to go.

Turning toward the Thames, gathering her strength, she flung herself out into the air.

SPECTATORS

Charlie and the Scourge were standing at the foot of a small mountain of bloodred cushions. At the top of them, a tall man with red skin and a white suit was lounging about as if he owned the place. Which, as it turned out, he did.

God of Rulers, God of the Dead. The Voice of the Void . . . the demon who stood beside them was saying. Or at least, Charlie supposed that it was this demon: it was always hard to tell when someone was speaking to you without their mouth moving. It (Charlie had decided to think of this demon as an "it") was about six feet tall, dressed in long robes, and was floating about thirty centimeters off the ground. Its head was squat and heavy, ridged with thick bones, and appeared to be much too big for its delicate body. It also had what Charlie could only describe as a *really* disgusting monster-type mouth; the four yellow inch-long hooks that crossed in front of its gob instead of lips had spread wide open as soon as Charlie and the Scourge appeared, exposing a truly revolting wet pink hole within. This demon, Charlie decided, was quite staggeringly ugly. Which, now that he came to think of it, was pretty much exactly what he'd been expecting demons to look like.

"His name is Gukumat," the Scourge murmured. "He has the power to replicate himself, and his consciousness is collective: each one of him is linked to the others. At this moment, hundreds, perhaps thousands, more of him are currently engaged in the upkeep and administration of every part of Hell and its dominions. Overminister Gukumat is a powerful ally indeed. And a useful friend."

Lord of Crossing-Places, Gukumat droned on pompously, in a weird, lots-of-people-talking-at-once voice that made the words appear directly inside Charlie's head. *King of All Tears, and Suzerain Absolute of the Dominions of Hell.*

The Emperor gave a vague wave of one cloven hand.

Sire, said Gukumat, turning slowly toward him, *allow me to present Khentimentu the Scourge.*

The Scourge made a low bow. Taking his cue, Charlie bowed too—though it hadn't escaped his notice that he hadn't yet been introduced.

There was a pause.

"I wonder, Khentimentu," said the Emperor, "is it *normal* for you to go around like this?"

"Like what, my lord?"

"Outside your vessel," said the Emperor, gesturing at Charlie with distaste. "I mean, it's almost as if"—he smirked—"as if you're not fully dressed!"

"I'm Charlie," said Charlie brightly, stepping forward.

"Well," said the Emperor, looking at the Scourge again and

ignoring Charlie utterly, "your personal habits are your own affair."

Charlie blinked.

"Gukumat!" barked the Emperor suddenly.

Yes, Excellency?

"What do you have for me and my guests?"

Jocasta is fighting the Ogdru Sisters in the pit, was the reply.

The Emperor gave a wide smile. "Gukumat," he said, "you know what I like."

There was a low rumble of shifting stone, then a crack of blazing white light opened out across the darkened room. Still dimly realizing that the Emperor had insulted him, Charlie turned, just as the whole of the wall behind him seemed to come away from the ceiling and slide downward. The air was suddenly filled by a sound unlike anything Charlie had ever heard in his life. It was quiet at first, like the distant hiss of a gas tap—but as the wall opened further the noise became louder, gradually resolving into a terrible boiling mixture of sounds: baying, barking, howling, jeering, rumbling, crashing, and screaming. Charlie stared out of the enormous hole where the wall had been, at what lay beyond it, stared—and gaped.

"Welcome to the royal box," said the Emperor.

Outside and far below them was the wide, blinding-white sandy-floored ring of an arena. The noise Charlie was hearing, he realized, was a crowd noise, coming from the unbelievable mass of spectators that rose, tier upon dazzlingly huge tier, around the arena's massive black walls. There were hundreds of thousands of demons out there, all apparently

different. There were things out there that defied belief: creatures that Charlie couldn't have begun to describe. For the
time being, however, strangely enough, Charlie wasn't really
looking at the audience. Like the rest of the spectators, his
attention was inexorably drawn to what was taking place on
the arena's floor.

Spread in an even circle around the ring was a pack of a
dozen or so of what Charlie immediately identified as velo-
ciraptors, or something very like them. They had the same
long, muscular bodies, the same loping movements, the same
beautifully balanced proportions of crouching torso and elegant, sinewy tail. Their eyes were quick and their claws were
sharp, and the only thing that was different about them was
the scythelike talons that protruded from the front of each of
their hind feet: apparently made of some kind of metal, the
talons glittered and flashed, occasionally sending bright little
reflections scurrying over the black stone of the arena walls.

Their opponent was something Charlie had never seen
before. It looked a bit like a rhinoceros: it had a similar sort of
humped, armored body—only instead of four legs it had six.
The creature's head was wide and flat: its brow and the length
of its snout were protected by a triangular plate of thick,
heavy bone. The skin that covered this part of the creature's
face was a raw-looking pink, covered in whorls and wrinkles.
Also, the creature was *huge*: its length covered more than a
third of the diameter of the ring, and the tip of its ridged back
actually reached *above* the line of massive stones at the arena's edge. The monster shook its heavy head and bellowed at

the nearest of the raptors, exposing a variety of businesslike teeth, and the raptors took a careful skip back out of snapping distance.

The big beast was breathing hard: the thick gray hide of its sides pumped in and out, tightening and slackening. Charlie noticed four wide gashes just behind the heavy bulk of its front left shoulder. The wounds were red, raw, and shining. As the terrible noise of the crowd fell suddenly to an expectant rumble, one of the raptors opened its wide mouth and squealed something, provoking a high, scratching cackle of unmistakable laughter from the rest of the pack. They bobbed on their taloned feet, enjoying the moment.

Jocasta's been wounded, said Gukumat, *but the two sides are still quite perfectly matched. The Ogdru Sisters have pack tactics and youth, but Jocasta has strength, experience, and . . . well.* The tall demon lifted a long, robed arm and pointed at the arena. *See for yourself.*

The audience gave a great roar of delight as six raptors suddenly and simultaneously leaped to the attack. At the same moment, the creature that Gukumat had referred to as Jocasta reared up into the air and—with a speed and accuracy that Charlie would never have believed possible from one so bulky—caught two of the raptors in her claws. In another second, the great beast slammed back down, pinning them to the floor with her full weight. The other four scratched uselessly on the big creature's armored sides and then fell back. The two that had been unlucky jerked on the ground as Jocasta took her weight off them—then lay still.

The remaining raptors abruptly abandoned the outflanking maneuver they'd been planning and slunk back to the shadows at the edge of the ring to rethink their tactics. Jocasta just bellowed at them contemptuously.

"What do you do for entertainment in your world?" asked the Emperor abruptly.

"Sorry?" said Charlie. The suddenness of the question had startled him—but the Emperor did not repeat himself. He just continued to stare at Charlie with his weird golden eyes.

"Oh," said Charlie. "Well, we have films. You know, stories. Games. Music. Stuff like that."

"I'm not talking about those things," said the Emperor dismissively. "Don't you have anything *physical*? Anything . . ." He gestured toward the arena, just as one of the raptors leaped into the air, its steel-shod talons flashing, only to catch Jocasta's double-spiked tail in the chest. The unconscious raptor was flung against the nearest wall-slab, where it slid down and landed in the shadows in a wet heap. The crowd went wild. "Like this?" finished the Emperor with a smile.

"Not really," said Charlie, doing his best. "Well, we have, er, *sport*, I guess. We compete against each other in running or swimming—or football."

"Football?" echoed the Emperor. In the arena, Jocasta had caught two more of the raptors in her front paws and was busily engaged in smashing them against each other. Again and again.

"Yeah," said Charlie awkwardly. "You've got, er, eleven guys on each side, they're on this big field, and they're only allowed to touch the ball with their feet. Right? And you've got a net at each end. That's the goal: whoever kicks the ball in there gets a goal, and whichever side gets the most goals . . . wins." Seeing that the Emperor's attention was elsewhere, he turned. Two lucky members of the raptor flock had got a hold under Jocasta's armor: they dug their talons in, hard. The big beast's mouth hinged open in a grimace of agony.

"But is there violence?" asked the Emperor. "Does anyone get hurt? Or die?"

"No," said Charlie uncertainly.

"Then what's the point of it? This . . . 'football'?" The Emperor made little quote marks in the air with his cloven hands.

"How d'you mean?"

"I mean," said the Emperor, rolling his eyes, "that this game you're describing is a test of strength. The best team wins, yes?"

"Er, yeah."

"Well, what greater test of strength could there be than *fighting*?"

Charlie stared. "But—"

"No physical trial could be more testing than fighting for your life. None. Therefore, any other physical trial is inferior. Correct?"

Now Charlie just gaped.

"So, if no one gets hurt," said the Emperor slowly, as if he were talking to a moron, "what's the *point*?"

Out on the arena floor, the fight was reaching some kind

of a climax. Jocasta, her face a mask of pain and rage, was swinging her great body from side to side, trying to dislodge the raptors. But they clung on stubbornly. Seeing their chance, the rest of the flock leaped to the attack. Another fell prey to a swipe of her tail—but the others were climbing all over Jocasta now, stabbing and slashing with their great steel claws, leaving raw red welts as they went. The crowd was screaming its approval.

"But . . . watching things kill each other—that's just wrong!" said Charlie.

Jocasta rolled, howling, onto her back, squashing all but four of the raptors, who managed to leap clear in time. But they came back as soon as she righted herself, clinging on even tighter than before, tearing and ripping at her in an ecstasy of fury—and the big beast was starting to weaken. The Emperor yawned.

"They're in pain!" said Charlie, his voice going high and reedy, which only made him more indignant. He felt the Scourge lay a restraining hand on his arm, but he wrenched it away and jabbed at the arena. "They're dying!" he said. "And for you it's supposed to be what—*fun*?"

Slowly, the Emperor turned to Charlie and raised an eyebrow.

"All right," he said. "First, I don't find it fun. Rather the opposite. I usually find the whole thing to be quite *dull*, if the truth be told. You see, it's always been this way, ever since the time of the ancestors."

He smiled slowly, at the Scourge first, then at Gukumat.

"It may shock these two veterans to hear it," he said, "but I think the Old Ones were wiser than they let on. We demons are a disparate lot and prone to violence, so making that violence a part of our culture—*officially*, as it were—was undoubtedly a very shrewd and clever idea. That's why I allowed it to continue, even after—your world presently excepted—we succeeded in conquering the universe.

"Second," the Emperor went on, "there *is* something in it for the combatants, if they win. Which reminds me—Gukumat? What is the Ogdru Sisters' favor?"

Charlie turned to face the arena again, and his eyes went wide. The fight was over. Jocasta lay on her side, a great pool of liquid spreading from the terrible wounds that the raptors had inflicted on her. Her eyes were open and apparently lifeless. The three remaining raptors were standing side by side, facing up toward the royal box, their front claws clasped in a gesture of what appeared to Charlie, astonishingly, to be supplication.

Nothing of great import or interest, my lord, said the tall demon. *I was going to grant their request without troubling you with it.*

"Please, Overminister, for the benefit of our guests: do tell us."

Well, Sire, said Gukumat. *It is rather amusing, I suppose. They wish to start a small . . . business.*

"Business? What sort of business?"

There is a settlement, near the borders of the Plains of Flame. "Gehenna," *they call it. There's not much there, no facilities to*

speak of, but the Ogdrus believe that the place has some poten-
tial as . . . well, a tourist destination.

"Really?" asked the Emperor, wrinkling his nose. "But all
that brimstone and so on! A bit sulphurous, I'd've thought.
Wouldn't you?"

Indubitably, Sire. But as my lord knows, with the High
Reaches demons one can never predict what fads and foibles
may catch on next. The Ogdrus propose to start what they call, I
believe, a "health spa."

"A health spa?" echoed the Emperor with distaste. "Gukumat, you amaze me."

Shall I grant their request?

"Fine," said the Emperor, suddenly losing interest. He
turned back to Charlie. "You see? The winner is granted a
boon from me." He leaned forward on his mountain of cushions.

"This is how things work here in Hell," he said. "If you
want something, you have to fight for it. Kill or be killed." He
yawned again. "You follow?"

Charlie nodded numbly, though he didn't—not in the
least.

"You may clear the arena, Gukumat."

At your command, Sire.

Gukumat bowed.

The arena floor seemed to ripple—

—and the remaining raptors, plus the body of their opponent, suddenly vanished. In another moment, the stains of
the battle were gone too. It was as if none of it had happened.

"Now," said the Emperor, settling back once more. "I've got something rather special lined up next, I believe. Gukumat?"

Sire?

"Is it time?"

Time for what, Sire?

"The boy," said the Emperor, annoyed. "Is he in position?"

Yes, my lord.

"Splendid." The Emperor looked down at Charlie, smiling again. "Here's something that might interest you." He gestured lazily at the next gladiator as he stumbled uncertainly out into the center of the arena. "This little chap arrived just after you did. Said he was a friend of yours. Now, what was his name?" He looked up at the ceiling as if trying to remember.

"Oh, God," whispered Charlie. "Jack."

"Oh yes," said the Emperor. "That was it. Jack. Gukumat?" he barked. "Open the other gates. Let's see what the little fellow is made of."

His grin widened.

"Quite literally, I should imagine," he added.

"Gladiator Jack"

Jack had been waiting in his cell when the jelly stuff came for him again. It had appeared from nowhere, swallowed him as before—and deposited him, this time in some sort of short passageway.

He was standing in front of a blank wall of cool, slate-gray stone. The passageway was empty and, apart from his breathing, entirely silent. Also, he had a knife in his hand.

The knife's blade was very short, an elongated half oval of glinting blue-gray metal. The black stuff the handle was made of was smooth and vaguely rubbery: against its dark surface Jack's knuckles looked whiter than he was expecting, until he noticed how tightly he was holding it.

His having a knife wasn't, he realized, particularly good news. He had not missed the Emperor's earlier words about gladiator pits. The knife meant, in all probability, that Jack was going to be expected to fight with it—and knife-fighting was not, as it happened, something that he had ever done before. Forcing his hands to relax, Jack tried a couple of jabbing and stabbing movements in the air and only succeeded in making himself feel very silly indeed. No, he decided: this whole situation was really getting worse and worse all the time.

That was when, with a low rumbling sound, the wall lifted to reveal what was beyond.

Gladiator Jack, step forward into the arena, please, said a voice in his head. The voice sounded bored and unfriendly, but suddenly, Jack wasn't really listening to it.

Step forward, gladiator. In accordance with the rules of the pit, if you do not step forward, you will be disemboweled, slowly and carefully. You have four seconds to comply.

Three.

Two.

One.

Jack blinked and stepped out.

Thank you. Please proceed toward the center of the arena and await the start of the bout.

Numbly, on legs that felt distant and rubbery, like they belonged to someone else, Jack did as he was told.

The arena was the size of a football pitch—bigger, probably—and surrounded all the way round by huge black slabs of rock, identical to the one that was rumbling down behind him, cutting off the only exit.

And above the slabs was the audience. Each and every row was filled to bursting by thousands—hundreds of thousands—of monsters. They were all looking at him. They were all screaming, howling, and jeering at him. The noise alone was incredible enough; the overall effect of the scene, Jack found, was really very alarming indeed.

As Gladiator Jack's opponent in this next bout, intoned the voice in his head (the crowd quieted a little, so Jack knew that the voice wasn't talking to just him anymore), *we present to you an undisputed master of the pit—the most feared fighter of our time. No quarter has he asked or given in a career that has now spanned some fifteen years.*

Terrific, thought Jack limply. *Oh, terrific.*

His speed is unmatched, the voice went on. *His cruelty is unparalleled. His name alone strikes ice-cold terror deep in the hearts of all who hear it. Fight fans, we present to you the Black Prince himself: LEO THE UNSPEAKABLE!*

Well, thought Jack, the name wasn't exactly the scariest he'd ever heard.

But now, on the opposite side of the ring from where Jack had come in, another of the black slabs was lifting.

It came slowly at first. Extending two long black—what? legs? feelers?—out into the blazing light, the thing seemed to test the ground, flexing. Then it took a whole step and moved into view.

It was a giant spider, and quite the most vile creature that Jack had ever seen in his life. Its body, slung at the center of its arched, oddly delicate-looking legs, was a good twenty feet long by itself, massively bloated and covered all over with spines like large screwdrivers. Its fangs glistened with slime, and its rows of eyes regarded Jack greedily.

BEGIN! barked the voice, and as Jack watched, the spider bounced once in a preparatory way, then began to scuttle toward him, its long legs striking eagerly at the sandy ground.

Jack was still staring at the spider, rigid with horror, when it *leaped,* knocking Jack flat on his back.

And now it was standing over him! It was bending down at him, blotting out the sky, and the distant roaring of the crowd was reaching a fever pitch. Jack's nostrils were filled with the spider's damp, musty smell. Layers of wet fangs split open like terrible flowers in front of him. There was nothing else in the world, nothing else to see but the dark maw and dripping fangs reaching toward him. And then—

"Stab me," said a voice.

There was a pause.

Jack had been screaming a bit. He screamed once more, but without quite so much conviction this time.

"Stab me," the voice repeated.

Jack stared. The dreadful mouth was still there, but it hadn't moved.

"Can you hear me?" asked the voice. The words were appearing in Jack's head, much as others had done before, but the effect was strangely soothing, as if soft, cool fingers were stroking his mind.

"Can you *hear* me?" the voice asked again.

"Y-yes?" said Jack aloud.

"Good," said the voice. "We don't have much time. Listen carefully."

As far as Jack was concerned, this instruction wasn't going to pose any problems. He had never listened more carefully to anything in his entire life, ever.

"The tip of your knife," said the voice, "is only a short

distance from my abdomen. If you drive your hand upward, right now, then you will stab me."

Jack did nothing, just gaped.

"Is there a problem?" asked the voice. "Can you move?"

"Er, yes," said Jack. "It's just—you *want* me to stab you?"

"Of course not. But it will be better for you if you are seen to put up a struggle, yes? So do it. Do it now."

Drawing on all his strength, Jack gripped the knife and jerked it upward. The spider had him pinned down; he couldn't see what effect the blow had had, but he felt something warm and slimy drip down and over his hand.

"Like—like that?" he asked.

"That's the best you can manage?" asked the voice.

"Yes," said Jack.

"Then it'll have to do. *YEEEEEEEEEEEEEE!*"

With a noise like hideously amplified chalk on a blackboard, the spider reared up over him, screeching. Jack watched the spider's massive black underside in awe as its legs twitched and shook, giving every impression of terrible agony. He could hear the crowd roaring and baying and clamoring, and for a moment he felt a strange kind of exhilaration.

Then the jaws came down. They closed around his neck.

And the spider bit him.

Jack could feel the spider's fangs in his neck, and a weird, wet, itchy dripping sensation as his blood began to well out around the punctures. But almost as soon as he had identified it, the feeling was gone. Jack wanted to scream some more—and why not? The situation certainly merited it—but he found he couldn't open his mouth. The blood seemed to be clogging in his veins, the breath was sticking in his chest, and Jack's vision was fading, filling with purple splashes that swam and spread, turning everything dark.

"There," said the spider. "Before you lose consciousness, I want you to know that—well, this isn't personal. I don't know you, I've never seen you before, and in any other circumstances it's quite possible that we might have become friends. I just want you to know," the spider repeated, "that I find that thought very distressing."

Oh, great, thought Jack weakly. *Thanks a bunch.*

"Goodbye, Jack," said the spider's voice. "Go with my blessing."

Then the purple patches spread to cover everything.

Well, Jack thought, *that's the last time I try and rescue anybody.*

Typical, he just had time to add. *This whole thing. It's absolutely bloody TYP—*

Then everything went black.

"Well," said the Emperor, looking down at Charlie. "That wasn't too exciting, was it? Really," he added, "was that the best you people can do?"

Charlie said nothing.

"I mean," the Emperor went on, gesturing out at the arena floor, "we've had shorter bouts, of course we have. But they've always been a bit more interesting than *that.*"

The Emperor was looking at Charlie carefully, studying his reaction. A small smile played across his lips.

Charlie didn't move.

"*Wait*, **Charlie**," the Scourge told him firmly, speaking directly into his mind so the Emperor wouldn't hear. "**Our time will come, but only if you *wait*.**"

"You may leave us, Khentimentu," said the Emperor, still smiling. "Now."

"**Thank you, Sire**," the Scourge replied. "**Come, Charlie.**"

They vanished.

When Charlie and the Scourge had gone, the Emperor relaxed on his mountain of cushions and munched meditatively on a sweetmeat.

Gukumat, at his side, bowed once more.

Shall I dispose of the small human in the usual way?

"No!" said the Emperor. "Heavens, no! What possible use could we have for a puny little blood-sack like that? I won't have my powers diluted, you know."

Indeed not, Sire, the Overminister replied. *How foolish of me.*

"Still," said the Emperor slowly.

Sire?

"Send him to Godfrey."

As you wish, my lord.

As soon as the command was given, it was done.

The Emperor settled back. Already the next combatants were entering the pit.

"He killed him," Charlie was saying. His eyes were unfocused: he was white and shaking. "He killed Jack!"

He and the Scourge were standing on the Needle again—the highest point of Hell, the place the demon had taken Charlie to first.

"Charlie—"

"Jack's dead!" said Charlie. "Jack followed me here, and now he's—"

"Charlie, listen to me," said the Scourge gently. "What do you want to do?"

Staring at the Scourge, Charlie thought about it.

He thought about staying up with Jack until four in the morning, watching zombie movies when they were supposed to be asleep.

He thought about the time in the Chinese restaurant with his dad: how he'd known Jack would come in with him and back him up, almost without having to ask him. Jack had always come with him, in all the time Charlie'd known him—even here, to Hell.

Jack's music taste was thoroughly dubious. His clothes were all bought by his mum. But Jack was Charlie's friend. And now he was gone. He was gone, and the Emperor had smiled.

Charlie drew one hand across his nose, wiping away the tears and snot onto the leg of his black jeans. He blinked.

"The Emperor," he said slowly, figuring it out. "I want to kill the Emperor."

"I do too," said the Scourge.

They looked at each other.

"Killing him," said Charlie. "That's what you—?"

"If we kill the Emperor," said the Scourge, "we can take his place on the throne. And then all his power—all Hell itself—will be ours, to do with as we wish."

"Can we do it?" asked Charlie. "Do you think it's possible?"

"As I said," the Scourge replied, "it won't be easy. But our chances will be greatly improved, I believe, if we work together."

Charlie sniffed again and looked out at the view. All around them, Hell glittered like dewdrops on a spiderweb. Already, the warm breeze was drying his tears to a crust.

"All right," he said. "Let's do it."

"Good," said the Scourge. "Very good."

ORIGINS

Holding steady in the air seven floors up outside Alembic House, Esme reached out one hand and knocked.

After a long pause, the curtains on the other side of the window slid open by perhaps a foot, and a white-faced, stunned-looking Felix loomed up out of the shadows of the room beyond.

"We have to talk," Esme mouthed through the glass.

Floating smoothly some two feet away from the wall, she slid through the air round the corner and came upon a small balcony, accessible from an open French window. Felix was waiting for her there. Esme spread her arms, drifted up over the balustrade, and touched down, her bare feet cold on the stone. Then she looked at him.

"Hi," said Felix, attempting a smile.

"Hello," said Esme.

"Are you up early? Or late?" Felix asked, once he'd closed the window. "I was just, ah, having a drink. The president of Paraguay has sent me some rather wonderful brandy. I don't suppose you'd—?"

Esme shook her head.

"Quite right!" said Felix awkwardly. "Very well, then. Do come through."

Silently, Esme followed him into the sitting room. The thick curtains were drawn tight: only one or two shafts of daylight betrayed the fact that it was early morning.

"All right," said Felix. "What can I do for you?"

"What do you know about a group called the Sons of the Scorpion Flail?" Esme asked bluntly.

Felix blinked. "Well," he said, "officially, they don't exist, of course. Off the record, I've heard . . . rumors. They started out as a branch of the Freemasons, would you believe. They've been peddling their supernatural cloak-and-dagger act all over the world for more than three hundred years. Why do you ask?"

"They've taken over the theater," Esme told him.

"Esme," said Felix slowly, looking at her, "would you mind telling me what's going on? The Scourge attacked me, and the next thing I knew I was lying on a table in the butterfly room. No one was around, so I called my driver and now—"

"The Scourge has escaped to Hell," Esme interrupted. "Raymond is dead."

"Oh, Esme," said Felix, shocked. "I'm so sorry."

Esme just shook her head. She wasn't interested in sympathy.

"Just before the Scourge killed him," she began, then stopped. The word *killed* seemed to have a physical shape: it left a tingling mark on her tongue. "It said something. It said that it's too late for me. It said that it's always been too late for me and that I should 'just ask Felix.' What do you think it meant?"

She looked at him. He had gone very still.

"It killed them all, Felix," she said, when he didn't answer. "Nick, Jessica, Raymond—everyone. But you woke up and went home like nothing had happened. It left you alive, Felix. Why?"

For another long moment there was silence.

"What did Raymond tell you," Felix asked, turning his glass in his hands, "about why I let out the Scourge?"

"He said that you did it for power," Esme answered. "He said you released the Scourge because the others in the Brotherhood were always better at stuff than you: you did it because you were jealous."

"Jealous?" echoed Felix with a sad smile. "Well, that's true in a way, I suppose. But I didn't release the Scourge just for power."

"No? Why, then?"

Felix took a deep breath. "I suppose it's time you heard the truth." Gesturing at another chair, he sat down and took a sip of his brandy.

Esme crossed her arms and just waited.

"A long time ago," said Felix slowly, "I . . . met someone." He looked up at Esme. "She was beautiful, clever, and thoroughly wonderful, and I loved her with an intensity that I scarcely would've believed possible. There was, however, one problem." He paused. "She was in love with somebody else."

Esme just looked at him.

"We worked together, she and I," said Felix, "so I was lucky enough to see her every day. I told myself I'd learn to be content with that. Perhaps I even believed it. But as time dragged past and my feelings didn't change, I began to become sick."

Felix sipped again.

"The color drained out of my life," he said. "My love was eating me up inside like a disease: sometimes I thought I could feel it killing me. And then, one day, one horrible day, I thought of something I could do about it."

"What?"

"Magic," said Felix simply.

Esme stared at him.

"Nick taught us to use our power in different ways," Felix explained. "Disguise was one. My attempts were always short-lived—partial, at best—but the potential of it began to obsess me. You see, with enough power, it seemed to me, a person could make themselves resemble *anyone*. You could even make yourself look so much like someone else that *nobody would know the difference.*

"Of course," he added, "I knew I couldn't do it alone. As you say, I just wasn't strong enough. But it occurred to me that I knew someone who might be."

"Who?" Esme asked.

"One night," said Felix, "that was all I wanted: one night with the woman I loved. And I realized that there was a way I could be granted that." He looked at Esme, hard. "For a price."

There was a pause.

"You don't—" said Esme.

Then, "No. You're not seriously telling me that's what you—"

Her brain was reeling. She could hardly get the words out.

"I mean, that's why you did it? *That's* why you let out the Scourge? So it could help you *pretend to be my dad* and . . ." She made a face. "With my *mother?*"

"I loved her," said Felix solemnly, "more than my own life. More than life itself—more than anything. And if I could have her love, even just once—"

"Even though she thought you were someone else?"

"Even though it was a lie," said Felix. "You're still young. You don't underst—"

"I understand pretty well. That's the weirdest, most disgusting, pathetic—"

"Call me names, if you like," said Felix. "You'll find it doesn't help. Believe me."

"But . . . you released the Scourge!" Esme spluttered. "You betrayed the Brotherhood! For—"

"Look," said Felix. "You know that phrase 'madly in love'? Have you ever thought about what that means? As long as I got what I wanted, I didn't care what happened! As long as I got," he repeated slowly and sadly, "what I wanted."

There was another pause. A long one this time.

"So, all right," said Esme, grimacing. "That's why you let out the Scourge. But that's got nothing to do with *me*, has it? What did the Scourge mean when it said it was 'too late' for me? That's what I'm asking."

"And that—I'm afraid—is what I'm telling you."

"Felix," said Esme, "I'm getting fed up now. Why don't you just tell me what you mean?"

Felix took a big swig of his brandy and swallowed hard.

"When I let the demon out," he said heavily, "it didn't make the break for the Fracture straightaway. The Scourge was weak to begin with: weak enough for me to think I could control it. It took over nine months before I found out how wrong I was. What a horrible mistake I'd made."

"Wait a second," said Esme. "Nine months? *Nine months* went past between you releasing the Scourge and it . . . ?"

Then suddenly, she felt a great rushing sound, like black wings closing around her. The world went dark, and all she could hear were voices.

There's something a bit special about you, said one.

*It's **always** been too late for her*, said another.

And then, with dreadful inevitability, something inside her clicked and fell into place.

"No," she said. "No. It *can't* be."

"Esme, I was afraid of this," said Felix. "For nearly fifteen years I've been hoping and praying it's not true. But I think . . ." He bit his lip. "I think the reason the Scourge left me alive is that it wants me to tell you."

He took a deep breath.

"What if Raymond wasn't really your father?" he asked. "I mean, think of your powers," he went on, leaning forward on his chair again. "Your flying. Your speed. Esme, I believe you were conceived while I was *possessed*. What if all your gifts don't come from your mother, or—or from me, but from . . . ?"

But to Esme, his mouth was moving but no sound was coming out. The only thing she could hear were the voices:

Something a bit special . . .

It's too late for her.

You're not human!

*It's **always** been too late for her. Just ask Felix.*

A strange pressure seemed to be building in the room: a dreadful focusing, as tremendous forces shifted and stirred.

"No," said Esme, breathing hard. Then she screamed it aloud. "NO!"

The voices, the black-wings sensation, and the pressure in the room all suddenly receded—and she could see Felix again, staring up at her, white-faced.

"You're wrong!" Esme told him. "Okay? You're just wrong, that's all."

There was silence.

Sleep, Esme told herself. Suddenly, she had to get some sleep.

"Look, do you have a spare room?" she asked.

"Seven of them," said Felix miserably.

"One without windows," Esme told him. "Sometimes when I have dreams I get . . . restless."

"Certainly," said Felix. "Whatever you want. Anything that's in my power to give, it's yours for the asking."

For another long moment Esme looked down at the little businessman.

An idea occurred to her.

"You know," she said, "actually, there is one thing."

"Yes?"

"It'll be simple," she told him. "You almost did it before. In fact," she went on, her skin beginning to tingle, "if my mother hadn't stopped you, you'd have done it already, instead of leaving it for the next sucker to do."

"Sorry?" said Felix. "I'm afraid I don't understand."

"They say that whoever the Scourge possesses can never really be freed," she told him. "Would you say that's true?"

"Certainly," said Felix. "In all the years since, there hasn't been a day that's gone past when I haven't felt its influence inside me. And as for the nights . . ." He shuddered.

"You're going to help me open the Fracture, Felix," said Esme.

Watching him gape at her, she smiled.

"I'm going after them," she told him slowly. "I'm going after the Scourge. To Hell."

TYPICAL

Blank.

There was nothing: no time, no sensation. There wasn't even enough of him to *tell* that there was no time and no sensation. Not, that is, until—

WHAM!

"Can you hear me, small human?" asked a high, elderly voice. "Hello in there? Hello?"

"What," asked Jack, none too politely, "do you want?"

"I have a couple of questions to ask. Are you ready?"

Jack said nothing.

"Splendid," said the voice anyway. "Well, it's like this. Since, as I think you'll agree, your last body was, let's say . . . somewhat underwhelming, I've decided to create you a new one. Before I begin, it seems only fair to ask if you have any preferences."

For a long moment, Jack thought about this.

"Sorry?" he asked finally.

"Now, I'm going to make some suggestions," said the voice,

"and all you have to do is tell me yes or no. All right? Let's start slowly. How about a tail?"

Jack said nothing.

"You can't go wrong with a tail," said the voice with sudden enthusiasm. "Extra balance in a fight. Prehensile, if you like. Or with spikes, a poisonous sting—whatever you like!"

"No," said Jack, with difficulty. "No tail."

"Claws, then," said the voice. "Retractable. Unbreakable. Good for climbing, hunting, or . . . hm . . . *close* work."

"No," said Jack. "No claws."

"As you wish," said the voice. "I think we can assume, however, that at the very least you'll be wanting a thicker *hide*. Hmmm. Bony plates on the shoulders, maybe."

"No."

"A thick, horny ridge on the head, strong enough to take a direct hit."

"No," said Jack firmly. "No horny ridge. No claws. No tail. Nothing! For Christ's sake, why can't you just leave me *alone*?"

There was an icy pause.

"Fine," snapped the voice. "See if I care!"

Then the darkness took him again.

"There," said the voice, sometime later.

Is he awake? asked another—one Jack remembered from the arena.

"He can hear us. It'll be a minute or two before he can respond."

Gladiator Jack, the second voice announced. *In accordance with the wishes of his most merciful Eminence the Emperor Ebisu Eller-Kong Hacha'Frav—*

With a soft click, the speech stopped dead.

"Enough of that for the time being, I think. Just open your eyes, please, and take everything in. Slowly."

Blearily, Jack did as he was told.

He was lying on a long, low couch in what appeared to be an ordinary hospital room. Beside him stood what looked, to Jack's eyes at least, like a man. The man looked old—his cheeks were sunken in, and his beard, though neatly trimmed, was shot with gray. He was wearing a rumpled tweed suit with patches on the elbows, a red woolen tie, and, Jack noticed, a gray woolly V-neck jumper.

"How do you do?" said the man. "I'm God."

Jack just looked at him.

Something of an awkward pause began to develop. The man frowned.

"You know," he began tetchily, "in most cultures, the polite response to being told someone's name is to reply with your own."

Jack blinked. "All right," he said. "I'm Jack."

"Yes," said the man. "I knew that, naturally. But I think it's important to observe the formalities, don't you? I mean, where would one be, otherwise?"

Jack blinked a couple more times. It didn't help.

"Am I . . . dead?" he managed finally.

"No. At least, not at the moment. I should've thought that was pretty obvious, to be honest."

"But you're God," said Jack, doing his best. "*The* God."

"Well!" The man's eyes twinkled. "That rather depends, doesn't it?"

"On what?"

"On which one of your lot's *funny books* you happen to prefer."

Jack stared at him.

The man made a *tsk*ing sound. "I should've known this'd be difficult," he said, and sighed again heavily.

"All right," he began. "If you're talking about belief in one all-powerful being who created the world, blah blah, then yes, technically I suppose you could say I'm 'the' God. After all," he explained, "it was me who created you."

"You . . . created me," echoed Jack, suddenly finding it hard to keep the sarcasm out of his voice.

"Not you personally," said the man. "Well," he added, "apart from just now. But I was there at the beginning: I caused it, you see."

"The beginning of what? Caused *what*?"

"Your world," said the man, grinning from ear to ear.

"It was a pet project of mine," he went on, while Jack gaped at him some more. "You know, like planting a tree. You put all the elements in place, all the things an organism needs to grow and flourish, and, well, you sit back and see what happens!"

"So what happened?" asked Jack.

"How d'you mean?"

"Well, assuming I believe you," said Jack.

"I can assure you," the man broke in, suddenly scowling, "it's never made the slightest difference to me whether you people believe in me or not."

Jack blinked. He'd clearly hit some kind of nerve there. *Whatever.* "What happened to you?" he persevered. "Why did you leave? And what are you doing here?" he added, his head beginning to hurt.

"Here in Hell, do you mean?"

"Well, yeah."

"My dear child," said the man. "Delighted as I am to be able to have at least a *semi*decent conversation with one of you at last, I must point out that this moment has been an extortionately long time in coming. As a species you really developed very slowly indeed, and the truth is . . . well, I got bored."

"Bored?"

"Life goes on, you know. I believe even *your* lot say that. And when the chance at the librarianship came up here, well, I took it. Much more interesting crowd, you see." He shrugged. "I'm sorry, but there it is. Now, how about taking a look at your new body, eh?"

Jack turned and looked down at the white sheet that came up to his neck. Parts of an earlier conversation about tails, claws, and so forth were coming back to him, and the religious implications of what he had heard suddenly didn't seem all that important anymore.

"Go on," said the man. "Take a look!"

Scared of what he might find, Jack yanked off the sheet. And saw—

"The same," said Jack. "It's the same."

"Mm." The man smiled a secretive little smile. "Looks that way, doesn't it? But I couldn't resist the idea of making just a couple of improvements. Tweaking you a bit here and there. You're a very old design, after all."

Jack was about to reply to this, when there was a soft *click* in his head, then—

May I remind you, Godfrey, that tampering with or inhibiting my telepathic transmissions is an offense punishable by—

"What's that?" asked "God." He winked at Jack, startling him. "What's that you say? I'm sorry, Gukumat, you're breaking up!"

I am not a fool, Godfrey. You would be ill advised to take me for one.

God just smirked. The voice behind Jack's eyeballs let out an icy sigh.

Is the gladiator ready to return to his cell?

"Oh yes," said God. "Quite ready. But Gukumat, could I ask you, please, not to bother me with things like this again? The Halls of Ages don't run themselves, you know."

Gladiator Jack, please be ready for transportation in three.

From nowhere, instantly, the jelly stuff had reappeared. It was slipping up under Jack's back.

Two.

The slime was encasing him, covering his whole body, sliding up over his face.

One.

Here we go again, Jack thought.

Zero.

And he was in his cell.

Jack sighed.

Then, very slowly and carefully, he began to feel himself all over.

It was a long process, and a strange one. After a while, he concluded that he certainly *felt* normal enough.

Finally, Jack settled down on the sandy floor as best he could. He lay curled up on his side, with his arm under his head: just then, that was enough. It had been a long day; he'd apparently come back from the dead, and any place to grab some kip was going to be fine by him.

Presently, he slept.

THE PITS

Jack was woken by a low grinding sound. He looked around and saw that one of the walls of his cell was moving—lifting, slowly and smoothly. The wall didn't stop at the ground, Jack saw: it continued straight down into it for a surprisingly long way. The yellow stone surface rumbled upward for about five seconds, then a gap appeared: a doorway.

Well, thought Jack, standing up, *after what I've had so far, what's the worst that can happen?*

He shuddered and told himself not to be so stupid.

Outside, across a thin strip of sandy floor, there was another cell, identical to his own—but Jack wasn't thinking about the cells anymore. He was thinking about their occupants: specifically, the coiled, sinewy shape on the floor of the cell that, as he continued to stare, suddenly *un*coiled itself a little, rose into the air, and looked right back at him.

"Fresh meat!" it exclaimed in a familiar scratchy voice.

The creature's face was wide and rubbery, with goggling bloodshot eyes. The rest of it reminded Jack, bizarrely, of a picture he'd seen once of the world's longest-ever tapeworm. The color was the same, a smeared mixture of rancid off-white and intestinal brown. Also, though Jack had never actually *smelled* a tapeworm, this thing was giving a pretty convincing impression of what that might be like—and a tapeworm not too long removed from its natural habitat, at that. Effortlessly, the beast nosed its way into Jack's cell: in a moment, its body had made a complete loop all around him—and still, Jack couldn't help noticing, a disconcerting amount of the rest of the creature's length remained behind it, on the floor of its own cell, its coils piled up, moist and glistening.

"Hello, fresh meat," it said, leering right in Jack's face— and the dizzying stench that came with the words almost buckled Jack's knees. "MMM-hmmm," it added, obviously liking what it saw. "Nice fresh thing. Nice fresh thing for Shargle!"

"Shargle!" barked a voice from outside, making Jack and the creature both jump. "Where are you? Get out here!"

A flash of annoyance crossed the hideous face, and the eyes turned in the direction of the passage outside.

"*Now*, Shargle. Or do you want me to tie your heads together again?"

"No, Inanna!" squeaked a voice from outside. "Not the tying! Not together! Not again!"

Jack stared. *Heads?* he thought dimly.

"I'm warning you, Shargle. My name's coming up, I can feel it, and I won't have my chances ruined just 'cause a long streak of pus like you won't come out of his cell!"

The worm creature made a furious hissing sound, then, with a sudden twisting movement, unwrapped itself from around Jack and backed out through the doorway.

"And whatever else is in there, you'd better follow him or I'll skewer you myself. Move!"

Jack obeyed without question. Still reeling from the smell, he stumbled out after Shargle. And his eyes went wide.

There were several reasons for this.

First, now that he was outside, he could see that his initial guess about his cell being just a part of something much larger had been dead right. He was surrounded by other doorways, leading to cells just like his own, stretching to either side as far as his eyes could see.

Second, he wasn't the only one coming out. Other creatures were too—all gradually forming up outside in the sandy passageway in an enormous and unruly line. He only had time for a quick glance each way, but what he saw was enough to make him feel very nervous indeed.

Third, well . . . when he looked up at what was standing in front of him, he couldn't *help* but stare.

Whoever she was, she was a good nine feet tall and unmistakably female. Her bulging torso was encased in some sort of black armored corset, a mass of straps, buckles, and—also unmistakably—weapons. She was festooned with swords and knives of every description, all arranged within easy reach of her hands. The hands themselves looked big enough to crush Jack's skull. She was completely bald, with some kind of tribal tattoo on her scalp. She had six silver rings in each ear and a silver spike through her bottom lip. Her arms were bare; muscles like bowling balls twitched and rippled all over her, and, oh yeah, she was *blue*.

She was looking at him.

"Inanna," she boomed.

"Er, sorry?" said Jack.

"Name's Inanna," the giant repeated. "And you are . . . ?"

"Jack."

"Bit small for this job, aren't you?"

"Um," said Jack. "Er . . ." But that was as far as he got. Quietly at first, a strange hissing sound began to fill the air. Somewhere, a long way away, a gong had been struck. Inanna shrugged, turned, and followed the line of monsters, who had begun to shuffle away along the sandy floor of the passage ahead.

"Move, fresh meat!" hissed Shargle into both his ears at once.

Flinching, Jack glanced round to find not one but two faces now leering into his.

Shargle has a head at both ends, thought Jack numbly— and, a moment later, an uncomfortable realization occurred to him as to why the creature's breath was so bad.

He started walking quickly.

Supplicants, boomed Gukumat's voice, *you have been summoned at the behest of Ebisu Eller-Kong Hacha'Fravashi, God of Rulers, God of the Dead, God of Darkness, God of Gods—*

"Yadda yadda yadda yadda," Jack heard Inanna mutter. "Come on."

This food you receive now is his gift to you, you penitents and seekers of boons. When you have taken your bowl, you may proceed to the dining hall.

"I take the bowl this time," hissed one of Shargle's heads suddenly. "*I* take the bowl."

"Uh-uh," spat the other quickly, rearing up to face its twin. "No way!"

"Yes!" squeaked the first. "*My* turn to do the eating! *You* do the other this time! MY TURN, MY TURN!"

Up ahead, something was making its way down the line—something unlike anything Jack had ever seen before. It basically consisted of six pale and disconcertingly human-looking legs, joined at the waist (knees pointing outward) to form a sort of arch shape. The place where the legs joined was wide and flat and held a tray on which were piled four tottering stacks of shiny black bowls: a pair of arms that sprouted from each side of the creature was busily handing them out. The legs walked with a rippling, spidery movement as the creature made its way down the row. Jack accepted his bowl, trying not to stare too much.

He could hear a long, low, rasping sound, a sound a little—no, a lot—like cheering. He kept walking, and the passage opened out into a space that took his breath away.

At the center of the dining hall was a vast and blazing bonfire. The floor of the hall sloped down gently toward it, and long curving tables of shiny black stone surrounded the fire in five concentric rings. Across the vast room from where Jack was standing, two more lines of gladiators were pouring out from other passageways beyond. But this wasn't where the cheering, which had seemed to double in strength when he emerged into the hall—was coming from. Jack looked up. The hall was like a massive chimney of black rock: being in it was like standing at the bottom of a dormant volcano. All around the wall of the room (though high enough to be well out of reach of any of the ground level's occupants) was some sort of observation deck. This upper level too was teeming with demons—some of them surprisingly smartly dressed, compared to the gladiators, but all of them cheering and yelling and waving and baying and barking and shrieking. Another packed observation deck was visible above it, and another above that. The walls stretched higher than Jack could see, and it was all he could do to tear his eyes from the sight and follow Inanna down one of the wide aisles to a table.

Presently, he sat down—and took a look at his dining companions.

Directly opposite him, in between a giant octopus and a thing like a big black praying mantis, sat a creature that looked, Jack thought, strangely normal. Mind you, he realized, his definition of "normal" had been pushed in some surprising new directions lately. The creature was a man, or at least he looked like one: he had only one head and a body not unlike Jack's own. The man's eyes were a bit blank and fishy looking, but he was looking at Jack interestedly enough, and—slowly, as if it were an effort for him—he smiled. Jack decided to take this as an encouraging sign.

"Er, hi!" he shouted. There had to be thousands of gladiators all around him, and most of them seemed to be banging their bowls on the table. "I'm Jack. What's your name?"

The man's grin got wider, but that was his only response.

Now, suddenly, Jack became aware that Shargle's heads had stopped squabbling with each other and were looking at him. The octopus and the mantis thing were too. Jack looked at the man again, and at that moment—

SPLOT!

The man's eyeballs dropped out of his face and fell into the bowl in front of him.

Empty eye sockets gaped at Jack like small wet mouths.

"Whee!" said the man. Then, louder, "*WHEEEEEEEEEE!*"

Then something nasty happened to his face.

It was as if his head were a balloon, and all the air had suddenly been let out of it. The dome of his narrow skull seemed to sag inward, provoking a considerable outpouring of greenish-gray goo that followed the eyeballs out of the sockets and into the bowl, joining them there. The mouth kept screaming and grinning until the head collapsed utterly, at which point the scream subsided into a choked, wet gurgle. The empty skin of the man's face sat between his shoulders for a moment—shivered—then *melted*, as the whole of what Jack could see of his body (shoulders, everything) suddenly turned liquid and slid out of sight.

Then there was a pause.

The giant octopus could barely contain its hilarity. Its great bulbous sack of a head was quaking and rippling, its tentacles draped over each other and twitching in helpless little paroxysms. The big black mantis creature was rocking itself back and forth so hard that it almost toppled over backward.

"HAAAAAAH!" said Shargle. "HAAAH HAA HAA HAA! Didn't you like that, fresh meat? That was *you*—see? Jagmat pretended to be *you*!"

Jack said nothing. He waited as, gradually, the laughter subsided.

"That's very clever," said Jack slowly. "Oh yeah, I'm *really* impressed."

At his words, the thing sitting opposite seemed to re-form itself. What was in the bowl turned pink and slid back with a hiss, and in another moment the creature had reared up in its true form, a frozen man-sized explosion of pink custardlike stuff. It wobbled and shook. Big bubbles formed and popped on its skin, belching out words.

"Fresh meat!" it burped. "Fresh meat! Fresh meat!"

"Whatever," said Jack—and sighed. *Yep*, he thought. *Gang up on the new guy.* In some ways, when it came down to it, Hell was really pretty predictable. He turned away to look at Inanna and found to his surprise that she was smiling. The smile vanished as soon as she saw him looking. Still, Jack couldn't help but feel a small glow of triumph. Maybe—just maybe—he was getting the hang of things.

"Chinj!" yelled someone off to Jack's right, interrupting his thoughts. In another second, the cry was taken up by the whole room. "CHINJ! CHINNNNNNNNNNNNJ!"

Jack, and everyone, looked up.

High up in the vaults of the gigantic dining hall, something was happening. Jack couldn't really see what was going on at first: it looked to him as if the shadows up there had somehow come to life. A strange rattling, clattering sound was gradually making itself audible, and as the great black mass of shapes sank toward the light of the fire, Jack saw what was causing it. The air of the hall was packed with a flock of small, black, birdlike creatures.

"CHINNNNNNNNJ!" howled the mass of gladiators. "CHIIIIIIIIIIIIIINNNNNNNNNJ!"

Jack watched the twisting, skittering flight of the creatures as they continued their descent toward the waiting hordes below. Lower they came, circling wildly. Now, one by one, individuals were breaking away from the group, plummeting like falling rocks to land on the tables below.

Patience! said Gukumat's voice in Jack's head. *Your patience, please! There are enough Chinj for each and every one of you. You'll all receive your share in good time!*

The first "Chinj" to land on Jack's table was having a hard time dodging the various limbs and appendages that whipped out to grab at it. Jack realized it was coming in his direction.

In the context of what Jack had seen of Hell's inhabitants so far, the Chinj was surprisingly pretty. Its daintily folded leathery black wings were batlike, but it was bigger than any bat Jack had ever seen or heard of, and much more solid looking: its glossy, fat little body reminded him of those large furry microphones on sticks that you sometimes see when people are being interviewed on TV. The creature had a button nose and a small, perfectly heart-shaped mouth. Its large furry ears looked endearingly ridiculous. Its big dark eyes were wide and trusting, and—as, with soft thumps that rapidly became a thunderous rumble, more and more of its fellows landed on the tables around it—it walked straight up to where Jack was sitting, looked up at him, and smiled warmly.

"Good evening," it said, not taking its big black bush-baby eyes off Jack for a moment—even as impatience and outrage finally overcame the blancmange monster opposite and the Chinj had to dodge a slicing grab from a quivering pink pseudopod. Calmly refolding its umbrellalike wings, the Chinj came back to earth just behind Jack's bowl.

"You're new to all this, aren't you?" it said in its clear, musical voice, and its eyes took on a winsomely sympathetic expression. "I can tell."

"Er, yeah," said Jack.

"It's no problem," said the Chinj. "There's nothing to it, I assure you. Perhaps," it added, taking a step toward him, "you'd be so good as to put out your hand."

"Why?" asked Jack. He'd just caught sight of what was going on around the rest of the table and was a bit distracted.

"No, look at me," commanded the creature, then smiled coyly as Jack did as he was told. "You're much nicer than the others," it said, still looking up at him through long, furry eyelashes. "I know we're going to get on famously, if you'll only just trust me. Put out your hand."

"Well, okay," said Jack, then, "What? OW!"

With a movement that had been too fast for his eye to catch, the little creature had ducked forward and fixed its fangs into his thumb, hard. The Chinj's jaws tightened: Jack felt the liquid slither of its tiny tongue and the unmistakable beginnings of a powerful sucking action. It was drinking his blood! He struggled to escape, but the chair he was sitting on had somehow changed shape, and more of that hateful jelly stuff he'd first encountered in the Emperor's throne room now had his body and both his arms in an inescapable grip. Plus, weird things—as in, even *more* weird things—were now going on all around him.

All over the room, and to the obvious delight of the howling company of assembled demons, the small winged creatures were *being sick*. To either side of Jack, a neat line of Chinj stretched all along the table, and every single one (except his own, obviously) stood bent, heads over the bowls, quietly but comprehensively regurgitating as if their lives depended on it. It was this that had distracted Jack earlier.

"What are you doing?" he yelled weakly at the Chinj that was sucking his blood. In actual fact, the pain had lessened after the initial bite, and the sensation of having his blood drained was really not much worse than getting an injection at the doctor's, but still some yelling was in order. "Get off me!"

It did. As suddenly as it had bitten him, the bat thing relinquished its grip and sat up. A tiny blob of ruby-red blood dripped from its mouth and hit the shiny black surface of the table. Now it too took up its position behind Jack's bowl—but all its earlier grace was gone. It moved uncertainly, with shuffling steps, and it was beginning to look unmistakably ill.

"There," it wheezed. "Sorry." Its small bulging chest pumped in and out, and words were clearly a struggle. "Had to—take a sample," it gasped, "before—I—'scuse me."

It broke off, bowed over the edge of the bowl—and let fly.

The way the little creature was being sick wasn't at all like the way that people do it. When human beings "blow chunks," "shout soup," or "do a Technicolor yawn," it comes out a bit at a time. The way the Chinj was doing it (or *were* doing it—for they were all at it) was in a constant stream, its mouth wide, its head back, projecting a pouring torrent into Jack's bowl like water out of a high-pressure hose. The small creature looked perfectly serene, its eyes closed. The stuff coming out of its mouth was pale pink, the consistency of smooth porridge, and—unlike what you'd normally expect from the contents of someone's stomach—it smelled surprisingly sweet.

Now, one by one, all over the room, the bat things were straightening up, their job done. Presently, Jack's Chinj too suddenly stopped—the torrent cutting out as quickly as it had started. A little stiffly, it drew itself up to its full height (its eyes were about level with Jack's chin) and passed a dainty wingtip across its lips.

"There," it said, its large, dark eyes shining with obvious pride. Its furry body had shrunk considerably, and it was huddling its leathery wings around itself as though to keep warm. "Enjoy your meal, sir," it said.

"Oh," said Jack, realizing. "Er, thanks."

The creature smiled and unfurled its wings, ready to take off—but then it stopped, looked up and down the table, and made a beckoning gesture with one of its tiny front claws. Much to his own surprise, Jack found himself leaning closer to hear what the small creature had to say.

"We're not supposed to know about things like this," said the Chinj, in a voice that lost none of its conspiratorial quality for the creature's having to speak quite loudly to make itself heard over the surrounding din. "But between you and me, sir, I think your number's up." It smiled up at him delightedly. "I think you're going to be in the games this time! Isn't that exciting?"

"Yeah?" said Jack.

"You're a very lucky fellow," enthused the Chinj. "I *do* so hope it goes well for you. Now, have you got your boon all worked out?"

"My what?"

"Your boon. Your favor to ask of the Emperor. You know," it prompted, its eyes flashing joshingly, "if you win!"

"Oh," said Jack. "Right. Yeah."

"The best of luck, sir!" squeaked the creature.

"Thanks," Jack repeated.

"And may I just say how *delicious* you are," the Chinj added, glancing up at Jack coyly. "I do so hope we'll meet again soon."

"Sure," said Jack. "Likewise, I guess."

"Well, must dash," said the Chinj, unfurling its wings and

shaking itself a little, preparatory to liftoff. "Goodbye—and good luck!"

"Thanks," said Jack. "See you."

But the Chinj had already leaped into the air and was arrowing its way back up to wherever it had come from. In another second, it had vanished from sight.

Jack's arms (and most of the rest of his body, in fact) were still firmly held by the jelly chair. When he looked round, he could see that all the gladiators were similarly restrained. The jelly chairs of the blancmange monster and the octopus were having serious difficulty keeping their charges in check, so impatient were they to get at their bowls. But then the massive echoing hiss of the gong came again.

Jack's arms were released.

And as each and every gladiator except Jack lunged forward and tucked straight into their dinner, all the cheering and baying and yelling cut out completely, and the massive room went suddenly, eerily quiet.

Jack looked around.

Inanna had taken her bowl up in both her skull-crushing hands and was gulping the contents: the impressively large blob of her Adam's apple pulsed up and down on her thick blue neck. Shargle's heads butted and hissed at each other, making disgusting gurgling and bubbling noises whenever one of them managed to stick itself under the surface and slurp at the substance within. Jack's eyes returned to what was sitting on the table right in front of him. His own bowl of Chinj chunder.

He looked at the weird pink goo and the faint wreaths of

fragrant steam that still rose from its depths and found to his horror that his stomach was rumbling. With a sense of resignation, he reached for the bowl with both hands.

It felt warm.

It smelled sweet and creamy.

So he held his breath, lifted the bowl to his lips—

—and took the first sip.

A shiver ran down his back, part revulsion and part something else.

Pleasure.

The stuff tasted absolutely *delicious.* Like cauliflower soup, only sweeter. Milky, with a hint of coconut—only the consistency was quite thick, more like a puree than a liquid. As he took a gulp, then another and another, the stuff ran over his tongue with a weird, oaty, floury texture, and little clumps and threads of it clung to his teeth.

He was drinking *sick*: a part of him knew this, a large part. But the stuff was warm and nourishing, and it was making him feel better than he'd felt in a long time. The warmth of the stuff spread down his insides, making him tingle all over. He found himself tipping the bowl back, getting it all down, and as the flow slowed to a dribble, he ended up shaking the bowl to dislodge the last few drips. He wished he could have had more.

But suddenly, the gong was sounding again.

Pray silence, the voice intoned sonorously, *for the keeper of the pits. The invincible. The awesome . . . LORD SLINT!*

Something large and heavy shifted in the massive bonfire at the hall's center, releasing a shower of upward sparks, and the room was suddenly bathed in an unearthly glow. Jack looked up. High up on the wall on one side of the great hall, between two of the observation decks, a bright rosette of light unfurled as a circular tunnel opened. The light that came from within was blindingly bright, but as suddenly as it had appeared, it was blotted out: the immense and sinuous shape of the giant flying shark slid through it and out into the air beyond.

Tremble, supplicants, Gukumat announced, *as you discover whom among you is to meet their doom at tomorrow's games, and what form that doom is to take.*

The giant shark made a swishing circuit of the hall, just above the heads of the crowd on one of the observation decks, eliciting an appreciative chorus of oohs and aahs. The jelly chair tightened around Jack again, as if anticipating trouble—and that was when he realized that the shark was not alone.

It was surrounded by something that looked, at first, like a strange kind of golden cloud. As, in wide, lazy circles, the shark descended through the air, Jack saw that the cloud was made up of a shoal of tiny creatures a little like, well, fish. They looked like angelfish, with the same strange, flat, almost triangular bodies and the same long, elegant whiskers pointing and trailing above and below. Their colors were very beautiful: alternating vertical stripes of glossy black and glittering gold that caught the light of the great fire and flashed it back and forth until the walls of the great hall shone with spots of light like a gigantic mirror-ball effect. There must have been hundreds of them, glittering and shimmering and whisking through the air around their master's every movement like a golden, hazy halo.

And each one, Jack could see, held something in its mouth.

Plink!

Something had dropped and landed in the bowl of one of the gladiators further up Jack's table.

Plink!

Another of the silvery objects flashed down through the air, to land in the bowl of the black mantis creature. They were falling all over the room now, like the first spots of a strange, tinkling rain—and the watching demons on the observation decks were howling and cheering again.

"Who'd you get, Qat? Who'd you get?" chorused both Shargle's heads at once.

The mantis clicked its slimy black jaws together and reached one of its alarmingly large claws into the bowl. It pulled out a small shiny disc with a word printed into the center. The word was like no word Jack had ever seen; it seemed to swim before his eyes for a second before it resolved itself into what, he guessed, was a name: something like—

"Svatog?" barked Shargle. "*Svatog?* Haaaah! He'll make mincemeat out of you!"

"Arse!" belched the blancmange firmly. "Qat's got what it takes, ain't you, Qat?"

The coin things were falling thick and fast now, and the air of the great hall sang with the high ringing sound of their impacts. The shark continued to circle overhead, and the babbling of the gladiators was reaching a crescendo again. So far, to Jack's relief, no coin had yet landed in his bowl. He turned to look at Inanna—and had a surprise.

She too was staring up at what was going on. But her whole posture had changed completely. Just then, Jack thought, she looked for all the world like a kid in class with her hand up, begging for the chance to answer some question that the teacher has asked. The whole of her massive blue body seemed to be straining upward: her whole being seemed to be begging the golden shoal that spiraled and glittered above them, begging them to notice her.

She wants it, thought Jack, her earlier words coming back to him. *She* wants *the chance to fight. But then—*

Plink!

A coin dropped into Shargle's bowl. And then—

Plink!

Something flashed past Jack's eyes.

Jack knew what it was, with a terrible certainty, without having to look. And when he did look, he wasn't wrong.

There it was, still shivering to a stop at the bottom of his bowl: Jack's own coin. The Chinj had been right. His number *was* up. And in the center of the coin was a word.

"HAAAAAAAAAAAAAAAAAAAH!!" yelled both Shargle's heads at once.

"Fresh meat and Shargle," Jack heard—barked, burped, and burbled by a multitude of mouths as word spread up and down the table. "Fresh meat and Shargle!" "Fresh meat and Shargle!"

"HEEEEEEEEEEE hee hee hee hee!" croaked Shargle, oily tears coursing down all four of his brown cheeks. "OOOOOh ho. No, that's too good. Hoo-HOO!"

The sound of the coins falling from above was drowned

out now as, for a moment, it felt like every single demon in the room was laughing at Jack.

"Oh, fresh meat!" Shargle crowed, wiping his eyes on his coils. "You won't *believe* what's in store for you. Just you wait! Why, I'll—"

But anything else the worm would have said was suddenly cut off by a terrible bellow from Inanna.

"NO!" she screamed suddenly. "NOOOOOOOOOO!"

As the whole of the room fell instantly, horribly silent, Jack looked up just in time to see the great shark, with three sinuous flicks of its body, rushing through the air back up to where it had come from. The golden shoal of fish things, their task completed, wasn't far behind. Already they too were vanishing back into the rose-shaped opening high above, right behind their master.

"NOOOOOOO!" shrieked Inanna again, her voice suddenly cracking with a despair that was terrible to hear. "Choose me!" she implored, straining up as her jelly chair struggled to hold her back. "CHOOSE ME!"

But the golden cloud was gone. The bright light of the wall's opening was blotted out as it closed. No more coin things were going to be dropped that night, even Jack could tell that. Now there was absolute silence in the room, as every single one of the thousands of gladiators waited to see what she'd do next.

Inanna closed her eyes, and for another moment her whole body was limp. Then she flung back her arms and exploded up out of her chair and onto her feet.

"It's a FIX!" she roared. "A FIX, I tell you!"

Jelly stuff was spreading and tightening around her, struggling to get her under control. Nonetheless, her words had already had their effect. A nasty murmur of agreement had spread around the hall of gladiators.

"Fix!" echoed the blancmange monster as the octopus began slamming its tentacles on the table.

"FIX!" roared the vast mass of demons with one voice. "FIX! *FIX!*"

Jack felt the jelly stuff that held him tightening the hardest it had yet, pressing and crushing in on him. The whole floor of the dining hall seemed to have gone soft and wet, as more and more of the stuff rushed to contain what was starting to look like a full-scale riot.

SILENCE! Gukumat's voice thundered in Jack's head, ringing in his brain and making big ugly blue flashes in front of his eyes. And indeed, the room did seem to be getting quieter, as each and every creature in it suddenly found itself locked in its own personal struggle with what held it.

You will all return to your cells, said the voice.

"Yeah?" someone yelled back. "And who's going to make us?"

You misunderstand, said Gukumat. *That was not a request.*

And at that moment, the pressure on Jack's body reached a climactic, terrible intensity. He felt like his brain was threatening to squeeze out of his eye sockets, much as the blancmange creature's had done earlier when it was trying to frighten him. He felt a hideous, bulging, *ripping* sensation—

—then darkness.

WEAPONS

The Scourge stopped walking and looked around. Apart from the way they'd come, three more vast corridors led away from the crossroads: ahead, left, and right.

The floor of the room they were standing in was marble, the center inlaid with a subtly repeating pattern of black and white tiles—but Charlie wasn't looking at the floor. The high ceilings were covered in lurid paintings depicting scenes from demon history in full and revolting detail—but Charlie wasn't looking at these, or at the giant fluted stone pillars that flanked the corridors either. He was looking at the Scourge.

"Up one more floor, I think," it said.

"We've been up about twelve already," Charlie pointed out.

"Seven, actually." The demon turned to him and held out its hands. "Ready?"

"Of course I'm ready."

"Well then," said the Scourge—and with that, they lifted smoothly into the air.

Charlie watched the pattern on the floor shrink beneath his feet and scowled.

"Look," he said, as yet another colossal balcony hove into view all around them, "are you going to tell me what we're looking for or what?"

They swung away to one side, lifting effortlessly over the balcony's wrought-stone parapet.

"**Weapons,**" the Scourge replied, as they came to rest soundlessly on one of the huge marble slabs that made up the floor on this level. "**To kill the Emperor, we're going to need weapons—though it seems a little unfair to call them that. We're looking for Ashmon and Heshmim—**"

"Ash-what and Hesh-who?"

"**My familiars,**" finished the demon.

The Scourge turned and set off toward the nearest of the pillars, which seemed to continue exactly from where the ones on the floor below had stopped. It bent to examine the large blank slab of polished black rock that was attached to the pillar's base. Charlie heard a soft *flump!* Then the surface of the slab began to fill up from right to left with line upon line of intricate, inch-high letters. The letters were red and seemed to flicker like tiny flames.

"Hey," said Charlie, coming over for a look. "That's kind of cool. What's it say?"

The letters vanished.

"**It** *says,*" said the Scourge, "**that if you can be patient for just a little longer, we are almost there. This way, I think,**" it added, and set off down the corridor.

"We are now," the Scourge announced, "in a part of the palace known as the Halls of Ages. To my knowledge, the Emperors of Hell have never once thrown anything away: the Halls of Ages are where everything is kept."

"Sounds like my house," said Charlie.

"This whole section of the palace is a network of halls and corridors like these. To either side of us are rooms containing all manner of wonders—an incalculably valuable physical record of the whole of Hell's history."

"Which is why no one comes up here," said Charlie.

"Precisely," said the demon. "Ah," it added, suddenly coming to a stop at the foot of yet another enormous pillar, which looked exactly the same as the others. "I believe we've arrived."

"Yeah?"

"Oh yes," said the Scourge, with a small shudder of pleasure, "most definitely." It made a gesture in front of the column, and a section of solid fluted marble wobbled for a moment, then vanished, to reveal a surprisingly ordinary-looking door, with a small brass doorknob.

"After you, Charlie," said the Scourge.

"All right," said Charlie dubiously. He grasped the cool metal, turned it, and the door swung open to reveal a small dusty room. At its center stood a solid-looking dark wooden desk, on which stood the green-shaded brass reading lamp that was the room's only light. Sitting at this desk, still holding the book he'd been reading, was a startled-looking elderly man in a rumpled tweed suit with patches on the elbows.

"Kh-Khentimentu," the man stammered out finally.

"Godfrey!" said the Scourge. "So good to see you."

"L-Likewise!" lied Godfrey, standing up.

"Charlie, Godfrey."

"Hi," said Charlie.

"Oh!" Godfrey looked at the Scourge. "He isn't another . . . is he?"

"Another what, Godfrey?"

"You know," said Godfrey, with a coy smile. "Human."

"He is human," said the Scourge. "Yes."

"Oh, but—fascinating! Really?"

"Really." The Scourge sighed. "Godfrey, time *is* rather against us. Ashmon and Heshmim—are they here?"

"Right," said Godfrey, suddenly nervous again. "Yes. Yes, of course." He got up and went over to the wall of small dark wooden drawers that lined the room from floor to ceiling. He reached into one, extracted something, and put it on the desk in front of Charlie.

"There we are," he said. "All present and correct."

"At last," said the Scourge in a quiet, breathy voice. "Go on, Charlie. Pick them up."

Charlie frowned. The two objects on the table were cylindrical and of equal size: two batons of perfect black, each maybe eight inches long and an inch and a half in diameter. Frankly, they didn't look very impressive. Still, Charlie shrugged and did as he was told, picking up one in each hand.

Instantly, he froze, horrified. At the first contact with his skin, the two strange objects seemed to melt, becoming oily and greasy in his hands. They were *warm* too, a sudden animal warmth that Charlie didn't like one bit. He made to drop them—and nothing happened! He shook his hands, palm down, over the surface of the desk, only to find that the two black objects clung to him obstinately. In another second they had lost their shape completely, running out and around his palms, a sudden oily welter of hot wet blackness that strung in ropy strands between his fingers, gluing them together. Now the stuff was running up his arms, two humped mounds of inky black, slithering round his shoulders, wriggling down his back, and playing in his hair.

"What the *Hell*?" he said.

"I present to you," said the Scourge, "**Ashmon and Heshmim. Ashmon and Heshmim? This is Charlie.**" At the demon's words, the two blacknesses suddenly sucked back into themselves, and all that was left were two small ferretlike creatures. They sat on Charlie's hands, staring at him intently with sharp, shining eyes.

"**Heshmim will defend you,**" said the Scourge. "**At a thought from you—or before you even think it—Heshmim will transform himself into shields or armor strong enough to repel almost any attack. Heshmim will also clothe you, with better than any of the rough garments you brought with you from your world.**

"**Ashmon,**" the Scourge went on, "**is for attack. He will assume the shape and properties of any weapon you can imagine.**"

"Not in here, though," put in Godfrey quickly. "Yes, practice with them *later.*"

"**You will find, Charlie,**" said the Scourge, "**that a steady purpose and a strong will are not all that are required to rule. Sometimes—**"

Hiss, flick, WHAM!

An object like a three-foot-long black javelin had struck, quivering, in the wall behind Godfrey, some three millimeters to the right of his left ear. The javelin thing remained in the wall for another moment, then melted as Ashmon reassumed his ferret shape and scampered back to his place on Charlie's right hand.

"Eep," said Godfrey.

"**Sometimes,**" said the Scourge, "**you have to** *act*."

"Coooooool," said Charlie.

"**You may go out into the passage and get used to each other. Godfrey and I have to talk.**"

"Sure," said Charlie. He was up and out of the door in about a nanosecond.

The demon and the librarian turned to face each other.

"So," said God. "How've you, ah—been?"

"**Much better, thank you,**" said the Scourge. "**Now.**"

"It's, er, nice to see you!" said the librarian with obvious effort.

"**Really?**"

"Yes," said God. "Yes, of course it is! Er, why wouldn't it be?"

"**I didn't think you would've expected to see me again,**" said the Scourge slowly. "**My return from exile on that little . . . experiment of yours must be something of a shock to you, I would imagine.**"

"Wh-what do you mean?" asked God.

The demon didn't answer.

"N-now hold on just a second!" said God, stammering again. "You know perfectly well that I had nothing to do with what happened to you—nothing whatsoever! You were exiled on Earth because no one knew the place existed, but it might just as well have been anywhere! You were bound by a power far greater than mine, as you well know, so *how* you could even *think* that I—"

"**Godfrey**," said the Scourge, "**shut up.**"

God did as he was told.

The Scourge planted its liquid hands on the desk: they pooled there, at the end of its arms, glinting green in the light from the lamp. "**If I knew for certain**," it began, leaning over the man in the chair. "**If I had so much as a shred of proof, Godfrey, that you had anything to do with my imprisonment on that world you created—do you know what I'd do to you?**"

God looked up at it.

"N-no," he said.

"**No,**" echoed the Scourge. "**You don't. But believe me, it would be far from pleasant. After all, I've had a very long time to work it out.**"

There was a pause.

"So," said God. "What are your, ah, plans?"

"**You know my plans,**" the Scourge replied. "**They have not changed.**"

"Oh," said God. "Oh dear."

"**With that human boy as my vessel,**" said the Scourge, gesturing out toward the passageway, "**I will kill the current Emperor and take my rightful place on the throne. Then, Godfrey, I will do what I originally set out to do.**"

"But surely," said God, "you *can't* still want to—?"

"I will awaken the Dragon," the Scourge told him, "and the Dragon will destroy the universe. All Creation shall be returned to the Void, and pure emptiness will reign once more.

"And this time," it added, standing up, "nothing is going to stop me."

THE PATH
OF VENGEANCE

Esme had lived above the theater her whole life. She knew every inch of it, every creak in every floorboard. The Sons of the Scorpion Flail had set sentries in case she came back, but they might as well not have bothered: Esme moved through the passageways like a ghost, in silence and darkness.

Look in my room, Raymond's voice echoed. *There's something for you.*

Part of Esme had been expecting that Raymond's room might have changed somehow. But of course it looked exactly the same.

It was full of him. Full of memories. There was his regimental photo from his SAS days, taken so long ago now that the Raymond in that picture was almost unrecognizable. Above that were his certificates from his years of brutal budo training with the Tokyo Riot Police. In the corner by the wardrobe, his outsized practice armor stood like the abandoned carapace of some giant insect that had molted and moved on.

She found what she was looking for easily enough, under the bed.

It was a rectangular narrow flight case—black, with steel-reinforced corners. The case was four feet long, a foot wide, and six inches deep.

When you're ready, when you know what to do, you use *it.*

Esme flipped the catches. As she lifted the lid, she was holding her breath. For a moment, she stared at what she saw, eyes wide, drinking it in. Then, still hardly daring to breathe, Esme reached into the case and lifted out what it contained. A strange sensation of pleasure spread up her arms and shivered through her whole body as she felt its weight.

At first glance, it looked a lot like her training sword—her bokken. The scabbard was made of the same plain, dark wood, and the overall dimensions of the sword were exactly the same too. But there was something unusual, she noticed, about the sword's tsuba. The disc of metal, which divides the handle from the blade and prevents your opponent's blade from simply sliding down yours and wounding your sword hand, was thicker than usual: a flat but solid-looking gold-colored lump, four inches in diameter at its widest points, cast roughly, but clearly, into the unmistakable shape of . . .

"A butterfly," said Esme aloud—and for a moment, then, she almost lost it.

Don't be soft, said Raymond's voice in her head. *Put it on.*

With a hard sniff, Esme slung the sword across her back. She adjusted the strap until it fit snugly and the grip lay close to her right hand. Then, reaching up without looking, Esme released the small catch that held the guard against the scabbard. It gave out a soft but deeply satisfying *click*.

In a fluid movement, she drew the sword. The soft hiss as it slid from the sheath was followed by a high, singing hum as the blade reverberated.

"Oh," she said. "Oh, Dad. It's beautiful."

Turning her wrists, she let the light from Raymond's bedside lamp play along the sword's edge. The warm glare traced the length of the blade from guard to tip: two feet eight inches of cold curved steel.

It was a pigeon sword—forged by Raymond's own peculiar process. For extra strength, it had been ground down and reshaped—*Seven times is my record*, she remembered him saying. It was the life's work of a master swordsmith, and it had been created just for her.

She let the sword dip once, twice in the air, in tiny, controlled chopping movements. The weapon, as Raymond had no doubt planned, was fractionally lighter than her training sword: it felt absolutely right in her hands.

"How do I look?" Esme asked aloud.

Deadly, Raymond's voice replied fervently. *Bloody* deadly.

The tears were coming freely now, but she smiled.

Less than two minutes later, she was back on the theater's roof. She unhooked the latch on the pigeon coop and flung it open. Esme stood there and watched the birds go: an explosion of wings, clattering off into the London night. Then, when she was ready—when she'd fully accepted that she (like the birds) might never come back—she followed them, dropping away into the dark.

By the time the Sons of the Scorpion Flail even got the door to the roof open, she was long gone.

"Esme, listen to me," Felix was saying presently, as they approached the ludicrous cream-colored pillars outside the Light of the Moon, the pub that was a gateway to Hell. "I've got to say, I'm really, *really* not sure about this. I mean, quite apart from the whole idea of you going on your own, I . . ." He winced inwardly, hearing the sound of his own voice. "Well, I don't know what it is you think *I* can do."

Esme wasn't even looking at him. She had her hands on the heavy padlock that held the pub's wide glass doors locked tight. There was a soft click. The padlock fell open.

"You're right about my never being really freed," Felix went on, "but if you think there's enough of the Scourge left inside me to help you open the Fracture, then—"

"Come on," Esme said, and set off into the darkness beyond.

Felix sighed heavily, and followed.

The pub had closed only a few hours before, and it stank, but it wasn't this that was making Felix uncomfortable. He was remembering the horror of the last time he had come here. The night when—through him—the Scourge had almost triumphed; the night when the woman he loved had died. Even in the dark, his footsteps led him unerringly on. Felix felt sick in his heart.

"Here," said Esme.

Felix put out a hand, and icy cold slid down his arm. There it was: the same cold space in the air, just above waist level. Beside him, he heard Esme take a deep breath.

"Ready?" she asked.

"Not really," said Felix. "No."

"Well, we're doing it anyway. *Go.*"

They both closed their eyes.

For six long seconds, nothing happened. Felix felt a stir of hope and relief. Perhaps the dreadful power that had taken him over all those years ago was really gone: perhaps there was nothing of it left inside him. "There," he was about to say. "Now let's go home."

But then, quietly at first, the whole room started to hum.

It was a sound that seemed to come from everywhere. The air thickened, tightening around them like polyethylene; then an eggshell-thin line of ruby-red light was appearing just in front of where he and Esme were standing. The crack in the air began to widen, revealing the freezing whiteness beyond. And in another moment . . .

It was done. The Fracture was open. All too easy.

Esme opened her eyes. Then she looked down at her hands.

"Esme?" said Felix.

"What?"

"The Fracture," said Felix, gesturing. "I didn't do any-thing."

"What do you mean?" Esme asked him. "It's open, isn't it? Maybe you did it without realizing."

"No," he replied. "I'm sure I—well, I think you did it by yourself."

They looked at each other.

"Esme," he began, "I—"

Esme cut him off. "Felix, if you're going to start telling me all that stuff about all my power coming from the Scourge again, then I don't want to hear it. All right? I know you don't want me to go. But I have a job to do."

She adjusted the strap that held the pigeon sword on her back. She checked the elastic bands holding her hair in place: they hadn't moved. She squared her shoulders and turned to face the gateway to Hell.

"Esme, wait!" said Felix.

"Goodbye, Felix," she told him. Already she was moving. She took one more deep breath, and she—

"FREEZE!" yelled another voice—one that definitely didn't belong to Felix.

She turned. The Fracture had lit up the whole room, which was now filling up with some forty armed men. It was the Sons of the Scorpion Flail. At last, it seemed, they had caught up with her. Esme blinked, and her chest and belly lit up with the bright red spots of laser sights as the men took aim.

"Wait, mademoiselle!" Number 3, the scar-faced man she'd spoken to before, was standing at the top of the steps: his mask was still off and his eyes were wild. "We can 'elp you!" he shouted again.

Esme just smiled grimly. No one could help her. She turned her back—on the men, on Felix, and on the world. She stepped into the freezing white light, feeling it take her—

—and she vanished.

"I am Ebisu Eller-Kong Hacha'Fravashi," the Emperor announced, sitting up on his throne. "God of Rulers, God of the Dead, God of Darkness, God of Gods. I am the Voice of the Void, whose breath is the wind and whose rage makes all worlds tremble. I am the Lord of Crossing-Places, the King of All Tears, and the Suzerain Absolute of the Dominions of Hell."

"Esme," said Esme. She was standing in the throne room, in almost the exact spot where Jack had stood when he'd arrived. "So," she added, "you're in charge here."

The Emperor's gaze narrowed and sharpened. "Yes," he said dryly. "I am in charge here. And what brings you to Hell, if you please?"

"I've come for the Scourge," said Esme.

"Really?" said the Emperor without much interest. "Why?"

"I'm going to recapture it and put it back in its prison," said Esme.

The Emperor's eyes went wide.

"Oh, but how *fascinating*!" he said, clapping his cloven hands.

"I'm glad that makes you happy," said Esme. "Now tell me, please. Where's the Scourge?"

"I'm afraid," said the Emperor, slowly and with relish, "that if you want a favor from me, you'll have to fight for it."

Esme looked at him. "What?"

"I won't let you see the Scourge without my permission. And if you want my permission . . ." The Emperor trailed off, smiling delightedly.

Esme blinked, then took a step toward the throne. "Fine," she said. "I'm ready."

"We shall see," was the reply.

Suddenly, Esme found she couldn't move. Some kind of jelly stuff seemed to have slithered up over the sides of the red carpet and trapped her feet. Already it was climbing up the legs of her combat pants. In another second it had pinned her arms to her sides and was slopping up over her shoulders.

"You will be taken to the gladiator pits," said the Emperor, sitting back on his throne, "together with the rest of the supplicants."

"I confess," he added, as the stuff covered her completely, then stiffened, ready for transport, "I can't wait to see you in action."

He gestured with his cloven hands. Esme disappeared.

Alone on his throne, the Emperor smiled. Really, the next day's action in the pits might prove the most diverting in a very long time.

AKACHASH

"Ah, *what?*" said Jack.

The jelly stuff had left him, but he wasn't at all where he'd been expecting to be. Instead of standing in the stone passageway again, he'd appeared in the auditorium's stands.

The banks of seats were filling up rapidly with other spectators: wherever Jack looked, sticky columns of jelly stuff were shimmering into being, then vanishing to reveal demons underneath. Dimly, Jack realized that he was going to need to find a place to sit down. But before he could search for any place other than where he was, which was practically next to the blancmangelike shape-shifting monster he'd met the night before, it was too late. It had noticed him.

"Hey!" it belched. "Wotsyerface!"

"Oh . . . hi," said Jack.

"Whatcha waiting for? Siddahhn. It ain't the royal box, but it's all we got, so . . ." The thing made a lashing gesture with one clammy pink flipper.

Reluctantly, Jack did as he was told.

"Jagmat," belched the blancmange monster.

"Jack," said Jack, hoping the creature had actually been telling him its name.

"Ehhh," it said, "about last night. You know, when I did all that . . ." Here the creature broke off, abruptly doing a sped-up version of the trick it had performed when they'd first met. It was every bit as disgusting as the first time, and Jack hadn't really needed reminding.

"Yeah?" he asked.

"Just a bit of fun, y'know. Someone always pulls some stunt on the fresh meat. S'traditional. Didnmeanuffinbyit."

"That's all right," said Jack distractedly. His attention had been caught by another demon settling itself down beside him: a flat-headed, oily-looking eel-like creature, about two meters long and as thick as Jack's leg. It nodded at Jack politely.

"Er, Jagmat?" Jack asked.

"Yep?"

"What's going on? I mean, I thought I was going to be fighting Shargle today. Not that I'm disappointed or anything," he added quickly.

"Big fight this time," was the reply.

"Yeah?" asked Jack. The auditorium was crowding up quickly, and before long he found himself pressed up a lot closer to his neighbors than he'd've liked.

"*Oh* yeah. The program's been all switched around. Even Inanna got a last-minute call-up."

"Really?"

"I reckon we're looking," the blancmange monster added, leaning even closer to Jack, "at an Akachash."

"A what?" said Jack. The word had left little moist pink spatters on his chin when Jagmat had said it. But the blancmange monster didn't answer.

Loyal subjects of the Emperor Hacha'Fravashi! boomed Gukumat's voice. A thrill went around the arena. *It gives me great pleasure to announce for you now that the next bout—*

"Whaddatellyou?" belched Jagmat.

—is an AKACHASH!

Instantly, Jack found he was standing up. He'd had no choice in the matter—the place was now so packed with demons that he couldn't have remained seated if he'd tried. Jack was in a bubble of sound, a cocoon of noise. All around him was hooting, roaring, baying, barking. His ears were battered with it.

SEVEN GO IN! roared the voice in his head, making stars blossom in front of Jack's eyes.

"ONE COMES OUT!" roared the crowd in answer, in a horrible clashing battery of tongues.

SILENCE! boomed the voice suddenly. As one, the crowd sat down.

First gladiator, the voice announced, as one of the arena's massive entrance slabs began to rise, *undefeated in seventeen straight bouts, with claws of steel and the cold of the Void itself in his heart—SVATOG THE CANCELER!*

"YAAAAAAAAAAGH!" yelled Jagmat. His whole wet pink amoeba body sprang into a glistening mass of thrashing tentacles, each one with a shrieking mouth at the end of it.

"Whoa," said Jack.

'Svatog the Canceler' shambled into the arena and stood there, blinking. He was a good size for a demon, perhaps eighteen feet tall. From the waist down, his body was glossy and black, a little like a horse's: his powerful-looking springy back legs ended in two great hooves that actually *smoked* (Jack couldn't help but notice) where they touched the ground. But it was Svatog's arms that tended to catch your eye first: they were *huge*. Forming a great horseshoe-shaped expanse of hulking muscle, they were so long that Svatog could comfortably lay each entire, massive, three-fingered hand out flat on the hot sand to either side of him. By contrast, Svatog's head looked almost comically small, not so much perched between his shoulders as set into his chest. He looked mean, Jack thought—mean and stupid.

"That's Svatog," Jagmat confided. "He's my mate, and he's going to KICK *AAAAAAAAAAARRRRRRRRRRRRSSSSSSE!*" The blancmange monster suddenly leaped up again on the last word, his voice rising to a roar. The demon in the ring apparently heard him, for Svatog's eyes narrowed, and one of his great arms suddenly lifted to point in their direction.

SHHINNNG!

Jack and Jagmat found themselves looking down two great yard-long spikes of gleaming steel that seemed to have sprung from the spaces between the Svatog's fingers.

"YOU THE BOSS!" shrieked Jagmat. "YOU THE BOSS!"

Svatog winked slowly and retracted his claws. As his arm

sank back down to his side, the wide slash of his mouth burst open in a wet and toothless smile.

Second gladiator, said the voice, *a firm favorite among fight fans in the years that she has graced the pits—GLADRASH THE BLUNT!*

From somewhere beyond the great raised entrance stone came a deep, rhythmic rumbling sound. Suddenly, to the accompaniment of a howl of ecstasy from her fans, Svatog's first opponent came rocketing out of the gate and into the arena, like—

You have to be joking, thought Jack.

—well, like a bull at a bullfight.

Gladrash the Blunt looked a lot like a bull: a heaving great brown-black mass of meat and muscle, with wild white rolling eyes and mountainous haunches that humped and sank as her hooves pummeled the ground. The main thing about Gladrash the Blunt that was different, however, from any bull Jack had ever seen, was her size: Gladrash the Blunt was big. Very big. About the size of a bus, in fact.

At the sound of their heroine's name, a whole section of the audience suddenly erupted in cheers and screams of delight. Svatog's smile vanished, his eyes narrowing into a gormless but vivid scowl as the great cow shot out of her gate and trampled past him, kicking up dust. Gladrash skidded to a halt on the opposite side of the ring, snorting as she pawed at the sand with one plate-size front hoof. Jack just stared.

Third gladiator, said the voice, *TUNKU THE SNOOL!*

Another entrance slab ground upward, and the audience

fell suddenly quiet. When Jack saw what came out next, he understood why. It looked like nothing more than a large floating jellyfish: as it drifted out into the arena, its dimpled tentacles trailed delicately in the air beneath it.

"But that's ridiculous," said Jack, echoing the sentiments of most of the crowd. "What chance has that third one got? That Svatog guy'll just *step* on it."

"Wait and see, kid," muttered Jagmat. "Believe me, just 'cos Tunku's invertebrate that doesn't mean he hasn't got it where it counts."

Fourth gladiator, said the voice, *RIPITITH GUNCH!*

The figure that strode out into the ring now was broadly human looking, if a bit on the tall side. Ripitith Gunch was wrapped in a long black cloak that covered him all over, even down to his feet. The skin of his face was deathly pale, and his head was thin and strangely elongated, culminating in a great foot-long shock of blinding white hair that stuck straight out of his head like a crown of spikes. The crowd started booing.

"Cheat!" shrieked the eel thing. "CHEAT!"

"I hate that guy," said Jagmat, getting an acknowledging wild-eyed nod from the eel.

"Why?" asked Jack.

"All that transfiguration crap, 'stead of a straight fight," snorted the blancmange. "Cowardly, I'd call it."

"'Sright!" yapped the eel thing.

"I see," said Jack—though he obviously didn't.

"No, no, *no*," snapped the Emperor, up in the royal box. "I asked for the *pickled* spleens today, not the sugared ones! I *specifically* asked for the *pickled* ones!"

"A thousand apologies, Your Excellency," gasped the small lizardlike creature beside him, shuddering beneath a silver tray that was bigger than itself. Charlie looked on in disgust.

"I would have Lord Slint chew your legs off," said the Emperor, "if I didn't think such a puny job might hurt his feelings." He sat up and beckoned to Gukumat. "Where *is* Lord Slint, by the way?"

He is preparing to make his entrance, Sire.

"Good, good." Scowling, the Emperor turned to the lizard creature, who was still trembling at the corner of the dais. "Are you still here?"

"S-Sire?"

"Didn't I just tell you what I want? Or are you waiting for me to have you *skinned*?"

"In-indeed, Sire," stammered the lizard. "I shall fetch them at once."

"Leave the tray," said the Emperor.

"As you wish, Sire," the lizard replied, grunting with effort as he set the tray and the greenish-gray pyramid of its contents down within his master's reach. "I live to serve you," it squeaked, bowing low once more before scuttling from the room.

"I think you'll find this quite interesting, Charlie," said the Emperor, selecting a sweetmeat and turning to Charlie with a wide grin.

"I can't wait," Charlie replied, doing his best.

Fifth gladiator, Gukumat's announcing voice boomed out, *fresh in from the twelfth-segment stench pits—the GRAKU-LOUS SLOAT!*

A gasp of delighted disgust rose up from the crowd as they saw what came into the ring next. Charlie barely suppressed a shudder. It was something between a centipede and a hedgehog. Some forty feet long, its cockroach-brown segmented body marched forward on a selection of disgusting, crablike pincers, and a ridge of shuddering black spines ran in a line down the center of its back. Emerging into the white-hot light of the ring, the hideous creature suddenly reared up on its hind legs, exposing a flat, disc-shaped head and two evil yellow eyes. Its mouth, a mass of dripping mandibles, hinged open to let out a terrible gurgling hiss. The creature eyed its opponents, then shook itself contemptuously, as if shrugging them all off.

"Ah, the Sloat," said the Emperor, chewing luxuriously. "I think we're going to see great things from him."

Sixth gladiator, boomed Gukumat's announcing voice: *a longtime supplicant, first-time entrant, give a warm demon welcome to . . . INANNA TWELVE-SWORDS!*

The rest of the audience fell quiet, content to gaze curiously as the big blue swordswoman strode into the ring—but the section of the auditorium where the uncalled gladiators were sitting erupted with cheers. Charlie watched the newest entrant. The dark blue, leather-clad figure was well built, muscular, and bristling with weaponry, but to his eyes she didn't look like much, not next to more imposing contestants like Gladrash, Svatog, or the Sloat.

"Remember what I said, Gukumat," said the Emperor, in an uneasy tone that made Charlie turn and look at him. "No surprise results."

Do not disturb yourself, Majesty. Lord Slint has been alerted to your feelings on this matter. It has all been taken care of.

"Good." The Emperor and the Overminister exchanged a look, then, still grinning widely, Hacha'Fravashi turned to look at Charlie. "I've another surprise for you," he said.

"Yeah?"

"A new acquisition for the gladiator pits," said the Emperor airily, though the golden slits of his eyes never left Charlie's for an instant. "She arrived yesterday. Another acquaintance of yours."

"Acquaintance?" echoed Charlie.

Still grinning, the Emperor settled back in his seat. Raising one immaculately suited arm, he pointed at the ring. Charlie looked—and his eyes went wide.

Seventh and final gladiator, boomed the voice, *a surprise late entry! Newly arrived from the as-yet-unclaimed planet of Earth, and perhaps the best opposition that world has to offer, show your appreciation for Miss ESME LEVERTON!*

FAVORS

Jack's mouth fell open.

It was her. His head filled with questions like, How did she open the Fracture? What was she doing there? Had she come to rescue them? But as he watched her walking out calmly onto the white sand of the arena floor in her red top with the hood up, the main thing Jack thought was—

Oh no.

Suddenly, he realized that everyone was looking at him. He had said the words aloud.

"Friendayours?" belched Jagmat, nudging him. The eyes— and other organs of attention—of the entire row seemed to swing round and focus on Jack as they waited for his answer. Jack felt the blood climbing up his neck and into his face.

"Yeah," he managed.

"Well, no offense, mate," said Jagmat, "but I hope she's better than you."

"She came," said the Scourge.

"Surprised?" said the Emperor.

"Yes," said Charlie, fighting to keep his expression blank. "Yes I am. Has she . . . said what she wants?"

"I'll be hearing her request officially in a moment," said the Emperor. He smiled. "But I think you already know what it is."

"She's come for us," said Charlie.

The Emperor's smile only widened.

"She will have to survive the Akachash first," said the Scourge.

As referee for this fight, said Gukumat, *O loyal subjects, we present to you none other than the keeper of the pits himself: the Clashing Jaws, the Potentate of Pain, the Undisputed Master of the Ring . . . LORD SLINT!*

A hatch screwed open in the wall just below the royal box, and the great shape of the flying shark emerged into view, blotting out half the scene below. With a single lazy swish of his horribly scarred tail, Lord Slint propelled himself down through the air toward the ecstatic crowds. As the seven gladiators waited, with varying degrees of self-restraint, the shark made three wide, lazy circuits over the audience, provoking a Mexican wave effect as he did so.

Svatog, Gladrash, and Gunch, Gukumat went on, *your requests are already known to the Emperor. Tunku: you do not wish your request known unless you win. As for you other three,*

His Highness the Emperor will now hear your supplications. Fifth gladiator, what is your boon?

The Sloat gave a great shudder. Rearing up on its hind legs once more, its disgusting brown jaws hinged open, its unspeakable poison-tipped mandibles mashing together as it ground out a single word: "FLESH."

A thrill shook through the crowd.

Inanna Twelve-Swords, state your request. Briefly, *please*, the voice added as Inanna strode forward, her great black-leather-clad torso bulging as she took a deep breath before she spoke.

"Demons of Hell," she shouted, "I have waited a long time for my chance in this ring, and this is the favor that I ask. I come from a far corner of the Demon Empire, a world called Bethesda. We are a peaceful people. A hardworking people. But the tithes and taxes we have been forced to pay lately are more than we can bear. Now, I'm going to give you," she went on, raking the other gladiators with a piercing glare, "a display of fighting you have never seen. And in return, I ask only that the Emperor and his Overminister relax the *grossly* unfair—"

Thank you, sixth gladiator.

"—and cruel demands they have—"

Thank *you*, *sixth gladiator*, the voice repeated, losing patience.

"—seen fit to inflict on a planet that never did them any harm!"

That will be all!

"MY PEOPLE ARE STARVING!" boomed Inanna in a voice that echoed round the great stadium even despite the booing and jeering of the crowd. "ALL I WANT IS THAT YOU PUT RIGHT WHAT YOU HAVE DONE!"

Sixth gladiator, said the voice.

The sand of the arena floor went dark around Inanna as Lord Slint settled, gently, in the air just over her head. Big as she was, Inanna would go down the great shark's gullet in not much more than a single mouthful. Looking up, she fell silent and her face turned grim.

You will hold your peace, or the consequences will be swift and painful, Gukumat told her, in a voice that only she could hear. Inanna scowled for a moment, then nodded curtly.

Seventh gladiator, you may speak, said Gukumat, in his announcer's voice again.

All eyes in the ring turned to Esme.

Esme just stood there at first, staring up at the royal box.

Speak, Gukumat repeated. *The Emperor is listening.*

Never taking her eyes off the distant bulk of the royal box, Esme took a step forward. She pulled back her hood, opened her mouth, and, in a quiet voice that everyone there heard quite distinctly, said, "It doesn't have to be this way."

In the royal box, the Emperor smiled. Then he got out of his seat.

Sire, Gukumat muttered, *keep back from the window. It's not safe!*

But the Emperor had already brushed the Overminister aside. He walked straight up to the great sandy sill and spread out his hands on it luxuriously. He leaned out into the open air and replied, "Oh yes? And why is that?"

Now the silence in the arena was intense. To the absolute and certain knowledge of every demon there present, the Emperor had never answered a gladiator directly in this way. Never.

"You could just give me what I want," said Esme.

"Which is what again? Remind me."

"The Scourge," said Esme, the steel in her voice sending a cold chill down Charlie's back. "Let me fight the Scourge."

A buzz of fevered speculation spread round the audience, quelling itself quickly when the Emperor opened his mouth to answer.

"I *shall* let you fight the Scourge," he said grandly. "*If* you win."

"I have no quarrel with you or these others here," said Esme, casting a glance around the ring at the six other gladiators. The Sloat rippled its legs listlessly, but the other, more experienced fighters did not react. "But for them, and for you, this is the last chance. Give me the Scourge."

In the rows around the royal box, a bit of guffawing and tittering broke out among the more aristocratic demons.

"I told you," said the Emperor, pretending to be surprised. "*If* you win!"

"Then everyone in this ring," said Esme simply, "is going to die."

For a moment, there was shocked silence.

Then, suddenly, the whole arena was laughing. Svatog even

joined in, the great foghorn grunts of his glee bouncing off the great black walls and echoing round the pit.

Esme's expression didn't change in the slightest—and the Emperor, despite himself, found his own smile beginning to fade.

"We'll see." He spun on his heel and went back to his royal seat. "She has courage, I'll give her that," he said, frowning as he settled himself. "Gukumat, I grow weary of preliminaries. Let's get this under way."

With pleasure, Your Magnificence, Gukumat replied with a bow.

GLADIATORS, his voice boomed in the heads of everyone present, *TAKE YOUR POSITIONS!*

Every demon in the audience began to stamp the ground in time. The rhythm was slow, unhurried, and merciless at first.

Crash. Crash. CRASH-CRASH-CRASH!

Crash. Crash. CRASH-CRASH-CRASH!

But it quickly got louder and faster, reaching an ecstasy of noise and thunder, and now, suddenly, the whole crowd was up for it, ready for the blood, ready for the carnage, ready to scream and howl and roar their guts out at the terrible battle that was about to take place on the shining white sand of the arena floor below. The noise of the crowd was like a solid thing, pressing on Jack until he was dizzy with it.

And, said Gukumat, pausing fractionally.

BEGIN!

THE FIGHT

As soon as the command was given, the cheering died away to an excited murmur.

Esme unstrapped the pigeon sword from her back: now she held it by her hip, in her left hand, her fingers loosely encircling the top of the dark wooden scabbard. She let her right hand fall easily to her side again: she bounced a couple of jogging steps on the spot, to ease a little of the tension in her legs—then she was ready.

Ninety-nine times out of a hundred, Raymond had always told her, *a fight'll be decided in the first few seconds.*

Esme glanced round the ring. Her attention was caught by Inanna, the tall blue woman: for a moment, they looked at each other—then Esme let her eyes flick onward as she waited to see which of her opponents was going to make the first move.

It didn't take much longer to find out.

To the delight of the crowd, Svatog the Canceler—standing some twelve yards off to Esme's right—was the first to lose his patience. With a heave of his arms, he lifted both his feet off the ground and *slammed* them down, hard enough to make the earth tremble under Esme's trainers. Turning toward Esme and flinging his arms wide (the gleaming steel claws sprang out to either side), he pushed out his great black chest—

—and screamed.

The sound was incredible. Like the blast of a steam engine, the acrid gust of his roar blew out at Esme with the force of a thirty-mile-an-hour wind. His squinty eyes bulged with rage and the roar continued, on and on, until it seemed it would never stop. Svatog's smoking hooves smacked into the ground, a step toward Esme, and another step. The crowd roared with him, waiting for blood, waiting to see the small human girl torn to shreds whenever Svatog chose to bring those clawed arms of his together.

Esme stood still.

Jack, frozen in his seat by helpless horror, glimpsed a blur of movement.

A glint of something flashing in the light.

Then, suddenly, the scream stopped.

The audience too fell silent. Why had Svatog gone quiet? Why was he just standing there like that? And *why* did the girl now have her *back* to him?

For a long, slow moment, nothing happened. Then, with a terrible, echoing hiss, something burst. The sand at Svatog's feet turned suddenly black. The eighteen-foot-tall demon sank to his knees, then fell on his face—hitting the arena floor with a ringing *smack*.

"What?" said Jack.

"Holy crap!" belched Jagmat.

One gladiator down, five to go.

The crowd erupted.

Esme just stood there, with the pigeon sword out in front of her. Outwardly she was perfectly composed—but inwardly her highly trained fighter's mind was working at full speed, alert to every detail of what would happen next.

Because then the battle really began.

Without warning, drawing one of her own curved swords, Inanna leaped sideways—and struck. For a second, as the wide blade bit into the fluttering black of his cloak, it looked like the bout was already all over for Inanna's neighbor, Ripitith Gunch.

But something strange was happening. The fourth gladiator's cloak was moving, shifting—changing. For one more long second, his narrow face seemed to hang in the air, his cruel mouth opening in a hideous grin.

Then the place where he'd been standing simply burst apart, into a boiling, tearing, chittering brown cloud of . . .

What?

Screaming with frustration, Inanna threw one of her arms up to cover her face as a swarm of locusts suddenly engulfed her. The swarm blasted past her in a tornado of beige insectile wings that seethed in the air and left a long black shadow on the arena floor, as her opponent—transfigured—sped out of her reach.

Meanwhile, with a bellowing scream, Gladrash the Blunt set off on a galloping circuit of the ring. The giant cow had not yet reached top speed by the time she reached Esme, but the thundering hooves would certainly have squashed her flat if she hadn't been watching. A leap, straight up into the air, tucking her legs under her into a smooth flip—and Gladrash's charge passed through empty space. Still, the giant cow kept on, kicking up dust, thundering toward her next opponent—Inanna.

The Sloat's legs gave a convulsive ripple, and it advanced away from the shadows at the arena's edge. Hissing nastily and grinning through its mandibles, it brought its face low onto the blinding white of the sandy floor, arching its long body up and over behind its head. The ridge of foot-long spines along its back began to quiver. As Esme dropped to her feet, the Sloat took a deep breath that made the membranous sacs on either side of its mouth bulge with effort—

—and it fired the spines straight at Esme.

Ripitith Gunch, rematerializing in the center of his cloud of locusts just behind Esme, with his long knife drawn and ready, transfigured himself back again suddenly as he realized his surprise attack was mistimed. As a flock of bats this time, he poured, shrieking, across the ring again, but not before several of his flock had been brought down, caught in midair, to expire, convulsing on the sand as the poison of the Sloat's stings worked its own awful magic. Gunch took himself in his bat-flock form to the far end of the ring, gathering the elements of himself into a shivering black column before he rematerialized fully. He looked down. There were three or four gaping holes in his cloak. He tutted and tossed the frayed edge of the cloak over one shoulder. Then, suddenly, he stiffened. His eyes bulged. His cold blood seemed to thicken and congeal in his veins. For a second more, he stood there shuddering—then he too fell facedown dead on the sand.

Two down, four to go. The crowd was in raptures. Tunku the Snool showed no reaction at all. The long, thin tentacle that had touched the transfiguration master on the back of the neck retracted up toward the floating watery sac of Tunku's jellyfish body, its poison exhausted. But there were plenty more where that one came from. Tunku the Snool sank back into the shadows, waiting.

And meanwhile, Esme was fighting for her life.

The Sloat's volley of poison-tipped spines was spread too wide: there had been no time to jump or dodge. Dropping the scabbard, Esme had taken the pigeon sword in both hands and—with a speed born of instinct as much as her years of training—she was knocking the spines away out of the air. The pigeon sword flickered in her hands. The air in front of her was a silvery blur, and the stings were clattering against the massive stone slabs to either side of the ring. But they were coming too fast, even for her.

Esme stepped back and, with a desperate outward blow of the pigeon sword, caught a low incoming spine and turned it aside. But now the sword was too far away from her body to catch the next one in time. She dropped flat onto her back. Twisting, she brought her right foot up for a kick that caught the last spine in midair, smacking it away.

But then, with a dreadful hiss, the Sloat charged.

Its dripping mandibles clashed shut in a blow that would have severed both Esme's legs at the thigh if she hadn't been fast enough: at the last possible moment, she flipped backward and up onto her feet, bringing her sword up in front of her with a desperate lurch. Confronted by the flashing blade, the Sloat reared up, hissing, giving Esme the precious seconds she needed to back out of striking distance.

Esme cursed herself inwardly. She'd been lucky: concentrating on an opponent's attack rather than the opponent was an amateur's mistake. Now too there were just too many factors, too many thoughts tearing at her concentration, demanding attention. She was watching the Sloat—but what about the other gladiators? She could track Gladrash by the sound of her hooves: the giant cow creature was making wild circuits of the ring, charging at whoever or whatever was in her way. But as to where any of Esme's other opponents were, why, one could be right *behind*—

Hold on: she'd had an idea. The corners of Esme's mouth twitched and lifted in the tiniest ghost of a smile. Then she attacked.

The gleaming blade of the pigeon sword hissed in the air. The Sloat ducked its broad, flat head, and Esme's stinging cross-body slash passed it harmlessly—millimeters from contact. Surprised, the foul beast danced back, its legs rippling. Holding the pigeon sword's long grip near the pommel for extra extension, Esme swung again, slashing downward. The Sloat counterattacked, snapping out at Esme's legs with its pincers—but they closed on nothing. Esme had sprung into another tight roll in the air, forward this time, whipping her feet round until they landed—

—hard—

—down on the top of the Sloat's head, driving it into the ground with a two-footed stomp that had her full weight behind it.

There was a gratifyingly nasty popping sound. The crowd roared its approval. Esme jumped clear, and both combatants staggered back from each other.

The Sloat backed away dazedly. One of its great mandibles was hanging off by a grisly flap.

Esme straightened up, breathing hard. The last move had taken a lot out of her, and she could see that while she'd wounded the Sloat, it wasn't seriously weakened. All she'd really done was annoy it. However, it was now quite close to the ring's edge—its hindquarters were plunged in shadow, some three yards from the black stone wall. It might be enough.

Suddenly, in a frenzy, the Sloat lunged, driving its wounded head straight into Esme's body, knocking her flat on her back. With two ringing *thunk*s, the Sloat jabbed each of its front pincers into the sand on either side of her.

Esme was trapped.

The monstrous creature regarded her unblinkingly. Fat milky droplets of putrescent slime were dripping from its ruined mouth, sizzling and spitting as they hit the sand, and the broken mandible dangled horribly. Still, the Sloat *hissed*, a deep hiss of contentment and delight. It reared up, looked down at Esme one last time.

And it saw she was smiling.

The crowd was in a frenzy now—roaring, screaming,

baying, barking. But under that, suddenly, the Sloat could hear another sound. A rhythmic, walloping, thundering sound, getting closer and closer. Now the smile on the small human morsel's lips had widened into a vicious, wicked grin: the Sloat's insect brain lit up with a flash of realization—

And then, with a terrible bellow of joy, Gladrash struck.

The Sloat reared up as the giant cow trampled it, its whole body an explosion of pain. Esme flung herself to comparative safety, the horrible *smutch* as the great hooves hit home still echoing in her ears. The Sloat's armored sides simply burst, spreading the creature's innards in a wide, wet circle, staining the sand. The Sloat's head and forequarters, comparatively unscathed, plucked at the arena floor weakly as what remained of the creature tried to pull itself toward her, staring at her wildly. It knew: it *knew* she'd tricked it.

But Esme had already turned her back on it—and in another moment, it was dead.

Strike three.

Esme allowed herself a deep breath. Then she was taking in the situation.

The giant cow's eyes were wild and bloodshot, and she was definitely favoring her front hoof. Ignoring the howls of her fans in the crowd, Gladrash lowered her wide black head, bellowing, as she charged again—at Inanna this time.

Esme watched.

The big blue swordswoman stood her ground as the giant cow thundered closer and closer. At the last possible second—when it looked to Esme like Inanna might let

Gladrash trample her too—she leaped to one side, bringing the curved blade of her scimitar round and down in a crashing blow that sent the giant cow almost to her knees.

Gladrash staggered on past Inanna and ran straight into the arena wall beyond. Her supporters—a whole section of the audience—let out a short gasping sigh and sank to their seats in horror. Gladrash the Blunt tottered back from the wall, swinging round to face her opponent, shaking her horned head as if trying to clear it.

Then she froze and fell and lay still.

Strike four.

Scowling, Inanna turned, with her back now to the line of shadow at the arena's sides. That was when Esme saw Tunku the Snool. The jellyfish slid from the darkness, tentacles outstretched. Almost before Esme knew what she was doing, the pigeon sword was out of her hand. It flew across the ring—

—passed straight over Inanna's shoulder—

—and nailed the third gladiator to the sheer black stone of the arena wall.

For a second, the crowd fell silent. Tunku the Snool just hung there, spitted. Its tentacles quivered for a moment, then dropped.

Strike five.

Suddenly, the whole crowd was up out of its seats again, screaming and howling and crying with delight. No one could remember an Akachash as good as this. No one.

Looking carefully at Esme, Inanna walked slowly over to the arena's edge, only taking her eye off the girl for a moment when she reached up to yank the pigeon sword out of the wall. As, with a soft *splotch*, the jellyfish demon slid to the arena floor behind her, Inanna took the weapon and hefted it, testing its balance. In her hands, the pigeon sword was like a toy. Then, with a snapping motion of her wrist that was almost too fast to follow, Inanna flung the sword back at Esme.

Esme put up a hand, and the pigeon sword's hilt slapped into it effortlessly. Then, as the crowd fell expectantly silent again, the last two gladiators eyed each other.

"I don't want to fight you," said Esme.

Inanna gave her a pitying look, then—*SHINNNG!*—drew her other scimitar. Now both her hands held the huge, curved blades. Slowly, deliberately, she took a step toward Esme.

"I mean, you've got a good reason to be here too, right?" Esme looked away from Inanna and called up toward the royal box. "Give us both what we want. This finishes now!"

Of course, there was no answer.

Some of the crowd started jeering and booing.

"Get on with it!" someone bellowed.

Slowly, the audience started their stamping, rhythmic crashing noise again, the sound that Esme had heard just before the start of the fight.

Crash. Crash. CRASH-CRASH-CRASH!

Crash. Crash. CRASH-CRASH-CRASH!

Inanna flexed her wrists, letting her scimitars spin and twist around her. The wide, curved blades glimmered and flashed as she sped them up, letting them cross and recross in front of her, a glittering whirlwind of razor-edged steel. She took another step toward her opponent: only a few more and she would be in striking range.

Esme didn't move.

"What's wrong?" asked the Emperor, up in the royal box. "Why isn't she defending herself? What's she doing?"

No one answered.

"Gukumat, if Inanna *wins*," the Emperor went on, his voice rising to an anxious whine, "I will be most displeased. Do you understand?"

The crashing got louder as the audience settled themselves back in their seats contentedly. What was coming next ought to be pretty good.

Jack, alone in the noise of the crowd, felt sick.

Wearily, grimly, Esme brought the pigeon sword up to a ready position. She sighed.

"All right, then," she said.

Inanna didn't answer, just lunged.

And in less than two seconds—

—two blurring, *lurching* seconds—

—it was over.

"I'm sorry," said Esme quietly.

Inanna froze, and the audience's rhythmic thumping died away in confusion as they saw her swords drop from her hands. She looked down from her opponent to the wound that had appeared down the length of her chest—a long, diagonal slash that stretched from her left shoulder down to her right hip. Then, still disbelieving, she looked back up at the girl who had just defeated her.

Inanna had waited a long time for her chance in the ring—her chance to ask the Emperor's favor. Now both were gone, in three moves.

The first had been a simple step back—the girl had been more ready than Inanna had realized. The blow itself had come in the second move. Esme had timed her attack exquisitely, reading the pattern in the swirling blur of Inanna's swords and striking at the exact point when her foe was unprotected—pulling herself clear (the third move) before the whirling blades could close around her and do any damage. It was, Inanna had to admit, beautifully done—and, strangely, she was glad.

Entertainment—that's what the crowd had wanted. They'd wanted her and Esme to get into some long and complicated battle—maybe even bantering with each other a little while they fought, trading witty insults as well as injuries: that sort of thing would have gone down well, for sure. Well, she was happy not to have given them the satisfaction.

Inanna's great knees buckled under her, and her head went light.

"I'm sorry," said Esme again.

Inanna just smiled. Then she died.

For a long second, Esme looked down at her opponent. She sniffed and, still holding the pigeon sword lightly with one hand, wiped a long brown arm across her brow. Then she glared up at the royal box.

"There," she said. "Are you satisfied? Is *that*," she added, gesturing at Inanna's fallen body with the sword, "what you wanted?"

"Marvelous," said the Emperor, relief at the outcome only adding to his delight. "Quite marvelous." He turned to Charlie. "And what was it again, in comparison, that you said you had in *your* world?"

Charlie looked at him blankly.

"Ah yes," sneered the Emperor. "Football."

My lord . . . ? asked Overminister Gukumat quietly.

"Oh yes," said the Emperor. "I think so, don't you? Definitely."

Congratulations, Gladiator Esme, said the Overminister's announcing voice. *His Highness the Emperor Hacha'Fravashi salutes a well-fought bout and has indicated that he may, in this instance, grant you one boon. What is your favor to be?*

"Riches!" cawed a scrawny, alligatorlike creature in the audience, jumping up and down. "Riches! Riches!"

"I told you what I want," said Esme.

Say it again, gladiator, the voice murmured in her head. *The audience wants to hear you.*

"The Scourge!" said Esme, exasperated. "Bring me the Scourge!"

Gladiator Esme has stated her boon, Gukumat announced grandly. *In view of her spectacular performance—*

Some of the slower members of the audience, who had blinked or otherwise failed to catch the last part of the battle (which was most of them), let out a great and disappointed *boo* at this.

—and her status as undisputed champion of this Akachash,

His Excellency the Emperor, in his infinite generosity, has decided to accede to her request.

"**We shall have to face her, Charlie,**" said the Scourge, in a voice only Charlie could hear. "**I'm afraid I see no other choice. Are you ready?**"

"All right," said Charlie, taking a deep breath. "Yeah. Okay. We'll do it."

"No," said the Emperor, "you won't."

THE CHALLENGE

Loyal subjects, said the Overminister, once Inanna's body too had disappeared like the others, *it gives me great pleasure to announce that, while the Akachash itself is over, Miss Esme Leverton has been granted permission for one more, final battle.*

Esme, standing in the center of the ring now, was concentrating on preparing herself. She retrieved the pigeon sword's scabbard and slotted it home. She reached up and felt the elastic bands that were holding her hair back: they hadn't moved. She straightened her spine and squared her shoulders; she jogged a couple of bouncing steps on the spot. She was tired. But now she was ready.

Gladiator Esme has come to Hell with one single purpose in mind—to wreak her vengeance on the one who is about to step into the ring.

A delighted anticipatory murmur spread through the crowd. In the royal box, Charlie stood up; the Scourge did too—

—then vanished, bursting suddenly into a whirling haze of powder-black vapor, which gathered around Charlie like his own personal storm cloud. The Scourge settled on him, taking hold: instantly, the curving hooks and spikes of the black tattoo began to boil and wriggle under Charlie's skin.

Most loyal subjects, Gukumat intoned, *I present to you a demon whose very name is the stuff of legend. Put your appendages together, my brethren, for the Prince of Darkness! The Sultan of Sorrows! The Dragon's Awakener, returned at last— KHENTIMENTU THE SCOURGE!*

Charlie stepped up to the window of the royal box and dove off.

Liquid darkness unfurled about him like a pair of enormous black wings. As the crowd roared its approval, Charlie descended through the air with regal grace and landed in the center of the arena. The darkness billowed, gathering itself around him into a sizzling, rippling tornado of black, then evaporated.

"Hi, Esme," he said.

"Charlie," Esme replied.

"You shouldn't have come."

Esme's lip curled. "Really."

Charlie sighed. "Look," he said, "you don't understand. Me and the Scourge—we're partners now. And we've got things to do here, important things."

Esme shook her head. "I'm going to give you one more chance," she said, taking a deliberate step toward him. "If you've got any vestige of self-respect, any shred of guts or decency, then you'll take it."

"What?"

"Concentrate," said Esme. "You can force the demon out. Make it let go of you. If you want."

Charlie didn't answer.

"Partners," Esme echoed, exasperated. "Look around you! And what about the announcement just now? I didn't hear *your* name—did you? Just the Scourge's!" She took another step toward him. "Charlie, if you don't help me now, then that's the way it's always going to be. You're a puppet," she added. "Nothing more. Is that really what you want?"

"No," said Charlie, frowning.

"Well, then . . ."

Esme held out her hand.

Watching in the crowd, Jack held his breath.

"No," said Charlie again, his frown getting deeper.

Esme looked at him, waiting.

"**No**," the word came out of his mouth again, and the black liquid patterns boiled and slithered in the skin of his arms.

Esme let her hand fall to her side.

"No," said Charlie once more, quietly. He shook his head. "This is too important. And what we have, the Scourge and me—it's not how you think."

"Then I'm sorry," said Esme, "but that makes you my enemy."

Crash. Crash. CRASH-CRASH-CRASH!

Crash. Crash. CRASH-CRASH-CRASH!

The crowd stamped out their excitement. Jack stared at Charlie and Esme—stared down at the two figures until they shimmered in front of his smarting eyes against the blazing white of the arena floor. Again he was surrounded by the cocoon of noise: it pressed and pushed and battered at him as the demons around him howled out for blood.

But the command to begin never came.

"What is it?" he asked, turning to Jagmat, as the crowd noise died away confusedly. "What's going on?"

Jagmat shrugged—an impressive and slightly alarming sight. "It's a private duel," he belched. "There'll be terms."

"What?"

"See for yourself," said Jagmat, gesturing with a wet pink flipper.

For a second more, Charlie and Esme looked at each other. Then they both vanished.

This duel, Gukumat announced, to boos and wails from the audience, *will be held in private, and at a later date. And now, on with the show!*

And that, it appeared, was that.

"What's wrong, sir?" asked Jack's Chinj later as, grimly, Jack sipped at his dinner. "You seem a little preoccupied, if you don't mind my saying so."

"He's scared!" shrieked one of Shargle's heads delightedly, seizing the opportunity to spread some misery now that it had lost the evening's battle over which end of the worm got to do the eating and which the . . . other function. "What's gonna happen tomorrow, fresh meat?" it crowed. "Maybe you die nasty! Maybe you don't come back!"

Jack ignored the worm utterly.

"It's my friends," he admitted to the small bat creature. "I'm worried about them."

"The two other visitors?" said the Chinj. "Esme and Charlie?"

Jack almost choked on his mouthful. "Yes!" he said. "Do you know something? What's happened to them? Nobody here knows anything!" he added, nodding at the serried ranks of guzzling demons that surrounded him.

"Well, of course they don't," said the Chinj primly. "They're gladiators."

"But you do?"

The small creature gave a secretive smile. "Finish your gruel," it ordered, "or I'm not saying a word."

Obediently, Jack raised the bowl of still-steaming goo to his lips and took another gulp.

"Tonight," whispered the Chinj conspiratorially. "It's happening tonight! Isn't that exciting?"

Jack put down the bowl. The Chinj was staring at him with wide eyes.

"I mean, can you *imagine*, sir?" it asked. "A real grudge duel, outside of the pits! A fight to the death, in the Emperor's own chambers no less! I'd give anything to be there, wouldn't you? It'll be thrilling!" it added, with an ecstatic little shiver of its wings.

So, thought Jack, it was true, then. The last little hope that maybe they weren't going to fight, the last ridiculous chance he'd been clinging to, winked out inside him and died. Jack gave the Chinj a long look.

"My friends are going to kill each other," he said slowly. "*Thrilling* isn't really the word I'd use to describe it."

THE EMPEROR

Charlie lifted his arm, and living darkness poured down over his hands. His fingers vanished under the velvety warmth, closing together and extending—and now Charlie held in his hands an exact replica of the pigeon sword. The long, curved blade glinted in the light, its tip lining up between his eyes and his opponent's.

"All right," he said. "Let's do this."

Charlie and Esme were standing in the Emperor's throne room, facing each other along the narrow strip of bloodred carpet that led up to the throne itself. The great domed ceiling loomed above them. All around them, the rippling jelly stuff that made up the rest of the room's floor heaved and subsided like an oily sea. Past Esme, the Emperor was lolling on his throne, grinning. For a second, Charlie looked at him.

Esme was standing between him and the throne—literally. The only way to get to the Emperor—the only way to avenge Jack and carry out the Scourge's plan—was through her. Charlie didn't want to hurt her. He didn't want to kill her. But Esme had followed him here. She had got in his way. And now there was no choice.

Esme's amber eyes remained fixed on his, her expression neutral. She held the pigeon sword by its dark wooden scabbard in her left hand, loosely, up near the hilt; her right hand was stuck nonchalantly in the pocket of her combats.

"You haven't drawn your sword," Charlie pointed out.

"Full marks for observation," she replied.

Charlie sighed. "Look," he said. Already he was angry with her. "Do you want to do this or what?"

Instead of answering, Esme gestured at him with the pigeon sword's pommel.

"That thing in your hand," she said. "You ever used one before?"

"Esme," said Charlie wearily, "just draw your sword."

"You think you're a match for me?"

"Draw your sword!" Charlie repeated.

"Or what?" said Esme. "What do you think you're going to do?"

"Fine," said Charlie, running the hand that wasn't holding the sword through his hair angrily. "*Fine.*"

He set his feet a little apart, spreading his weight.

"Ready or not, then," he said, with a smile that showed his teeth, "here I come."

He took his sword in both hands, leaped into the air, and flew at her.

SHINNNG! *WHUD!*

Warding Charlie's blade off easily with her still-scabbarded sword, Esme had stepped toward him. Her whole body weight, therefore, plus whatever forward momentum Charlie had put into his attack, was concentrated in the heel of her right hand as it struck the point of Charlie's chin, palm open, hard. She'd hit him that way before—in exactly the same place, in fact—one of the very first times they'd fought.

Charlie's head snapped back. The force of the blow lifted him off his feet. He sailed a clear ten yards back through the air—and crashed, eyes wide with surprise and shock, on his back.

"You're an idiot, Charlie," she told him.

Still without drawing her weapon, Esme advanced on him. Her amber eyes flashed down at him fiercely.

Charlie got to his knees, then his feet, pointing his sword toward her, frowning uncertainly as she approached.

"I gave you a chance to start making up for what you've done," Esme said. "You rejected it. If it wasn't for that, I might almost be feeling sorry for you right now. As it is, I'm just sick of the sight of you. You're an *amateur*," she spat, knocking his blade almost out of his hand with the still-scabbarded pigeon sword. "An *accident*," she added, dealing Charlie's blade another smacking blow. "And this—"

SHANG!

"—has gone on—"

SHING!

"—long *enough*."

Charlie was holding his sword high up in front of his chest, expecting her to hit it again. He was completely unable to defend himself, then, when Esme took her sword by its grip and lunged, low and hard.

The steel-capped tip of the pigeon sword's scabbard crashed into his stomach. Doubled up around her blow, Charlie flew back again, the breath driven out of him in a long and undignified gasp. When he next looked up at her, he was grimacing with pain.

The black tattoo—its curves, its hooks, its spikes—was spreading under his skin, pouring down his arms like oil, running up into his face.

"When you're ready," Esme told him.

Bristling with rage, Charlie got up and started toward her.

Esme's thoughts went something like this.

All she needed, she knew, was an opening, a chance to strike at Charlie before the Scourge could take over and protect him. To get it, she planned to needle Charlie, probing mercilessly at his swollen pride until she provoked him into an error big enough to give her the opportunity she wanted. Then she would take her chance and . . .

And what? Kill him?

Esme frowned, not moving, as she watched him getting closer and closer.

The only way to get at the Scourge, she told herself—the only way to do what she'd spent her whole life training to do—was through the boy. She knew this. And the boy was an idiot. He was stupid and selfish and seemingly entirely lacking in self-control.

But—and this was the problem, now that it came down to it—did being an idiot mean that Charlie deserved to *die*?

Suddenly, when he was still outside normal striking

distance, Charlie made a snapping motion with the wrist of his right hand and flung something at her.

It wasn't the sword—at least, not anymore. In the fractions of a second that it took to cross the space between them, the weapon in Charlie's hand had somehow lost its shape, the glinting steel vanishing and stretching and liquifying. Whatever it was now, it was long and black, and it hissed through the air with something like eagerness. Esme stepped smoothly aside, expecting the weapon to pass her, but it turned to follow her—

—and caught round her neck! It wrapped right round her throat, then constricted, its coils tightening and crushing inward round her neck like a snake's coils on its prey. Excruciating pain flashed and fizzed through her whole body like a thousand-volt dose of electricity. Instantly, Esme drew the pigeon sword and severed the whatever-it-was just inches in front of her chin. Dropping the scabbard, she reached up with her left hand, grabbed the wriggling black tentacle thing that still clung to her neck, and flung it away. Spreading her arms, she leaped backward, out of Charlie's reach.

Something was wrong with the places where the weapon had touched her—badly wrong. The skin of her neck when she felt it had that deadened, bulbous feeling that comes just before blistering. Where she'd touched it, her fingers were numb, cold, as if they were frostbitten. Holding the pigeon sword up in front of her, she stepped back, stepped back from Charlie for the first time—and stared.

Leaving no mark, the ink-black severed part of the weapon

slid across the carpet in a liquid blob. Just before reaching Charlie it transformed, becoming a strange kind of ferretlike creature, scampering back up Charlie's leg before vanishing into the blackness that now bulged and rippled all over his body.

Charlie smiled.

"Cute," said Esme, through her teeth. "Very cute."

Still smiling, a smile that was horrible with the way the tattoo was now swarming up into his face, Charlie started to walk toward her again.

"That's quite some toy you've got there," Esme told him. "Something the Scourge gave you, maybe? Like it knew you couldn't do anything to me with an actual *sword*?"

Charlie shook his head as if to clear it but kept walking.

Well, there was no way she could risk another blow like that. So, no mercy, then. No more games.

Without any further warning, she attacked.

With an echoing *crack*, Charlie found himself parrying a sizzling slash that—if he had stopped to think instead of instinctively lifting one demon-reinforced arm to block it— would certainly have ended the fight there and then.

Esme frowned.

CHING! CHING! CHING! CHING! CHING!

Esme launched a stinging succession of lightning blows, but Charlie's reinforced arms seemed to move by themselves as they caught and blocked them.

She feinted and spun, shaping for a wide cross-body slash but suddenly converting it into a roundhouse kick that struck

Charlie hard in the ribs. He staggered back. But not as far as she'd hoped. He was protected, shielded—*armored* somehow—by the same liquid stuff as his weapons.

So Esme did the feinting kick.

She began the move in textbook style, leaping off her left foot into a spinning midkick with her right. With utter predictability, Charlie lowered his hands to protect himself, at which point Esme folded her right leg into a further 180-degree spin, letting her left foot scythe up over Charlie's guard, striking him in the face.

Bingo. Charlie flew back a good ten feet—

—twenty—

—and smacked into the nearest wall. He sank to his haunches, propped there, his head lolling. There. Now, before things got any worse, it was time to finish it.

Esme leaped, flinging herself through the air toward her enemy. She let out a scream, raising her sword over her head with both hands as the bloodred strip of the throne room floor slid past underneath her. She brought the pigeon sword out and down, concentrating all her speed and strength into the two feet eight inches of hissing steel and the enemy that would die at its edge.

The curves and hooks of the black tattoo seemed to bunch in Charlie's face. Charlie's still-open eyes rolled up in his head, showing only the whites. Charlie's hands came up. The palms slapped together.

And the blow stopped, two inches short.

He had caught her blade between his hands.

"**There,**" said the Scourge, through Charlie's mouth. Eyes filled with darkness locked on Esme's. "**That's enough.**"

Charlie's body swung upright, the steely grip on the sword never loosening for a moment. The pigeon sword's point was now just an inch from Charlie's right eye, but Esme found herself forced to step back or lose her grip on her weapon completely.

"**Again,**" said the demon inside him, "**it comes down to this.**"

Esme gave an extra wrench on the pigeon sword. The blade was pressed flat between his palms with a superhuman strength. Apart from flexing the sword slightly, her efforts had no effect whatsoever. Esme pulled and twisted as hard as she could, but the sword might as well have been trapped in stone.

"**Give the weapon to me,**" the Scourge told her.

"No!"

"**Give it to me,**" said the demon quietly. "**Now.**"

"Never!"

The air between them began to flare and smoke as the demon's magic coursed out and around her—a bulging, crackling field of power. Her hands were still clasped around the pigeon sword's hilt, clinging desperately to Raymond's last gift to her, but the air around her was closing in, clamping down all around at her. Suddenly, she felt her feet lifting off the ground. She felt her grip beginning to weaken, her strength giving out, and then, horribly, it was over. Her fingers left the sword. Now she was flying through the air, flung back and upward by the Scourge's power from one side of the throne room to the other, and in the long slow moment, the moment before she hit the opposite wall, she realized what it was that had defeated her.

Herself.

WHAM!

The impact stunned her. She slid to the ground, her legs folding under her, and the world turned black in front of her eyes.

There was a sound in her head like the sea, whispering in her ears. For a whole second she felt like drifting away on it. But she shook her head, hard. Tasting blood in her mouth, warm and coppery, she opened her eyes, and looked up.

"You are beaten," said the Scourge, through Charlie's mouth. The demon was standing over her. The pigeon sword was at her throat.

"And you know how," it told her. "You know how, in fact, every time you fight me, you're going to lose. Look," it said, making a small gesture in the air with the hand that wasn't holding the sword. "Look at yourself."

Esme didn't want to. She knew what she'd see. But she looked. And she saw.

There was a pool of darkness, quivering, under the skin of her palms. In another second, it was moving, spreading: the long, graceful curves and the scalpel-point hooks were already beginning to form.

"You're *marked*, Esme," said the Scourge. "You've always been marked. You just never knew yourself before."

The black tattoo was swarming up her arms. She could feel

it under her skin, all over her body. It had been waiting inside her all her life, and now she could feel it moving.

There's something a bit special about you, echoed Raymond's voice in her head.

You're not human! echoed another.

It's already too late for her, echoed the Scourge's. *It's always been too late for her. Just ask Felix.*

"No," she whispered.

"There," said the Scourge, watching her reaction. "I believe you're beginning to understand."

Esme stared up at the thing behind the boy's face, stared up at it helplessly.

"All your power," the Scourge told her, "your speed, your flying, your strength—all of it comes from *me.*"

The demon regarded her carefully.

"You are fighting yourself," it said. "How can you expect to win," it asked, and there was an odd note of kindness in its voice, "if you are fighting yourself?"

Esme lay there in Charlie's shadow. Her mind was swarming with darkness: her whole body felt *thick* with it, so that she could hardly breathe. She could recognize the power of the demon inside her. And for the first time, in perhaps the whole of her life, she began to be scared.

"The night you were conceived, I could have made my escape," said the Scourge. The point of the pigeon sword rested on the carpet now, with Charlie's hands on the pommel. The demon spoke slowly, taking its time. "Felix had released me, and in return I had granted him his wish of that one night with your mother. At long last, I was free to do as I pleased. But instead . . ." It paused. "I stayed."

Esme stared up wordlessly.

"For nine months I waited," the Scourge went on. "And even after you were born I remained. Watching you through his eyes. Seeing you grow. Wondering about what you might become. Why do you think that was? I'll tell you." The demon leaned over her.

"I stayed because I could not help myself." The eyes stared down at hers.

"My child," it whispered.

Esme felt the dark inside her quicken at the words—and shuddered.

"You've ruined my life," she said softly, almost disbelievingly. "Before I was even born, you ruined my life."

The boy with the demon inside him, the great dome of the throne room beyond him—all of it was turning blurry and dark.

Remember your mother. . . .

"But I swear," she said, "I'll make you pay for what you've done."

She stared up at the demon, her amber eyes flashing fiercely.

"I'll have my revenge," she hissed. "I *will* have my revenge. I *swear* it."

Her breath choked in her throat.

She fell back.

And for Esme, everything went black.

"Bravo!" said a voice, and the throne room resounded with slow, ironic handclaps. "Bravo!" said the Emperor again.

With regal slowness, he stood up from his throne.

"That went even better than I'd hoped!" he said. "The battle. The great revelation. Truly, that was all most amusing. But now, I think, it's time to proceed to more important matters." He waved one cloven red hand, and his Overminister shimmered into view beside him. "Gukumat?"

Sire?

"Bring the boy. You know, the other one. Let's have all three of these tiresome earthlings in one place. It's time to get this whole thing wrapped up."

At your command, Sire.

The air in front of the throne seemed to bulge for a moment—then Jack appeared.

For a second, as the jelly stuff slithered off him and slipped over the sides of the carpet to join the rest of the pool, Jack just stared at Esme's limp body. Then he ran to her and knelt by her side.

"You've killed her," he said, looking up at Charlie.

The Scourge made Charlie's head swivel toward Jack. It looked at him.

"**No**," it said, "**I have not. And this state she is in now is not of my doing. Believe me**," it added, "**I have no wish to harm her.**"

"Khentimentu," the Emperor interrupted. "Let's start with you."

Charlie's head swiveled to face the throne.

"I've let you have your fun for long enough," the Emperor announced. "It's time to add this girl's powers—and yours—to my own. Gukumat?" he added. "Put Miss Leverton into the pool."

There was a pause.

"*What?*" said Jack.

"**I can't let you do that,**" said the Scourge.

"Come, come, Khentimentu," said the Emperor, smiling again. "You didn't seriously think I'd allow you to run around Hell making plans behind my back, did you?"

He gestured at Esme.

"You and that girl are connected by a special bond, as you've just proved. By adding her essence to my collection," he went on, indicating the slowly rippling pool of jellylike matter that rose and fell all around them, "I will take your powers and add them to my own, just as I have with any other demon who poses a threat to me, and any gladiator who showed any promise." He smiled.

"Hold on," said Jack. "You mean *that's* where the jelly stuff comes from? It's all"—he grimaced, staring around at the oily liquid, hardly believing it—"*dead demons*?"

"Even in death, my subjects continue to serve me," said the Emperor, his golden eyes glinting. "Oh." He frowned, pointing at Jack. "Except for *you*, of course. You're no use to anyone, alive or dead, quite frankly."

Jack blinked.

"**Your powers are a sham, Hacha'Fravashi,**" said the Scourge, squaring Charlie's shoulders. "**You are weak and decadent, and you do not have the strength to stop me from fulfilling my destiny.**"

"Which is what again?" asked the Emperor, raising his eyebrows. "Remind me."

"**I will awaken the Dragon,**" said the Scourge. "**Its breath will be destruction. Its fury will cleanse the firmament. Its gaping jaws will swallow us, every one, and at last all Creation shall—**"

"Oh yes," said the Emperor, pretending to stifle a yawn. "Boring."

Then he struck.

His handsome face sharpened into a scowl of pure rage, and his right arm flashed across his chest in a vicious backhand slap. At the same moment, a kind of undersea explosion lit up the surface of the throne room floor, and something like a ripple in the air passed between the Emperor and his victims. Though they were twenty feet apart, Charlie's body suddenly bent double, as if something large and heavy had smashed into his midriff. Flung back across the throne room, he hit the wall again, a full thirty feet up off the ground this time. Then he slid to the floor in a helpless heap and lay there, unconscious once more.

Jack just gaped.

Standing where Charlie had been was a man-shaped blob of blackness. The Scourge sank to the floor, shuddering with pain, looking at itself as if in sheer disbelief at what had just happened.

With a single blow, the Emperor had completely separated the Scourge from its host body.

"There," said the Emperor, lifting into the air. He floated smoothly over and touched down on the carpet in front of the Scourge. "Perhaps now you'll realize how much trouble you're really in." He looked down at the demon at his feet. "How's it feel," he asked, "being forced outside your vessel? I imagine you must be feeling a bit . . . exposed. Defenseless, even."

On the word *defenseless*, the Emperor leaned over the Scourge, staring down hard, his golden eyes livid with super-human concentration. The jelly stuff around him lit up again—and suddenly the Scourge was writhing in soundless, convulsive agony. The Scourge lost its man shape, turning into nothing more than a splatter of black, jerking and flapping on the carpet in front of the Emperor's spotless white shoes. Just as suddenly, the Emperor stopped what he was doing and stood upright again.

"Gukumat, did you hear me or not?" he snapped. "Put the girl into the pool!"

Obediently, Gukumat floated over, reaching toward Esme with long, elegant fingers.

"No!" said Jack, his voice coming out in a kind of squeak. "I mean, leave her alone!" he added, as gruffly as he could manage.

Now everyone in the room was looking at him.

"Yes," said the Emperor, regarding Jack with obvious dis-taste. "I suppose we'll have to do something about you too. Lord Slint!" he called, looking round. "Where *is* he? Ah, there you are. If you'd be so kind . . ." He gestured vaguely in Jack's direction.

Jack turned, just as the giant flying shark slithered in through the throne room's double doors. He caught a pinkish-gray glimpse of a widening mouth.

"Oh, *shi*—" Jack just had time to say as he was lifted off the ground.

And then, with a great sweep of his tail, Lord Slint swam away through the air, powering his way up toward the vaults of the throne room's roof, where he could devour his freshly plucked morsel in peace. Jack hadn't even had time to scream.

In the shadows over by the wall, Charlie stirred. Across the throne room, the Emperor and the Scourge faced each other.

"Now," said the Emperor. "Time to have some *real* fun." And he lashed out with his power again.

The world spun crazily. The walls of the throne room slid past at hideous speed—but Jack's thoughts, strangely, were quite clear.

The shark hadn't bitten him seriously yet: for the time being, it was only carrying him, but Jack wasn't really thinking about that. What he was thinking, in between things like *AAAARGH!* and *SHARK!*, went something like this:

How come *he* didn't get to have superpowers that made him be able to do cool things?

How come *he* didn't get to face his enemies on equal terms? Or have sword fights or do kung fu?

And this! said his brain, with mounting indignation. Look at this latest situation! He'd thought having to go to Hell was bad. Getting bitten by a giant spider—well, at the time, that had seemed about as low as you could get. But oh no, *his* luck had to go one better, didn't it?

This whole situation, Jack was deciding—not just this latest development but pretty much everything, stretching back in an unbroken line for what seemed like most of his life— was infuriatingly, excruciatingly, incandescent-apoplexy-inducingly UNFAIR.

What this was, Jack decided, what this whole situation *was*, really, when you came down to it, he thought, the realization hitting him with almost as much force as the shark had—

—was *typical*.

Jack's mind lit up with a freezing-white blast of clarity.

And now, suddenly, he was angry. Very angry indeed.

In his hand, much to his astonishment, was his knife. He must have got it out before the shark had grabbed him. His arm was free, trailing below the giant flying shark's lower jaw. So Jack reached up with the knife—and he struck.

The first blow almost jarred the knife's handle from his grasp as it hit Lord Slint's hard snout. Jack took a stronger grip.

"NO!" he shouted as he stabbed down again.

"NO. NO. NO!" he shouted, stabbing down on each word, oblivious to the soft *thunk*s of the puncturing sounds echoing in his ears.

"I'm NOT!" he yelled.

"GETTING!"

"BLOODY!"

"KILLED!"

"AGAIN!"

On the last stab, Jack heard a soft and unforgettably revolting *smutch* as his knife hit home. Then several surprising things happened at once.

Lord Slint's gray-pink mouth hinged open in a grimace of sudden and terrible agony. He stopped swimming. His marblelike eyes rolled back in his head.

And slowly, but with gathering speed, Jack and the giant shark demon began to fall.

"Oh no," said Jack, feeling gravity take hold.

"Oh *no!*" he repeated with feeling, as he kicked himself loose from the shark's vile mouth.

And then, suddenly, they landed.

"It is *you* who are weak," the Emperor had been saying. "*You* who are overconfident." On each "you" he flashed his power out again, making the Scourge jerk helplessly where it lay.

"Now . . ." He paused, raising his hands for the killer blow. "Now it's game over."

Then he froze.

Wham! With a sudden and stunning impact, Jack struck the soft carpet—just a few scant inches from the jelly stuff.

Ker-*splash!*

Lord Slint, in comparison, wasn't so lucky.

Whether the giant flying shark was alive or dead before he hit the pool, it's hard to say. Lord Slint did not have time to struggle or fight before the seething jelly stuff picked him clean. In another second, even his great skeleton was gone, and there was nothing left of his carcass but an evaporating stain on the surface. But Jack wasn't looking at that.

"*Huk,*" said the Emperor—and stood there rigid, his golden eyes bulging out with shock.

There was a long, slow moment of silence in the room.

The Emperor had been poised to destroy the Scourge—poised to wreak final destruction on this mythical creature and add its powers to his own—when, quite by accident, he'd been distracted. As the small gladiator—this "Jack"—had fallen from the roof, followed by Lord Slint, the Emperor had paused in what he'd been doing, to watch. In that moment, while his attention was elsewhere, something extraordinary had happened.

Ebisu Eller-Kong Hacha'Fravashi, Suzerain Absolute of the Dominions of Hell, looked down at his chest. Specifically, he looked down at the long spike of cold steel that had suddenly appeared there. Already the area around the wound was filling up with blood, a spreading stain of bright red, made brighter still by the shining whiteness of the suit he was wearing.

"What?" asked the Emperor. "How . . . ?"

In answer, Charlie put his head up from behind the Emperor's shoulder, clenched his neck in the crook of his arm to get a better grip—

—then rammed the pigeon sword home, further still.

"YES," hissed the Scourge, rising up weakly from the floor.

"*No!*" gasped Jack, watching from where he'd landed. What Jack saw on Charlie's face at that moment appalled and horrified him. This time, unlike before, there was no sign of the black tattoo. This time, Charlie's killing rage was nothing but his own. And there wasn't just rage on his face: the fury was matched in equal measure by a savage kind of glee. It was obvious to Jack—it was written, truly, all over his friend's face—that for the first time, Charlie was enjoying this new power he had found, unaided: the power to kill.

"It's not fair!" the Emperor whined, drips of bright blood coming out with the words, making even more of a mess of his suit. "It's . . . not . . . *fair!*"

"**You are weak, Hacha'Fravashi,**" the Scourge repeated, putting its face right up to its enemy's. "**Weak and decadent. You, and those before you since I was banished, have turned from the one true path. With Gukumat's help, I will awaken the Dragon. The whole universe will be brought to an end, and at last all Creation will be returned to the purity of the Void. And *you*,**" the Scourge finished, "**you and everyone else no longer have the power to stop me.**"

As if in answer to the Scourge's words, the Emperor's golden eyes rolled up in his head. His whole body went suddenly rigid in a last paroxysm of agony—then limp.

Into the pool, said Gukumat.

"**Yes, into the pool,**" echoed the Scourge, its husky whisper a shred of the commanding voice it had always used before. "**Do it, Charlie. Do it now.**"

Slowly, wordlessly, Charlie let the pigeon sword's point tip forward, further and further, until finally the weight of the Emperor's body made it slip off the end—flopping into the jelly stuff with a splash.

It hissed delightedly as it received him. The surface seethed and boiled. There was a loud electrical sizzling sound. Then silence.

Ebisu Eller-Kong Hacha'Fravashi was gone.

The Emperor is dead, said the Overminister in his strange, multitudinous voice. *Long live the Emperor.*

Charlie looked up. Slowly, as if his mind were coming back from some place far away, his eyes regained their focus.

"Huh?" he said.

All hail to Charlie Farnsworth, Gukumat intoned. *God of Rulers, God of the Dead, God of Darkness, God of Gods. The Voice of the Void, whose breath is the wind and whose rage makes all worlds tremble. Lord of Crossing-Places, King of All Tears, and the Suzerain Absolute of the Dominions of Hell.*

"**Hail**," the Scourge answered, bowing deeply.

Jack just stared.

But then, slowly—

—warily—

—Charlie started to smile.

TRUST ME

"Not being funny or anything," Charlie was saying, sometime later, "but—when I thought you were dead? It really . . . sucked."

Jack looked at him.

"Being on the receiving end wasn't all that great either," he replied. "But, you know, thanks."

There was a pause.

Behind Jack, the blazing light of the Fracture beckoned and shrieked. In front of him stood Charlie, smiling in a way that Jack suddenly found completely and utterly exasperating. Past Charlie's shoulder he could see the Scourge, making a great show of conversing with Gukumat but doubtless listening to every word he and Charlie said.

Suddenly, he didn't care.

"At the risk of stating the completely bloody obvious," he began, "this is a staggeringly bad idea. Don't you think? I mean, for one thing, what the Hell am I going to tell your folks?"

"Huh?" said Charlie.

"Your parents," Jack prompted. "Remember them? Come on, man, they're going to be frantic!"

Charlie's face darkened. "Tell 'em whatever you like," he growled.

"Sure," said Jack. "I'll tell them that you've gone off to become Emperor of Hell—"

Acting *Emperor of Hell*, said an officious voice, and Jack realized that Gukumat was looking at them. *He has not yet been crowned.*

"Whatever," Jack muttered. He looked back at Charlie.

"Come on," he told him. "Come back with us."

"I want to stay, Jack," said Charlie, shaking his head. "I'm telling you, there's nothing for me"—he gestured at the Fracture—"over there."

"Oh yeah?" said Jack. "And what's for you here?"

"Anything I want," said Charlie simply, and smiled.

Jack looked at that smile.

"Well," he said, "I suppose this is it, then."

"Yeah. I guess it is."

There was another pause.

"Listen," said Jack. "You're not going to get into anything *evil* here, are you?" He was trying to keep the tone of his voice light and joshing, but the effect sounded pathetic, even to him.

"Trust me," said Charlie, smiling.

Yeah, thought Jack sadly. *Right.*

"Well," he said, "good luck."

"Yeah," said Charlie, sticking out a hand. "You too."

They shook.

"But I think you're making a big mistake," Jack told him.

Charlie tore his hand out of Jack's and stalked off, scowling. Jack sighed.

"Mr. Farrell," said a voice.

Jack whirled round, and there—its ink-black face mirroring his own—stood the Scourge.

"**What I'm going to say is quite obvious,**" it said, "**but I thought I'd make it clear to avoid any . . . misunderstandings.**"

Jack just looked at it.

"**I have been merciful with you this time. If our paths cross again, I can't guarantee I may be so again. I would earnestly advise you, therefore, not to interfere in the future.**"

"Is that right?" said Jack, doing his best. "Well, I guess that depends on what happens between you and my friend over there, doesn't it?" He gave the Scourge his most threatening look—and saw from his reflection that it wasn't very impressive.

"**You humans,**" said the Scourge. "**So melodramatic. And so dreadfully, *dreadfully* predictable. You have been warned, Jack Farrell.**"

It turned and drifted smoothly away.

"Yeah," said Jack to its retreating back, "what*ever!*" But it didn't turn round.

Jack sighed again and put his hands on the bar at one end of the ordinary-looking hospital trolley that was standing beside him with Esme laid out on it.

Esme's face was completely blank, utterly, horribly lifeless except for the rhythmic rise and fall of her breathing. There was nothing anyone could do, God had said. Physically, there was nothing wrong with her—and it wasn't magic either. Her unconsciousness was somehow self-induced, self-inflicted: she could wake up at any time, or she might never wake up at all. Personally, Jack had his doubts about this analysis, but his opinion, as usual, didn't seem to count for much.

He looked back at Charlie, who immediately looked away, pretending not to have been watching him.

Jack sniffed. If he was going, it was time to go.

He turned his back, took a deep breath, and started pushing the trolley.

Its wheels squeaked, with a low keening sound almost like a human voice. The squeaking stayed audible for a surprisingly long time as the boy and the girl passed into the crackling whiteness of the Fracture—

—and vanished.

Charlie watched them go. Then he turned away.

END OF

BOOK TWO

"THERE IS NOTHING ELSE INVOLVED. YOU EITHER DO IT OR YOU DON'T. THERE IS ONLY ONE PURPOSE IN ATTACKING THE ENEMY—TO CUT HIM DOWN WITH FINALITY."

MIYAMOTO MUSASHI,
FROM THE BOOK OF FIVE RINGS,
AS INTERPRETED BY HANSHI STEPHEN KAUFMAN

BOOK
THREE

THE MASTER OF NONE

THE CATCH

Charlie Farnsworth stood on the edge of the Needle and looked out over Hell.

The gargantuan mountainlike shape of the palace seemed to swell out beneath his feet. Beyond, the glory of Hell's fantastic landscape seemed barely contained by its purple-blue horizon. Everything Charlie could see—the sea of fire, the five great roads, all of it—now, supposedly, belonged to him. But Charlie still wasn't happy.

"What did Gukumat mean?" he asked the ink-black figure standing beside him. "What was that about my just being 'acting' Emperor of Hell, exactly?"

"It is just as the Overminister said, Charlie," the Scourge replied carefully. "You have killed Hacha'Fravashi. You have taken his place on the throne. But you have not yet been crowned Emperor."

"So? What's the holdup? Why can't you just crown me and get on with it?"

"I'm afraid," said the Scourge, "that it's not quite as simple as that."

"Why?" asked Charlie, rounding on the demon. "*Why* isn't it as simple as that, exactly? You promised me if I killed the Emperor we could rule Hell together. You *promised*! And now what're you doing? Backing out on me! Using me again, to get what you want!"

Inwardly, the Scourge sighed.

"**We can both have what we want,**" it told Charlie slowly. "**You can still become Emperor, and the demons will follow you until the end of the universe.**" It paused. "**There is, however, a catch.**"

"I *knew* it!" Charlie stamped his foot.

"**There is something you have to do first,**" said the Scourge.

"Oh yeah? And what's that?"

"**You must make a decision, once and for all.**"

"What decision?"

"**If you truly wish to become Emperor of Hell—**"

"Yes?" said Charlie. "Yes?"

"**—then you can never go back to your world.**"

There was a pause.

"That's it?" asked Charlie. "That's the catch?"

"**That is the catch,**" said the Scourge. "**Understand me, Charlie: after this, there is no turning back. If you want to become Emperor, I can make it so. The price, however, is that you must give up your past life and all it entails: friends, family—everything. You must choose, Charlie,**" it emphasized. "**Them or us. One or the other. Forever.**"

Charlie blinked.

"**You will, I'm sure, want to make a last visit to your home world before you decide,**" said the Scourge. "**This has already been arranged for you.**"

"Wow," said Charlie, pouting. "You've really got this all figured out, haven't you?"

"**Time is short,**" the Scourge snarled. "**If you want to become Emperor, you must learn to expect some decisions to be made for you. That is the way for those who rule. If you find this *objectionable*, perhaps it would be better if—**"

"No!" said Charlie quickly. "No, that's okay."

It was the first time the demon had lost its temper with him like that. He was surprised and, he realized, more than a little frightened.

"**You can have one night,**" said the Scourge. "**One night in your world—we can't spare you for longer than that. You can then choose to return here or stay, as you wish—though if you choose to stay on Earth, you will naturally have to give up your powers. At any rate,**" it added, "**the choice will be yours.**" It paused. "**What do you say?**"

Charlie looked up at the demon standing beside him, this magical being that had come into his life and changed it utterly. Reflected in liquid darkness, his own eyes blinked back at him nervously.

Them or us, he thought. *One or the other. Forever.*

"Sure," Charlie heard himself say. "One night on Earth. Why not?"

"Very well," said the Scourge. "**Gukumat?**"

At his master's command, the Overminister shimmered into view.

"**Prepare the Fracture.**"

As you wish, my lords, said Gukumat, bowing. *As you wish.*

INTRUDERS

London. The West End. 10:24 p.m.

"That's it," the enormous security guard announced. "I'm going to have to ask you to leave."

Number 3 looked up at the man, who stood a good foot taller than him (and a good two feet wider). The single button that the bouncer had managed to do up on his jacket was showing serious strain from the job of holding back his massive chest.

"Come on, mate," said the bouncer, "let's have you outside. You don't want any trouble, believe me."

Number 3 sighed, reached up, and pushed his mirrored sunglasses a little way down his nose. Thanks to a scuffle with a vampire some years ago, his right eye was false, but his left one was looking up at the bouncer—hard.

"Listen, please," Number 3 told him. He crooked a finger, and the other man bent obligingly forward. Number 3 rewarded him by opening his coat a little and giving him a brief glance at the small but efficient-looking 9mm machine pistol currently strapped under his left armpit. The bouncer's eyes went wide.

"I represent an organization called the Sons of the Scorpion Flail," said Number 3. He spoke quietly, with a pronounced French accent. "You 'ave not 'eard of us, and I would advise you now to forget you ever did. But call your boss, call the police, call the prime minister if you like: they will all tell you the same sing. Leave me alone, please. *Now.*"

For another long second Number 3 and the bouncer looked at each other, as the pub's denizens went about their business around them.

Number 3 disliked this place. He never drank, so he supposed he wasn't really qualified to comment, but even if he did drink, it wouldn't be in the Light of the Moon. Night after night, the pub was packed with beery civilians, until the overworked bar staff could hardly keep up. All that meant to Number 3, however, was that Number 2 had made a serious operational error in not closing the place down. Because this pub, though it looked no different from the many other places just like it in London's West End, had a secret.

The tiny speaker embedded in his sunglasses crackled for a second. Without breaking off his staring match with the bouncer, the Son pushed the shades back into position.

"Three 'ere," he said.

"We're reading activity in the Fracture," said a voice in his ear.

Despite his years of experience, Number 3 felt his heart rate beginning to speed up.

"Copy," he said. "Go away, please," he told the bouncer. "Sank you." He turned and focused his eyes on a spot at the far end of the room. Smoothly, the lenses of his shades switched down through the ultraviolet and thermal levels to a deeper, more sinister spectrum that reduced everyone and everything in the room to pale green smudges—everything except that spot, which, as Number 3 watched, began to whiten and swell outward.

The Light of the Moon looked like a bad West End pub. It sounded and *smelled* like a bad West End pub. But as well as being a pub, it was something else: it was a gateway to Hell. And the gateway was opening.

Number 3 watched as the spot in the air that marked the Fracture went greenish-white, then began to send out lazy little tendrils of magical power—power that only Number 3, at that moment, with his special lenses, was able to see. Slowly, he let his right hand creep up and under his coat, toward where his weapons were waiting. Then, abruptly, his view was blocked by a hulking shadow, and his wrist was caught in a strong grip.

"Oi! Just stop right there."

"Let go of me, please," said Number 3 politely.

"I don't care who you think you are," said the bouncer, "but I'm not letting you get your popgun out in here. There are people about. See?"

"Let go *now*, please," said Number 3. "I 'ave no wish to 'urt you."

Past the bouncer, a burst of whiteness filled Number 3's vision: for a moment, the bones of the bouncer's rib cage stood out like an X-ray against the light before the lenses' protective layers reacted and dimmed down the transmission to a dull glow.

"Listen, mate," said the bouncer, "you don't—OW!"

Number 3 was already moving. In less than a second he had shifted his weight, breaking the bouncer's grip, spinning the man round, and driving the arm that had held his up the man's broad back in a vicious and immobilizing half nelson. With his left hand (Number 3 could shoot just as well with his left), he yanked out a second, identical machine-pistol, already drawing a bead on the thing that had emerged from the Fracture, tracking its flapping, desperate flight across the room.

But already, Number 3 knew, he was too late.

The intruder shot past, right over the oblivious pub-goers' heads, and up over the wide steps. It burst straight through one of the big plate-glass doors and out into the London night, leaving nothing but tinkling splinters behind it.

Shoving his gun back into its holster, the Son of the Scorpion Flail applied a nerve-pinch to a certain spot: the bouncer slumped to the floor without protesting. The drinkers nearest the shattered door were only now just starting to scream.

"*Merde*," said Number 3, with feeling.

Whatever it was that had just come through from Hell— he'd lost it.

Alembic House. Same night. 3:47 a.m.

Felix sat up in bed, coming awake instantly in the darkness. He was breathing hard, he was sweating, and as he felt for the lamp on his antique bedside table, his hand was shaking helplessly.

He'd been dreaming. It was a long, slow, freezing kind of

dream, full of darkness and falling and cold that squeezed stony fingers round his heart. It was a frightening dream. It was also a dream that Felix had had before: he knew what it was, and he knew what caused it.

He was being summoned. The darkness still inside him from all those years ago was calling him again, and he knew he was powerless to resist. Felix sat up, sighing as he put on his glasses.

And some time later, he was across the street from the Light of the Moon, standing in the shadows, watching the two men who were now guarding the door.

"This is crazy," Number 12 was saying.

His partner, Number 9, just sighed. This was the fourth time his fellow sentry had made this observation that night, and they'd only been on duty outside the Light of the Moon for about an hour and a half.

"I'm serious," Number 12 went on. "If Number Three couldn't do anything, then what good can *we* do? Next time something comes through, it's gonna take more than the two of us to stop it."

"Orders are orders," said Number 9 primly.

Number 12 scowled. Since Number 9's recent promotion up the ranks and into single figures, he was really becoming insufferable: all the years they'd worked together, and now it was "Orders are orders." Suddenly, Number 12 decided that hinting at what he wanted to know wasn't going to be enough: he'd have to ask his partner out straight.

"It's tonight, isn't it?" he said. "That's why they won't

send more of us. They're bringing Project Justice in tonight."

"What do you know about Project Justice?" asked Number 9.

"Come on," said Number 12, enjoying the chance to scoff. "You don't think I've heard the rumors? They've done it: the Star Chamber finally pulled off the deal with the Russians. And now, if this Fracture thing really goes where they say it goes, then *we* can go in with a nuke!"

"Why don't you shut up?" suggested Number 9. "Before I—"

A simultaneous crackle in the men's ears cut him off.

"Nine here," said Number 9. The signal was faint and full of interference. Both men cupped their hands to their earpieces in an effort to make it clearer.

"Repeat, please," said Number 9, in a voice loud enough to get both Sons of the Scorpion Flail noticed if anyone had happened to be passing at that moment. "You're breaking up! Hello?"

Silence.

"I think," began Number 12, "he said there was movement round the back."

"I know what he said!" snapped Number 9. Actually, this was a lie: he was glad Number 12 had been there to make sense of the message, though he would never have told him so to his face.

"Well?" asked Number 12, looking at him.

"All right," said Number 9. "Let's check it out. But remember, look casual, okay?"

Number 12 sighed again, but he followed Number 9's lead. The two men set off.

Felix watched them go. It would take the Sons at least two

minutes to get round the block to reach the rear door of the pub and the same again to get back: more than enough time. As he crossed the road, he smiled. That had been the first time he'd used magic since . . .

His smile faded. He'd enjoyed himself for a moment there, but when he remembered the last time, his expression turned grim once more.

Noting the broad wooden board that had been chained over the shattered pane of glass, Felix put his hands round the padlock that held the doors shut and concentrated: it fell open with a soft click. Felix straightened up, brushed his lapels, did up the button on the jacket of his impeccably expensive suit, and stepped through.

The darkness inside him, a darkness blacker than that of the empty pub around him, was stirring: Felix could feel it. Unbidden, his feet took him to the spot at the end of the room, and his hands began the gestures by themselves. He watched, with a strange sort of detachment, as the Fracture's dull red glow widened to a fierce, freezing whiteness.

Then he was there, in Hell. He was standing in a broad, tall, blood-colored dome-shaped room, with a round, raised dais at its center. On the dais was a throne. On the throne, sitting comfortably, was what had woken him.

"Good evening, Felix," said the Scourge. "Thank you for coming."

"You say that like I had a choice," Felix replied.

"My dear fellow, do let's be civil. After all, we've known each other quite a long time."

"You destroyed my life," said Felix. "And now the only person left that I care about in the world is lying in a coma, because of you."

"You destroyed your own life," the Scourge replied evenly, "when you made your bargain with me. Everything that has happened to you, you've brought upon yourself. Don't tell me all this time you've been pretending otherwise, *please*."

"All right," said Felix, after a moment. "Then how about you tell me what I'm doing here?"

"I think you know the answer to that," said the Scourge. "You're here to die."

Felix and the demon looked at each other. Once again, the Scourge was right about him: Felix had known this was the end. He'd known since he'd woken up.

"But first," the Scourge went on, "there's something you're going to do for me."

The demon settled back on the throne, and there was a short pause before it spoke again.

"It's about Esme," it said. "You're going to give her a message."

The Palace Theatre. Same night. 4:49 a.m.

Darkness. Freezing, black, bottomless. The darkness slid past her, through her, taking her down, and a soft voice said—

We're the same.

What?

We're the same, it repeated, you and me. In fact, there is no "you and me." I'm you. You're me. You've always been me. And the only reason I'm speaking to you like this is that you just won't admit it yet.

Black water. Cold, darkness, and falling. There was a pause, then the voice spoke again.

You know what I can offer you.

Esme said nothing.

You can feel it, said the voice. **In your body, your blood: strength without limit. Power beyond imagining. And all you have to do is accept me.**

Open your heart, the voice told her, and Esme couldn't help but listen. **Open your heart, and LET ME IN . . . YES!**

Then, suddenly, urgently, as if its owner were standing right next to her, another voice said, *Remember your mother.*

Esme's eyes fluttered, then opened.

She was wearing nothing but a long white cotton T-shirt, she realized: one of hers, an old one, one she never usually wore. Also, she saw, she was strapped to the bed. Three thick brown padded leather straps stretched from one side to the other: one across her legs just above her knees, one across her hips (with loops for her wrists), and another across her chest. The buckles on the straps were done up quite tightly, so Esme closed her eyes, reached inside herself, and concentrated. The air in the room turned thick for a moment. There was a soft clinking sound as the straps fell loose. Then Esme sat up.

There was a door at the foot of the bed, with a thin crack of light beneath it. Hugging herself because the floor was cold under her feet, she walked over to it. She waited for a moment, listening, then she turned the handle. A young man was standing outside, dressed in black from head to toe, with a gun on his belt. On seeing Esme, he turned pale.

"Oh," he said. "You're . . . uh—"

"Where is it?" asked Esme. Her voice came out in a kind of croak.

"I'm—I'm sorry?"

"Where *is* it?" Esme repeated, already losing patience.

"Where's what?" asked the man, genuinely puzzled.

Esme frowned. She let her head fall to one side: a thick clump of her wild black hair swung down over one eye while the other fixed him unblinkingly.

"Listen," said the man, suddenly having trouble getting his words out. "I've, ah, got to call someone. If you just stay right there, then—"

Esme's arm shot out and she caught the man's hand when it had barely moved toward his hip. He found himself being pulled toward the girl as her hand crushed, mercilessly, on his. His vision was turning dark, but he could still see her face and her burning amber eyes.

"**Where. Is. It?**" asked Esme, and her voice seemed to blossom like black flowers in his head.

"I don't—I don't—" said the man, the last vestiges of his training making him reach, with his other hand, for his gun.

Esme sighed—and the man flew back, smashing into the wall and landing in a heap on the floor.

Esme looked down at the prone body for a moment. Then, still dressed only in her long T-shirt, she stepped over the guard and set off down the corridor.

The next few minutes—

"Freeze, or I'll—*AAAGH!*"

—passed in a sort—

"I repeat, subject is . . . NO! *PLEASE!*"

—of blur. Esme was beginning to recognize her surroundings, but the loud alarm sounds were unfamiliar and, she found, quite irritating. Plus, there were all these *people*. At one point, on the landing outside the butterfly room, twenty-two more of the black-clad men fanned out and surrounded her. They were wearing gas masks and body armor. They were shouting. Their guns made a lot of clicking noises as they pointed them at her. It was all, she found, very irritating indeed.

A burst of harsh light blasted in around the edges of the butterfly room's double doors, and Number 2 looked up just as, with a heavy *crump*, the doors buckled inward.

He stood up, facing the doors, nodding to the two men he had stationed to either side, who took up position, waiting.

The doors opened, and Esme came in.

Her wild black hair stood out all around her. Her hands, as she stepped over the unconscious body of one of the men who had tried to get in her way, opened and closed on the empty air by her sides. Her amber eyes flicked once around the room, taking in her old dojo and the way that now it seemed to be filled with men and machinery. Then they fixed on Number 2.

"So," said the Sons' leader unhappily. "You're, er, awake, then."

Esme just looked at him.

"Now," Number 2 went on quickly. "There's no need to get, er, overexcited. For the last day or so you've been in . . . well, some kind of a coma. We had no idea when, or if, you'd wake up, but we thought—for your own protection, of course—that it might be best to put you in . . . well, in restraints. I can see that that might not have been quite the right thing to do, and I apologize, truly, so please, there's no reason for any violence. All right?"

Still Esme said nothing.

"This," said Number 2, gesturing at the oblong metal box behind him and the racks of improvised laboratory equipment that surrounded it, "is a, ah, rather dangerous piece of equipment."

Esme raised an eyebrow.

"All right," said Number 2. "I'll tell you. It's a bomb. It's rather a powerful one. We are, at present, engaged in quite a delicate stage of its preparation. So, you know, perhaps if you'd be good enough to wait outside or in your room for another twenty minutes or so, then we'd be able to discuss things a little more—"

Esme brushed the cloud of words aside. "Where is it?" she asked.

Number 2 frowned. "I'm sorry," he said slowly. "I'm not sure if I under—"

"WHERE IS IT?" wailed Esme suddenly, as the sadness clawed at her.

Number 2 stared. Some sort of horrible change had come over the girl. Her face was stricken with grief. "I'm afraid I don't understand what you're talking about," he finished uncertainly.

"Look," said Esme, trying again. She looked down at her

feet. Her hair swung down over her face again, and her eyes were going a bit watery. She bunched her fists and straightened up. "It was taken from me, all right? The Scourge took it, and I've got to have it back." She opened her hands and held them out, empty, trying to show how important it was.

"It's all I've got—you see?" she explained. "It's all I've got left from . . . from Raymond." Her voice had gone wobbly again. The men were just looking at her blankly. She felt a stab of impatience. "I'm going to ask you again," she said. "Then I'm going to get angry. Where is it?"

Suddenly, the air in the room was heating up—the pressure building. Number 2's eyes narrowed, and he nodded to the two men standing behind her.

Instantly, before Esme could react, they fired.

The glowing tips of the Tasers hit home at her back, on either side of her spine. Esme's body began to convulse, and the bursts of bright current began to run in weird blue splashes down her T-shirt and her bare brown legs. The men kept their fingers pressed on the triggers of their specially adapted weapons. But Esme was still asking.

"WHERE IS IT?" she cried, and again. "*WHERE IS IT? WHAT HAVE THEY DONE WITH MY SWORD?*"

The equipment rattled on the shelves.

Everyone winced.

Then, suddenly, she fell.

"Tranquilizer," barked Number 2. There was a long, soft hiss as the injection was applied to the girl's neck. It was a large dose. It would have to be.

FRIENDS

Jack was in a foul mood.

When he'd come back from Hell the day before, stepping out of the Fracture wheeling the trolley with Esme's lifeless body in front of him, he hadn't exactly known what to expect. Not flags and a brass band to welcome him or anything, of course not: the most he'd hoped for, he supposed, was a chance to get Esme back to the Brotherhood's headquarters before he decided what his next move should be. But no. Oh no. As had been the case, it seemed, with so much in Jack's life, things had naturally turned out worse.

What he'd got instead was a surprise encounter with a bunch of black-clad men in gas masks, all of whom seemed to be pointing guns at him. They'd whisked Esme off to who-knows-where before Jack barely had time to protest, and any attempts he'd made since to ask after her—let alone get to see her—had been met with total indifference from his captors. The men had proceeded to spend most of the next twenty-four hours grilling Jack for his story, making him go over it again and again while at the same time clearly not believing a word of it. They'd refused to explain who they were or what they were doing there. They'd refused to let him call his parents, and they had locked him in one of the rooms at the theater.

And as if all of that weren't enough by itself, he felt sick.

He'd first noticed the feeling just a couple of hours after his return from Hell: it hadn't been too bad at first—just a light, nagging sensation in the pit of his stomach, particularly whenever he looked at food. Over the following twenty-four hours, however, the feeling had got steadily worse. There was a feverish sort of tingle in his shoulders and under his arms. His mouth tasted furry and his stomach kept gurgling and twisting itself up, like he'd swallowed a snake and it was eating him alive down there, eating him from the inside.

Typical, he thought. What a time to get ill. How absolutely bloody typ—

He froze, staring.

A patch of shadow in the corner of the room was moving, rippling—solidifying, as he watched, into a manlike shape of purest liquid black. The darkness vanished, and a figure stepped out of the shadows.

"Charlie," said Jack.

"Hey," said Charlie. He had a sword strapped to his back, and he looked very pleased with himself. "Got a minute?" he asked.

"I suppose so," said Jack dryly. "I'm not exactly in the middle of anything here."

"Cool." Charlie grinned again and reached out a hand.

There was a sensation of huge black wings closing around them. Then Jack and Charlie were standing in the open night air.

Jack looked around himself. They had reappeared on some kind of rooftop: a high one too—he could tell because of the breeze.

"Where are we?" he asked.

"We're on the roof of Centre Point Tower," said Charlie.

Jack walked to the edge. Of course Charlie was right.

Built in the 1960s out of ribbed concrete and glass, Centre Point Tower used to be one of the tallest buildings in London. It's still one of the ugliest. Nonetheless, Jack had to admit, there was a pretty good view from the roof. London's streets were spread out all around him like the glittering threads of a spiderweb, the Thames cutting through them like a slash of darkness.

"Well?" Jack prompted, still in no mood to mess around.

"Well what?" asked Charlie, who was now sitting cross-legged on the concrete.

"You want to tell me what this is all about?" asked Jack. "I thought you were staying in Hell with the Scourge." It was difficult to keep the bitterness out of his voice—and to be honest, he wasn't trying very hard.

"I'm just . . . visiting," was Charlie's faint reply.

"Really!" said Jack, with heavy sarcasm. "Staying long?"

"Just tonight," said Charlie, attempting to make it sound casual and once again failing pathetically. "Just tonight," he repeated, and he let out a single hollow laugh. "Huh."

Jack looked at him. "What?" he asked.

At last, Charlie looked up. His eyes glinted.

"This is it, Jack," he said. "This is my last visit. After tonight, if I go back to Hell, I can't ever come back here again."

Jack blinked.

"How come?" he asked.

Charlie sighed. "I'm just too important," he replied, "apparently."

Jack rolled his eyes in disbelief.

"I guess it's kind of like with the prime minister or the queen or something," Charlie explained blithely. "Every move I make'll be planned in advance, and they simply can't put the arrangements in place to guarantee my safety with the way things are over here. You know how it is."

"Oh, *sure*," said Jack. "Sure, I know how it is." But the sarcasm flew over Charlie's head—again. Jack sighed. "So?"

Charlie looked surprised. "So what?"

"So, are you going to do it?" asked Jack, losing patience. "Are you seriously telling me you're going to stay in Hell for good?" He paused. "Or—or what?"

Charlie looked down at his lap again before answering, and his hair swung forward over his eyes.

"I dunno," he said distantly.

"Maybe," he added.

"Yeah," he finished. Then he flicked his hair back, shrugged at Jack, and smiled.

For another long moment, Jack stared at Charlie, getting what he wanted to say in the right order. It was difficult.

"Do you know?" he began finally. "There's something I've been thinking about you for a while now. I think it's time I told you, because you really ought to know."

"What's that?" asked Charlie.

"You're a complete and utter *git*," said Jack.

Charlie stared at him.

"What do you want me to tell you?" asked Jack. "Am I supposed to beg you not to go? 'Don't go, *mate*—I'll miss you.' Would you like that?"

Charlie shook his head. "Jack—"

"No, really," said Jack, hitting his stride now. "I want to know. Would it make any difference if I told you again how stupid you're being? I mean," he asked, "what about your parents?"

"It'll be dealt with," said Charlie. "I've got a plan."

"Ooh, a *plan*," echoed Jack, with utter contempt. "Well, hooray for that."

He sighed. His anger was cooling now. Truth be told, Jack wasn't very good at being angry, even when he had a right to be. Being angry was too much bother: he could never manage it for long.

"So what's the deal here?" he asked wearily. "What exactly has the Scourge promised you?"

Charlie perked up visibly.

"Well, it's like this," he said. "I can't tell you very much, it's kind of a secret, but me and Khentimentu are going to perform this ceremony."

"What ceremony?"

"There's this old temple kind of thing, in the deepest part of the palace. No one's even been down there for thousands of years."

"Uh-huh," said Jack, already not liking the sound of this at all.

"When everything's all set up, we're going to do this, like, ritual. It's called 'waking the Dragon.' And after that, every demon in Hell will do whatever I say."

"But this ritual," said Jack. "What does it involve? What happens?"

Charlie shrugged and grinned. "What do I care? I mean, it's just some public-relations thing, right? Me and the Scourge do a bit of hocus-pocus, some bogus religious ceremony, then all the demons'll follow me forever!"

"That's it?" asked Jack. "You're sure that's all it is? I mean, how do you know?"

"I know," said Charlie heavily, "because the Scourge told me."

"The Scourge told you," echoed Jack. "It actually said to you, 'This dragon business means nothing.'"

"Yes!"

"Those exact words."

"Yes!"

Jack waited.

"Well," said Charlie, "no. But I promise you, Jack, it's no big deal."

The two boys looked at each other.

"All right?" prompted Charlie.

"Not really," said Jack. "There's obviously more to it than that. Something's happening, and you don't know what. And," he added, seeing Charlie shaking his head again, "I don't trust the Scourge."

"Well, I do," said Charlie. "I *do* trust the Scourge!"

The boys looked at each other. There was a pause.

"Look," said Charlie, shuffling himself a little closer toward Jack across the gritty concrete. "You don't know what it's like. I've tried to tell you, but you just won't believe me."

Jack looked at him.

"Meeting the Scourge is the best thing that ever happened to me," said Charlie. "Do you understand? Since that day I took the test, it's like every part of my life—every step, every breath—is magical and important and *real*. Now, I'm asking you, man, what is there here that could possibly be better than that? Go on," he prompted, when Jack didn't answer straightaway. "Tell me."

Jack still didn't answer. Charlie smiled.

"When's term start again?" he asked. "A couple of weeks' time? So are you seriously telling me I should come back to school, on top of everything else, when I could be, like, ruling the universe?"

Still Jack said nothing.

"That's the choice," said Charlie. "I can rule in Hell—or come back here and be . . . *ordinary*." He snorted. "As for my parents . . ." He smiled bitterly. "Well, like I said, I've got a plan. The whole thing's going to blow over. Pretty soon, no one'll even remember I've gone. So there's nothing for me here," said Charlie, edging closer to Jack. "You see? Nothing. Except you."

There was another long pause.

"You know," said Charlie, "you could always come and visit me. I'll always make time for you, mate. You know that, right?"

"Come on, man," he added when Jack still didn't reply. "Say something!"

For another long, slow moment, there was silence between them. Then Jack did say something.

"You're an idiot, Charlie."

Charlie blinked.

"I can't believe you can't see how stupid you're being," said Jack. "And it just makes me sad, because whatever I say, whatever I do, you're just going to go ahead and do this stupid, *stupid* thing, and there's nothing I can do to stop you."

He looked at Charlie.

"That's right, isn't it?" he asked. "There's nothing I can do?"

"No," said Charlie thickly. "There isn't."

"Then," said Jack, standing up with an effort, because he was fed up and sad and sick and his feet had gone to sleep, "you might as well take me back to the theater."

Charlie sniffed.

"You go," he said, still sitting, his face obscured by his hair. "I've got stuff to do."

"You're going to make me walk?" asked Jack.

"No. You don't understand. You're going back. You'll be there in less than a second. Don't worry about it."

"Oh," said Jack, doing his best not to. "Okay."

"Goodbye, Jack," said Charlie. "I'm sorry it has to be like this."

"Bye, Charlie," said Jack. "I'm sor—"

He felt a rush of blackness, then he was back in the locked room.

"—ry too," he said to the empty air. And that was when it occurred to him that he could have asked Charlie to put him wherever he liked. *Typical.*

On the roof of Centre Point Tower, Charlie sat cross-legged for perhaps another minute and a half. On his shoulders, two ink-black shapes suddenly hunched outward, then Ashmon and Heshmim ran down his arms and nibbled at his fingers with their sharp little teeth. Charlie stroked their shiny black bodies absently for a while.

Well, he thought, *that* hadn't exactly gone as well as he'd hoped.

Them or us. One or the other. Forever.

Frankly, the choice didn't seem like such a big deal. At any rate, if the world was going to persuade him to stay, it would have to work pretty hard to impress him now.

Charlie stood up. His familiars vanished into a cloak of darkness, and as the cloak spread billowing about him, he walked to the edge of the roof. For a moment, he looked out over the city. Then he stepped off, plunging into the night.

THE LAST NIGHT

Number 27 was thinking of pastries. Specifically, he was thinking of mille-feuille, his favorite pastry, and just how delicious it was. He was beginning to doze off, when a single red light on his control panel suddenly started to wink.

Instantly he was awake, reaching for the radio on his desk with one hand even as the other was punching the relevant display up onto his monitors.

"Two here," said the radio.

"Sir," said Number 27, "we have a problem."

At that moment, every one of the newly installed speakers dotted all over the top floors of the building let out a dreadful rising shriek. The intruder alarms had kicked in.

"Monitors?" barked the radio.

"Sorry sir?" said Number 27.

"Anything on the *monitors*?" repeated Number 2.

"Nothing sir," said Number 27. "Except—wait."

"Yes?"

"There's something coming up the stairs. No . . . No, not coming *up* the stairs."

There was a pause.

"What?" asked Number 2.

Number 27 just sat back and rubbed his eyes. But when he looked again, he could see that what was happening was, unfortunately, still happening.

"Twenty-seven, I'm waiting."

"It's going *through* them, sir," said Number 27. "Whatever it is, it's coming through the walls!"

"Put the whole team on full alert."

Number 27 didn't need telling twice.

On the landing outside the butterfly room, Charlie paused, frowning. He'd set off the intruder alarm almost a minute ago now, and still no one had appeared to try and stop him. What sort of response time did they call this? Tutting exaggeratedly, he set off for Esme's room. Rather than have to bother with all the stairs and corners, he went straight through the walls.

Charlie had been doing this a lot lately, back in the palace in Hell. The novelty of the sensation—the sudden damp feeling of the cold, old stone as it passed through him even as he passed through it—had worn off quite quickly. Scaring the pants off the people in the rooms beyond, though: that, he found, was the fun bit.

There had to be about twenty of these goons camped out in each room, packed like sardines in their little rows of sleeping bags. The effect of his appearance on them as he rose up through the floor, letting his cloak ripple about him and fill the room with a flood of crackling darkness, was, Charlie found, very satisfactory indeed. Grinning to himself, he slid through the ceiling, leaving chaos and screams in his wake. Once inside Esme's room, however, he stopped and frowned again.

He looked around the room, pointlessly checking all its cushion-covered surfaces. It was dark in there, but that wasn't a problem for him. The problem was, the room was empty.

Hmm.

He opened the door and stepped out onto the landing outside, just as some five or six Sons of the Scorpion Flail finally got there to intercept him. He was greeted by a chorus of ratcheting safety catches, orders for him to freeze, and so forth. It was so like something off the telly, it was really very funny.

"You," said Charlie to the one standing nearest him, who hadn't even managed to get his gas mask on properly yet. "Where is she?"

"Er, wh-who?" stammered Number 16.

"The girl, stupid," said Charlie, reaching into the man's mind when he didn't answer straightaway. "Thank you," he added, when he'd got what he wanted, and with (though he said it himself) a pretty credible burst of manic baddie cackling, he whirled his cloak about himself and vanished, reappearing at Esme's bedside.

He looked down at her.

She looked awful.

It wasn't just that she was tied to the bed with a frankly

bewildering array of straps, buckles, and (now) chains holding her in place. It wasn't even that she was attached to an intravenous drip full of (Charlie noted with a superhuman glance) enough tranquilizers to stun a whale. Her eyes were scrunched up like she was in pain. Her arms were covered in long clawed scratches that she'd obviously done herself. Her hands, strapped down to either side of her, were bunched into small fists. She was pale and sick looking and desperately, desperately sad.

For the first time in a while, Charlie felt a pang of something a little like regret.

But it was okay, he told himself, because that was why he'd come.

He'd been in the room perhaps three seconds at most. The ceiling and the walls rang with the impact of boots as the Sons ran down to catch up with him: it was time to do what he'd come to do. He reached up and took off the pigeon sword, sliding the strap from his shoulders. Gently, carefully, he laid it by Esme's right side and closed her fingers around the hilt. Her hand was warm, and he held it for a fraction of a second longer than he needed to.

"There you go," he said quietly.

Instantly, Esme stirred. Her eyelids fluttered—and Charlie stood back, watching her uncertainly. Suddenly, he realized, she was holding the sword for herself, clasping it to her chest in both hands now, until her knuckles bulged white against the dark wood of its scabbard.

The Sons were battering at the door. Great heavy blows

threatened to knock it off its hinges—yet the small and uncontrollable shiver that Charlie gave as he watched Esme begin to wake was nothing to do with them.

The door burst open—

—but Charlie was gone.

For a long, delicious moment, Charlie soared through the orange-tinged sky over the West End. His cloak of liquid darkness rippled about him, and he laughed with delight as the wind of his passing grew hot on his face.

He vanished again and reappeared standing in his room.

It was his bedroom, in the house in Stoke Newington—the place where he'd grown up. All his stuff—his games, his comics, his film collection—was all exactly as he'd left it. After everything that had happened, Charlie found this inexplicably annoying.

How lame and paltry it all looked now, especially with the thin layer of dust that had already started to form over all of it. When he'd thought about this moment before, he'd imagined he'd be tempted to take something as a keepsake, despite the risk that it might be noticed. Now he was here, he wasn't tempted in the least. There was nothing worth coming back for, nothing compared to what was waiting for him in Hell. Sneering, he sank through the floor.

He appeared in his parents' room, by their big four-poster bed. Like Esme's room had been, it was empty. Charlie frowned and sank through another floor, ending up in the passage that led to the sitting room. Now, at last, he could see light, escaping round the gaps at the edges of the door. He stood outside in the passage for a moment. Then he took a deep breath, held it, and slid through.

The wood of the door was old and hard and had what must have been about forty different layers of paint on it. The way his eyes were now, he could even see the little lines that his parents had marked off on the doorway over the years, to show how much he'd grown.

He'd found her. His mum was asleep on the sofa. Charlie just stood there and looked at her.

She didn't look good either. She was pale, her lipstick was smeared, her mouth was open, and her head was lying at an angle that would obviously give her a very sore neck in the morning. The floor surrounding the sofa was covered in scrunched-up tissues; there was an empty glass and a half-drunk bottle of white wine on the table in front of her, and the TV had been left switched on, though very quietly. Across the floor stretched a long cord that led to the telephone, which lay at her side on the cushions, under her hand.

She'd fallen asleep waiting for it to ring: waiting for him, Charlie, to call.

Charlie felt bad then. For a long second the bad feeling ran all the way through him like a slow electric charge, and all he could do was stand there.

But then, after a moment, another urge took hold of him, the urge to get out. He had a way to fix everything, quickly and—he reckoned—cleanly. He was going to leave the whole mess, everything, behind him. He could do that. He was going to do that. He *had* to do that.

"Bye, Mum," he said quietly. Then he vanished again.

This time, he reappeared outside Blackhorse Road Underground station.

His father had moved into a flat near here with his new . . . "girlfriend," as Charlie supposed he had to call her (he grimaced). This was where his dad had been living since leaving Charlie's mum. Charlie could remember the address all right: the problem was that since he'd never been there before, he didn't know how to find his way there. Tutting slightly, because it was annoying that even a superhuman like himself still had to stop for directions, Charlie looked closely at the local map that was outside the station. There. That was where it was. Moments later, he was outside the building.

Floating smoothly upward through the summer night air, he began to look in through the windows. On the south-facing side, the side where he'd materialized, all of them were dark except one. Luckily (or unluckily), that turned out to be the one he'd been looking for. Six floors up off the ground, Charlie froze.

They were standing in the middle of the kitchen: his dad and the woman Charlie hardly knew. They were hugging each other.

It wasn't the kind of hug he'd ever seen his dad and his mum give each other: Charlie knew that straightaway. His dad's face was pressed deep into the side of the woman's neck. The woman was running her hands very slowly across Charlie's dad's back, high up, up near his shoulders.

The kitchen looked bright and new and amazingly clean, as if it had never been used before. The glare of the bare strip light on the kitchen's ceiling gave the place a harsh, antiseptic appearance. Outside, staring in from the darkness, watching them, Charlie felt his stomach knotting into icy twists of loathing and disgust.

Charlie remembered what his dad had told him that time in the Chinese restaurant: *When the chance came up for me to be really happy, I had to take it.* He smiled fiercely. Maybe the two people he was looking at thought they were happy now. Maybe they were even right. But it wasn't going to last. Soon they'd be sorry. When they found out about what he was about to do, they'd be sorry for the rest of their lives. And that, Charlie decided, was fine by him.

"God, Sandra," said Mr. Farnsworth finally, lifting his head to look at her. His eyes were red and puffy. "What if he's done something stupid? What am I going to do? I just wish he'd call."

"I know," said the woman doggedly. "I know."

But Charlie didn't hear this. He was long gone.

This time, he reappeared on Hungerford Bridge.

Of all London's bridges across the Thames, this was Charlie's favorite. From Hungerford Bridge you can see most of the city's landmarks, and the looping golden-yellow lights on either side of the river at that point are really quite lovely. Charlie looked down at the black, silent Thames moving below him, cold and deep and merciless, and for a second he felt that the bridge—the whole city with him on it—was moving, and that the river itself was still. Then he pulled himself together. Dawn was on its way now. If he was going to finish what he'd come to do, he had to act fast. He took a step back from the railing and began to use his magic.

Even at that time of night, there were still a few people on the bridge. His first priority, therefore, was to prevent anyone from seeing him and what he was about to do. Charlie frowned, and the space around him began to shimmer: for the next few minutes, until he was ready, the eyes of anybody who looked would simply slide past him as if he weren't there. Now he was free to get on with the real business at hand.

The air started to thicken and go hot as Charlie coaxed it into giving him what he wanted.

The trunk came first—an ugly, solid clump that he massaged into shape with a grimace of disgust, smoothing it with his fingers. With quick, careful movements, he extended the arms and legs, focusing his concentration on the bones, the sinews, and the blood vessels as they whispered into being behind the delicate layers of the skin. Next, still frowning, he looked at the gap between the shoulders—and it began to glisten and bulge. In another moment it was inflating: swelling as it filled with bone and blood and, finally, brain. Still Charlie concentrated, smoothing and whittling and working at the surfaces until at last his hands fell to his sides, and he stood back and looked at his handiwork.

He gripped the railing, suddenly dizzy. His stomach felt watery, his temples twitched, and his whole body ached with a kind of shock at what he had just pulled out of himself.

But there. It was done. It would do.

Floating in front of him, standing stiff like a mannequin, pinned in the air by Charlie's power, was a replica of himself. Charlie hadn't bothered to copy all his moles and freckles and so forth, but apart from those, the replica was exact in every detail: hair, blood type, fingerprints, even his teeth, in case Charlie's dental records were used to identify him.

It felt quite strange, looking at himself like this. For a moment he almost felt sorry for this body of his and what was going to happen to it on its journey down into the cold and the dark. But then he remembered.

He'd come there to kill himself. And it was time to finish the job.

Charlie transferred his watch to the body's wrist. He took out his mobile phone and stuck it into the back pocket of the identical black jeans the body was wearing. He gave the new version of himself a last, critical look—then pitched himself up, over the railing, and into the river. There was a soft splash from below, and his body vanished, to be washed up some-where downstream.

The Emperor was dead. Long live the Emperor.

It was done. His last links to the world he'd grown up in were severed. There was nothing else to keep him there, so he closed his eyes, opened them again, and then he was standing in front of the Fracture.

There were some more of the goons from earlier, shouting and firing guns at him, but he paid them no mind. He just stepped through, back into the quiet, seething whiteness that seemed to reach out and beckon him in. In another moment, he was back in the throne room.

"Sorry I'm late," he said.

The Scourge stood up, walked quickly down the steps of the dais, and took Charlie's hands in two of its own. Its touch was smooth and cool.

"**I'm so glad to see you,**" it said. "**I can't tell you how glad. We have big things to accomplish, you and I.**"

"Yeah," said Charlie, and smiled.

He felt great. All the pent-up frustrations of his life were falling away: he could feel them streaming off him like water when you climb out of a swimming pool. All the tension and the rage and the fear and the hurt were slipping away until all that was left was himself and the demon and their future together. He felt strong and fit and full of excitement: he felt better than he'd ever felt in his life.

"Let's do it," he said. "Let's go to work."

And inwardly, triumphantly, the Scourge smiled.

Arm in arm, the boy and the demon walked out of the throne room.

Charlie didn't look back.

PERSONAL DEMONS

When the dreadful noise of the intruder alarms finally stopped, Jack noticed a tapping sound—coming, he realized, from the window.

"*What?*" said Jack aloud. What the Hell was it now? Scowling, he stood up and yanked open the curtains.

There, on his windowsill, sat a small, batlike creature.

It was Jack's Chinj.

It was looking at him.

Jack stared. He hadn't been expecting to see the Chinj again: certainly not here, on Earth, in London's West End, on the windowsill of the Palace Theatre. The small creature's smile of delight widened to a look of near-ecstasy as Jack opened the window.

"Sir!" it breathed. "I can't tell you how glad I am to see you!"

"Er, hi," said Jack. There was a pause. "Um, if you don't mind my asking, what are you actually *doing* here?"

"Why, sir," said the Chinj, obviously hurt but trying not to show it. "You can't seriously be suggesting that I should have abandoned my sacred duty to you simply because you decided to leave our realm? But of course," it joshed, nudging Jack's arm with one leathery wing and looking up at him slyly, "you are joking with me."

"What do you mean," asked Jack, grim-faced, "'*our*' realm?"

"Why, our *home*," said the Chinj, its jaunty expression beginning to slip.

"The pits," it added, seeing that its point wasn't getting across.

"Hell," prompted the Chinj finally, giving Jack a puzzled look. "Sir."

Jack stared at the Chinj. Then he rubbed a hand over his eyes.

"Listen," he said, "I think there's been some kind of mistake. *This*"—he pointed past the Chinj and out at the London night—"is my home, where *my* kind come from. I know we met there and everything, but I'm not actually from Hell. I mean . . ." He tried a smile. It didn't come out very well. "I'm not actually a demon or anything. Okay?"

The Chinj frowned.

"Yes, you are, sir," it said. "Or part demon anyway."

"Er, no," said Jack. "I'm not."

"Of course you are."

"*No*," said Jack, quite firmly now. "I'm *not.*"

"Sir," began the Chinj, holding up one tiny finger. "If I might point out, I *have* been performing most of your digestive functions for you for some time now."

"*What?*" said Jack.

"And I think I can claim to know what I'm talking about. Yes, sir, you *are* a demon. At any rate, you certainly need to feed like one."

"Look," said Jack, "I'm not going to argue about this. It's nice to see you again and everything, but if you don't mind,

I'm having a miserable night and I really, really want to go back to bed. I'm sorry about your wasted journey. But, you know, good night."

He reached for the window, ready to close it again.

"You are sick?" asked the Chinj quickly.

Jack froze.

"You have aches and pains in your limbs? Your stomach keeps rumbling?"

Jack said nothing.

"You are always hungry, yes?" the Chinj went on. "But there is nothing to eat here that seems to satisfy you?"

"Yes," said Jack quietly.

"Well," said the creature, unable to keep the note of triumph out of its voice, "why do you think that is?"

There was another pause.

"I'm just ill," said Jack, with a sudden and horrible uncertainty. "Upset stomach. You know, something I ate, that's all."

But the Chinj was shaking its head.

"Oh, sir," it said sadly. "I had no idea."

"No idea what?"

"That you didn't know," said the Chinj. "It must come as a bit of a shock." It reached out a leathery black wing and touched Jack softly on the arm. "It's all right, sir. I'm here now. And I'll take care of you. Always."

Jack stared at the Chinj, too stunned to be angry anymore. He looked into its wide, dark eyes. The Chinj felt sorry for him, he realized. This threw Jack completely.

"If I may say so," said the small creature quietly, "you

really don't look at all well. Little wonder," it added, "when you haven't fed properly in so long. If I might suggest . . . ?"

Smiling kindly, the Chinj gestured with its eyes to a place on the floor somewhere behind where Jack was standing.

Jack turned and looked. All he could see in the direction the Chinj was indicating was a small bright blue plastic bucketlike object, an empty wastepaper bin, sitting in the corner of the room. He looked back at the Chinj.

And it was then, with a falling sensation in his heart, that Jack realized what the creature meant to do.

His stomach let out a growl so astonishingly loud that Jack was suddenly scared that it might alert the guards outside. The growl went on for what seemed like an eternity, a long, gurgling ripple of deep sound that finally tailed off into a high, soft series of murmurs. Obviously, there was no choice. Jack bent down and, with shaking hands, picked up the empty bin. When he turned back, the Chinj was already in position, its wings folded neatly behind its furry back to keep them out of the way. As Jack did his best to hold the blue plastic bin steady in front of it, he watched as a momentary spasm of something like pain crossed the face of the small creature.

Then it opened its mouth and let fly.

Jack closed his eyes. He didn't want to watch any more. Hearing the thick splatter as the stuff hit the plastic bottom of the bin—feeling the occasional droplets that splashed back up onto his hands in tiny, warm spots—these sensations were enough for him. When at last the Chinj had fulfilled its sacred duty, the edges of the bin were heavy in his hands and the smell was thick and strong in his nostrils.

"There," said the Chinj, with quiet pride.

Jack opened his eyes and looked down. He looked at the porridgey stuff lurking darkly in the shadows at the bottom of the bin. To his horror, he found that he had never wanted anything so much in his entire life. His whole body was gripped with a deep, physical need that was so strong it shocked him.

Nervelessly, he lifted the edge of the bin to his lips, staring with a strange fascination at the reluctant, bulging way the stuff crept up the side as he tipped it up toward his eager, suddenly slavering mouth.

"There," murmured the Chinj again soothingly. "Long swallows, sir. Nice and steady, that's the way."

And time went slack.

Charlie and the Scourge reappeared in darkness. They were traveling downward and at tremendous speed, but even with Charlie's eyes as superhumanly powerful as they were now, he could see nothing anywhere, in any direction. He could smell nothing, feel nothing. Apart from the demon's cool liquid hand holding his, there was only darkness.

"Okay," said Charlie. "How about you tell me where we actually *are*? And, like, what we're actually doing here?"

"We have now passed beyond Hell's foundations," the Scourge answered. "We are reaching the heart of Creation: the sleeping place," it said and paused, "of the Dragon."

Charlie considered this for a moment.

"And this," he said, "means what to me, exactly?"

"It means everything, Charlie," the Scourge replied. "This place is where it all began, and this is the place it will end. The being that sleeps here created it all. And from here too Creation will be unmade."

There was a pause while Charlie gave this his best shot.

No, he decided, he still wasn't getting it.

"So, this Dragon, it's . . . what? Another God?" he asked.

"That would be one name for it," the Scourge replied, "yes. But it would be better to leave the old stories of your world behind. The truth of the matter is this: the Dragon created everything. Then it slept."

"'On the seventh day He rested,'" quoted Charlie mechanically.

"Well," the Scourge admitted, "that part of your folklore is surprisingly accurate. But that's where the resemblance ends. After creating the universe, the Dragon slept, but it did not wake up."

"It didn't?" asked Charlie, doing his best to get his head round it.

"No," said the Scourge. "It has been asleep since time began."

Charlie was going to say something about this.

But then a thousand voices spoke in unison, and all thought ran out of his head.

Only one for whom the Void is pure in his heart, said the voices, *can awaken the Maker of All.*

The words had come like a series of explosions behind Charlie's eyeballs. He was stunned by them. Even so, it occurred to Charlie that—was it possible?—he recognized who was speaking.

Charlie Farnsworth, said Gukumat, *are you that one?*

There was a long silence. Charlie looked in vain to where the Scourge's face should have been, but all around him there was still nothing but darkness.

"Is this the, er . . . ?" he whispered. "Do I—?"

"**Say yes, Charlie**," said the Scourge.

"Yes!"

"**'The Void is pure in my heart.'**"

"The Void is pure in my heart!"

Approach, boomed Gukumat's voices, in the same eerie, thunderous unison.

And instantly, the darkness blazed into light.

"I know why the Scourge was exiled," Felix began. "I know why it was imprisoned."

Felix had returned from Hell. He'd had no choice in the matter. And now he was delivering the Scourge's message.

Esme stood in the butterfly room's ruined doorway. She was dressed in black—black combats and a black hooded top with the sleeves pulled well down—and she held the pigeon sword clasped to her chest.

The rest of the room was filled with men with guns. Their last attempt to keep Esme sedated had ended badly: there had been a number of casualties, and now the Sons of the Scorpion Flail had decided on a policy of keeping a discreet and careful distance. They looked nervous. But Felix only had eyes for her.

"Go on," said Esme quietly.

"Well," said Felix, "we in the Brotherhood always believed that if the Scourge were ever allowed to escape and make its way back to Hell, it would form an army of demons and lead it back to conquer the Earth." He shrugged. "We were wrong."

"Tell me, Felix," said Esme.

"All our religions are false," Felix said. At this, a couple of the Sons began to shift awkwardly. Felix ignored them and pressed on.

"There's no benevolent Creator watching over us all. There's no divine justice, no grand master plan. There's just this . . . *being* that made the universe and has been asleep ever since. The demons call it the Dragon."

He took a step closer toward her.

"I've seen it," he said. "The Scourge took me to the lowest part of Hell, far below where the demons live, and showed me where it sleeps."

His voice dropped almost to a whisper.

"It's huge, Esme. You can't imagine how big it is: the brain just can't take it in. All of Hell is built on its back, and I don't think it's even noticed. And now the Scourge is going to wake it up."

"So?" said Number 2.

Felix gritted his teeth.

"The sole purpose of the Scourge's existence," he explained, "is to wake the Dragon. For the whole of its life—longer than we can possibly imagine—it's been trying to do this one thing. Once, before, it almost succeeded: instead, the Scourge was sent into exile—imprisoned, here on Earth. But ever since then it's been biding its time, waiting for another chance. And now, thanks to this boy, Charlie, that chance has finally come."

"The chance for what?" asked Number 3 quietly.

Felix didn't want to say it. It felt too much like another betrayal.

He took a deep breath.

"The Scourge hates all living things," he said. "Even—it seems—itself. The Scourge will use Charlie to help it wake the Dragon, and if the Scourge succeeds, if the Dragon wakes . . . the universe will come to an end."

He paused.

"The whole of Creation will be wiped out: *everything will cease to exist.* Instead, there will be only Void: nothingness. 'Purity,' the Scourge calls it. Forever."

There. He had said it. Immediately, the thing inside him woke up and began its work. Felix could feel it. There was no turning back now.

It was an odd sensation. When the Scourge had told him what was going to happen to him, he'd been expecting to panic when the time came. Now that it was here—now he could see it happening and feel the slow seeping cold moving all the way through him—he felt strangely calm. He looked down at his hands. Already they were becoming translucent. Another moment, and a dull metallic line began to make itself visible through the flesh of his wrists. The line was the other side of the handcuffs the Sons had put him in when they'd found him as he stepped back through the Fracture.

When he'd returned from Hell, Felix had brought his death with him. Now he was fading away. Literally.

"My message is this," he said. "The only thing that can stop the Scourge from waking the Dragon—the only thing that can stop the universe from being destroyed—is you, Esme. This is what I was summoned to tell you. Either you return to Hell and face the Scourge again, or, well . . ." He shrugged miserably. "You get the picture."

The handcuffs fell to the floor with a dull clank.

"That's it," he said. "That's the end of the message. I don't know what the Scourge wants with you: it's obviously a trap. But as you can see," he said, holding his hands up in front of his face, "I had no choice."

His hands were completely transparent now. Through the thin misty shapes that were all that remained of them, Felix and Esme looked at each other.

"I'm sorry, Esme," said Felix, keeping his gaze on her thirstily for as long as he could. Esme was, after all, the only person he cared about in the whole world—even though she was the one person who could never have cared about him. He didn't mind, he realized. He loved her anyway, just the same: he *loved* her, he told himself, and the realization cast a last wisp of warmth through the freezing, creeping cold inside him.

Esme stared back at him. Her eyes were bright.

Then suddenly, silently, Felix disappeared.

The Brotherhood of Sleep was finished: the last surviving member of the generation that had let the Scourge escape was gone, and the demon's vengeance on its jailers was complete.

Almost.

"Jack," Esme whispered.

"What?" said Number 2.

"Jack," she told him. "I need Jack."

The Mission

"So . . ." said Jack to Esme later. "What's the plan again?"

They were standing in the Light of the Moon. It was late in the evening of the following day. Number 2 had finally bowed to Number 3's repeated requests and closed the pub down: the place was deserted apart from Jack, Esme, and the Sons of the Scorpion Flail, who were busily checking their equipment.

The Sons looked tense. Fair enough, Jack decided: when he'd made his first trip to Hell, he'd done it without thinking. These guys, by contrast, had had a whole day to worry about what they were getting themselves into.

Esme adjusted the strap of the pigeon sword on her back and gave him a tired look.

"Jack," she said, "we've been through all this. Until we go in, we don't know what we're dealing with. I've got to tackle the Scourge—we know that much. You've got to do whatever you can with Charlie." She sighed. "That's all we can say for sure at this point."

"But what about these Sons guys?" Jack asked quietly, taking a step closer to her. "D'you really trust them? After they, like, chained you up and everything?"

Esme bit her lip.

"I was dangerous," she said. "They didn't know what I might do." She shivered. "*I* don't know what I might do. Besides," she added, banishing the thought quickly, "Jessica sent for them. They can't be completely useless—can they?"

"I suppose we need all the help we can get," said Jack dryly.

"Not all the help," Esme replied, looking around. "Too many and I'll have to be watching their backs, as well as yours and mine."

There was a pause.

"So," said Jack. "That's it, then."

"What is?"

"The plan." Jack tried a grin. "The plan is there is no plan."

"That's about the size of it," said Esme, with, Jack was glad to notice, a grim but definite smile. "Yeah."

"Business as usual, eh?" Jack quipped. His own smile faded. "Listen, there's, er, something I've got to tell you. It's about Charlie."

"What about him?" Esme asked.

Jack took a deep breath. "Esme," he said, "you can't kill him."

"Now, I know how it is," he went on quickly. "If it's a straight choice, Charlie or, like, saving the universe, then I guess you've got to do what you've got to do. But before things get that far, I just wanted to say . . . well . . ."

He looked at Esme.

"Charlie's an idiot," he told her. "I know he's an idiot. He's stubborn, impatient, arrogant, pigheaded, and, you know, sometimes he's a bit of a knob. But"—he shrugged help-lessly—"he's my friend. He's got into this thing and it's gone over his head: he doesn't know what he's doing. And I want you to know that . . . well, whatever happens, I still think there's a chance we can save him. Okay?"

There was another pause.

Jack didn't claim to know very much about girls. He couldn't figure out what Esme was thinking. Her expression at that moment was, to him, unreadable.

"Jack," she said, "I don't know if we'll get the chance later, but . . ." She trailed off and looked down at her feet.

"What?" asked Jack.

"Well," said Esme, "I just wanted to thank you."

Jack stared at her.

"What for?"

Esme looked up at him, and Jack found himself trans-fixed by her amber eyes. Suddenly, he noticed a strange kind of tightening in his chest. His right kneecap, of all things, seemed to be twitching uncontrollably by itself: he hoped she didn't notice it. She really was, he decided again, very pretty indeed, actually.

"You brought me back," she said.

"Back?"

"Back from Hell," Esme prompted, smiling now. "When I was unconscious. That was you, right?"

"Oh," said Jack. "Er, yeah."

"Well, you know . . . thanks," Esme told him.

"'S'allright," Jack managed.

"I'm glad you're coming with me," said Esme.

And suddenly, she was giving him a hug! Esme was giving *him*—Jack!—a *hug*, and a stray hair from her elastic bands was tickling him on the nose! But just as suddenly as the hug had begun, it was over. Esme stood back.

"Good luck," she told him, looking into his eyes again. "And try to stay out of trouble, all right?"

"You too," said Jack. His ears were going red.

Esme smiled bleakly and turned away.

"Last check, gentlemen," said Number 2, and instantly the big pub was echoing with the nervous clicking and clinking of equipment—guns, ammo, who knew what else?—being rechecked for what must have been about the seventeenth time. Jack heard a flapping sound, then the Chinj swooped down to land on Jack's shoulder. Looking around, Jack caught its eye. The creature had arched one bushy eyebrow: it was smiling and giving Jack what looked suspiciously to him like a saucy look. Jack scowled. Then he noticed that the fiddling sounds of the Sons and their gear had stopped abruptly.

"What, may I ask," said Number 2, marching up to Jack in the sudden silence and pointing at the Chinj, "is *that*?"

Jack sighed. "It's a Chinj," he said gamely.

"How do you do?" asked the Chinj.

"What," said Number 2, still managing not to shout, "is it doing here?"

"He's not very polite, is he?" said the Chinj.

"It's kind of a long story," said Jack quickly, "and I figured it would only hold things up if I mentioned it before. The main thing is, it's coming with us."

"It most certainly is not!"

"And since it actually comes from Hell, it might be able to, I don't know, show us around a bit," Jack finished.

"I think you'll find I can really be quite helpful," put in the Chinj with a winning smile, doing its best.

For a moment, Number 2 just stared. His face was going a strange gray-red color, and Jack could see some goodish-sized veins standing out on his neck.

"I am *not*," began Number 2, "going on this mission with—"

"Hey," said Esme, walking up to Number 2 and looking up at him, right in the eye. "Me and Jack and . . ." She paused. "His, ah, friend here are going on this trip no matter what. As for you and your men . . ." She raked the room with a piercing gaze. "I still haven't decided yet whether I want *any* of you to come along—at all."

Number 2 stared at her and gaped.

"B-but," he spluttered. "But . . ."

Esme's amber eyes narrowed. Her hard hands lifted fractionally from her sides.

"Problem?" she asked.

Number 2 fell silent.

"Thought not," said Esme. "I'll let you take"—she considered—"three men. And you'd better stay out of our way. Now if you'll excuse us, we have a job to do."

She stalked off, over toward the cold spot in the air that marked the Fracture, leaving Number 2 standing there seething.

"Civilians," he said finally, and shook his head. He looked at his men and clicked his fingers: "Number Three? Number Nine? Number . . . Twelve? You're all with me. The rest of you, guard the Fracture till we come back." His face darkened. "*If we come back.*"

"Sir! Yes, sir!" barked the Sons—while the ones he'd called stepped forward.

"All set, Number Nine?" asked Number 2, with a significant look at the enormous pack the younger Son was carrying. "Everything five-by-five?"

"Yes, sir!" Number 9 snapped back proudly. The mysterious black rectangle on his back was so large that it stuck out all round his head, making his face look almost comically small. "Cocked and locked and ready to rock! Sir!"

Jack winced.

"Good man," said Number 2. "Suit up, gentlemen. It's time to hit the road."

Four black gas masks were pulled into place with a simultaneous whisper. Looking at the effect, Jack had to admit it was a good one. With the simple addition of this one prop, the Sons had ceased to look quite so terrified and had become— well, if not actually terrifying, they certainly looked a lot more formidable than they had before.

Gesturing at the Fracture, Number 2 turned to Esme. "After you, Miss Leverton."

Esme didn't bother to acknowledge this. She didn't even turn round. She just lifted her hands, and immediately the patch of air in front of her took on its glowing sheen.

Jack sighed. *Well*, he thought, *here we go ag—*

"This is it, gentlemen," said Number 2, interrupting. "This is what we've been training for. You," he added, turning to his men—and conspicuously ignoring Jack, "have been picked for this mission for one simple reason: you're the best. You hear me?"

"Sir! Yes, Sir!" barked the three Sons, their voices now muffled by their gas masks.

"Make me proud," said Number 2.

Wallies, thought Jack conclusively.

The Fracture began to open, and the dull red gave way to crisp, whispering white. Number 2 took a step forward, so he stood shoulder to shoulder with Esme.

"Let's do it," he said.

They stepped into the light and vanished. The three other Sons went after.

"Here we go, sir," murmured the Chinj in Jack's ear. "Home sweet home."

"Sure," said Jack, not looking at it. *Right.* He stepped into the whiteness, feeling it take him.

When he opened his eyes, he was in the throne room.

"And Mr. Farrell!" said a voice. "*What* a surprise."

A glance around the great red room was all it took. Jack saw that the Sons had already been unmasked and were now struggling in the grip of the same jelly stuff he'd encountered on his first trip to Hell.

The Scourge stood up from its throne.

"Overminister," it said, **"if you'd be so good, I'd like these people transported to the gladiator pits."** It glanced at Jack. **"That's where they belong, after all."**

My pleasure, Sire, Gukumat replied.

"Esme, you're coming with me. Take my hand, please."

And that, really, was when Jack began to be scared.

Esme was standing before the throne. Her arm was lifting as if it were being pulled by invisible strings. As Esme put herself into the hands of her enemy, all Jack could do was watch in horror. Then, together, they disappeared.

Jack sighed bitterly. More jelly stuff was already climbing his legs, running up his back, surrounding him all over from head to toe. He felt an all-too-familiar squeezing sensation—a moment of unbelievable tension—then Gukumat, the Sons, and the throne room all vanished, and Jack found he was back in his cell.

The Chinj wasn't with him, he realized. It was the first time Jack had thought of the little creature since they'd stepped through the Fracture, and for a moment he felt a little guilty: he hoped it had got away all right. To be honest, though, as he reflected, looking around himself, he had enough problems to be getting on with on his own.

The cell was exactly the same. He was surrounded by the same sandy-colored walls, the same ceiling—or lack of one;

there was the same floor. It was almost as if he'd never left.

"Can anyone hear me?" he shouted quickly before his voice betrayed him. "Hello? Is anyone there?"

For a long moment there was silence. Then—and the sound was like two pieces of sandpaper rubbing together—Jack heard laughter.

"Well, well, well," said a voice. "If it isn't fresh meat."

Jack did not reply.

"How are you, fresh meat?" asked Shargle. "Did you miss me? I sure missed you."

Jack walked over to the nearest wall and leaned against it. Then he let his legs sag and his back slide down it, until he was sitting on the floor in the corner. *Oh, perfect*, he thought, this was just perfect. Of all the demons in Hell he could've had for a next-door neighbor, it had to be this one. How completely, utterly—

"I knew you'd come back," the worm hissed through the wall. "I've been waiting. And we're going to have fun, you an' me. I know it."

Well, thought Jack, that was that. His second trip to Hell had already gone about as well as his first. He sighed, rested his head on his hands, and waited for whatever was going to go wrong next.

BLOOD

"I'm glad you decided to come," said the Scourge.

"You didn't exactly leave me much of a choice," Esme replied.

"Perhaps not. But before that, before Felix passed on my message, you had already made another choice, had you not?"

Esme could feel warm air slipping by on the bare skin of her face. Although the darkness surrounding her was total, she knew they were traveling downward, and at great speed. The Scourge's hand was still holding hers; it was cool and smooth and nothing like a human hand at all.

"What are you talking about?" she asked.

"When we last fought, when I showed you what you are, you reacted strangely," said the Scourge. "For a while, I was even afraid that you might not recover. Your attempt to deny the truth about yourself might easily have destroyed you utterly. Instead, you woke up—and that is a choice, of a kind. The question is, Why?"

"Why do you think?" asked Esme through her teeth.

"I was hoping," said the Scourge, "it was because you've accepted the situation: you've understood what you are at last, and you've realized it's pointless to resist me."

"Guess again."

"But in fact," the Scourge went on wearily, "you've only come back because you still think you can defeat me."

"Bingo," said Esme.

"Oh dear," said the Scourge. "How tiresomely human of you. Well, we shall see."

A glimmer of light appeared far below them, quickly growing to a chilly white glow as they continued their plummeting descent. Esme now saw they were traveling at blurring speed down an arterial red–colored tunnel. The tunnel was becoming narrower and narrower, until there was barely enough room to pass without touching its moist-looking sides. Then it opened out suddenly into a space so vast that for a moment it took Esme's breath away.

Beneath Esme's feet, to begin with, was nothing more than a kind of steamy red mist: wherever the floor was, it was too far away to see, and the same was true of the walls. The ceiling, the only part of the room she could make out so far, seemed to stretch out forever in any direction she looked. It was made of the same wet-looking fleshy red stuff as the tunnel. All across it ran a series of meandering raised strips, like gigantic dark blue pipes of some kind. What Esme was seeing wasn't making a whole lot of sense to her, so as she and the demon hurtled on downward, she waited as calmly as she could for whatever the Scourge was going to show her next. But when at last the floor of the vast room *did* finally loom into view, Esme found herself staring again.

From here—from the altitude she was at now—the raised bluish pipe things didn't look like pipes anymore. They were more like blood vessels. *Veins*, she realized. Vast as it was, the room looked like it was alive. And gigantic. Bigger than anything she could possibly have imagined.

"**The heart of the Dragon**," said the Scourge.

For the past few minutes, Esme had noticed an odd sensation inside herself. It was a kind of quickening: a shivering sense of electric anticipation, spreading through her whole being, sending rushes of goose bumps up her arms and the back of her neck. It wasn't fear or nerves—she'd learned to control those. It was something else. Something—

"**Yes!**" said the Scourge delightedly. "**You feel it. I knew you would.**"

"Feel what?" said Esme, and scowled at her own stubbornness forcing her into so weak a lie.

"**Don't you know what that is? That sensation?**"

"No."

"**I'll tell you. It is the demon in you.**"

"Yeah, right."

"**This place,**" said the Scourge, gesturing grandly with its free hand, "**is where our power comes from. This is where our people began: the first people, the rulers of Creation, and the ones who will bring it to its conclusion. All that is strong and good in you—all that is demon—has its origin in here. That is why you're feeling what you feel now.**"

"Why don't you just cut the nonsense," Esme suggested,

"and show me whatever it is you want to show me?"

"**All in good time**," said the Scourge.

Far below, the veins on the floor of the chamber were getting bigger—bunching and bulging and knotting together. Before much longer, Esme could see what they were leading to: a plateau, huge and roughly circular, that swelled out of the surrounding meaty red flesh like some bulbous growth or excrescence. As they got closer, Esme began to make out more details.

Every inch of the plateau's fleshy red surface was covered, it seemed to her, by thousands of tall figures—each one of them apparently identical. Each and every one of them was dressed in flowing robes and floating off the ground. Each and every one of them had conjured a magical globe of light and was holding it, patiently, suspended over their long fingers to show the way.

Gukumat: all of the army of strange floating figures were Gukumat. As Esme and the Scourge made their final approach to the plateau, the Overminister's multiple bodies parted simultaneously, drifting back with a rustle of silk to form a place for the two of them to land. Trying hard not to boggle too obviously, Esme touched down, only a yard or so away from the boy the Scourge had brought her to see.

"**Charlie**," said the Scourge. "**How are you?**"

"Oh, hi," said Charlie vaguely. "Yeah, I'm okay. How are you?"

Charlie was standing in front of a strange hump in the plateau's surface: a thick cylinder about the size of a petrol drum, made of meat. It was gnarled and twisted by the bone structure and blood vessels behind its fleshy exterior: like the plateau and everything else since the tunnel, it didn't look built, it looked *grown*.

Strangely, Charlie didn't seem to recognize Esme or even know she was there. After answering the Scourge, Charlie's eyes had gone blank: he just stood there, frozen, like a shop-window dummy waiting to be positioned, while the black tattoo writhed listlessly under his skin. Esme frowned.

"I now have complete control of his mind," the Scourge explained. "He will respond only to the stimuli I choose for him. He can't hear or see or sense anything other than what I allow him to. Including, of course, you."

"Nice," said Esme. "How did you manage that?"

"He wants to become Emperor of Hell," said the Scourge, with a smirk in its voice. "The fool wants it so much that he has abandoned everything from his life before he met me and put himself entirely into my hands. In short," it added, "he trusts me."

Esme looked at Charlie. She waved a hand in front of his eyes and only succeeded in making herself feel very silly indeed.

"All right," she said. "Well, what are you going to make him do?"

"We're going to wake the Dragon," said the Scourge. "This heart chamber, when the Dragon wakes, will be flooded for an instant with its lifeblood. In that instant, the Dragon will unmake what it created, and the purity of the Void will be complete once more."

Esme smiled mirthlessly. "That's a Hell of a story."

"Indeed," the Scourge replied. "It is, nonetheless, true."

Esme thought for a moment. The air in the chamber was moist and still. She was conscious of the vastness of the space around her and of Gukumat's eyes on her: all of them.

"Let's say I believe you," she began.

"I assure you," said the Scourge, "if you don't, then by the time you realize your mistake, it will already be too late."

"Sure. But this 'waking the Dragon' business," Esme went on slowly. "Can anyone do it, or is it just you?"

"Only I have the power to awaken the Dragon," said the Scourge, with quiet pride. "It is my greatest gift: the purpose of my life and the cause of my years of exile."

"But you can't do it *alone*," Esme pursued. "Can you? You have to have a puppet—some sucker to be your hands and do your dirty work for you. Am I right?"

"I cannot do it without a willing host body," the Scourge replied. "That is correct."

Esme thought some more. "Well," she said—

—and drew her weapon. The pigeon sword whispered through the air and stopped, millimeters from Charlie's throat.

"What if I just kill him?" she asked.

There was a pause.

No one had tried to stop her. Neither the Scourge nor Gukumat had moved in the slightest—and as for Charlie, Esme doubted whether he'd even noticed how close to death he was. Esme kept her blade at his throat. Her eyes became rooted to the rhythmic pulse of the artery in Charlie's neck.

She could strike him dead in a heartbeat. But she did not.

"You can't," said the Scourge gently. "Can you?"

The point of the blade shook fractionally as, for a second, Esme tried to force herself. Then, slowly, she took the sword away from Charlie's neck.

"Now you see how weak your humanity has made you," said the Scourge. It turned to the nearest Overminister. "Let us begin."

At once, Gukumat's voices rose in unison.

Blood will decide it. Blood will begin it. Seal your intention with blood.

Charlie blinked, and his eyes came into focus. He was still looking at the Scourge.

"What happens now?" he whispered.

Esme shook her head. It was pathetic.

"You must cut yourself, Charlie," the Scourge explained.

"You want me to *what*?"

"Cut yourself. Let a few drops of your blood fall onto the altar. This will"—it paused—"prove your determination to rule. Your left thumb would be a good place."

The Scourge made a small gesture, and an ink-black shape hunched out on Charlie's right shoulder: Ashmon scampered down his arm, and by the time the ferret creature reached his hand, it had become a scalpel-like knife. Surprised, Charlie looked down at the knife, then he looked back up at the Scourge.

"You, er . . ." he said. "You really want me to . . . ?"

"Trust me," said the Scourge.

"Well," said Charlie, "okay."

He wiped his left thumb on the leg of his black jeans, then brought it up toward the knife. The short, gleaming blade was now just a millimeter or two away from his skin.

Suddenly, weirdly, Charlie found that he was thinking of his body—falling into the river, dropping away endlessly into the cold and the wet and the dark. Then Charlie thought of his mother, still waiting for him at home. There was an odd feeling in his stomach—something warm and bright—and he realized that a big part of him didn't really want to do this. So, quickly, before he could think too much—

—he did it anyway.

The knife was so sharp that it didn't even hurt at first. It was only when he pushed the blade upward, opening the wound, that it started to sting. Charlie bit his lip and held his hand out over the cylinder thing. With a clicking sound that was surprisingly loud in the silence, fat droplets of dark blood fell onto its surface. The droplets began to form a pool.

Then it started.

With a sudden gurgling sound, the pool of blood simply vanished, sucked away out of sight. Surprised, Charlie took a step back—or rather, he tried to and found that he couldn't: his feet seemed to have disappeared into the ground.

There was a strange rustling, whispering, stretching-splitting-crackling sound, as unseen tendrils of flesh and sinew began to grow and thicken all around him. Something big was emerging from the floor behind him, a rearing shape like a shadow made of flesh, molding itself around Charlie's body. When the stuff reached his elbows, caressing him encouragingly, he flinched: but then, as he was gently but firmly pulled back into the chair—the throne of blood and bone that had been prepared for him—he smiled uncertainly. Seated now, his hands resting on great red swelling pillows of sticky meat, he rode the throne upward, grinning like an idiot, and all Esme could do was watch.

"CHARLIE!" she yelled. "*CHARLIE!*"

Of course, Charlie didn't answer. The Scourge took her hand. There was a sensation like huge black wings closing around her.

Then Esme opened her eyes, and she was somewhere else.

She was sitting on the edge of a bed. It was an ordinary single bed, but it looked quite strange to her just then, because apart from the bed there was nothing else in the room except white-ness—blank, bright, and surrounding—and the Scourge, standing before her.

"There," it said. "Now, for the first time, I think I see why living things are so strangely attached to their short and pointless little lives."

Esme just looked at it. "Excuse me?" she said.

"I have been waiting for that moment," said the Scourge slowly, "for longer than you could possibly imagine. It has been my one purpose in life, and my lifetime has lasted many thousands of times longer than the longest of humankind."

"Yes?" Esme managed. "So?"

"Through years of exile and imprisonment, I have been waiting to finish my task. And now—now, when the end is in sight—I find, to my astonishment, that I am thinking of renouncing it. Do you understand me?"

"Not really," said Esme. "No."

"Of course you don't." The Scourge shook its head. "How could you? How could you possibly grasp the enormity of what—"

"Okay, look," Esme interrupted, pointing at her face. "See? I'm bored now. Why don't we just fight and get this over with?"

"Because," said the Scourge, "I think . . ." It paused.

"I love you."

Esme stared at it with wide eyes.

"*What?*"

"You heard me."

"Yeah, I heard you," Esme spluttered, "but I don't know what the Hell you think you mean. What—what are you talking about?"

"You are my child!" said the Scourge, with sudden fervor. "Crippled, twisted, stunted by your humanity—but my child, a child of mine nonetheless."

It stood closer to her, leaning over her.

"I can help you," it murmured. "I can help you to become whatever it is in you to become. You are unique, my poor one. Since time began, there has been nothing to compare with you. And with me at your side you can—"

"All right, that's *enough*," said Esme. She shuddered.

The Scourge took a step back.

"I told Felix you could stop me," it said, sounding strangely . . .

hurt all of a sudden, Esme realized. "I didn't lie: here are my terms. If you will agree to stay with me here in Hell, I will stop the ritual. I'll release the boy. I'll abandon the very purpose of my existence, and the Dragon's sleep will remain unbroken."

Esme just stared.

"You are my daughter," the Scourge told her. "We belong together. If you can accept that, then the universe will be spared. If not, well . . ."

The Scourge shrugged.

"Think about what I've said. But don't take too long to decide."

It vanished, and Esme was left in the freezing whiteness, alone.

THE GATHERING

This is ridiculous, thought Jack, finally slumping on the sandy floor.

How the Hell was he supposed to rescue Charlie when he was trapped in a cell?

Come to that, how the Hell could Jack possibly find Charlie, even if he were able to get out? Thanks to the teleporting properties of the jelly stuff, Jack knew next to nothing about Hell's geography: he wouldn't've known where to begin to look.

Face it, he thought, if saving the universe was something someone like *him* was capable of doing, then everyone would be at it. It was as simple—as typical—as that.

It was at that moment that he heard a soft rumbling and creaking sound. The large stone wall was lifting again.

Jack sat up. The outside of his cell was in shadow: beyond the wall he could see nothing but darkness. He stood, walked over, and, gingerly, put his head out.

That was when Shargle grabbed him.

Thick coils of muscle dropped around him and tightened.

Jack struggled, but he couldn't move: his arms were crushing against his ribs, and one of Shargle's unspeakable heads was looming toward him, eyes glinting gray-blue in the dark.

"Hello, fresh meat," said the worm, grinning delightedly. "Remember me?"

"Of course I remember you, Shargle," said Jack, with exasperated effort. "But what the Hell do you want?"

"I'll tell you what I want," said Shargle, leaning closer. "I want to see your insides. Yes! Your nasty little innards, squeezing out of you! Fresh meat, you owe me a death!"

"What are you talking about?"

"You were promised to us!" whined Shargle's other head, rearing out of the darkness to Jack's left. "You're ours! It said so on the coin!"

"So?"

"Everyone's always so *mean* to Shargle," said the first head, pouting.

"Name-calling!" said the second.

"Hitting us!"

"Tying us together!" The heads looked at each other, shuddered in sympathy, then smiled. "But now," both of them chorused, "now, at last, *Shargle* can be mean to *you*!"

Heaven's sake, thought Jack. "Shargle," he began, "this really isn't a good time—"

"For us," announced Shargle's first head, "any time is a good time."

"But the universe is about to end!" Jack gasped, doing his best. "The Dragon is about to wake up!"

For a moment, all four of Shargle's eyes widened in sur-prise—then scowled.

"'The Dragon,'" one head snorted. "*That* old story!"

"No one believes in the Dragon anymore!"

"Now beg us for mercy!"

"Yes, beg." The worm's coils wrenched tighter.

"Whine! Cringe! Squeal!"

And now Jack could feel his bones grinding together. Great gouting blue fireworks were going off behind his eyeballs; his head felt ominously tight, like a tube of toothpaste being squeezed without the cap being taken off, and when he tried to breathe all there was was the nauseating stench of the worm. As Shargle's heads leaned toward him, the revolting wet brown holes of his mouths opening wider and wider, Jack's vision seemed to shrink down until he could see nothing else, but then . . .

Then, suddenly, there was a burst of light, and a thunderous, echoing voice said,

CITIZENS OF HELL, YOUR ATTENTION PLEASE: THIS IS OVERMINISTER GUKUMAT. YOU ARE SUMMONED, ONE AND ALL, TO AN ANCIENT CEREMONY. PREPARE FOR TRANSPORTATION, EACH AND EVERY ONE OF YOU, IN THREE—

There was a rising hum in the air: jelly stuff winked into being and began, instantly, to spread.

TWO, boomed the voice.

"EEEEEAAAAAAAAAAAAGHlllp!" Shargle shrieked out his frustration from both of his heads but was abruptly cut off as the shimmering substance swallowed him.

ONE.

The jelly stuff stiffened, went thick.

And for a moment, everything was black.

Shargle and Jack had been transported together: Jack was still wrapped in the worm's coils. Shargle's grip had loosened—a little, not much—but the weird thing was that Jack couldn't feel the ground. He seemed to be floating.

"Where are we?" Jack managed. "What's happened?"

"Jack?" said a voice with a French accent he recognized. "Jack? It is you?"

"Number Three!" said Jack. "Where are you? Oh, *Shargle*," he added, struggling in the dark, "for God's sake, why can't you just get off me?"

"No!" squeaked Shargle nervously. "Shan't! No! Fresh meat can just—"

ATTENTION, SCUM OF THE GLADIATOR PITS!

Everyone fell silent.

You are here, said the voice, *not because we wish it but because the ritual demands that all demons in Hell be witness to the Dragon's awakening. You should see your presence here for what it is—an unspeakable honor for ones such as yourselves—and act accordingly.*

"Arse," belched another familiar voice.

You have been brought into the presence of the most holy and omnipotent DRAGON, Gukumat went on. *The Eater of Worlds: Alpha and Omega—the Creator and Destroyer of*

All. Look on your god, you supplicant scum. Look on your god and TREMBLE!

"Gah!" said Jack—and everyone else—as the darkness suddenly flooded with light. Jack's seared retinas took several moments to adjust. But the next thing he said was, "Whoa." The word didn't cover it. No words did. So for a while, Jack just stared.

Jack and Shargle were being held in a bubblelike field of what was, presumably, magic of some kind. As well as Jack and the worm, the bubble was big enough to hold all four Sons of the Scorpion Flail and a large pulsating blob that Jack was able to recognize—to his surprise—as Jagmat. Jagmat, Jack, Shargle, Number 3, Number 2, Number 9, and Number 12 were all floating around in the bubble like snow in a recently shaken snow globe. The Sons looked scared. They had a right to be. But Jack wasn't paying attention to his companions. The surface of the strange magical bubble thing that was now imprisoning them was transparent: Jack was looking out of the bubble at what was beyond.

He gaped.

The bubble was suspended from the ceiling of a gigantic red chamber—so big that Jack wasn't even sure it qualified as a single room. Other bubbles just like it, containing various numbers of unhappy gladiators, were strung around the ceiling in a vast, necklacelike ring.

Waiting below them, on the floor of the chamber, was what had to be every single demon in Hell. The entire demon population was laid out below Jack in a huge, dark, crawling circle. There were creatures down there that defied description. But he wasn't looking at these either.

In the center of the chamber was an enormous plateau, made out of the same bulging fleshy red stuff as the ceiling and floor. All across it stood a mass of identical white-robed figures. And in the center of that—at the center of everything—were two who Jack knew well: Charlie, seated on a throne of meat, and the Scourge, standing beside him.

DEMONS OF HELL! boomed Gukumat's multitudinous voice. *This is a day that has been long in coming! Only once before, since the beginning of Creation—only once, since the most holy Dragon first fell into its ancient slumber—has the whole mass of our people been gathered together as we are at this moment. And WHAT A SIGHT WE ARE!*

The gladiators' bubbles actually shuddered in the air at this; the giant chamber rang with the sound as all the demons on the ground roared their approval.

SINCE TIME BEGAN, IT IS WE WHO HAVE HAD POWER IN THE UNIVERSE!

The crowd was in ecstasy.

IT IS FOR US THAT THE PLANETS TREMBLE IN THEIR ORBITS!

Delirium. Pandemonium.

AND IT IS WE, said Gukumat, *BY DIVINE RIGHT, WHO WILL BRING ALL CREATION TO AN END!*

Strangely, on this line, the riotous applause from Hell's assembled population seemed to die down a little.

"Jack?" asked Number 2 suddenly. His face was pale, his

eyes were bright, and his voice was high and tight sounding. "Could you possibly tell us what's going on here, please?"

"Quiet," said Jack.

For too long, Gukumat went on, *the universe has been allowed to continue, filling the Great Darkness with its chatter and its noise. For too long we, the true guardians of Creation, have allowed it to wallow in its trivial and pointless pursuits. My brothers,* said the voice, *it is time to bring history to a close. It is time to awaken the Great Swallower and let darkness reign supreme once more! It is TIME,* the voice screamed, *reaching a pitch of feverish intensity, FOR A RETURN TO THE PURITY OF THE VOID!*

On uttering this, Gukumat raised every single one of his sticklike arms, ready to greet the rapturous thunder of acclaim that the Overminister was naturally expecting.

He didn't get it. Instead, the vast crowd murmured and blustered in confusion.

Gukumat's thousands of hands dropped to his thousands of sides. His thousands of shining robes flashed white as he turned his backs on the crowd—and bowed once, inward, low.

My demon brethren, he said, *there is one here who will explain what you are about to witness much better than I ever could. It is, therefore, my peculiar honor to present to you your one true Emperor. The Voice of the Void, whose breath is the wind and whose rage makes all worlds tremble. The Lord of Crossing-Places, King of All Tears, and the Suzerain Absolute of the Dominions of Hell. Demons, I give you—*

"Get *on* with it!" belched Jagmat.

—KHENTIMENTU THE SCOURGE!!!

Breaking scuffles on the ground suddenly became good-size riots: the crowds of demons were jostling for position, trying to get a look at what was going on.

Helpless, Jack just watched.

"But what about *me*?" whined Charlie suddenly.

The Scourge had been just about to speak. Now, distracted, it turned to look at the boy on the red throne. Charlie was scowling and tugging, weakly but insistently, at the demon's liquid-black arm.

"Hey!" said Charlie. "Aren't you listening? What about *me*? I mean—I'm going to be the Emperor, right? Not you."

"We're coming to you, Charlie," said the Scourge soothingly. **"In fact, I was just about to mention you."**

"No tricks," said Charlie. "*I'm* going to be Emperor. I am! Right? You promised."

"Indeed I did, Charlie," said the Scourge, resting a cool, liquid hand on the boy's cheek. **"Indeed I did."**

Charlie felt a soft pressure in his brain—a pushing sensation so slight that he barely noticed it.

And instantly his ears rang with an echoing storm of noise.

It was the crowd!

And they were chanting something! A rhythmic chant, two simple syllables, making the vast room reverberate as they repeated them again and again. What were they saying? It was hard to make it out. It wasn't—was it? Yes!

CHAR-LEE! they roared. CHAR-LEE! CHAR-LEE! CHAR-LEE!

"Your true Emperor, who will lead all Hell into a new era of peace and prosperity!" *said the Scourge, the chant already collapsing into a surge of delirious noise.* **"CHARLIE FARNSWORTH!"**

And the crowd went wild!

Charlie smiled, tears coming to his eyes and running down his face. He raised an arm, acknowledging the wave of respect, admiration, and, yes, love that was coming at him then, a wave that threatened to lift him up and sweep him away on a tide of unspeakable happiness. They loved him! They really loved him! And what was even better, of course, the best thing of all, was that they'd always love him—forever and ever! Unlike, say, his dad for instance (he grimaced), *the demons would never leave or decide they preferred someone else. They would never get tired or fed up or sad or change in any way whatsoever: they would love him unconditionally, forever. And Charlie and the demons would be happy together! Safe and happy until the end of time! Safe and happy and—*

The Scourge looked at the boy on the throne. Charlie's eyes were open, but they were glazed, their attention turned inward, lost in the trivial yet apparently necessary delusion that had taken perhaps two seconds to construct and position in the child's primitive mind.

You don't deserve the universe, thought the Scourge, disgusted. **None of you do.**

It turned to face the assembled masses.

"My fellow demons," it said, **"the time has come."**

"Shargle, get off me!" said Jack for what felt like the millionth time as he continued to struggle in the worm's quivering coils.

"The Dragon!" shrieked one head.

"It's real!" shrieked another. "The Scourge'll wake it up! We're doomed!"

"Shargle, give it a rest, will yer?" belched Jagmat, rippling a frill of his blancmangelike body to propel himself through the magic-charged air toward Jack.

"Whotsyerface!" he boomed, dealing the still-trussed Jack a blow on the shoulder with a burly pink pseudopod that sent him careening helplessly into the magic bubble's wall. The wall bulged, fizzed, but—luckily, in view of the vertiginous drop onto the waiting horde below—held.

"Jagmat," Jack managed. "Hi."

"Ain't that your friend down there?" Jagmat remarked, pointing at the distant figure of Charlie with a tentacle.

"Yeah," said Jack. "I'm afraid so."

"Him'n the Scourge ain't gonna do what I fink they're gonna do, are they?" Jagmat asked. His tone was light, but Jack could hear the seriousness underlying the question.

"Yeah," said Jack. "I think they are."

"Well, holy crap!" belched Jagmat, swelling up and turning pale. "We're in some trouble here and no mistake!"

But Jack didn't reply. He was distracted. At the top of the bubble something weird—as in, even more weird—was happening. A strange black spot had materialized in the air. For a moment, Jack thought he was imagining it, but the spot was getting bigger—until suddenly, before Jack's astonished eyes, a *face* had appeared: a tiny face, just hanging there.

It was the Chinj.

"There you are, sir!" it said. Its dainty features creased into a delicate grimace. "Erm, I'll be right with you."

For a moment, the extraordinary spectacle outside the bubble was forgotten. Jack, Jagmat, Shargle, Number 3, and the rest of the Sons all just stared as the strange hole in the air suddenly widened to a kind of doorway.

Beyond the doorway was darkness: it clearly led to somewhere else. And it was big enough for a person to get through easily.

With a flutter of its wide black wings, the Chinj emerged into the bubble with them.

"What?" began Jack, his head beginning to hurt. "How did you—?"

"I'm afraid explanations will have to wait, sir," said the Chinj firmly. "Suffice it to say, I had help. Now . . ." It gestured behind itself. "This mini-Fracture will take us to a secure location in the Dragon's lymphatic system."

"Sorry?" said Jack.

"We should be far enough away for Gukumat not to be able to find us. However," the Chinj pursued grimly, "this Fracture is, I'm afraid, only temporary. If you wish to escape from your imprisonment here, you need to come with me. Right," it added, "now."

"Where're you going?" To Jack's surprise, it was one of Shargle's heads that had spoken.

The Chinj frowned. "It's no concern of yours, gladiator," it said primly. "But Jack and I are going to the Parliament."

"Parliament?" echoed Jack.

"It's our only hope," the Chinj announced. "We must speak with the Grand Cabal."

"No!" shrieked Shargle, unwinding his coils from round Jack at last and propelling himself to the furthest side of the bubble. "Not the Cabal! Not the Parliament! Not that!"

"I 'ate to admit it," belched Jagmat quietly, "but the worm's got a point: fink I'd rather take my chances with the Dragon."

"There's no time to argue," said the Chinj, turning to Jack. "Sir, if you want to help Miss Esme—if you want to stand any chance of preventing the Scourge from awakening the Dragon—then you simply must come with me this instant. I promise you," the Chinj added quietly, looking deep into Jack's eyes. "There's no other way."

"All right," said Jack. He turned to look at the Sons.

Even with his previous experience of Hell, Jack was finding the current situation alarming enough; the effect it was having on the Sons was clearly nothing short of catastrophic. The four grown men were floating and tangling and clinging helplessly to one another, a confused huddle of limbs, military equipment, and miserable scared faces.

"Come on," Jack told them. "Let's go."

"I am with you," said Number 3 after a moment, detaching himself and swimming over toward him through the magic-charged air.

"No *way*!" Number 2 spluttered, staring after him. "No way! There's no possibility on Earth that I'm following a kid and a . . ." Words failed him. "A *thing* into who-knows-what just because they say so. We're all staying here to, uh, assess the situation." He recovered himself. "That's an order."

"Sir," began Number 3, "with respect, we are not 'on Earth' any longer." He gestured outside the bubble, at the scene below. "We are out of our depth here: far out of our depth. Jack and his friend seem to know what zey are doing. I believe we should—"

"Three, I forbid you to follow them." Number 2 crossed his arms. "That's final."

"Look," said Jack, with sudden fury. "I don't know what you people have come here for. It's obviously some big secret, since you haven't told me what it is. Frankly, I couldn't care less. But I'll tell you why I'm here." He paused. "I'm here to help my friends and—it sounds like—save the universe. And I could do with a little help. Now, are you coming with me or what? Because if you're not, then you can just get stuffed!"

Get stuffed? echoed Jack's brain jeeringly. It was typical, really, just typical that he hadn't even managed to swear properly. Still, he'd said his piece: it was up to them now.

"Hell, I'll go," said Number 12, with a nervous glance at Shargle and Jagmat. "Anywhere's gotta be better than here—right?"

"Roger that," said Number 9.

The Chinj was looking at the portal, the edges of which

were vibrating and quivering ominously. "Sir," it said warningly.

"Just coming," said Jack.

"Well, I'm not!" said Number 2. "And you can't make me! There's no way you can—AAAGH!"

Number 12 and Number 9 had grabbed his shoulders roughly and thrown him. Helplessly, he slid through the magic-charged air. The Chinj fluttered daintily aside as Number 2 approached the mini-Fracture and plunged through it before he could stop himself.

The other Sons followed. Then Jack. Then the Chinj.

"Nutters," belched Jagmat.

But they'd vanished.

BLACK WINGS

For a long time Esme sat where the Scourge had left her, staring into whiteness, alone.

Then, a strange dark spot materialized in the air. The spot widened—and a small old man appeared.

The man was wearing a rumpled tweed suit with patches on the elbows and a large leather flying cap with big earflaps. He also wore fingerless gloves made out of purple wool, and he was rubbing his hands vigorously, producing an odd soft scrunching sound in the silence of the weird white room.

"I can't stand this place," he said, looking around.

"Sorry?" asked Esme.

"This *place*," snapped the man, who clearly hated repeating himself. "I can't stand it! Why the Scourge insists on taking people here, I simply can't imagine." He paused, looking nervously from side to side. "It's definitely gone. Hasn't it?"

"What's gone?"

"The Scourge!"

"Oh. Yes. Yes, it's gone."

"Well, that's something, at any rate. Oooh, it's cold in here." The man went back to rubbing his hands for another moment or two. Then, suddenly, as if noticing her for the first time, he looked up at Esme. "How do you do?" he said, beaming delightedly. "I'm God."

Esme's eyes narrowed. "Hi," she said carefully.

"I've been meaning to speak to you for quite a while, actually," said God. "I've helped your friend, and now it's your turn, but . . . well, it's much too cold for me in here." He gestured behind him at the extraordinary hole in the air, which was now wide enough for them both to pass through. "Why don't we step into my office," he asked, "as it were?"

Esme looked at him.

"I'm sorry," she said, feeling very strange, "but really, I have to stay here."

God's hand fell to his sides. "Don't tell me," he said. "You've got to save the universe."

"Well, yeah," said Esme, surprised.

"Well, believe me," said God, "you certainly won't be able to do that alone, so please, why don't you stop wasting my time and—*unkh*!"

He made the last noise because Esme's hand was suddenly around his throat. Pulling God toward her easily, Esme showed him she was serious for a moment: his eyes bugged outward and his little arms flapped in the air in a very satisfactory manner. Then she relaxed her grip enough to let him breathe.

"You know," she said, "I'm not feeling very patient or

polite right now. In fact, I'm not in a good mood at all. So how about you just tell me what you want?"

"It's not what *I* want," said God, with obvious difficulty. "It's what *you* want. What I can offer you."

"And what's that?"

"Knowledge," said God.

Esme just looked at him.

"I'm the archivist here," God explained. "I have records of everything that has happened—and I do mean everything—since time began. If there's anything you want to know—anything at all—then I can help you!"

Esme frowned. "You can tell me how to beat the Scourge?"

"Maybe."

"Maybe's no use to me."

"Maybe's all I've got," snapped God.

Esme stared at him, surprised again: he was annoyed at her, she realized, not because she had him by the throat but because she'd disrespected his job and what he knew.

"All right," she said, and released him.

"*Thank* you," said God. "Now, shall we?" He held out a hand.

Esme took it uncertainly, and they stepped through the hole in the air, out into whatever was beyond.

Esme blinked: the whiteness of the strange room had vanished, and it took a moment for her eyes to adjust. They were hovering, she realized, in midair, in the center of a tall, chimneylike structure. The chimney was very wide, and its walls were made of thousands of huge slabs of black rock, fitted one on top of the other. High above, Esme saw a tiny pinprick of gray light. Darkness yawned below her feet.

"We are now," God announced proudly, "in the central shaft of the palace. It stretches all the way from the Needle, at its summit, right down to the Dragon's heart—a distance of some seventy thousand—"

BOOM! He was interrupted by a sudden deep burst of noise coming up from somewhere below them. A jarring series of rippling shock waves shook the rocks, massive as they were, in their places.

"Ah," said God, as loose dust and soot fell pattering around them. "Oh dear."

"You want to tell me what that was?" asked Esme.

"It's the Dragon," said God, as if it was obvious. "The Dragon's juices have been released, and they are now eating away at the foundations of the palace. Soon all Hell—and all its inhabitants—will be digested, converted into raw energy so that the Great Swallower can wake itself up. The Scourge must be further along with the ritual than I thought. We'd better hurry."

"Hurry where?" asked Esme.

"That way," said God, jabbing one mauve-gloved finger upward. "And quickly, if you please. As fast as you can."

Esme pursed her lips but did as she was asked. The massive slabs of black rock in the chimney sides began to blur together as she picked up speed. After a few seconds, she turned to look at her companion.

"Is this right?" she enquired. "We keep going like this?"

"No," said God, shaking his head. "Stop a minute. Please, just stop."

Puzzled, Esme did. Soon they were perfectly still once more, hanging in midair over the yawning chasm below.

"I thought," said God, with elaborate sarcasm, "that you were supposed to be *fast*."

"Sorry?" said Esme.

"You're kin to Khentimentu!" said God, as if he were talking to a moron. "When it comes to speed, in all Hell's long history there's never been a demon to match the Scourge. And here you are," he added, "toddling along like we've got all the time in the universe!"

"You want me to go faster?" Esme asked. "Is that what you're saying?"

"If it's not too much trouble," said God, with a sneer.

For another long moment, Esme just looked at him. Then, "Fine," she said—

—and took off at high speed straightaway. The old man's fingers tightened around hers in an effort not to be left behind. She forged on, blasting her way upward, until noise of the air resistance building up in front of her began to roar in her ears.

"There!" she shouted. "How about that?"

But to her surprise, God was shaking his head again.

Incredulous, Esme slowed to a stop once more, just as—

BAKHOOM! Another great shudder of noise from below rippled the very air around them. When the walls stopped shaking, Esme saw that God was almost incandescent with impatience.

"Didn't you hear me?" he asked. He gestured round them. "Didn't you hear that? We have places to go! Things to do! And all you do is dawdle!"

"I wouldn't call that dawdling," said Esme.

"I've known Chinj who could fly faster than you're going," God spat. Then he sighed. "I thought you had a real chance against the Scourge. I thought you might have what it takes." He looked her up and down, then shook his head. "Obviously, I was mistaken."

"Look," said Esme, feeling herself losing patience again. "I don't know what it is you want from me exactly, but I'll tell you: it's not possible to fly any faster than that."

"Oh, great!" said God. "Perfect! Now we're going to get into an argument about what's 'possible'! And what a wonderful time and place for it, I might add!"

Esme stared at him.

"Don't you know anything?" said God. "The Scourge can be faster than *light*. The molecules simply part around it: the very fabric of reality would get out of Khentimentu's way if that were its wish. And here's *you*, arguing with *me* about what's possible."

"Hang on," said Esme. "You're saying I can be as fast as the Scourge?"

"Hallelujah," said God theatrically. "I do believe the penny is starting to drop."

"Faster than light?" echoed Esme.

"And things like walls won't stop you either," said God. "Now, are you going to get a move on or aren't you?"

Esme bit her lip and thought about it.

"All right," she said. "I suppose I could try. But there's just one thing. If I can really be as fast as you say, how will we know where we're going?"

"My dear girl," said God. "You just keep to your side of things, and I'll worry about mine. All right? I just need you to get up to speed."

Esme shrugged. "Okay, then. Let's go."

"And put your back into it this time!" squeaked God.

But suddenly, they were going so fast that the wind whipped the words from his mouth.

Still frowning, Esme took herself up to what she'd considered up till then to be her top speed and stayed there. Words echoed and spun in her head.

The Scourge could move faster than light.

There's something a bit special about you.

Strength without limit. Power beyond imagining—

Was it true? she wondered. Was it really true that all along she had only been using a fraction of her potential? Perhaps it was. But if she did let her power out, if she did use her potential, wasn't that . . . well, dangerous? If her power came from the Scourge, then perhaps she wouldn't be able to control it. Perhaps it might make her evil: perhaps it might mean that the Scourge could control her. Even now, with so much at stake, that was too much of a risk. It was just too dangerous—wasn't it?

But . . .

A real chance against the Scourge.

You still think you can defeat me.

You're not human!

Remember your mother.

Esme concentrated. She felt the air resistance on her face like a weight, pressing at her all over, but she forced herself to ignore it. She ignored the strange old man with his hand in hers, she ignored the walls of the great chimney flashing past—she ignored everything, in fact, and turned her attention inward, forcing herself to concentrate only on each moment and the moment that followed it, one at a time. She closed her eyes, feeling the tension of the air, its reluctance to let her pass.

And she let her mind find a way through it.

Suddenly, every molecule in her body began to dance and tremble. It was a little like the sensation she'd felt in the heart chamber, only this time it was stronger. She could feel, inside herself, the power that had waited all her life as it began to wake, uncurl itself, take hold.

Now Esme let it happen.

"Yes!" shrieked God. "Yes! *Yes!*"

But Esme didn't hear him. All she could hear was the rushing scream of the air as it grew red-hot—then white-hot—then, finally, as it gave up its resistance and let her through.

There was silence.

Black wings closed around them both.

And when Esme opened her eyes, she was somewhere else.

"Not bad!" said God, grinning at her slyly. "Not bad at all. For a beginner."

Esme didn't reply.

"Set us down over there," God suggested, gesturing past the large stone balustrade that had appeared around them. "Go on. Take a moment to get your bearings."

She did as God said, slipping smoothly through the air, over the balustrade, bringing them both to rest, gently, on the cool marble floor that lay beyond it.

Blinking a bit, Esme looked around herself.

"Welcome," God announced, "to the Halls of Ages! The single greatest repository of history in the universe!"

A deep rumble from below them greeted his words, and God suddenly turned rather pale.

"Whatever you've brought me here to see," said Esme, "you'd better show it to me right now."

"Yes," said God, grimacing. "I think you may be right. This way, please." And with that he scuttled away, down one of the vast, arched corridors that led away ahead of them.

Esme sighed, but she set off after him.

THE PLUNGE

Number 2 picked himself up from where he'd landed, brushing nonexistent dust off his uniform with great care, while the other Sons and Jack watched him apprehensively.

"The device," he said finally, snapping his fingers.

Number 9 frowned. "Sir?"

"The *pack*, soldier!" growled Number 2. "Give it to me! On the double!"

"Sir! Yes, sir!" said Number 9.

"Now," said Number 2, when the giant black pack's mysterious weight was settled on his back to his satisfaction, "I want you all to listen to me very carefully."

He looked at his men one at a time, conspicuously ignoring Jack and the Chinj.

"In view of current, uh, circumstances"—he eyed the narrow, moist, pink-walled tunnel they'd appeared in with distaste—"I'm going to pass over what happened just now and pretend that it never took place. But I will say this." He fixed each member of his team with a glittering glance. "If any one of you punks even thinks about pulling a stunt like that again, you'll have me to answer to. And believe me, when I'm done, Hell's gonna look like the teddy bears' picnic. Clear?"

"Sir. Yes, sir," said the other Sons.

"I am ranking officer here," said Number 2, with great emphasis. "I'm in charge. That means no one decides what we're going to do except *me*. Understand?"

"Sir, yes, sir."

Number 2 sighed, turned, and looked at the Chinj, who was now perched on Jack's shoulder. "So, uh, where to next?" he muttered.

"That way," said the Chinj, stifling a smirk and pointing down the tunnel with one wing. "In my opinion," it added politely.

"This way, people!" Number 2 announced loudly, gesturing in the direction the Chinj had just indicated. "Come on, let's move with a purpose."

They set off.

The tunnel was quite narrow, so the group had to walk in single file.

The floor sank slightly with every step, a little—but not quite—like wet sand. Jack, touching one of the walls briefly with one hand, couldn't help noticing that as well as being rather slimy, it was also unnervingly warm to the touch.

"The passage," he whispered to the Chinj. "It's almost like . . . like it's alive."

"It is," the Chinj replied.

Jack turned to the creature perched on his shoulder and gave it a level look.

"Okay," he said, "you're definitely going to have to explain that one."

"With pleasure." The Chinj cleared its throat. "Over the millennia since the universe began," it announced, "Hell has vastly outgrown its original size. Its foundations, nonetheless, were built upon a system of living tissue."

"What living tissue?" asked Jack. "Not . . ." He thought about it for a moment. "Not the Dragon?"

"That's right," said the Chinj encouragingly.

"So Hell is part of the Dragon?" asked Jack, doing his best.

"A very small part, yes. A bit like a mole, or a . . ." The small creature paused, obviously struggling to find the right word. "A growth."

"Wait a second," said Jack. "Are you seriously trying to tell me that the whole of Hell is just, like, a spot on the Dragon's *bum*?"

"I beg your pardon, sir," said the Chinj icily, "but the heartland of the Demon Empire is rather more significant than a—what did you call it? A 'spot.' And as to which part of the Dragon's anatomy Hell is situated upon, why, that's one of the fundamental mysteries of the universe. The greatest Chinj theologians have debated that very point for—"

"But Hell grew out of the Dragon," pressed Jack, interrupting, "and this Dragon is so big that it didn't even notice—right? That's what you believe?"

"It's what I know."

"How do you know?"

"Because I'm part of it too."

"You're *what*?" said Jack.

The Chinj sighed. "Look," it said. "In your body you've got all sorts of . . . pathways. You have a nervous system, blood vessels, digestion—right?"

"O-kay," said Jack slowly.

"Well!" The Chinj gestured at the pinkish-red walls around them and at the sloping floor that was becoming increasingly warm and moist and squelchy the further downward they progressed. "That's what we've got here! Now, when we first met and I took that sample of your blood, I noticed that it contains a number of specialized cells that ferry essential supplies around your body—oxygen, that sort of thing. Correct?"

"I guess."

"Well, that's what we Chinj do for the Dragon," said the creature.

"Sorry," said Jack. "You've lost me."

"But it's simple, sir!" squeaked the Chinj exasperatedly. "Think about it: think about us and what we actually do. We carry essential nutrients to the various parts of the demon population. We feed the body politic! In essence, there's no difference between we Chinj and your blood cells—it's simply a matter of scale."

Jack gave this his best shot—and failed.

"No, I'm not getting this at all," he said. "How come you're awake and the Dragon isn't? How come, if you're part of the Dragon, it was okay for you to leave and come to Earth to get me?" *And how come I'm even* asking *questions like this?* he added, though not aloud.

"I told you," the Chinj replied. "If you stayed away, I'd just have to come back here every day. And to answer your other question: well, your body keeps going when you're asleep, doesn't it?"

"Yeah, but—"

"You remain alive even when you're not awake, don't you?"

"It's not the same thing. We're talking about being asleep since *time began.*"

"That's true," said the Chinj, "but the Great Depositories—the stores of eternal nourishment to which all Chinj must return to replenish themselves—are bigger than you can possibly imagine. They're a long way off running out yet. Perhaps," it added, with a mischievous nudge of one leathery elbow, "one day, if we survive this, I may even show them to you. But there, now: I'm talking about secrets that even demons do not know."

"Really?" asked Jack, frowning. "The demons don't even know this stuff?"

"Of course not," said the Chinj, shocked. "Why, none but the Chinj may know the secrets of the gruel. In fact," it went on, its small furry face taking on an unmistakably guilty expression, "strictly speaking, it's only the Chinj themselves who are allowed to enter these tunnels. On pain of death, actually."

Jack gave the Chinj another long look.

"Well, I'm sure it won't happen in this case," said the

Chinj, a little too enthusiastically for Jack's liking. "I mean, these are rather particular circumstances, don't you think?"

"Hmm," said Jack. "Who's in charge down here?"

"The Grand Cabal," said the Chinj loftily. "The Parliament"—it paused—"of the Chinj."

"Oh!" said Jack. "Just you Chinj, then."

"Naturally."

Jack let out a sigh. "Phew. That's all right, then. I thought for a second you were telling me we were in trouble here."

The Chinj flared its tiny nostrils and shot Jack a look of surprising venom.

"Do *not*," it said, "underestimate the power of the Grand Cabal. We Chinj have guarded our secrets for longer than you could ever understand. Why do you think the demons are afraid to come down here? Because only a fool would risk the wrath of the Parliament of Chinj."

"Sure," said Jack distractedly. "Right."

He was concentrating on the floor. The passage was now so steep that he was finding it hard to keep his footing—and the Sons were having the same problem. He looked ahead, just in time to see Number 2—

"*Gah!*"

—slip, and bring the full weight of the pack down with him as he fell. *Wham!*

"I'm all right!" he said, flinging off the helping hands of Number 3. He shuffled around to face Jack and the Chinj; Jack struggled to wipe the smile off his face in time, but he wasn't quite fast enough.

"Mind telling me how much more of this stuff there is to deal with?" Number 2 growled.

"These passageways are not usually navigated on foot," the Chinj replied sniffily.

"Is it going to get much steeper?"

"Yes," said the Chinj. "I'm afraid so."

"Terrific," said Number 2. "So how do you suggest we continue? Besides on our arses, I mean."

"That," said the Chinj, drawing itself up to its full height on Jack's shoulder, "is *your* problem."

For a long moment, the man and the Chinj looked at each other.

"Let's keep going," said Jack quietly.

"What did you say?" asked Number 2, his eyes flashing dangerously.

"I said, let's keep going. We can't solve anything by standing about here."

"You know," said Number 2, "I think I've had just about enough of you. You're not here to give orders. In fact," he added, "why *are* you here? I wish someone would tell me why we've got to have a *kid* along, because I'd really like to—"

"Jack is right," said Number 3, from up ahead. He shrugged. "Let's go."

For a second, Number 2 seemed so enraged that Jack thought his eyeballs were going to pop right out of his head. This was no figure of speech: Jack had seen it happen to someone once before, after all. But when Number 2 had got himself and the pack turned back round again, all he said was, "All right. Let's keep it moving. But watch your step now."

They continued in silence down the passageway.

Now Jack found himself having to turn his feet sideways to stop himself from slipping completely: the sides of his trainers seemed to bite a little way into the soft pink surface of the wall, giving him a precious bit of extra traction, but soon just trying to stay upright became a hard enough task, even without the effort to keep going. The walls were close enough for him to support himself with his hands: the passage was now so narrow that Jack could barely see past the struggling figure of Number 2 and his pack.

Jack was looking at the pack, still trying to guess what it might contain, when, suddenly, Number 2 lost his footing again. His big boots slid out from under him. The pack hit the floor, and in another second he was plunging down the tunnel.

Number 3 didn't stand a chance: Number 2 scythed helplessly into him, then the pair of them vanished from sight.

Jack looked behind him at the two remaining Sons— Number 9 and Number 12. Both were wearing identical horrified grimaces on their faces.

"Great!" said Number 12. "Now what're we going to do?"

"We go after them," said Number 9. "Obviously."

"Wait!" said Jack. He turned to the Chinj. "What's down there? Is it safe?"

The Chinj shook its head. "I—I couldn't say. I've always flown this way before. Perhaps the impact might—"

"Look, we've got to go after them!" Number 9 repeated. "We've got to. Right?"

"I think the landing should be soft enough," said the Chinj. "I'm just worried that all this noise might—"

"'Kay," said Number 9. "Let's go." He shoved past Jack. He reached his hands out to either side of him and took as good a grip of the slippery pink walls as he could. Then he swung himself once and set off.

Jack and Number 12 exchanged a look. Sheepishly, the last Son squeezed past Jack, shrugged, sat down, and gingerly pushed himself off, following his comrades out of view almost instantly.

There was a pause.

"Humans," said the Chinj. "So impetuous. As bad as demons, really."

"I guess we're going to have to follow them," said Jack.

"I see no other option," the Chinj replied. "They'll definitely get into trouble without us."

"Why? What's down the end of this thing?"

"It's not what's down there," said the Chinj. "It's what all their noise is going to bring. Look," it added distractedly, frowning and gesturing with one wing, "you'd better go."

Jack looked down the tunnel.

"Oh, Hell," he said, but he sat down.

"Piece of advice, sir," said the Chinj into his ear from behind him. "There's a bit of a drop at the end. My guess is that you'll minimize any injuries you sustain if you keep as relaxed as possible. All right?"

"What?" said Jack.

But with a sudden leaping movement, the Chinj had knocked Jack's hand away from the wall. Jack scrabbled to get his grip back, but already, inexorably, he had begun to slide.

"Good luck, sir!" Jack heard the Chinj call after him. "And remember! Do try to relax!"

Jack picked up speed quickly. Once he'd forced himself to take his hands in from the sides and fold them in his lap, he began to go faster still. The tunnel was now almost vertical: the walls were accelerating to a smooth pink blur—and Jack found, to his surprise, that he was enjoying himself.

It was better than any water chute he'd ever been on. Still the tunnel continued, an apparently endless tube of glistening fleshy red. The only sound was the soft hissing from where his jeans and T-shirt were still making contact with the sides— and soon even that had faded away, because the chute was now so steep that he was barely touching them. There was a long, drawn-out moment of absolute silence, a silence in which Jack had time to reflect that whatever was at the bottom of this thing had better be *unbelievably* soft, when, suddenly, without warning, the pink walls of the tunnel abruptly vanished, to be replaced by . . . nothing.

AAAAAAAAAAAAAGH! said his brain, not unreasonably. Darkness and emptiness gaped around him. The trickles and droplets of thin, clear slime that had eased his descent seemed to thicken in the air, drifting up past his face as he fell. His arms began to paddle and flap. He waited, plummeting for long, aching moments, and then—

WHUDGE!

He hit something.

There was a thrashing of darkness, warm and wet. It streamed past every inch of Jack's body. Gradually, he felt himself slow, then stop falling—and then, of course, he had another problem. He couldn't breathe. His chest was going tight and his ears were beginning to sing. The thick, squidgy liquid seemed reluctant to let him through. Jack struggled and kicked, struggled and kicked. Then, suddenly, he caught a glimmer of light. He flung himself upward. Strong hands had grabbed him. The dreadful slime burst over his head—and he was out.

He gasped, sucking in a great glob of gunge with his first breath, which made him start coughing all the air out again.

"There," said Number 3's voice. "Just breathe. You are safe."

Jack hacked and spluttered some more. "Blimey!" he managed finally. Then he fell silent, looking at Number 3's face, which loomed palely at him out of the surrounding darkness. Jack saw the expression there change from concern to relief. Number 3 was actually glad he was all right: Jack found that oddly touching.

"Did, er . . ." he said, once he'd got himself together. "Did everyone make it all right?"

"They are all 'ere," said Number 3, gesturing with his torch.

For a second Jack didn't recognize them, covered as they were in the same tarlike substance he could feel dripping from his own ears, hair, and everywhere else. The other

Sons were all taking a moment. Number 2, who'd presumably had an especially difficult time, what with the pack, simply sat, breathing hard, with his oil-black legs sticking out in front of him.

The floor was strange. It crackled and crunched like shingle when Jack moved. He reached underneath himself and picked up a bit of it. Whatever the object was, it was too big to be a pebble. It felt hollow and delicate, and it was an odd shape: his probing fingers suddenly slipped into two little holes in the thing, and Jack hurriedly shook the object off with a shudder he couldn't explain.

"Is anyone hurt?" he asked quickly.

Hearing him, Number 2 looked up and took a deep breath.

"Everyone okay?" he barked. "Everyone still five-by-five?"

"I don't know about anyone else," said a voice in the darkness, "but—far as I'm concerned? This mission sucks."

"You shut your mouth, Number Nine," said Number 2.

"I'm Number Twelve, sir," said the voice. "*He's* Number Nine."

"I don't care what your number is, soldier," Number 2 snapped back. "I'm telling you, if you don't shut your mouth, you'll . . . you'll be sorry!"

"Um, where's the Chinj?" Jack asked.

No one answered.

Well, Jack thought, the Chinj could look after itself. It would be back soon enough—he hoped. He sighed. Suddenly he decided he'd had enough of the darkness.

"Do any of you have anything stronger than these

torches?" he asked, doing his best to ignore the way his voice was echoing. "What about a flare or something?"

There was a rustling sound, and torch beams danced overhead as the Sons checked their pouches and pockets. "I've got one," said Number 9.

"Well, don't keep us in suspense, soldier," said Number 2. "Light it up!"

There was a soft *flump*! Then the room was bathed in red light.

And Jack's mouth fell open.

At the center of the room, lapping sluggishly at the shore of crunchy stuff, was a lake of what appeared to be oil of some kind. It was completely black, except for where it reflected the burning red of the flare, and the ripples moved eerily slowly across its surface. But it wasn't this that Jack was looking at, really. What he was looking at was the roof.

The room was big: a gigantic hemisphere of shining black rock, arching overhead. He could see at least a dozen tunnel openings, high up the sides. Between these, the ceiling was entirely covered by a carpet of dangling, leathery black egg-like objects, packed together very tightly. As the flare continued to burn, Jack stared at them—stared until the light began to flicker, then went out, and the darkness was filled with the big blue splashes on his retinas.

At the last moment, some of the egg things had started moving.

There was another soft *flump* and another. As two more flares lit up the room, Jack saw that his earlier impression had been right. The strange dangling objects *were* moving, in a rippling motion that quickly spread across the whole of the ceiling.

"What on Earth?" began Number 2 as a soft, high-pitched squeaking began to fill the air.

"Put out the light," said Jack. Realizing he was whispering, he said it again, as loud as he could. "PUT OUT THE LIGHT!"

The two men holding the flares looked at him for a moment.

Then the ceiling seemed simply to drop.

"GET 'EM OFF! GET OFF ME! *AAAAAAAGH!*" someone screamed, as everything vanished in a welter of wings and fangs. Long, clever fingers were clutching at Jack's neck, feverishly groping for something; whatever it was, they obviously found it, because Jack felt a sudden nervous pressure that made his whole body go limp and floppy. Curled up on the floor, in the last, wild second before losing consciousness, Jack glimpsed the "pebble" he'd picked up earlier. The strange holes his fingers had got stuck in *looked back*, and he realized that it was a skull.

His head filled with darkness. It was as if a second passageway had opened up beneath him and he was plunging again, as helplessly as before.

This time, however, it was bottomless.

THE STAFF

"Right," said God. He pulled his gloves off and dropped them on the table, next to the brass lamp with its green glass shade. Then he held his hands out and closed his eyes.

The air in front of God's hands began to wobble and shake. The effect was a bit like heat haze, but it only lasted for a moment, because just then a shadowy shape appeared, a shape that instantly began to thicken and stretch. The shape was long and silvery: a small flash of light trickled along its length as it materialized.

Esme looked at the magical staff that had formed in God's hands. Her throat seemed to have gone strangely dry.

God opened one eye. "You've seen one before."

"Yes," said Esme. Nick's "test" suddenly seemed a long time ago. "But—"

"In here," said God, "is the answer you're looking for." He closed his eye again. "For what it's worth."

Esme took a deep breath. "All right," she said. "I'm ready."

"We'll see," said God.

Esme put her hands out: already her fingers were curling around the magical staff. Slowly, carefully, she let them curl a little further, and a little further still, until she could almost feel the cool of its metal on her skin. Then she closed her fists on it.

It was like being hit by a wave of cold water. The shock of the first images almost stopped her heart in her chest.

Death.

The images flickered and spun.

Death.

The images wouldn't stop coming.

Death.

And before she knew she was doing it, she'd let go of the staff, gasping.

"*God*," she said. "That was—"

"Yes," he replied. "That was your mother."

"I don't . . ." Esme was breathing hard. "Why are you showing me this?"

"Because, even though she failed, it's the last time the Scourge came close to being defeated," said God. "Because it's time you knew the truth—and the truth, I'm afraid, always hurts. Now, have you seen enough? Do you understand what you have to do?"

Esme stared at him. Her head was full of what she'd just seen, the glimpses of it. Still, she took another deep breath, forcing herself back under control.

"Show me the rest," she said.

God looked at her, blinked, and bit his lip.

"Actually," he said, "I'd rather not."

"I'm sorry?"

God pouted. His eyes, Esme noticed, were shining strangely.

"If you must know," he said, "I find it all rather upsetting. It upsets me," he repeated, "personally. All right? So if it's all the same to you, I think I'd really prefer it if—"

"Show me," said Esme quietly. "Now."

"Oh, all *right*," said God—and sniffed heavily. "Hold out your hands, then."

Esme did. She closed her eyes. She took hold of the staff, and as the magical vision took her up like a wave, she held on tightly.

And this time, she saw everything.

A young woman was lying on a concrete floor.

Her skin was very dark, her orange caftan was very bright, and her strong brown feet were bare in a pair of knackered old sandals. Her hair fizzed out all around her face like a black halo. Her amber eyes were dim with pain, and thick blood was running from her nose and mouth. The young man kneeling beside her pulled down his sleeve and dabbed at her uselessly.

"She's bleeding internally!" he said, panicking. "I can't stop it!"

"Belinda," said Nick, standing over the woman, still dressed in his customary black. "I—"

The woman scowled and deliberately looked away from

Nick, turning her gaze instead on the kneeling man. A hand reached up and pulled him toward her with a fierce, feverish strength that surprised him.

"Raymond," she whispered.

"I'm here, petal," breathed the big man.

"You," said the woman, with difficulty. "Not Jessica. Not Nick. *You*." She took a breath. "Teach her," she said. "Look—" The word rattled to nothing. "Look after her." She was breathing fast now, the breaths coming in little shallow gulps that made it hard for her to form the words. "Tell her I l—"

She tried again.

"Tell her I l—"

It wouldn't come out.

"I'll tell her, love, I swear it!" said Raymond. "I'll tell her every day!"

And when the woman heard this, she smiled. Slowly, she drew her hand down the big man's rough, wet cheek—and the quick breaths suddenly ceased.

Then she died.

"There," said God, as the magical staff wobbled and disappeared. Tears dribbled freely down his wrinkled face. "*Now* are you satisfied?"

Esme just looked at him. She felt numb inside—cold. Still, she had enough strength left to ask the first question that had to be asked.

"How do you know all of this?" she said.

"What?" God sniffed. "You think I *faked* it?"

"What proof," asked Esme, with infinite patience, "can you give me that all that really happened?"

For a moment, God stared at her as though dumbfounded.

"Hell's teeth!" he shouted, stamping his foot and gesturing at his face. "Look what that did to me! Are you made of *stone*?"

But Esme just stared back at him, waiting. Her own tears were long dry now. A ball of something hard and bright and cold and heavy had formed inside her; she could feel it, the shape of it, tight against her ribs when she breathed. Her expression as she stared at the old man then did not waver in the slightest. She met God's eyes: met them until he had to look away.

He sighed. "Look, I told you," he said. "I'm the archivist of Hell. I'm your *god*: I know everything, that's how I got this job."

Esme was still staring at him. Still waiting.

"All right!" said God, throwing his hands up. "I don't have any proof!" He thought of something and, smiling a thin smile, he added, "You're just going to have to take it on faith."

There was a long pause.

"Okay," said Esme. "Then I've got a few more questions I'd like to ask."

"Shoot," said God.

Esme took a deep breath, because for a moment, to her surprise, it seemed that the tears might come back. But then she said it.

"They didn't stand a chance, did they?"

God looked up. "Who? The Brotherhood?"

"Everybody," said Esme. "If it hadn't been Felix who let the Scourge out, it would've been someone else."

"Yes," said God. "I'm afraid that's probably true."

"So why was the Scourge imprisoned on Earth?" asked Esme. "Why put it among people, when it was obvious that one day someone would let it escape?"

God sighed. "Nobody knew or cared about my little planet." He shrugged. "It seemed the safest place. But the fact is, wherever Khentimentu was imprisoned, it was only ever going to be a matter of time before it got out." He smiled mirthlessly. "That's the problem with dealing with something that can't be killed."

"But why put it among people?" Esme repeated. "I mean, how could you do that to them?"

"It wasn't *my* decision!" God bit his lip. "Besides," he huffed, "I've helped you now. Haven't I?"

Esme sighed.

"All right, then," she said slowly. "Well, what about how to defeat the Scourge?"

God stared at her. "I thought *that* was pretty obvious," he said. "Didn't you? I'm certainly not going to show you the vision again."

"I don't want you to," said Esme, her patience beginning to wear thin. "I just want you to tell me something I can use, like you promised."

"But I showed you!" said God, exasperated.

"Showed me what?" said Esme, her voice rising despite herself.

"The answer!"

"What answer? Why can't you just tell me?"

"DUH!" said God. "What's wrong with you people? Did you all turn stupid after I created you? The only way to defeat the Scourge—the only way to make the magic strong enough to trap Khentimentu in the staff—is through—"

"Yes?" said Esme.

"Through . . . well . . ." God trailed off suddenly.

"*Yes?*"

"Through sacrifice," he finished.

There was a pause.

"What?" asked Esme.

"I think that someone has to die," said God. He looked up and, seeing Esme's expression, added: "I'm sorry, but there it is." Then he looked down at his feet.

There was another, longer pause, as Esme considered this.

She'd known, she supposed. At least, she always should've known.

What else was there for her, anyway? She was neither one thing nor the other, not demon and not human: she belonged nowhere.

This was her job. One job she'd trained her whole life to do: one chance to have her revenge.

Boom! The room shook, and a million glass bottles rattled in the boxes on the walls.

"You, er . . ." God looked guiltily at his feet again. "You don't have much time."

Esme squared her shoulders.

"All right," she said. "I'll do it."

TO THE DEATH

"There," said the Scourge, turning to the nearest Gukumat. "I believe we are ready to proceed. Is everything in place?"

The Overminister bowed. *Yes, Sire. It's just—*

"What is it?" The Scourge was suddenly aware of all of Gukumat's eyes looking in its direction.

Gukumat bowed again and folded his long-fingered hands in front of his robes in an awkward, self-effacing gesture. *One hates to question Your Worship at a time like this,* he said, *but the situation being what it is, one can't help but feel a little . . . concerned.*

"Say what you mean, Gukumat," said the Scourge, beginning to understand why Hacha'Fravashi had disliked him so much.

Very well, Sire. It's the boy. Gukumat gestured toward Charlie, who was still sitting bolt upright, a blissful smile on his face. *Are you quite sure he's . . . safe?*

"The boy is in my power," said the Scourge, as patiently as it could. "He is, I assure you, perfectly 'safe.'"

Your Worship's words are most reassuring, said the Overminister.

However, the fact remains that when he realizes what is to become of him, he—

"Charlie is not your concern, Gukumat," snapped the Scourge. Then, in a more conciliatory tone, it added, "Please, leave him to me. Now, is everything ready for the next stage?"

For perhaps three whole hundredths of a second, Gukumat thought about this.

At that moment, the Overminister was engaged in a number of simultaneous activities. The Carnotaur—arguably the most dangerous of the gladiators—had lost what little patience its pea-size brain possessed and was busily attempting to break out of its magical bonds. A detachment of twelve clones was subduing it with fire lances while another fifteen were combining their powers to shore up the bubblelike wall of its makeshift prison. At that very instant too some seven thousand other Gukumats were also engaged throughout the vast heart chamber in similar containment activities with Hell's increasingly unruly populace. Demons were an impatient breed and not given to waiting in one place for long: there had already been casualties. However, these were well within acceptable limits. In fact, as the Overminister had discovered, having Hell's entire population in one place actually made it a lot easier to deal with—logistically speaking, at least.

It is, Sire, he answered.

"Splendid," said the Scourge. "Then—"

A ripple went through the humid air, a soft susurrus of power that set the silken robes of the surrounding Gukumats rustling. The Scourge paused, distracted. Some twenty feet away across the wet pink fleshy floor, a patch of space seemed to bulge suddenly, condensing, taking shape.

Then Esme appeared.

She stood with her hands at her sides, the hilt of the pigeon sword jutting over her shoulder. The nearest Gukumats opened their hooked jaws and hissed at her, but they might as well not have been there. Her eyes were closed, but as soon as the haze of molecular disturbance in the air had dispersed around her, she opened them and looked at the Scourge, hard.

The Scourge folded its liquid-black arms. Though it showed no outward sign of it, it was smiling.

"So," it said. "You've taken the first step. You're beginning to realize what you can become. My congratulations: you're clearly a fast learner."

Esme said nothing.

"Am I to understand that this means you have decided to accept my offer?"

Esme looked around herself slowly. She looked at the gladiators, trapped high above in their bubbles of magic. She looked at Charlie, frozen, staring, on his throne of meat. She looked at the massed ranks of the Gukumats and the clamoring horde of demons spread across the landscape far below.

"You've been busy," she said.

"We have," agreed the Scourge. It gestured in Charlie's direction with long, inky fingers. "The boy is about to complete the ritual," it said. "You're just in time."

"How does it work?" said Esme. "If you don't mind my asking?"

"Not at all!" said the Scourge. "It's like this: before awakening fully, the Dragon must first be convinced that the universe is ready for its own annihilation. Do you understand me so far?"

Esme grimaced but nodded.

"Well," said the Scourge, "the reason I need Charlie is that he's going to play the part of the universe's *representative*."

Esme frowned.

"In just a few moments now, Charlie will be offered a choice. He will be granted a glimpse of the whole of Creation, and the Dragon will ask Charlie, as the universe's spokesman, what he, Charlie, wishes should be done with it. In that instant, the fate of us all will rest solely in Charlie's hands."

"And?"

"Naturally, Charlie will be so obsessed with his own little preoccupations that he won't have the wit to understand what is being offered. With—I assure you—only the slightest of nudges from me, he will answer the Dragon's question in exactly the way I want him to. Then, at last, the awakening will be unstoppable."

"By *mistake*?" said Esme, incredulous. "You're saying that Charlie's going to cause the destruction of the universe by *mistake*?"

"You could call it a mistake on his part, perhaps," said the Scourge. "There will, I promise, be no mistake on mine.

"So," it added, after a moment, "what do you say?"

There was a pause.

"Let me get this straight," said Esme. "If I agree to what you said, then you're going to stop all this?"

Abruptly, every single one of the Gukumats seemed to stiffen.

"You're going to abandon the idea of waking the Dragon," Esme went on, "and never even think about ending the universe again, *ever*. Right?"

"**That was my offer,**" the Scourge replied. "**Yes.**"

A ripple of consternation spread through the ranks of Gukumats.

My lord! the Overminister began. *I—!*

"I don't believe you," said Esme.

There was another pause.

"**What?**" said the Scourge.

"It's quite simple," Esme began. "If I really believed that taking up your offer—that acting"—she wrinkled her nose—"as your 'daughter' was actually going to stop you from doing what you're doing, then believe me, I'd agree like a shot."

She smiled fiercely.

"I'm not going to lie to you: I wouldn't like it. In fact, the idea of having to call you 'Daddy' is just about the single most repulsive thing I can think of. But if it was really a straight choice between that and letting you kill everyone, then repulsive or not, there'd be no contest, obviously. *However*," she added, continuing to stare at the Scourge, trying to gauge what effect her words were having (its liquid-black face remained smooth and impassive, just as it always did), "that's not really the situation here—is it?"

No one answered.

"You know," said Esme, taking her time, "there's one thing about this that makes me very angry indeed."

Neither Gukumat nor the Scourge spoke.

"It's not the blackmail," said Esme, "the 'love me or else!' thing—though to be sure that certainly is pretty irritating.

"It's not even," she added, "the fact you've murdered my family and put a blight on my entire life.

"It's the fact," she went on, the cold, tight sensation in her chest brightening, hardening, "that you've asked me to *trust you afterwards.*"

She glared at the demon.

"Do you really expect me to believe anything you say, after all you've done?" she asked. "Do you really expect me to believe that you can keep a promise, after the lies you've told and the lives you've ruined?"

"I gave you my word—" said the Scourge.

"Yeah, and maybe you even believed it," said Esme. "But the point is, *I don't.* And if you thought I was going to, you're obviously a lot stupider than I imagined."

"You reject my offer, then?" asked the Scourge.

"You're damn right I reject your offer."

Esme's hard brown hands lifted fractionally from her sides. Her amber eyes glittered as she faced her enemy, and the Gukumats around her all backed away—away from the girl and the way that she smiled.

"No tricks," said Esme. "No more lies. You and me are going to fight this out to the finish. Right now."

THE GRAND CABAL

Jack came to, or thought he did—it was so dark it was hard to tell—to the sound of voices.

"Didn't even get a shot off," said one.

"Twelve," began Number 3 wearily.

"Hello?" croaked Jack.

"Jack!" said Number 3, relieved. "You are all right over there?"

"Um, yes. I think so." In actual fact, Jack wasn't at all sure. He could wriggle his fingers and toes, but everything else seemed to be stuck. Even turning his head was apparently impossible: he pushed, quite hard in fact, but the only result was a soft, resinous creaking sound from whatever held him. His whole body was throbbing, as if a great weight were pressing on it.

"Well? What the Hell is this place, kid?" burst out Number 2, to Jack's annoyance. "Just where the Hell are we now?"

"Where the Hell do you think?" said Jack grimly. "We're in Hell."

"But what's going to happen to us? Why's it so dark?"

"Because in Hell," muttered Jack, "no matter how bad things get, you know they can always get worse."

"Listen to the smallest of you!" said an unfamiliar voice suddenly. "He shows wisdom! It's a pity that he didn't show this wisdom earlier—before you all committed the crimes that will result in your death!"

There was an answering chittering sound that came from all around them: a sound, Jack realized, like laughter.

"Bring lights for the soup-suckers!" said the voice. "It's time for them to see who they've offended!"

There was a soft *flump*; then there was light. The cave they were in was not big by Hell's standards, perhaps fifty or sixty feet high—but Jack and the Sons were *stuck to the ceiling*. Directly below them was another pool of mysterious liquid, this one pale and frothy looking, the color of sour milk. Ranged around the pool, clinging to the floor and walls of the cave staring up at them with a million shiny black bush-baby eyes that glinted in the light, were more Chinj than Jack could ever have guessed existed. The ranks of leathery-winged bodies stretched as far as Jack's eyes could see.

"*Gluttons!*" screeched the voice. "Soup-slurpers! Vulgarians! See the grisly fate that awaits you—you and all who trespass in the sacred byways of the Chinj!"

Jack looked for where the voice was coming from: its origin wasn't hard to find. On the far shore of the frothy sour-milk stuff, three long steps had been cut roughly into the sheer black walls of the cave. At the center of the top step, flanked by a squadron of fierce and, with their graying fur, oddly venerable-looking bat creatures, stood a lone, pale figure.

This elder Chinj was almost white with age. Its wings were ragged, peppered with holes. The fur all over its body had fallen out in places, and great ugly patches of its gray and wrinkled skin had been left exposed to the elements. Its ears, by contrast, were crested with large and luxuriant snow-white tufts of hair, growing straight out of the tips as well as, Jack noticed, from the insides. A thick milky cataract dulled one of the Chinj's eyes, but the other blazed up at them with a hatred that was astonishing to see.

"You who have feasted on our holy works!" the Chinj shrieked. "You who have suckled at our treats! You, who've grown fat on the fruits of our toils and yet now have violated our most sacred trust!"

There was a chorus of angry squeaks from the rest of the flock.

"Gruel gobblers!" howled the elder Chinj. "Chunder-munchers! Let the trials," it screamed, "commence!"

It was at this point, unfortunately, that Number 2 burst out laughing. Soon, the walls of the cave were ringing with it—hard, brash gales of laughter that were made all the more ugly by the obvious edge of hysteria to them.

To Jack's surprise, the elder Chinj just waited until the laughter died away.

"You find us amusing?" it asked quietly.

Number 2 made a snorting sound in his nose. "What is all this?" he said.

The elder Chinj's stare did not waver. "I'm quite certain that you don't need reminding," it said. "But just for the record, I will state your crime. You were caught trespassing in the nursery pits, where none but the Chinj may go."

"And this means what to me, exactly?" said Number 2.

"There is but one penalty for this offense," said the elder Chinj, drawing itself up to its full height, which, it had to be said, wasn't very high. "Death," it announced.

The word spread around the cave like an echo, carried by the squeaking voices from a million furry throats.

"Death!" the flock chanted in time: "Death! Death!"— and now it was Number 2's turn to wait until the noise died down.

"Cut us loose, short stuff," said Number 2. "Don't mess with us: you might get stepped on."

Number 12, glued in place beside him, guffawed loudly. Jack gritted his teeth.

"Yes," said the elder Chinj, with dignity. "I will cut you loose. I think first, however, it's time for a little demonstration of who, exactly, is 'messing' with who." It turned to the squadron of thickset Chinj standing on the step below it. "Start with the one to the noisy one's left," it said, indicating Number 12 with a skeletal front paw.

As one, the squadron leaped into the air. In seconds the creatures were swarming all over him, until it seemed the Son had simply vanished under a mass of leathery bodies—but then, suddenly, and with an eerie precision, the Chinj stopped what they were doing and flapped back down to their places on the steps. In another moment, an excited, barely maintained silence had returned to the cave.

Jack waited, holding his breath.

"Are you ready, soup-sucker?" asked the elder Chinj quietly. "Are you ready for your death?"

"You know what?" Number 12 asked back, with a smug glance at his colleagues. "I've had just about enough of this. Why don't you just cut me loose and—"

There was a soft ripping noise, and before Jack knew what had happened, Number 12 had fallen into the pool.

There was a long moment, then the hapless Son bobbed to the surface, coughing and spluttering. Whatever the milky stuff was, he was covered in it from head to foot. Thick curds of it clung to him all over: he looked like he'd been sprayed with cottage cheese.

Quietly at first, the Chinj were chanting again: a single word, getting louder all the time. "Death," they said. "Death. Death. *Death*. *Death*. DEATH. DEATH. *DEATH!*"

Number 12 was looking down at his hands, frowning at something. The white stuff that covered him was beginning to take on a strange, pinkish quality. The pink turned to soft red as it started to happen.

Jack's eyes went wide.

No, he thought.

Oh, God. Yes! It was true!

Suddenly, unstoppably, Number 12 was being *dissolved*.

With horrible speed, his hands seemed to melt—to shrink and then vanish into fat pinkish-red droplets that fell to the surface of the frothing, milky pool. Now his whole body was disappearing, and the skin on his skull was sizzling away to reveal the raw, wet bone underneath. As Jack stared down, unable to look away from the hideous spectacle, Number 12 helplessly turned his now-empty eye sockets upward at Number 2.

His lipless jaws had just hung open to scream when he sank from sight.

The chanting of the Chinj broke down into a feverish chorus of cackling and cheering. All that remained of Number 12 was a spreading, pinkish stain. In another moment that too had gone, and the elder Chinj raised a front paw for silence.

Jack gaped.

"You see?" crowed the chief Chinj, once relative silence had returned to the cave. "You see who you have offended?"

"Wh-what?" stuttered Number 2. "What have you done with my man?"

"You have blundered," said the elder Chinj, "into the belly of the beast. You and your comrades will be made useful for perhaps the first time in your guzzling little lives: you shall be broken down!" it announced, hopping from one long three-toed foot to the other. "You shall be dissolved in the holy juices of the Dragon! Your bodies shall be among the first to become fuel for the Awakening—an unmerited honor for the likes of you, I might add! So, prepare yourself, soup-sucker!" it finished, leering toothlessly. *"You're next!"*

The flock was already all over Number 2. He'd all but disappeared under a blur of leathery black bodies, but his screams were still as clear as anything.

"Wait!" he screeched. "God! No! For the love of Christ, please, *wait!*"

Smiling broadly, the old bat creature made a signal with one wizened forepaw. Instantly, the flock drew back.

"This isn't . . ." began Number 2, then tried again. "This isn't right!"

"'Not right'?" scoffed the elder Chinj, its eyes bulging. "Are you in our sacred chambers or not?"

"But we didn't know about the—the sacred places," Number 2 wailed. "It wasn't our idea to come here!"

Er, hang on, thought Jack.

"Really," said the elder Chinj. "Then whose was it, may I ask?"

"Number Two," hissed Jack. "Shut up!"

"We were led here!" said Number 2, his voice reaching a sort of ecstasy of whining. "We were led here by a *Chinj*!"

The word echoed around the cave. Bat creature looked at bat creature in stunned dismay, dismay that turned to outrage, outrage that echoed from a million furry throats in a rising, chattering tide.

"Who," managed the elder Chinj, its forepaws actually quivering with fury. "*Who did this?*"

"Me," said a voice from the far end of the cave. "I did it," said Jack's Chinj.

The whole room went instantly quiet.

The elder Chinj turned. Its good eye took on a laserlike intensity that would have reduced even a full-size demon to jelly. However, Jack's Chinj stood firm, meeting its ruler's gaze with a look that managed to be defiant yet respectful at the same time.

"What is your designation, young Chinj?" asked the eldest bat creature grimly.

Jack's Chinj stood to attention. "Second division, third under-Chinj, rating B-thirty-seven-stroke-six! Sir!" it recited, then bowed deeply.

"Chinj B-thirty-seven-stroke-six," said the elder Chinj, acknowledging the bow with a curt nod, "you have been accused of leading these creatures into our most sacred places. This constitutes high treason, the most heinous crime it is within the power of our people to commit. I will ask again—and I want you to think carefully before you answer. *Did you lead them here?*"

The silence and tension in the room were palpable: the air was thick with them—or maybe it was the smell that was all that was left of Number 12; Jack didn't really want to think about which.

"I want to tell you why," said the Chinj.

In the tension-filled hush the elder Chinj looked around the cave. "Go on," it said.

"I did this," said Jack's Chinj. "I broke the most important rule of our people because I believed it was the right thing to do." It paused. "Every Chinj here knows what I'm talking about. You've all, every one of you, known it for ages."

"Reach your point, young Chinj," cautioned the elder. "Our patience grows thin."

"The Dragon is about to awake," said Jack's Chinj.

A small murmur spread through the flock at its words— though what sort of emotion the reaction represented it was impossible at that moment for Jack to tell.

"As you say," said the elder Chinj carefully. "We know this. What's your point?"

"My point, Sire," said Jack's Chinj, "is that this cannot be allowed to happen."

The murmur rose to a rumble of dissent, and Jack's Chinj had to struggle to make itself heard.

"I brought these people here because I believe they can stop the awakening! We should help them, not kill them!" These last words were lost under a sudden tumult of squeaking and flapping from the flock.

"QUIET!" roared the elder Chinj. "I MUST HAVE QUIET!"

It thumped its stick on the platform until the hubbub died down a little.

"You astonish me, young Chinj," it said. "You seem to forget: we *are* the Dragon. It lives through us. Its wakening and final triumph should be our ultimate goal! I mean . . ." The elder Chinj looked incredulously around at its flock. "Don't the rest of you *want* the Dragon to wake up?"

Jack was working out what all the fuss was about. While it was true that some of the Chinj supported the elder, it was obvious that at least an equal number of the creatures weren't at all so certain. Squabbles were breaking out all over the cave, and the air was filled with anxious screeching and cackling as the flock began to fight.

"Listen to me!" shouted Jack's Chinj. "If the Dragon wakes, it'll mean the end of *everything*. The end of the demons! The end of the universe! The end of *us*!"

"This is heresy!" roared the elder Chinj. "All our lives we have suffered the indignity of serving the demons! Now at last the time of judgment is at hand! We shall take our rightful places at the cornerstone of Creation and plunge gladly into the Great Void from whence we came!"

"I don't *want* the Great Void," snapped Jack's Chinj, to a dangerous chatter of agreement from the flock. "I like being alive!"

"You call what we do *life*?" replied the elder. "All we do is feed the soup-suckers!"

"I like being alive!" repeated Jack's Chinj stubbornly. "The Dragon's awakening can't be allowed!"

"It is *right*! It is fate! It is how the universe was ordained!"

"RUBBISH!" screamed Jack's Chinj.

Anything further in this exchange was drowned out utterly as the whole of the gigantic flock of bat creatures finally flew into confusion.

In all this, it seemed, Jack and the rest of the Sons had been temporarily forgotten.

Quickly, Jack tried his bonds—not too hard, obviously. He was still stuck fast. So were the three remaining Sons. All the men were doing was staring helplessly. The Sons were going to be no use at all. So, of course, it was down to Jack. *Typical.*

He took a deep breath, then shouted at the top of his lungs.

"HEY!"

He was bigger than the Chinj. He was definitely noisier. A good third of the flock suddenly stopped arguing and looked up at him. The others were still at it, so he tried again. "HEY! HEY, *YOU*! *HEY!*"

The noise died down a bit more. Now even the elder Chinj was looking in his direction.

"Listen," said Jack. "I've got a proposition for you."

"I don't believe this," said Number 9, later. He and Number 3 were making an inventory of whatever equipment had survived their journey.

Number 3 didn't answer. After a last vain attempt to clear the black slime out of the barrel of one of the two rocket launchers the team had brought with them, he tossed it aside with a scowl.

"I don't believe that kid!" said Number 9. "Where'd he learn to bargain like that? I mean, that was beautiful! Number Two gets left here with the pack, so Project Justice is still game on—and it's all down to Jack! Who'd've guessed it?"

Suddenly, Number 3 stopped what he was doing and straightened up, his expression darkening.

"Number Three?"

"I told you," Jack was saying to the elder Chinj. "You've got my promise."

"And what use is that? The word of a *soup-sucker*."

"And you've got a *hostage*," Jack finished through gritted teeth.

"The Grand Cabal finds your terms to be acceptable," said the large Chinj standing to the elder's right. It turned to the elder. "May I remind you, my lord, that the Parliament has made its decision. The Chinj peoples have spoken—and you, I'm afraid, must abide by their wishes. Your truculence is unseemly."

"But this is *wrong*, my brother," said the elder Chinj. "You cannot expect me to stand idly by and watch the long-awaited awakening being jeopardized."

"Look," Jack interrupted. "This is a no-lose situation for you. If we do stop the awakening, then you've still got your consolation prize: you've got my promise that I'll come back, and I've left you Number Two as security."

"Believe me, young human," hissed the elder Chinj, "your agony shall give me considerable pleasure."

"Fine, dissolve me, whatever, I don't care—but you never know," Jack went on. "If we fail, then you get your awakening thingamajig anyway. So you'll still be happy. All right?"

"Hmph," said the elder Chinj.

"Now if you'll excuse me," said Jack, "I've got to go and help someone save the universe. Before it's too late," he added grimly.

"We too must make our preparations," replied the Chief Grand Cabal SpokesChinj. "We shall meet again."

"Count on it," said Jack.

He watched as the council head and the elder Chinj leaped into the air and flapped off back down the tunnel. His own Chinj stood by him, also watching them go. Then it looked up at Jack.

"Sir," it began.

"Jack," said Jack. "Call me Jack."

"Jack, then," said the Chinj. "I must say, I don't think I understand you very well. Not at all, to tell the truth."

Jack looked at the bat creature. "It's pretty simple," he said. "I figured either you Chinj get me, or the universe comes to an end. I'm stuffed either way, so what difference does it make how it happens?"

"Well," said the Chinj, "I suppose if you put it like that . . ."

It paused.

"Do you know, sir?" it said—and by the time Jack had thought to correct it it had already gone on—"I think that there may be more demon—more *gladiator*—in you than you suspect."

They looked at each other. The Chinj was smiling. After a moment, Jack found that he was too.

"Come on," he said. "Let's go find the others. I want to introduce you to an interesting human invention."

"Oh yes?" asked the Chinj, polite but dubious. "And what's that?"

"Guns," said Jack, and smirked darkly to himself. "Lots of guns."

He set off down the tunnel.

The Chinj shrugged its small shoulders and set off after him.

THE LAST BATTLE

For another moment, the Scourge stared at Esme.

"**You still think you can win?**" it asked. "**Even after your failures before?**"

"Stop talking and find out," was Esme's reply.

"**As you wish.**" The Scourge unfolded its liquid-black arms.

It took two steps, blurred into motion, and before Esme had time to realize what was happening she felt a blow that took her breath away.

It was like being swatted with an oil tanker. She was hurled back a clear forty feet straight through the air, landing with an impact that drove the air from her lungs. In front of her eyes, the air shimmered, shook, and the Scourge reappeared again. Now cool liquid fingers held Esme by the throat. Looking down the shining black surface of the Scourge's arm, she caught her own startled expression reflected in its face. Carelessly, easily, it jerked her into the air. Feeling her trainered feet leaving the sticky pink ground, Esme looked downward.

She was dangling over the edge of the plateau.

"Now," said the Scourge, its voice completely casual, "**are you beginning to realize what a mistake you've made? Or do you need me to show you some more? Hmm?**"

Esme felt the dreadful grip loosen on her neck. Her windpipe released, she gasped for air. "You're—" she managed. "You're—"

"**Yes,**" said the Scourge, enjoying the moment. "**My strength has returned. I'm now quite capable of defeating you without the boy. So *you*,**" it went on, the grip going tight again, "**have lost what little chance you had. Haven't you?**"

Esme closed her eyes. Her head was pounding, her vision was closing in: dark shadows were swallowing everything. As the seconds stretched out, Esme knew she couldn't wait: whatever she was going to do, she would have to do it now. Forcing herself, she reached down inside herself. She felt a shifting sensation—

—then the Scourge's grip was gone, and she could breathe again. She staggered, looking around herself. She had reappeared on the other side of the platform, away from the edge. She could see the Gukumats, backing away all around her. She could see Charlie still sitting frozen on his throne. And as the air bulged and shook and a liquid-black shadow materialized in front of her, she could see the Scourge.

"**Good,**" it said. "**You're learning. It's a shame, really, that this thing between us has to come to an end. But it *is* going to end. Now.**"

And with another blur of movement that was faster than the eye could catch, it launched its attack.

Esme caught the first blow on her forearm, blocking it without thinking. Another blow instantly came lashing at her face and she swerved back to dodge it, swinging her elbows round and together to block the demon's follow-up to her body. Every blow that followed she managed to block, but every block she managed still *hurt*—and step by driving step, she knew, the Scourge was forcing her back across the plateau, away from the center, back toward the edge once again. Esme tried a leap—

—and a muscular piston of darkness shot out from the liquid-black body, catching her by the waist and dragging her back down easily, even as a clubbing roundhouse punch swung in toward the right side of her head to punish her. She caught the blow again on the outside of her forearm: the impact drove a flare of pain right through her shoulders.

But then, with her left, she struck.

It was a solid blow: though it only traveled about a foot or so, it carried all her weight and strength behind it.

It landed smack in the center of the Scourge's face.

For a moment, Esme could actually feel the darkness spreading around her fist, taking her in. She pulled, and a tiny ripple of black spread around the spot where she'd struck, but her fist was now trapped—stuck fast.

The Scourge's body began to shiver and shift. When the darkness resettled, an ink-black hand was on the point of her elbow, and the place where she'd struck had become another hand, gripping her at the wrist.

Esme's arm was straight out. She had time to realize what was about to happen—when the demon retaliated.

With a soft *crack!* the Scourge broke her arm once, snapping it back at the elbow by simply pushing against the joint.

With a rippling *pop!* it took her trapped wrist and twisted it, a full one hundred and eighty degrees.

It jabbed on her hand, shoving the bones back. By now, Esme's mouth was opening to scream. So then, only then—it released her.

Esme fell on her back, paralyzed by pain, her arm flopping weakly by her side. The sharpened fractures had punched straight through the skin of her elbow, and the bone was sticking out by a clear inch. She stared at the wound. Then she looked up. The Scourge was towering over her.

There was a pause.

"Hurts, does it?" it enquired.

Esme stared back, blinking, eyes wide with pain—but, determined not to give the demon the satisfaction, she said nothing.

"These fighting skills of yours," it said, raising an admonishing finger, "they might work on Charlie, but they're not going to be of any use on me. Not now."

Esme concentrated, concentrated on using her power to heal herself, but it was hard. The pain was incredible; it blanked out everything—everything except the Scourge's voice.

"'Ninety-nine times out of a hundred,'" it was saying, "'a fight'll be decided in the first few seconds'—isn't that what Raymond used to tell his students?"

Esme closed her eyes, and with a terrible, twisting *push*, the bones in her arm began slowly to move back to their positions.

"He was wrong, of course. Fights are more usually won—and lost—before they even begin. For instance, I would say that it's always a good idea to make sure you know *how* to win before you *can* win, yes? Otherwise," the Scourge added, turning its back on her and walking a few steps away, "you're going to lose. Painfully."

It was done. Blood still ran from the wound, but the bones themselves were back in place, the fractures healed, the torn muscles beginning to mend. Sour adrenaline flushed through Esme's body, making every part of her feel heavy. But her arm and her fingers were working. She got to her feet.

"What's next?" the Scourge asked. "What would you like to try now?"

Esme was thinking. She hadn't bargained on the Scourge being so powerful outside Charlie: in this respect, it was true, she had miscalculated. Despair was clawing at her heart, a sense of doom and failure that a less disciplined fighter might have allowed to overwhelm her. Shoving the feeling aside, forcing herself to concentrate, Esme accepted the mistake and began to consider what it was she could actually *do* about it.

There was only one answer. Esme shut her eyes—and reappeared somewhere else. It didn't occur to her that the skill was coming to her more easily each time she used it: there wasn't time. She reached up, drew the pigeon sword, and, at a speed that hurt to watch, she charged, now—

—at Charlie.

With the fight going the way it was, there was no other option. Mercy was a luxury she could no longer afford. She would find a way to make her peace with what she was about to do later, when the stakes weren't so high. It was, after all, a straight choice now: Charlie or the universe.

One of them had to die.

Charlie's eyes were glazed: he was utterly oblivious. Before the Gukumats could stop her, Esme had blasted past them like a thunderbolt. She raised her arms for the killing stroke. The girl and the sword become one long, glittering streak in the air.

With a ringing *crack* and an impact that traveled up Esme's arms and shook her to the core, her stroke was parried, stopped dead in midflight, less than a foot from the target.

"No, no, *no*," said the Scourge. "That's quite out of the question, I'm afraid."

For a moment, Esme froze.

The demon had caught her easily: it had simply appeared at the last moment between her and Charlie and had met the edge of the pigeon sword with a swordlike object of its own. The shape mirrored that of her own weapon—it had the same graceful curve and proportions of the classical Japanese katana. But it, like the Scourge, was still a glossy ink black. As she watched, with a last oily shimmer the darkness of the blade seemed to ripple away: it was only then that the cold steel was revealed beneath.

"Swords, is it, next?" asked the Scourge, without much interest. "Very well. If you insist."

It took a step toward her, its liquid feet pooling on the soft pink floor, and Esme sprang back into a guard position, watching carefully, waiting. With a rustle of silk, the Guku-mats formed two rows, a long line of space to either side of the combatants.

"Ready?" asked the Scourge.

Esme said nothing.

"Then let's begin."

Instantly, the space between them turned to a scissoring blur of steel.

It was impossible for a bystander to tell where one attack ended and another began. One by one, all the gladiators that were trapped in the bubbles above gradually stopped trying to escape and stared instead at the dreadful combat that was taking place below them. All Hell seemed to fall silent, except for the stinging hiss of sword on sword.

Esme was fighting on instinct—instinct and her years of training. If she'd stopped to think out each move, she'd've been lost, instantly. As it was, the battle was all going her opponent's way, because all she could do was react. Each swirling, whistling block and parry sent little ripples of fatigue up her arms. Each deft dodge, left, right, up, down, back—sometimes the Scourge came so close that she could actually feel the air move as her opponent's blade slid past her face—left her a little slower, a little more tired.

Obviously, she realized, she was going to lose.

It wasn't a question of pessimism. The Scourge was keep-ing pace with her easily: though it seemed to take every ounce of her speed and strength to meet those of her enemy, every attack *she* launched was parried and riposted smoothly and, apparently, without effort. As she began to tire—as the speeding blades slowed until the sharper-eyed bystanders found themselves actually able to tell the swords apart from each other—it seemed the Scourge was even slowing down with her.

"**Really,**" it said, meeting a lunge from Esme with a twisting movement that all but jerked the pigeon sword from her fingers. It followed it up with a vicious slash at her legs that Esme had to jump to avoid. "**Is this the best you can do?**"

In reply, Esme spun on her feet. Leaning forward into the stroke, she dropped her hands: she brought the sword round in a blow at the demon's waist that would have sliced a man in two.

The blade did pass straight through the demon, right where a man's waist would be. But the ink-black body simply sealed itself up after it, and, with a movement that was almost too quick for Esme to catch, the Scourge repaid her for her trouble with a straight-arm punch in the face with the pommel of its sword. She blinked and shook her head, momentarily stunned.

That was when the Scourge struck again, stabbing Esme through the shoulder of her sword arm.

The pigeon sword fell from her fingers.

Not bothering to remove its own weapon from her body, the Scourge advanced toward Esme; as she staggered back, shuddering at the pain, it put one glistening foot on Raymond's last gift where it lay and snapped the pigeon sword cleanly, up near the butterfly-shaped guard. Then it stopped and looked at her.

"I'm sorry if this offends you," it said, "but I must be honest: I'm beginning to lose interest."

With another ripple, the steely glint of the Scourge's weapon vanished, swallowed under glossy darkness, and the part of the thing that had impaled Esme suddenly changed shape. Widening and twisting in the wound in her shoulder, the demon lifted Esme upward until she was teetering on tiptoe, and though her jaw was set and her lips bitten shut against crying out, tears were running down her face.

"You're better than this," said the Scourge, bringing its own face up to hers. "Aren't you?"

With a soft, sucking sound, the darkness retracted. Esme dropped to the ground like a sack of potatoes, next to her shattered sword.

"Surely we've passed the point where physical violence is going to solve anything, don't you think?" the Scourge asked. "Punching. Kicking. Going at each other with pointy objects. It's all so *limited*.

"Come on," it added, leaning over her. "Why don't you show me what you can *really* do?"

But then . . .

AWAKENING

For Charlie, now, there was silence: absolute silence except for the low thump of his own blood pumping in his ears. Seated on his throne, he looked down at his arms, at the black tattoo shapes still swarming and pulsing there—and then he looked out at his kingdom.

He saw the ranks of Gukumats, stretching in every direction. Beyond that, he saw the vast serried legions of the demon peoples—the whole gross, adoring mass of his subjects, screaming and cheering from all around him. The view changed: for a second, all Hell seemed to expand and bulge—and now, suddenly, he could see further still.

Darkness slid through him like icy water, glimmering and glittering with tiny points of light that Charlie was suddenly able to identify as . . . *stars*. Planets and galaxies swam past like beautiful jellyfish, twinkling in the surrounding blue-blackness of space, close enough to reach out and touch. Black holes opened in front of him like flowers. Suns—whole solar systems—blazed into being, then shrank and winked out as he watched.

At the same time, the noise in his head was changing. The sound of his own pulse in his ears had gone, mixing with the crowd noise, mutating and modulating downward into something darker, thicker, deeper. It was all around him: throbbing and seething, and all the time it was getting louder and louder.

Ba-BOOM!

Ba-BOOM!

Ba-BOOM!

Ba-BOOM!

It was inescapable, dreadful, unspeakable, the noise. It was as if every creature in the universe were banging on a drum and screaming at him at the same time. The noise assaulted him on every level, getting more and more irritating the more irritated he got.

And suddenly, Charlie found himself wishing he could do something about it.

Here he was, at what should have been the proudest moment of his entire life, and what happened? There was all this noise, interrupting.

All there ever was for him was noise and interruptions.

Whenever things went well for him, there was always something going on to spoil it. Esme and Jack were a prime example: they could've left him to get on with stuff, they could've trusted him a little—but no! Of course, they'd had to interfere.

His *dad* too, instead of messing everything up, could've—

Surrounded by light and life, sitting on his throne in the center of the universe, Charlie blinked.

Dad, he thought.

He thought of his mother's expression at the breakfast table that morning when his father had told them he was leaving.

He thought of his dad sitting alone in a Chinese restaurant and how Charlie had told him he was "*never going to forgive him. Never.*"

He frowned.

Well, he told himself, he didn't care about that—not anymore. He'd taken steps. He'd left all that behind. And there— it occurred to him—was the answer.

The universe shimmered and roared around him, waiting for whatever Charlie was going to think next.

This, he thought—the noise, the lights, the stuff going on around him now—was all no different. His days of weakness, of being at the mercy of events, were gone. He alone— he, Charlie—had the power; he was in complete control of his destiny. Nothing was going to get in his way or hurt him anymore in any way whatsoever—he wouldn't allow it. He could just decide, and whatever he wanted would be so.

Well, the noise and the lights were getting to him.

He'd had as much as he was prepared to take.

So he decided.

Let it out, a voice echoed in Charlie's head. *Let it all out, open your heart, and LET ME IN. YES!*

It would all . . . just have . . . to STOP.

As soon as he'd completed the thought, he felt something move inside himself. The thing that had been waiting inside him, waiting for this moment for longer than Charlie could possibly have imagined, suddenly seemed to give a great, convulsive LEAP.

In front of his eyes, the vision was sucking back into itself like someone had pressed rewind. The black holes slammed shut, the suns brightened and went out again, and the planets and galaxies were flung past him and back into their appointed places. The view shrank and collapsed.

Then he was back on his throne, and at last the horrible noise was dying down.

Charlie let out a big sigh, glad it was all over. He had an odd taste at the back of his mouth—a strange, coppery taste that he couldn't identify at first—and to be honest, he was feeling a bit weird. He made to lift his hands to rub his eyes and found to his surprise that he couldn't: his arms seemed to be stuck to the throne somehow, as if they'd been glued there.

Odder still, the black tattoo seemed to have vanished: of the great swirling pattern of curving blades and hooks, there was now no sign whatsoever. All there was was his own bare skin and the nasty taste that stayed in his mouth no matter how many times he swallowed.

Blood, he realized suddenly. It was blood.

Something's wrong here, he thought, beginning to panic: something was definitely wrong. Everything looked different. The Gukumats weren't looking at him—no one was. And underneath him, behind his back, the throne was moving again. With a speed that was shocking to Charlie, he saw that it was growing again. Tonguelike petals of moist-looking meat were curling upward in front of him, closing inward, blotting out the scene outside. Charlie gave a last, great effort to escape his throne: his left arm came slightly free of its armrest—

—and his eyes widened in horror.

The movement had released a pool of dark red liquid. Two thick dribbles of his blood just had time to run over the edge of the armrest before thin tendrils of pink shot out, lassoing his arm and yanking it back into position.

The throne went back to what it had been doing. It went about its work with redoubled strength now, battening down hungrily until Charlie's flesh quivered with each terrible *suck*. The realization, when it came to Charlie, was sudden and devastating.

The charade was over. The throne was killing him.

And now, at long last, Charlie began to get an inkling of just what an idiot he'd been.

MAGIC

Suddenly, a great thunderclap rang out. Rolling around and back from the distant walls, it was loud enough to silence the entire hordes of Hell. Everyone—Esme included—looked at the throne. In this sense, Charlie had finally got his wish, but the petals of meat had already closed, blocking him from sight.

In the silence, a strange, rushing, gurgling sound became audible, getting nearer and nearer until it seemed to be coming from all around. Closer it came, an encroaching silvery tinkling hiss, quickly growing to the thunderous roar of an approaching torrent.

Abruptly, a frothy, milk-colored liquid burst in from all sides of the room. The back rows of the assembled demons were caught completely by surprise, dissolving to nothing where they stood.

The Dragon's juices had reached the heart chamber. It was the demons' turn to be broken down into energy for the awakening. Already the flood of pale fluid was darkening into a nutrient-rich, bloodred broth.

There was a moment of horror, then the screaming started.

"Oh *crap!*" barked Jagmat, high up above proceedings, still trapped in his magical bubble. Suddenly this didn't seem such a bad place to be, not compared to what was happening to the rank-and-file demons on the ground. As one, in a blind panic, the population had lunged for the center of the room, trying to get as far away from the surrounding tide of juices as they could, trampling anyone and everything in their path in a headlong charge of storming feet, tentacles, pseudopods, fins, coils, and whatever else they used to get around. It wasn't going to do them any good: the climb to the top of the central plateau was all but impossible, as it was protected by magical barriers that Gukumat had constructed for the very purpose of preventing any escape. Jagmat stared downward, horrified, as the foremost of the demon hordes scrabbled frantically up the sides of the central platform, only to fall back and vanish into the teeming, howling mass that followed them.

The walls, the floor, the entirety of the chamber gave a long, rippling shudder. All over the room, gigantic veins and blood vessels began to twitch and convulse as each and every part of the heart chamber began, slowly, to come to life.

The air was hot with carnage. Esme stood there, stunned by it, hardly able to make sense of it all—

—and in that moment, the Scourge *laughed*.

It was a dreadful sound, like no laugh Esme had ever heard. It was husky, like dry bones scraping together, yet it was also high and screeching, like the brakes on a bus full of screaming children just before it plummets over a cliff. It echoed through the surrounding noise, chilling her to the quick, and in another moment the Overminister—all seven thousand of him—joined in.

They were enjoying this, the Scourge and Gukumat. They were enjoying their moment, savoring a triumph that, for them, had been a long time coming.

Esme set her jaw, shaking off the last of the pain of the Scourge's stab wound. It hadn't healed up properly yet, but she wasn't thinking about that. The shoulder would work: that was all that mattered.

She stood up.

The Scourge saw her and, with an effort, managed to stop laughing.

"**There**," it said, gesturing behind itself at the throne at the center of the plateau, which was still sealing and tightening—slowly—around its victim. "**If you're planning any last-minute heroics, Esme, I should tell you, there's no longer any point. Charlie has served his purpose. The Dragon is waking.**"

"We're not dead yet," said Esme. "That means there's still a chance."

The Scourge looked at her, then shrugged, the movement making its shoulders and neck drip together in long, tarlike strings.

"**If you could get to the throne in the next few moments, you could still rescue Charlie, I suppose. Perhaps you might even convince the Dragon to return to its slumber—though it would certainly want your life in Charlie's place.**"

"Fine. Whatever it takes."

"**Still,**" said the Scourge, "**two further problems remain for you. First, you don't have much time.**"

"And second?"

"**Second, I won't let you.**"

"Then I guess I'd better pull out all the stops," said Esme.

She could feel it now, feel it inside herself. This was the last battle. This was what she'd been waiting her whole life to do.

Magic. She would have to use magic.

Already the power was rippling through her, coursing in her veins until the very ends of her hair crackled with it. And now, for the first time, she recognized what it was and where it came from.

Remember what I told you about your mother, said Raymond's voice in her head. *Remember your mother. And don't ever forget . . . well, that I love you.*

It was Raymond who had brought her up, Raymond who had trained her. *Raymond* had made her what she was, not the Scourge. And *her mother's blood* ran in her veins, every bit as strong as anything else that was there.

Almost without realizing she was doing it, Esme lowered her hands to her sides. She lifted, rocking forward slightly, until only the tips of her toes remained in contact with the fleshy red ground below her. She closed her eyes.

"At last," said the Scourge. "**At long last, the moment of tr—**"

In that second, before the demon could finish what it was saying, Esme struck.

The air over her hands heated up, rippled, and burst into light. Her feet left the ground and she rose into the air, but she had eyes for nothing but the face of her enemy. Bringing her hands up, concentrating her hatred and determination, summoning every ounce—every drop—of the unstoppable, bottomless desire for revenge that seemed at that moment to consume her entire being, Esme flung her magic at the Scourge.

Jagmat, high above, glimpsed a smoking streak run a line between the girl and the demon. It left a black scorch mark on the fleshy red ground, and for a second, as whatever it was struck the Scourge's outstretched palms, it seemed that nothing else was going to happen. Then—

KER-BLAM!

Spreading from the line, widening and swallowing all in its path, a sudden, shatteringly bright light expanded, searing every sense in Jagmat's jellylike body. The magical bubble that held him rattled and shook; he and Shargle bounced around inside it like dice in a cup; and when Jagmat next was able to see what was happening, he saw that the Scourge had vanished and a great ring of the Gukumats—hundreds of them— had been flung back from the blast. There was a wide, clear space around where the girl and the demon had been standing, swept clean in a spreading wave as if from an explosion. Those Gukumats at the edge had been knocked straight over the precipice. The robes of many that remained were on fire; shrieking, they thrashed and slapped at themselves as they tried to put out the flames, and some just lay where they'd been flung.

"Whoa," said Jagmat, with his usual understatement. Then, "I wonder which ones were lookin' after the—*AAAAAGH!!*"

Abruptly, as soon as he'd articulated the thought, the walls of his bubblelike magical prison simply flickered out of existence, and the hapless demon found himself plunging toward the ground.

And then all Hell broke loose.

Howling with a mixture of terror and sudden delight, the wave of rank-and-file demons that at that moment had been scrabbling up toward the central platform suddenly found that their way was no longer blocked by the Overminister's magic. They poured in a black screaming rush over the edge, overwhelming the first line of Gukumats before they had time to put up any resistance.

Those Gukumats behind the outside lines were no luckier: the ring of glowing bubbles holding the gladiators had failed, and now the air was filled by a sudden plummeting deluge of grudge-filled and angry fighting demons. The Carnotaur, in particular, was not satisfied with the score or so of flattened Gukumats that cushioned its landing: it had disliked the Overminister for a long time, and now, it had decided—unsheathing its claws, glands seeping acid from every pore—that some serious payback was due.

Gukumat had a full-scale rebellion on his hands. And suddenly, for the first time in its millennia-long life, his hivelike mind found itself uncomfortably uncertain of what the outcome was going to be.

Slowly, in the weird calm at the center of all this chaos, Esme came down to earth. She was breathing hard, but she forced herself back under control. There was no sign of the

Scourge. Ignoring the fierce battle that was beginning to rage around her, she looked all over the place, checking the smoking heaps of lifeless Gukumat bodies that seemed to have piled up at the edge of the blast.

She had never used her power like that. She had never known it could be used like that, or how powerful she really was. Truth to tell, she had scared herself more than a little, but she forced herself not to think about that now. The Scourge wasn't dead—it couldn't be dead. All she had done, she knew, was strike the first blow—and she wasn't sure if she had the strength to strike a second.

Well, now was her chance. She closed her eyes and took a deep breath. She was just on the point of disappearing, ready to find Charlie and see what she could do to stop what was happening, when she felt, without looking, the air in front of her face as it rippled and went hot.

The blow came instantaneously.

Her eyes flew open, and she watched with a sort of detached weariness as she was thrown back another twenty feet. She hit the ground hard, and by the time she'd skidded to a halt, the Scourge was standing over her again.

"Not bad," it said. A stinging slap to her face made Esme's world explode into stars. "Not bad at all," it added, swinging at her again.

But when it struck this time, the blow landed on thin air. The Scourge froze, staring, but Esme had vanished. And when it heard her voice again, she was behind it.

"Khentimentu the Scourge," said Esme quickly, wiping the

blood from her mouth in a long streak down her arm. "To roots that bind and thorns that catch I consign you."

The demon shook a little—wobbled—but stood firm. It turned to face her. So Esme said it again.

"Khentimentu the Scourge," she said. "To roots that bind and thorns that catch I *consign* you."

"You still don't understand, do you?" it said. **"Those words have no power over me, not from you. You can't banish me. You *are* me. All that you can do—all that you've learned—comes from me!"**

"That's not true," said Esme. "My mother defeated you before, and I can defeat you now: Khentimentu the Scourge, to roots that bind and thorns that catch I—"

"No," said the demon, wrapping one liquid-black hand around her throat, **"you *can't*."**

And once more, it started to squeeze.

THE END

"Now, are you absolutely sure that you've got me all right?" It was something like the seventeenth time Jack had asked this question, he knew. A part of him even suspected that the Chinj might be becoming a little impatient with him, but he didn't really care. At that moment, he was being carried, bodily, high over a horde of demons that—when they weren't being horrifyingly dissolved by a rising tide of juices—were busily engaged in massacring each other in a variety of creative and enthusiastic ways. Given the situation, the question of whether the flock of batlike creatures had a firm grip on him or not was one that he needed to hear the answer to, he found, both urgently and often.

"You are not . . . as heavy . . . as the other humans," said the nearest Chinj into his ear, with some difficulty. "I suppose . . . we should be thankful . . . for that."

Jack was surrounded by them. If anyone down below had chanced to look up (which, thankfully, they were all too busy to do) they would have been hard-pressed to make Jack out amongst the rattling, clattering flock. The Chinj had carried him a long way already. The glimpses that Jack caught in between the heaving, flapping, furry bodies were enough to tell him that they need only go a little further.

The radio in his ear crackled suddenly.

"Jack?"

"Yep."

"They cannot take me any further; I am dropping now," said Number 3.

"Are you on target?" he asked. "Are you close enough to the center?"

"Can't see. No time. They're—"

The signal dissolved into a burst of static, or possibly the clattering of wings.

"Number Three!" said Jack. "Number Three, can you hear me?"

The radio crackled again, but there was no answer.

"Good luck!" called Jack—immediately feeling very silly indeed. If the Chinj had dropped Number 3 into the mass of demons, then he was going to need a lot more than luck.

But suddenly, it was his turn.

"We are close to the center," said the voice in his ear. "Going down now. Do not . . . forget your promise to us . . . small human."

The landing, when it came, was surprisingly gentle. In less than a second, it seemed to Jack, he was standing on his own two feet on the eerily squishy arterial-red ground, and the fluttering black flock was opening around him, peeling away in a great spreading tornado of dark furry bodies and leathery wings.

Now, finally, he could take in the scene.

An explosion off to his right was the first thing that attracted his attention. A blast wave full of something wet and sticky passed over him, and when his vision cleared, he glimpsed Number 3 backing away from the crowd toward the center of the plateau, covering his escape with a hail of fire from his MP5.

Jack couldn't see what was following him, not at first. For a moment it seemed as though the mass of demons—still fighting one another—were going to leave him be. But then the crowds parted—the impromptu barricade of prone and still faintly smoking Gukumat bodies was roughly shoved aside—and Jack realized that Number 3 was in trouble.

The demon that was after him wasn't especially big, but it looked strong. Its squat, barrel-like body was covered in a gray-green scaly armor of some kind: it swatted at Number 3's bullets with its long-fingered razor-clawed hands as though the gunfire were a cloud of mosquitoes. It rattled forward on its stumpy legs with a terrible eagerness: its small head, not much bigger than a pair of fists held side by side, was split up the center by a disgusting vertical maw of hooks and thrashing tentacles, and its long bony arms grasped out for the Son as he backed away.

Jack watched, frozen, as Number 3's first gun ran dry. The creature lunged—and the Son leaped to one side, drawing a heavy Sig Sauer automatic pistol from his hip and shooting several fat bullets into the creature's face at almost point-blank range. The demon staggered back a yard or two, physically driven back by the force of the shots—but Jack could see, with a terrible detached certainty, that it was stunned rather than actually hurt.

With a smooth movement, Number 3 pulled the rocket launcher that was strapped to his back round to a firing position. He raised the long, tube-shaped weapon up onto his shoulder and, without even appearing to take aim, let rip.

The rocket hit the demon in the chest, lifting the hapless creature off its feet and carrying it bodily right over the improvised barricade and over the battle raging below, until it vanished from sight.

"Number Three!" yelled Jack, screaming to make himself heard over the dreadful wave of noise that seemed to assault his ears from every direction.

The Son didn't hear him.

Jack thought about yelling again. Then he stopped himself.

Number 3 couldn't help him. There was no one who could help him. Somehow, his desperate plan had worked, and he was through to the center of the room, alone. There was no telling how long he'd be left that way. He had a job to do, and here was the chance to do it.

He turned and faced the killing throne.

"Oh no," gasped Esme, catching sight of Jack as he started off up the steps. "Oh, God, no—Jack!"

The steps were steep: slippery and disgustingly warm to the touch, they pulsed with dreadful life under Jack's bare feet—but he kept going. The vile meaty purple petal things that now surrounded the throne almost refused to move aside for him. He had to dig his fingers into their slimy rough edges and yank at them, hard, before they'd get out of his way. It was like trying to unwrap a giant artichoke: no matter how many of the tonguelike objects he managed to pry away, there always seemed to be another one underneath. The noise of the battle sank to a dull roar behind him, muffled by all the layers. Then, suddenly, the last one parted, and he saw what was waiting for him in the center.

He didn't recognize Charlie at first. Or rather, he knew it was Charlie, but what sat in the throne as the tentacles caressed and sucked at him looked like a mannequin—a model of Charlie, not the real thing. His face was drawn, his cheeks shrunken. His arms and hands were skin and bones, and his eyes, shut tight, looked like peeled hard-boiled eggs in their sockets.

Then Charlie opened them and looked at him.

"Oh, Charlie," said Jack. "You *berk* . . ."

"Jack," croaked Charlie, stretching toward his friend with two fingertips—all he was able to move. "Jack . . ."

"Well, okay," said Jack, with a confidence he didn't remotely feel, "let's get you out of this thing at least." And he strode toward the throne. Trying not to flinch too much, he grasped one of the slimy, pinkish-gray tentacle things that was sucking at his friend's arm and yanked it away. The tentacle wriggled and thrashed, its nasty leechlike mouth parts opening and shutting convulsively on thin air. Charlie shuddered.

"Don't," he said.

Jack stared at him. "What?"

"Don't."

"What the Hell do you mean? Do you want to get out of this mess or what?"

"The Dragon," croaked Charlie. "It's—"

But something strange was happening. All over Charlie's body, the sucking writhing tentacle things were letting go, releasing him. Charlie slumped in the throne, unable to move, his blood still dripping listlessly from a hundred different wounds—but the thing that had done this to him was changing, shifting before Jack's eyes.

Suddenly, it seemed to Jack that the throne—the tongues, the tentacles, everything—was looking at him. It was all pointed in his direction. And then, in a voice from the bottom of a pit . . . something began to speak.

"**You,**" it said. The voice was like the Scourge's, only older. Deeper. Stronger.

"**You,**" it repeated. The voice didn't seem to be coming from any particular place, but Jack heard it with every fiber of his being.

"You have forced your way into my throne room. You seek to deprive me of my rightful victim. Explain yourself."

"Er," said Jack. "Um . . ."

"Do you wish to stop the awakening?" prompted the voice.

"Er, well, yeah," said Jack, grabbing at this chance and hardly believing that it was being offered. "Yes, actually," he said, putting more effort into his voice this time. "I want to stop the awakening. Yes."

"This child has paid for the awakening with his life. The price for preventing it will be the same. Do you, then, offer your life?"

"Er, what?" asked Jack.

"Blood will awaken me," explained the Dragon patiently. **"Blood will send me back to my slumbers. All dealings with me must be sealed with blood. Do you, then,"** it repeated, **"offer your life?"**

Jack stared.

Then he scowled.

For Heaven's sake! he thought (only he didn't use the word *heaven*). If this didn't just beat everything. Here he was, with the existence of the universe now—apparently—depending on him. Against all the odds, he had got his chance: he could save Charlie, he could save the day—but of course, it had to hinge on him volunteering to die. How completely, *utterly*—

"All right," he said, stepping up. "Okay. I'll do it."

"Do what?" boomed the voice.

Jack scowled again. "I'll 'offer my life' or whatever! Come on, let's get on with this!"

"Then take the boy's place on the throne."

"Right," said Jack.

The tentacle things didn't resist him now. They fell away easily. What resisted him was Charlie.

"No!" said Charlie, plucking weakly at Jack's arms as Jack lifted him out of the throne—and dumped him, none too ceremoniously, on the fleshy red floor.

"Shut up," said Jack, "and listen to me. You have a job to do, and it's time for you to do it."

Charlie stared at him, stunned by the strength in Jack's voice. For the first time ever, Jack realized, Charlie was actually taking him seriously.

Jack sighed.

"You've got to go out there," he said, gesturing past the purplish, tonguelike layers of the walls, "and you've got to help Esme."

Still Charlie stared.

"You've got to do what you first said you were going to do. Remember? You've got to help her defeat the Scourge. You've got to do it," said Jack, staring right back into his eyes. "For me."

There was another pause.

"Oh, mate," said Charlie. "I'm so sorry. I—"

"Save it," said Jack, sitting down on the throne. "Just go. Let me get on with this."

He closed his eyes, not wanting to look at Charlie anymore. This whole situation was, after all, entirely Charlie's fault.

To his credit, Charlie didn't try to say anything else. And when Jack opened his eyes, Charlie was gone.

Right, thought Jack, and waited for the next bit.

It wasn't long coming.

"Khentimentu the Scourge," said Charlie, from Esme's side. "To roots that bind and thorns that catch I *consign* you."

The demon froze. "**You!**" it said.

"Hi, Charlie," said Esme.

"Hi, Esme."

"Glad you could make it."

"Don't thank me," said Charlie. "Thank Jack."

Esme looked at him and nodded slowly. "Well," she said. "Let's make sure he didn't waste the effort."

"Ready when you are."

"On three, then," said Esme. "*One.*"

The air in front of Charlie and Esme suddenly wobbled and shook; then a long, glistening, stafflike object was forming between them, stretching across in front of them, under their hands.

"**Charlie?**" asked the demon, and for the first time in its long life, it suddenly sounded uncertain. "**Charlie, let me explain.**"

"Two."

"**You can still be Emperor. I can still give you everything you wanted! Charlie, *you'll be sorry!***"

"I already am," said Charlie, then closed his eyes.

"Three," said Esme. The magical staff was fully formed now: a last gunmetal glint passed down its length, then it was ready for the job it had to do.

"**KHENTIMENTU THE SCOURGE!**" said Esme and Charlie

both at once, and their combined voice was so loud that all Hell suddenly found that it had stopped what it was doing and now had no choice but to listen to the boy and the half-demon girl and hear what they had to say next.

The Scourge trembled.

"TO ROOTS THAT BIND—"

The words echoed around the heart chamber. The magical staff glowed blinding white.

"—AND THORNS THAT CATCH—"

Now the demon was screaming—a terrible sound, a sound like tearing in your head, a maiming scream that went on and on.

"WE *CONSIGN* YOU!" roared Esme and Charlie at once. *"GET YOU HENCE, AND TROUBLE US NO MORE!"*

And with a final, piteous shriek, the liquid darkness that was Khentimentu the Scourge was sucked, helplessly, toward the burning magical staff that Charlie and Esme held in their hands. It swirled around them, a nimbus of pure black, rushing and hurtling and twisting and rippling.

Then, with a final clap of thunder—

—it was gone.

Exhausted, Esme sank to the floor.

They'd done it! They'd trapped the Scourge in the staff! Now if Esme could only get the demon back to Earth and reimprison it, she would have succeeded at last where Nick had failed. Hardly believing it, she turned to smile at Charlie.

But he wasn't there.

"Been here—*ow*," Jack said aloud, as the Dragon began to suck out his life. "Done this," he added, doing his best to put a brave face on things—though to be honest, at that moment, he wasn't sure why he was bothering.

"You are . . . very strange," said the Dragon suddenly.

For a moment, Jack was too surprised to speak, but it didn't take him long to recover himself.

"No," he replied. "I'm normal. It's *you* who's strange."

"What . . . do you mean?"

"I mean," said Jack, with an effort, "this business of you creating the universe and falling asleep, then waking up and destroying it."

"Yes?"

"Well, what kind of a routine is that? If all you were ever going to do was sleep through the whole thing, why bother creating the universe in the first place? It just . . ." Jack shook his head. "It doesn't make any sense!"

Suddenly, to Jack's surprise, the sucking sensation stopped. The throne still held him tight: the tentacle things still gripped his arms—but the blood was no longer being leeched out of his body.

"Your question is a fair one," the Dragon said, considering. **"You're about to die, so I shall let you in on a secret."**

Jack held his breath.

"I have not been asleep."

"So?" asked Jack, annoyed. "What've you been doing all this time? Pretending?"

"My slumber was a convenient fiction," said the Dragon

smugly. **"It was necessary, to preserve the conditions of my experiment."**

"What experiment?" asked Jack.

"When I created your universe," the Dragon announced, **"I also created its nemesis: an immortal being that thrived on the worst in people—a being that, if it were given the chance, would have the power to bring my Creation to an end."**

"The Scourge," said Jack.

"The central question of my experiment, then, was this," the Dragon went on. **"Could the other sentient creatures work together to prevent this catastrophe from occurring? Or would they be so wrapped up in their own concerns that they would allow themselves to be destroyed?"**

"I don't understand," said Jack.

"That question has now been answered," said the Dragon, regardless. **"The Scourge succeeded. The awakening was not prevented."** It paused. **"You failed."**

Jack thought about this, following through the implications of what he'd just heard.

It took several seconds, but when he finally got his head round it, he felt an emotion that was so strong he couldn't actually identify it at first.

"Hang on," he said. "Let me get this straight. This whole thing—the whole history of the universe—was just some kind of . . . test?"

The Dragon did not reply.

"But that's insane!" said Jack, with rising fury. "Are you seriously telling me, after everything that's happened, that it's all been, like, a game for you?"

"Not a game," the Dragon replied. **"An *experiment*. And now the experiment is over."**

"But—I don't *believe* this!" said Jack. "All this effort, all this pain and suffering, and it's just so you can prove some *point*?"

"That is correct," said the Dragon simply.

"Well," said Jack. There was, he found, only one more thing to be said.

"You SELFISH GIT!"

"*What?*" said the Dragon, astonished. **"*What* did you just say?"**

"I think you heard me," said Jack, disgusted. "Well, I've got a question for you too. Where do you get off playing with people's lives like that? What gives you the right? *Who*," he added, reaching a pitch of righteous rage, "*do you think you are?*"

"I am THE DRAGON," roared the Dragon. **"I am your Creator. It is an unspeakable, immeasurable honor,"** it went on, **"for an insignificant speck such as yourself to have the opportunity to converse with one such as me. You are here as a penitent, offering your pitiful life in exchange for a stay of execution for your universe. I would think, therefore, that a little *respect* is—"**

"Hang on," said Jack suddenly. "Say that again."

"I said," said the Dragon, **"I am the Dragon. Your Cr—"**

"No, after that."

"After what?"

"After all that crap you just said," said Jack, another ugly thought beginning to occur to him. "What do you mean, *my* universe?"

"I'm sorry?" asked the Dragon.

"You said, 'your universe,'" pursued Jack doggedly. "What exactly did you mean by that? Are there others? And come to think of it, what do you mean by 'one such as me'?"

"You must have misheard me."

"No," said Jack. "Your voice is pretty loud, and I'm quite sure you distinctly said—"

"It is not for one such as you to question the utterances of the Dragon!"

"Just tell me this," said Jack quickly. "If you created us— the universe, everything—then who created *you*?"

"No one!" said the Dragon. **"I created myself."**

"Nope. Sorry," said Jack. "I don't believe you." He shook his head, actually smiling to himself now. "Blimey!" he said. "You gods—you're all the same. You must just think we're all stupid!"

"Wh-what do you mean?"

"I mean, look at what you do, going around 'creating' things. Why do you do it?"

"My motivations are like me: infinite and mysterious. A puny mortal could not—"

"Oh, *save* it," said Jack. "Please, just give it a rest, will you? If you don't have the guts to tell me yourself, then I'll tell you what *I* think—all right?"

"**Very well,**" snorted the Dragon. "**Amuse me!**"

Jack took a deep breath.

"I don't think," he began, "that when you—and people like you—go and start something like this, you do it with some grand master plan in mind. You do it," he said, "because you're bored. That's my guess.

"Yeah," Jack went on, liking his idea more and more the more he examined it. "You do it because you think it'll be fun. You do it because it might be interesting. You do it," he finished, "because you've got *nothing else to do*!"

There was a long silence.

"Am I right?" asked Jack. "Or what?"

"**That's . . .**" said the Dragon—and paused. "**Actually,**" it conceded, "**that's rather acute of you. Intriguing. Go on.**"

"Well!" said Jack. "In that case, it follows that you don't actually want *my* universe to end. Do you? I mean, if that happens, then you'll have to find something else to play with!"

The Dragon did not answer.

"In fact, I reckon you'd be pretty pleased if you didn't really have to destroy us. In *fact*," Jack added, hardly believing in his own audacity, "you don't really want to kill *me* at all either!"

There were another few seconds of silence—seconds that felt, to Jack, very long indeed.

Then Charlie shoved his way into the throne room. Esme appeared beside him.

"Jack!" they shouted. "Jack! *No!*" And they set about trying to rescue him.

Charlie—Jack was surprised (and at the same time kind of pleased) to notice—was crying: his eyes were red and puffy, and guilty tears were pouring down his cheeks. Even Esme looked worried—but she was the first to catch Jack's eye and interpret the few frantic and secretive gestures he could manage, glued as he was to the throne.

"It's all right, mate! I'm coming! We'll just get you out of— ow! What?" sputtered Charlie, when Esme grabbed him and roughly pulled him a couple of steps back. "What are you—?"

"Wait," said Esme.

There was a rumbling from all around them, and a whispering, crackling, rustling sound as the fleshy walls began to shrink back.

"I have decided," the Dragon's voice announced, **"that on this occasion the universe shall be spared. I have also decided"**—Jack held his breath—**"to allow this boy to live."**

"I like you," it added, in a quieter voice that Jack knew only he could hear. **"You're *interesting*. However, your enquiring nature has made you most impertinent. If your universe had more like you in it, then I might have to destroy it for my own peace of mind. Do I make myself clear?"**

"No problem," said Jack fervently.

"The Dragon has spoken," said the voice. **"Be sure of what you want of me, foolish mortals, before you disturb my ancient slumber again."**

Not wanting to push his luck any further than he had already, Jack kept his mouth shut.

Then, for a long moment, he thought about it.

He thought about God, and the god who'd created God, and the god who'd created the god who created God, and so on. He thought about what it all might mean for himself and his life and his place in existence. He thought, in that moment, about the meaning of it all—and wondered, briefly, whether there actually *was* one. But then the throne released him.

And *then* Esme threw her arms around him.

And suddenly, Jack found that, actually, he didn't really care.

"So," said the elder Chinj, much later, "you have fulfilled your promise. You have returned to throw yourself upon our mercy— to prostrate yourself," it added, "before the righteous wrath of the Grand Cabal. I confess, small human, I am surprised."

"Yeah, well," said Jack. "A promise is a promise."

"And let me remind you," said the elder Chinj, "and all those here present, of what that promise consisted!"

"Get on with it!" squeaked a voice from the back row of the flock, to a dangerous chatter of agreement.

"You have agreed, in accordance with our most holy laws," intoned the elder Chinj, scowling furiously, "to pay for your heinous crimes. You have promised," it added, "to make good your gross violation of our most sacred byways. YOU HAVE SAID," it shrieked, reaching a fever pitch of ferocity, "THAT WE CAN DO WHATEVER WE LIKE WITH YOU!"

"That's right," said Jack, when the flock had quieted down enough for him to make himself heard. "I did."

"Well," said the elder Chinj, suddenly going quiet. "The Parliament of Chinj, in its infinite wisdom, has decided to be—*muhnuhmuful.*"

It coughed, covering its mouth with one withered paw.

"I'm sorry?" said Jack. "I didn't quite catch that."

"We've . . . decided to be . . . *mmmuhful,*" said the elder Chinj, with obvious reluctance.

"I'm really sorry," said Jack politely. "But I still didn't—"

"We're going to let you live!" snapped the elder Chinj. "All right? Satisfied?" It turned and stumped its way out of the cave, which, by now, was ringing with cheers.

"There," said Number 3, from beside where Jack was standing. "At last. It is all over."

"I couldn't have put it better myself," said a voice—and they all turned.

There, some twenty yards down the passageway, standing beside a large, but still pack-size, technological-looking metal shape—

—was Number 2.

"It's no good trying to stop me!" he screamed (though in fact, as yet, no one had). "The countdown has begun. In thirty seconds, all that's going to be left of this place is a mushroom cloud the size of New York!"

In the silence that greeted this announcement, Number 3 sighed.

"Number Two," he began.

"No, wait a second," Jack interrupted. "You mean, that thing in the pack was . . . a bomb? A nuclear *bomb*?"

Number 2 grinned widely, and his eyes glittered: "Project Justice," he said, with a gesture at the device. "As soon as the gateway to Hell was discovered, I gave the order myself. The first away-team to make the trip was to go in with tactical nuclear capability. That way, if Hell's inhabitants proved hostile, we could strike decisively while we had the chance—eliminating a potential threat at its source, and saving the human race!"

"You . . . plank!" Jack spluttered. "You stupid, half-witted—"

"Number Two," said Number 3 again. His voice was quiet, but something in its tone made Jack stop talking suddenly. "This is unnecessary."

"Don't you try and tell me what's unnecessary, Number Three," said Number 2. "You know your orders, and the situation's been clear ever since we got here. This whole place is a threat to our world and our way of life, and the only chance we've got is to strike first and strike hard. So, listen, any last words you got? You'd better say them now, because in"—he consulted the readout on the device—"less than eighteen seconds, you'll have missed your chance. Permanently."

"Would someone mind telling me what's going on here?" asked Esme. She pointed at Number 2. "This man's not really going to do what he says he's going to do, is he?"

"*Non*," said Number 3. "He is not."

"Watch me," said Number 2. "Here we go! Two! One! MOMMYYYYYYYYYYY!" he screamed, crouching and covering his ears while everyone—Number 3, Number 9, Jack, Charlie, Esme, and the numberless Chinj—just stared at him.

Beside him, the machine beeped twice, then fell silent.

After another few seconds, Number 2 opened his eyes.

"Number Two," said Number 3, "for some time now it 'as been my belief that your judgment as a Son of the Scorpion Flail 'as been less than . . . reliable."

Number 2 stared at him, eyes wide.

"I must say," Number 3 went on, "my observations of your performance on zis mission 'ave certainly borne out my suspicions. Wi' zis in mind, I took the decision to remove Project Justice's security key." He held up the object: it dangled from his gloved hand. "A fact you would 'ave noticed if you 'ad checked for its presence before attempting to detonate the device."

"You . . ." said Number 2. "Wait a second. What the Hell *is* this?"

"Number Two," Number 3 continued, "you are 'ereby relieved of command, and your membership of the Sons of the Scorpion Flail is rescinded pending a full enquiry."

"Yeah? Well, I've got news for you, *pal*," said Number 2, standing up. "You don't have the authority. Only Number One himself has the power to fire me—and his true identity's so top secret that nobody even knows what he looks like!"

Number 3 allowed himself a small smile. "That is not," he said, "ze case at all, I am afraid."

"What do you mean?"

"Well," the man Number 2 had always thought of as his subordinate pointed out, "*you* know what I look like, do you not?"

For another moment, there was silence.

Number 2 turned sheet-white. "Y-you don't mean . . ." he stammered. "No, I don't believe it. You mean, all this time—all these years—*you* . . . were . . ."

Still Number 3—or Number 1, to give him his proper designation—said nothing.

"What the Hell's going on?" whispered Jack.

"W-well, IT MAKES NO DIFFERENCE!" shrieked Number 2, whipping out his own Sig Sauer and pointing it at his superior officer. "See? Who's in charge now, huh? *Who's in charge now?*" In three quick steps he moved away from the machine, the fat black hole at the end of the gun's barrel looming ever closer in Jack's vision.

"I'm going to count to three!" said Number 2. "If you haven't given me that security key and got down on your knees by then, I swear to God I'm going to shoot you in the face."

"And what difference will that make if you're just going to blow us all up anyway?" asked Jack brightly.

"SHUT UP!" screamed Number 2. "Just *SHUT UP!* ONE!" He pressed the barrel up against Number 1's forehead.

"Two!"

Nobody moved.

"Thr—*uhn!*" Number 2 grunted, as the large rock that had been dropped from above landed on his head and he fell to the ground.

"There," said Jack's Chinj, fluttering into view and finding a perch on the back of its prone victim. It looked up at the others. "I *did* enjoy that," it said—and winked.

INTERLUDE

Mr. and Mrs. Farnsworth were standing side by side.

Mr. Farnsworth was pale: his jaw was clenched, and his lips were pressed together in a bloodless line. Mrs. Farnsworth's eyes were wide and red, and she was blinking a lot: her knuckles were white where she gripped her handbag.

The two of them were standing in the morgue of Charing Cross police station in London's West End, in front of a mortuary slab. They'd come to identify a body that had recently been found floating in the Thames.

However, except for a rumpled white sheet, the slab in front of them was empty.

"But . . . I don't understand it!" said the attendant. "It was here! It was here not thirty seconds ago, when I went to open the door for you! And now it's—"

"It's what?" asked Mr. Farnsworth, with heavy emphasis.

"Gone!" said the attendant. He got a grip on himself.

"I'm so, *so* sorry," he said. "I've been helping people to identify bodies for over fifteen years, and I assure you, nothing like this has ever happened before. It's extraordinary! It was here not two minutes ago, and now it's just . . . vanished!"

"Not 'it,'" said Mr. Farnsworth.

"Pardon?"

"Not 'it!'" Mr. Farnsworth repeated, his voice rising dangerously. "Stop saying '*it*'! That's our *son* you might be talking about, you bl—!"

At that exact moment, a phone rang.

It was a mobile phone. There was an embarrassed pause, as first the attendant and then Mr. Farnsworth huffed, sighed, patted their pockets, checked their phones—and frowned.

Blinking, Mrs. Farnsworth took her mobile from her bag. She looked at the screen, pressed the button, and, numbly, held it up to her ear.

"Mum?" said Charlie. "Mum? It's me."

THE TREE

"Here," said Esme. "This one."

"What, really?" asked Charlie, surprised. "But it's just like the others!"

"That's the whole point," said Jack, "I imagine."

"Looks safe enough," acknowledged Number 1. He looked at Esme. "We do this now?" he asked.

Esme said nothing. She took the staff—which had grown strangely dull and rusty looking, like an elderly scaffolding pole—and strode ahead of them into the undergrowth surrounding the large and gnarled-looking oak tree that stood a little way up the small slope beside the battered tarmac path. Pausing only to look around to make sure no one happened to be watching, Number 1 and the boys set off after her.

They were in a certain park, in London. It was early autumn now, but the sky was a pleasingly clear pale blue and the sun was warm on Jack's back, casting long shadows on the ground in front of him as he followed the others into the shrubbery. It was a good day to be in a park. A five-a-side football match with jumpers for goalposts was going on some three or four hundred yards away. People were flying kites, walking dogs, throwing Frisbees and doing other park-type things. No one saw the little group disappearing off the path—or if they did, they didn't think anything of it. In another moment, Jack was sloshing through the piles of leaves as the air around him (under the shade of the tree) turned dark.

"Looks old," he said, looking up at it.

"Yeah," said Esme. "No one knows how old." Her face turned sad. "At least," she added, "not anymore."

"Well," said Charlie. "What happens next? How does it work?"

Esme didn't answer. She was circling the tree, the leaves making soft scrunching sounds under her trainers. The trunk of the tree was wide and solid looking, covered in bulbous lumps like petrified cauliflowers, or possibly, Jack thought, brains.

"Here," said Esme finally, taking up a spot some four or five feet away to Jack's right. With a sudden smooth movement, she lifted the staff and struck it into the ground. For a fraction of a second, Jack actually thought he could feel an impact tremor vibrating up through the soles of his trainers. But then he told himself he must be imagining things.

Esme tested the staff, which was now sticking straight up into the air, but it remained where it was.

"All right," she said. "We need to get around the tree. If we stretch out, I think we should be able to hold hands."

Before he could do anything about it, Jack found himself

holding hands with Charlie and Number 1, having missed his chance. With hideous predictability, he'd ended up on the opposite side from Esme and the staff—out of sight of whatever was about to happen. *Typical*. He sighed.

"Ready?" he heard Esme ask.

"Er . . . sure," he said hurriedly.

"Then we'll begin." Esme took a deep breath.

Jack suddenly noticed that all around them, all the noises of the park—the people, the traffic from the road beyond, even the birds—seemed to have gone strangely silent.

"**Khentimentu the Scourge**," said Esme quietly, and her voice seemed to set off small flowering explosions behind Jack's eyeballs. "**To roots that bind and thorns that catch, I consign you.**"

Number 1's and Charlie's hands grew warm in Jack's own. He was standing very close to the tree, facing inward, and his nostrils were filled with the dark, earthy, wet smell of the leaves and the mossy bark of the tree in front of him. The smells were strong, sweet, and—suddenly—almost overwhelming.

"**By the light of the world**," said Esme in the same clear voice. "**By the strength of my will and the curse that first stilled you, I command that you return to your prison. Get you hence,**" she finished, "**and trouble us no more.**"

From far away at first, but coming quickly closer, Jack felt a low, bubbling, sizzling sensation. It traveled up his arms and rushed through his veins, a tide of something hot and dark. It was like being hit by a wave of warm oil, but oil that was somehow alive, scrabbling and rippling and seething all through him in a frantic last effort to take hold. Jack held on tight to the hands that held his. The circle remained unbroken, and . . .

And then, as quickly as it had come, the sensation vanished.

For another long second the four of them stood there like that. Then . . .

"There," said Esme.

Charlie let go first, Number 1 a moment after that, and Jack found himself standing in front of what still looked like an ordinary tree, with his hands tingling.

He walked round to join the others, noticing as he did so that the staff that Esme had been carrying had now vanished.

"Is that it?" he asked.

"Yes," said Esme. "Yes it is."

"And is it . . . safe?" asked Charlie.

"As safe as it can be," said Esme. "Yes."

"Only we know ze secret," said Number 1. He looked around the little group, unsmiling. "Only one of us, or someone that we tell, will be able to release ze demon."

"Yeah, like *that's* going to happen," said Charlie, and shuddered.

For a moment, there was silence among them.

Jack was looking at Esme. Suddenly, she just looked incredibly, utterly tired. Come to think of it, he felt the same way.

"So," said Charlie, with a casual tone that was blatantly false. "What's next?"

Jack had to admit, it was a good question.

To his surprise, it was Esme who broke the silence.

"I've been fighting the Scourge," she said, "my whole life. There's nothing I've done—not one single thing—that hasn't been totally taken up with that."

Jack looked at her. He hadn't thought of this, but it was true. All the time he'd spent in Hell, all the time since this whole thing had started, only really amounted to a few days in real time. Esme had been fighting since before she was born.

Suddenly, she smiled.

"I'm going to learn how to live," she said. "That's what I'm going to do next. And maybe you'd all better do the same." She turned to Charlie. "Especially you."

"Yeah," said Charlie, looking at his feet. "I guess."

"I've got to go," said Esme, coming toward Jack and giving him a quick hug that was over before he'd even realized that that was what she was going to do. With her hands on his shoulders, she looked into his eyes. "See you round?" she asked.

Jack was blushing furiously, but he managed not to look away. "Er, sure," he managed, then immediately felt very silly indeed.

"Bye now," said Esme to the others.

Then she vanished.

"I too must go," said Number 1. Ignoring Charlie, he looked at Jack. "It 'as been a pleasure," he said.

"Thanks," said Jack, surprised.

Smiling at Jack, Number 1 nodded once—and walked away.

Then Charlie and Jack looked at each other.

"Well," said Charlie finally, "apart from thinking of something to tell my folks, I guess that's it."

"Yeah," said Jack. He felt strangely empty. Almost . . . disappointed, somehow.

"You taking the Tube?" asked Charlie.

"Sure."

"It's not quite as quick as dematerializing, but it gets there in the end."

"Fine."

"Let's go, then."

The two boys emerged onto the path and set off toward the nearest Underground station.

They didn't look back.

EPILOGUE

Three weeks later, Jack was back at school. He was sitting by the window, in a double history class.

Jack hated double history. He'd spent the first ten minutes of the class drawing little dashes around the edge of his history folder for every single minute there was left. Next, he'd started crossing them out as they passed. In about five minutes' time, he knew, he was going to be exactly an eighth of the way through the double class, and that wasn't anything like far enough for him.

He was in a foul mood. And really, he thought, who could blame him? Being forced to sit through the best part of two hours' tiresome waffling about Tudors and Stuarts seemed like a pretty poor reward for recently saving the universe. Plus, naturally, there was the fact that nobody knew about it: there was nobody he could tell. He wouldn't have known where to begin even if there *were* anyone he could tell. *You* try explaining to someone that you know Hell exists because you've been there, that you've met God (and God's god) and that the universe only continues to keep going because of decisions and actions that *you* made. See how far it gets you.

At first, Jack had been pleased to be back. His parents had been so wildly (and guilt-inducingly) relieved to see him that they'd accepted his story about running away with Charlie and spending a few nights in a hotel, almost without question. To his further surprise (perhaps it was something to do with his meeting with the Dragon), he'd found he was able to eat proper food again rather than Chinj vomit, which had obviously been a plus too.

But then—very soon after, in fact—the problems had set in.

He felt . . . detached from things. It felt to him as though a sheet of clear plastic lay between him and the world. He found he was wandering around in a sort of daze, going about the daily stuff of his average-fourteen-year-old's life like a robot, or maybe a puppet. And slowly, grimly, he'd begun to realize why.

No one has adventures every day.

This, he realized, was what was "typical." Not the fact that everything that could possibly go wrong for him always seemed to do so—he wasn't sure he really believed that anymore. What was typical, what was really typical, was the universal truth that no matter what amazing things you've done, what incredible adventures you've had, you've still got to come back to reality afterward. You've got to go to the toilet, you've got to do the washing up—you've got to go to double history, even when, if it wasn't for you, the Tudors and Stuarts would have become even more pointless and irrelevant than (it seemed to Jack) they are already. And this, Jack decided, was even worse.

There. Five minutes gone. He could now cross off an entire chunk of the dashes around his history folder. Hell, he thought, he might even color them in—anything to help pass the time.

His reverie was interrupted by a soft tapping at the window beside him.

Jack looked up. On the other side of the glass, standing on the windowsill, was a large, furry, batlike creature wearing a pair of wraparound sunglasses. It was waving at him.

Very slowly, Jack looked around the room. Mr. Hildegast was still droning on. Everyone else in the room still looked bored beyond belief. No one appeared to have noticed the Chinj's appearance.

He looked back at the Chinj, which was making a series of pointing and jabbing gestures with its small front paws, its wings flapping dangerously.

The meaning was obvious. Jack nodded once. The Chinj grinned, bowed, and dropped out of sight.

Jack turned and put his hand up.

"Ah, Mr. Farrell!" Mr. Hildegast beamed at him. "Do you have a question?"

"I'm sorry, sir," said Jack. "But I was wondering if I could be excused."

Mr. Hildegast's expression turned sour and thunderous. "Mr. Farrell! Are you seriously suggesting," he asked, and his voice held the beginnings of what Jack grimly realized was going to be one of his drearily predictable climaxes of indignation, "that I should let you disrupt my class—that I should let you *disturb your colleagues*—just because of your bladder? You should have gone before you came in!"

A few appreciative titters spread around the room at this, and Jack was aware of everyone looking at him.

He didn't care.

"Sorry, sir," he said, "but I'm . . . not well. I think it's something I ate. And I really need to be excused, right now."

The tittering went up a notch.

"Heaven's sake, man," said Mr. Hildegast, "why didn't you say so? Go! Go quickly!"

"Thank you, sir," said Jack, and the laughter of the rest of the class followed him out down the passageway, until the door to the classroom banged shut behind him.

He made it to the toilets, got into the cubicle at the end that had the window, opened it, and sat down.

"All right," he said, "this had better be important."

"I'm very happy to see you, sir!" squeaked the Chinj, bobbing up and down on its long toes as it clung to the cubicle's tiny windowsill.

"You too," said Jack. And it was true: it was good to see the small bat creature. "Nice sunglasses," he added.

"Thank you," said the Chinj modestly. "Miss Esme gave them to me."

"They look good on you."

"You're too kind."

"And how is Miss Esme?" Jack asked, a little pointedly. He hadn't heard from Esme since the business at the tree. He'd tried ringing the number at the theater, but it always seemed to be busy—and he'd begun to feel more than a little hurt.

"She's well," said the Chinj judiciously, "but she's been a bit busy. In fact, that's rather what I wanted to talk to you about."

"Oh yes?"

"There's a problem," said the Chinj, "at the Fracture."

Jack's expression turned grim. "What sort of problem?"

"Well, it's like this," the Chinj began. "Thanks largely to your efforts, Hell's been going through some rather big changes lately. For one thing, ever since . . . what happened, the new Emperor and I have—"

"New Emperor?" echoed Jack. "Who?"

"I was coming to that," said the Chinj. "As I was saying, the new Emperor and I have been approached by a number of parties who've been enquiring about the possibility of . . . well, *emigrating*, as it were."

Jack looked at the Chinj. "What are you talking about?" he asked.

"There are some demons," the Chinj replied patiently, "who want to come and live here, in your world."

"*Here?*" asked Jack, incredulous. "Why?"

"I honestly couldn't tell you," said the Chinj. "I mean, I was prepared to travel back and forth for you, of course, but I really can't see what merits the place has to offer by itself. To be honest, it seems rather"—it grimaced daintily—"well, boring, actually. No offense," it added quickly.

"None taken," said Jack.

"But these demons just won't listen to reason. We've been positively *flooded* with enquiries about the Fracture. One enterprising lot even set up a company, offering the chance for rank-and-file demons to book holiday tours—"

"*What?*"

"Though I'm sure I need hardly tell you," the Chinj went on hurriedly, "all requests to use the Fracture have been vehemently denied. It's under constant guard in case anyone is foolish enough to attempt to go through without permission."

"So?" asked Jack. "What's the problem?"

"The problem," said the Chinj, "is that the Emperor himself has expressed an interest in visiting."

"Oh yes?"

"In fact," the Chinj admitted, "he's already come through."

"Is that right?"

"Actually, there's a rather heated scene going on as we speak. It's becoming difficult to prevent other humans who don't . . . 'know the score,' as it were, from seeing things that they probably shouldn't."

"I can imagine," said Jack distractedly. Much as he was enjoying talking to the Chinj, he was uncomfortably aware of how much time was passing. Soon, no doubt, he was going to have to go back to his double history class and pretend that nothing had happened. "So," he asked, "what does this have to do with me?"

The Chinj hopped awkwardly from one foot to the other.

"The Emperor has asked for you personally," it said. "In fact, his Royal Highness has indicated that he will tear every part of the Light of the Moon into tiny pieces with his tentacles unless you come and explain to everyone how he once fooled you into thinking he was a human."

"Jagmat," said Jack, realizing. "*Jagmat*'s the new Emperor?"

"I believe," the Chinj went on, with obvious exasperation, "he thinks that this will somehow convince Esme and the Sons to let him take a look around. At any rate, you'd better come and talk to him."

"Well, fancy that," said Jack, pleased for the blancmange-like demon.

The Chinj looked at him doubtfully.

"How soon can you get away from this place?" it asked.

Jack looked up at the small creature, seeing his own reflection in the lenses of its sunglasses.

He didn't reply straightaway. A part of him was telling him that he ought to say no, that he should probably go back to double history and get on with the rest of his life.

But the other part of him was already working out how he could escape.

"Tell them I'm on my way," he said.

And then, for the first time in quite a while—

—he smiled.

ACKNOWLEDGMENTS

I am particularly grateful to the following people for their help with this book.

First, and most important, to my lovely girlfriend Laura, and my stalwart flatmate Simon, for putting up with me and for giving *Black Tat* merciless critical savagings whenever it needed them, which was often. To my brother Jack: when it comes to draft-readers, I'm really very lucky. For fight scene advice, "Sifu" Sid and "Swordmistress" Suze: any technical errors I've made in the fights in this story certainly aren't for want of effort on their part. To Kelly and Lucy at RHCB and Liesa and Eloise at Razorbill, for their sensitive and eagle-eyed editorial input. To Maggie, for waving her wand and changing my life. To the staff (past and present) of Blackwell's bookshop on London's Charing Cross Road, for their support and encouragement. To Douglas Hill—grandmaster of SF thrills for young people—for being an inspiration. To James Long and his fine novel *Silence and Shadows* for the idea behind the pigeon sword (and to Simon M. for knowing how much it would appeal to me!). Finally, to my friend Antonia, for being *Black Tat*'s number one fan when there was no number two. In June 2003 I'd all but given up on this book: if it wasn't for her insisting she find out how the story ends, then you wouldn't be reading this now. Thank you. Thank you all.

Musically, *The Black Tattoo* was written under the combined influence of a lot of brutal drum-and-bass abuse (old-fashioned to some, but it still does the job for me) and the soundtracks to many of my favorite films (you've read the book, you can probably guess which ones I mean!).

"Write the exact book that you yourself would be thrilled to read," Lee Child once said. That's still the best piece of writing advice I've ever heard.

All best wishes to you,
Sam, 12th Jan. 2006
www.theblacktattoo.com
Password: "Fetid"

Read an excerpt from Sam Enthoven's second novel

TIM DEFENDER OF THE EARTH!

SECRETS

LONDON. Admiralty Arch. Within sight of Buckingham Palace. The black ministerial Mercedes turned out of Trafalgar Square and purred smoothly to a halt. The driver leapt out, opened the passenger door, and snapped to careful attention as his passenger emerged.

David Sinclair had been Britain's prime minister for less than twenty-four hours. Already he'd found something about the job that he didn't like.

"Why the hell don't I know about this already?" he asked, setting off for the Admiralty's entrance without waiting. "Why wasn't I told about this before?"

"Because," said Dr. Alice McKinsey behind him, for what had to be the thirtieth time at least, "it's *classified*. What you're about to see, Prime Minister," she added, only just catching up, "is the single most sensitive scientific project that the UK has ever been involved in. Only myself, my team, and a very select few others have the slightest idea of its existence. To keep it that way, it was decided early on that only the *most powerful person in the land* could ever be let in on the secret."

She looked at the PM as she held the Admiralty's door for him, waiting for the flattery to work its magic. David Sinclair was the third prime minister to discover what she'd been working on all these years: she was getting used to the breed and the way they operated. Sure enough, this one seemed no different.

"I understand that, Dr. McKinsey," said Sinclair. "There's not much you need to tell me about national security, believe me. But I was expecting . . . I don't know, key codes to our nuclear arsenal, access to special bunkers in case of attack, that sort of thing—not what you've been telling me. I mean . . ." he added, his voice rising again, "it's fantastic! You couldn't make it up!"

"One moment, Prime Minister," said Dr. McKinsey. By now they had reached the life-size portrait of Winston Churchill that stood at the end of one of Admiralty Arch's echoing passageways. Long years of habit made her check her surroundings before she touched a certain spot on the picture's ornate gold frame.

"Identify yourself, please," said a voice from Churchill's mouth, making Mr. Sinclair flinch. Dr. McKinsey leaned toward the painting.

"Dr. Alice McKinsey plus one. Password: Leviathan."

"Voice pattern accepted," Churchill announced. "Password verified. Stand by . . ."

Titanium bolts slid back in their sheaths with a sound like

distant thunder. The painting swung forward to reveal a small room behind it, luxuriantly upholstered in comfortable-looking old red leather with thick pile carpet underfoot.

"Shall we?" asked Dr. McKinsey.

"After you," said Mr. Sinclair.

Dr. McKinsey pressed a button on the brass panel on the wall. Churchill's portrait—now revealed as the front of a foot-thick door of what looked like solid steel—swung back into place. Then the elevator began its descent.

"How long has this project of yours been going on?" asked Mr. Sinclair. The acceleration was smooth, but he could feel they were traveling at high speed.

"It was Stalin who gave Churchill the idea originally," said Dr. McKinsey, glad of the rare chance to explain the history of her life's work. "In 1926 a group of Russia's top scientists were assigned to the task of producing a kind of 'supersoldier,' bred and trained from birth to be incredibly strong, insensitive to pain, indifferent to what they ate—in other words, *invincible*. Imagine it, Prime Minister," she went on, her eyes lighting up as she warmed to her theme, "an entire army capable of marching for days on only the most minimal of supplies. Soldiers who could fight tirelessly and unstoppably without pain or fatigue. That was the original basis for our program." She smiled.

"So . . . this creature," said Mr. Sinclair. "Are you saying it was once . . . a man?"

"No, no," said Dr. McKinsey. "Stalin's scientists experimented directly on living humans and animals, but since I came on board, we've never attempted anything like that here. What we've done instead is directly manipulate DNA—the building blocks of life—to create something completely new: a creature *based* on living, or once-living, things but that is in fact *entirely different*. Up until sixty-five million years ago, dinosaurs walked the earth. But while the superficial resemblance is definitely there, nothing like what you're about to see has *ever existed before*."

"Indeed," said Mr. Sinclair with a thin smile. He was perfectly certain that what Dr. McKinsey was talking about couldn't be even a quarter as impressive as she was making it out to be. Whatever trick she'd managed to pull on previous PMs to make them carry on providing such massive amounts of funding for her ludicrous scheme, it wasn't going to work on him.

But Dr. McKinsey, for her part, had seen similar thoughts go through the minds of two of Mr. Sinclair's predecessors. She knew that the prime minister's air of cynicism would vanish once he saw what she'd brought him here to see, so she wasn't worried—not yet.

Seventy stories below the center of London, the elevator slowed smoothly to a halt. The door opened, and Dr. McKinsey watched Mr. Sinclair's expression carefully as he took in the scene beyond.

They were in a laboratory. It wasn't the biggest laboratory in the world, but it was a decent size—six rows of long work tops filled with computers and equipment. Eighteen technicians stopped what they were doing and stood up—white coats rustling—to look in the prime minister's direction.

But he wasn't looking at them.

Mr. Sinclair's mouth had fallen open. Like a zombie, he shuffled forward straight past the lab and its contents while Dr. McKinsey and her teams exchanged knowing smiles. When at last the prime minister reached the thirty-meter-long strip of reinforced glass that was the laboratory's far wall, he stopped and stood there, gaping at what lay outside it.

"It's . . ." he said finally, turning to Dr. McKinsey and pointing at it. "It's a monster. A *giant monster*. Here, under London."

"That would be one way to describe him, yes," Dr. McKinsey answered. "But we call him something else. Prime Minster," she went on, "allow me to present the Tyrannosaur: Improved Model. Tim for short."

Mr. Sinclair just stared. What he was seeing seemed to stop at his eyeballs and go no further: his brain simply couldn't take it in.

Beyond the glass lay a vast concrete chamber. The observation window where Dr. McKinsey and the PM stood was about halfway up one of the smaller sides: the sheer drop into the colossal space outside the window was dizzying by itself.

But the creature the chamber had been constructed to contain took up a full third of its volume.

It was a dinosaur—or it looked that way to Mr. Sinclair's eyes. The creature's skin was gray-green and scaly: it had two hind legs, each one the size of a battleship, and a long and muscular tail. Its shoulders were surprisingly broad and powerful-looking: arms the girth of redwood trees led to huge hands with curving claws. The creature's head alone, with its elongated jaws full of stalagmitelike teeth, was bigger than any living thing the prime minister had seen before this moment. A ridge of short bony plates led up along the creature's tail and spine, culminating finally in a small lump on its bony forehead, a little above its eyes. The giant was lying on its side. Its eyes were closed. Its legs were drawn up; its arms were crossed on its chest; its sides heaved in and out colossally.

Dimly, the prime minister began to be aware of how closely Dr. McKinsey was watching him. He turned.

Dr. McKinsey was more than seventy years old, but at that moment you would never have guessed it. Her smile was like a young girl's as she savored the prime minister's reaction.

Mr. Sinclair cleared his throat.

"It . . ." he began.

"He," Dr. McKinsey corrected gently. Her smile widened.

Mr. Sinclair blinked and frowned.

"He, then," he said. "He's . . . drugged? You keep . . . 'him'—drugged like this? So he can't escape?"

"Oh no," said Dr. McKinsey. "Tim's not drugged. He's just sleeping."

She gestured out of the window—and just then, the enormous beast stirred. Leathery lips peeled apart, exposing more fangs. One huge clawed forelimb slashed listlessly at the air, and the sinuous tail lifted—curled—then slapped the floor. There was a distant rumble, and Mr. Sinclair felt an impact tremor through the soles of his expensive shoes.

"Ah, look!" said Dr. McKinsey. "He's *dreaming* again. Isn't that sweet?"

Mr. Sinclair did not reply.

"Tim first hatched back in 1995," Dr. McKinsey explained quickly, collecting herself. "It had taken us well into the eighties to create a DNA chain that was stable enough, and to get him to the egg stage took even more work, as you can imagine—but that was the date he hatched: August 7, 1995. And now"—she paused—"Tim is reaching puberty."

"Puberty," the prime minister echoed.

"That's right," said Dr. McKinsey. "Tim's a young teenager. He's growing extraordinarily fast: in fact, he's more than doubled in size in the last six months alone. It's not surprising that he needs a lot of rest." She gazed fondly out of the window.

Mr. Sinclair examined the face of the woman standing beside him. Dr. McKinsey's smile was filled with pride. Not just pride in a job well done, either: her pride was more like . . . it wasn't, was it? It was! She looked like she felt almost *maternal* toward this creature, this leviathan slumbering below the streets of Britain's capital. And the beast had "doubled in size in six months"! What (Mr. Sinclair wondered with rising dismay) was supposed to happen in *another* six months? Or the six months after that? Was Dr. McKinsey *insane*?

He swallowed. Time to get a grip on the situation.

"Am I right in thinking," the prime minister began, "that this . . . 'Tim' is the only one of his kind?"

"That's . . . true," said Dr. McKinsey. She tried to keep her smile in place, but she could feel it slipping a little. She knew what was coming.

"So in all this time, only *one* of your . . . experiments has produced anything like the result you wanted, and this 'Tim' is it. Am I correct?"

"We've never been able to replicate the original gene sequence," Dr. McKinsey answered. "We've tried everything to simulate the exact conditions of the experiment, but . . . something's missing somehow. It's as if that one time, something strange took place. Something extraordinary. Something *unique*. But . . ."

While Dr. McKinsey was talking, Mr. Sinclair turned his back to the window. The sight of the giant monster outside was putting him off, and he wanted no distractions while he made his next point. It was time to say what he'd come to say—what he'd wanted to say ever since one of his civil servants had taken him to one side and explained how, for the best part of a century, a full ten percent of Britain's tax revenue had been siphoned off into a top secret military project.

"But all your other experiments in this direction have failed," he put in.

"In that direction," Dr. McKinsey admitted, "yes. We've tried thousands, possibly millions of different DNA combinations, but Tim is the only one that has resulted in a living creature."

"I must say, Dr. McKinsey," Mr. Sinclair continued, "that's not a terribly high success rate for all these years of work—and funding," he added with heavy emphasis.

"Tim may be the only living result of our work here, Prime Minister," said Dr. McKinsey carefully. "But I think you'll agree, he's quite . . . impressive."

"Indeed," said Mr. Sinclair. "But impressive or not, in view of the costs involved, one could be forgiven for expecting something more by way of *benefits*."

"Sir?"

"I mean, this creature of yours . . ." said Mr. Sinclair. "What does he actually *do*, apart from sleep?"

Dr. McKinsey took a deep breath. "In the course of this project we've made some staggering scientific advances, Prime Minister. Why, in the field of gene research alone, we're *far* in advance of anything the rest of the world has to offer, and—"

"Yes, yes," the prime minister interrupted. "But if I remember correctly, the original purpose of this program was a *military* one. Am I right?"

"That's true, but—"

"Well?" asked the prime minister.

"We . . . haven't had a chance to test Tim in the field," Dr. McKinsey admitted. "Frankly—as you can imagine—the security implications make that pretty difficult. It's not as if we can just take him out somewhere and put him through his paces. Not without the world noticing."

"Quite," said the prime minister.

"So for the last ten years—before we pursue that particular line of inquiry—we've been waiting for him to . . . mature," said Dr. McKinsey. "At this point, we don't know what he's capable of. The potential, as you can see, is staggering. But . . ."

She took another deep breath.

"Well . . . as you may have noticed, he's beginning to outgrow our current facilities. To be honest," she added, "we're not sure how much longer we can keep him here. Like any youngster, Tim can sometimes become"—she paused—"well, rather *exuberant*."

The prime minister stared at her.

"So," Dr. McKinsey rushed on, "if you'll only agree to the next bit of extra investment, then I think we'll be seeing some very real developments very soon. The next few years ought to be thrilling!" she added enthusiastically while wincing inwardly at the pleading in her voice.

"Dr. McKinsey," the prime minister began. "Alice," he

added, striving for a little intimacy to soften the coming blow.

Her heart sank.

"I want to congratulate you—and the rest of your team—on everything you've achieved with this project. Really: I'm quite staggered by what you've done. It's a great shame in a way that your work has remained such a secret, because the whole of the scientific community owes you a huge amount of respect and admiration for your lifetime of selfless work.

". . . But I'm afraid I must be frank with you," he went on. "Britain can no longer afford to support you in your endeavors. I simply cannot," Mr. Sinclair said, "in all good conscience, allow such a fantastic amount of this nation's taxpayers' money to be spent on . . . a *giant monster*. Especially," he added darkly, "a *teenage* one.

"I'm afraid this project can no longer be allowed to continue. I'm transferring your funding to an alternative program. You are to close down your facility here and, naturally, ensure that all evidence of your activities is prevented from ever reaching the hands of anyone outside our shores."

"What does that mean?" Dr. McKinsey asked. "What about Tim?"

"I'm afraid that means *destroy it*," said the prime minister bluntly. "Unless you can think of something else to do with your . . ." Words temporarily failed him. "*Pet*. Good night," he added, and started walking back toward the lift.

"Wait!" said Dr. McKinsey. "Prime Minister! Wait!"

"Don't worry," said Mr. Sinclair, "I'll show myself out."

"But I have to ask . . ." she cried, "what 'alternative program'? Who will our funding be going to?"

In the lift, Mr. Sinclair turned. He smiled bleakly as he pressed the button on the brass panel. The doors began to slide shut.